Also by K L Stockton

Awakened By You

SHATTERED BY YOU

K L STOCKTON

authorHOUSE®

AuthorHouse™ UK
1663 Liberty Drive
Bloomington, IN 47403 USA
www.authorhouse.co.uk
Phone: 0800.197.4150

© 2016 K L STOCKTON. All rights reserved.

No part of this book may be reproduced, stored in a retrieval system, or transmitted by any means without the written permission of the author.

Published by AuthorHouse 01/29/2016

ISBN: 978-1-5049-9806-2 (sc)
ISBN: 978-1-5049-9805-5 (hc)
ISBN: 978-1-5049-9807-9 (e)

Print information available on the last page.

Any people depicted in stock imagery provided by Thinkstock are models, and such images are being used for illustrative purposes only.
Certain stock imagery © Thinkstock.

This book is printed on acid-free paper.

Because of the dynamic nature of the Internet, any web addresses or links contained in this book may have changed since publication and may no longer be valid. The views expressed in this work are solely those of the author and do not necessarily reflect the views of the publisher, and the publisher hereby disclaims any responsibility for them.

For Lorraine Milench

My beautiful Mum. This one is for you.
Love you to the stars and moon… and back.

Acknowledgements

A huge thank you to my Mum, Lorraine Milench, if it wasn't for your comment "I didn't want the story to end" after reading Awakened by You, I would never have thought about continuing Skye's story. You planted the seed in my imagination and it has grown and grown.

To both my Mum and sister, Donna Turner, once again thank you for your honest and constructive feedback.

To my husband, Ian, your encouragement and patience is boundless. I love you and thank you.

A massive thank you to Sharon Rollisson-Slaughter, Debbie Shipman and everyone at the THE BIKER GUIDE® Facebook group for helping me decide which is the best kind of motorcycle for my heroine to ride.

CHAPTER ONE

CLAYTON

"Mr Joshua Blake has arrived sir"

Helena's voice ringing through the intercom shatters the quiet ambience of my office, I take a deep breath and let it out slowly. I feel like I've been swimming under water for a long time when I take another refreshing deep breath and close down the spread sheet I've been working on for the last two hours. I stand and stretch, my back muscles and spine creak from being hunched over the desk for so long.

"Send him straight in" I punch the intercom button, settling back into my chair. A distant memory of Skye on her knees under my desk, sucking me off springs to mind. My dick stirs, it's been too long since we last played in my office and the fault is all mine. I must remedy that. I mentally run through my schedule to see if I can make time. I don't get far when the door bursts open.

"Tell me baby bro, what do you buy a woman who has everything and wants for nothing?" Joshua, my eldest brother says as he saunters across to my desk with a huge smirk on his face.

His overly gleeful smug look doesn't alter as he settles into the plush leather chair on the opposite side of my huge mahogany desk. The bastard is trying to wind me up, if it wasn't for the fact I respected the hell out of him I'd have smacked that smug smile off his handsome face before his ass made it to the chair, but it's me who's going to have the last laugh, I'll soon swipe the self-satisfied look off his face. I lean back in my chair, the leather creaks and groans as I push back into the reclined position, and grin evilly back at him.

"My dear brother, you are about to find out. I'm just waiting for someone else to join us" Joshua raises an expectant eyebrow for me to elaborate, which I ignore I'll let him stew for a few more minutes "have you got your costumes for the party?" I ask deliberately changing the subject.

For our first wedding anniversary, Skye suggested since it was also my birthday and Halloween we hold a fancy dress party celebrating everything all in one hit. It was a huge success, so every year since we've held a party. In a few days we will celebrate five years of wedded bliss.

"Yes, although Lucas and Sam keep changing their minds" Joshua chuckles "you know Elizabeth threatened the pair of them yesterday that she would decide for them. Lucas pipes up "I know what we can go as. I'll dress up as Dad and Sam you can go as Uncle Clayton" then Sam says "Cool that means I get to spend all night with Aunty Skye." Then the little buggers started arguing because Lucas decided he wanted to go as you instead."

I laugh at that as I imagine the scene. Both my nephews are crazy about Skye, they've been smitten from the first day they met her. Now at eight years of age the twins are even worse, they hero worship her! As they got older and understood exactly the kind of work Skye did and how she is the creator and designer of the characters in their favourite video games in their eyes she is the coolest adult alive. Just last week they got Skye to give a talk to their classmates on 'Bring a Parent to School Day', they didn't want Joshua or Elizabeth to go, oh no! It had to be Aunty Skye.

"I should feel insulted that neither son wants to go as me" Joshua shakes his head "but I don't envy you as you'll be fighting them off all night just to get near Skye"

"I'll get Paul, Bruce and Alan to set up an exclusion zone around Skye, that'll keep them at bay" I deadpan.

"You would as well" Joshua barks out a laugh, he's right I would if I could get away with it.

The only thing stopping me is the fact Skye would bitch slap me to high heaven when she found out, there was no 'if' about her finding out, somehow she would and the consequences didn't bear thinking about. An involuntary shudder goes through me just at the thought of being cut off. A knock on the door and Helena walking in brings an end our conversation. I stand as I see Billy behind her.

"Sorry I'm late Mr Blake the traffic from the airport was terrible" Billy says shaking my hand.

"Don't worry about it, thank you Helena" she nods and closes the door "Joshua, this is Billy Quinn"

"The property guy" Joshua says rising and shakes Billy's hand "I've heard a lot about you over the years, nice to finally meet you" Billy blushes, his eyes flick to me and I can see uncertainty in them.

"This is my brother, Joshua, who is also my lawyer" Billy nods in understanding "please take a seat" he sits in the chair next to Joshua "can I get you a drink?"

"Water please" Billy says as he starts to take out documents from his satchel "do you mind if we use your computer Mr Blake? The battery on my laptop has died" Billy looks sheepish as he says this. I know the guy well enough to see that he's also embarrassed, in all my dealings with him Billy is the consummate professional.

"Of course" I say placing his drink on the table and slide the keyboard over to him then turn the screen so we all can see it.

Billy quickly brings up a property agent's website "I found three possible properties. All of them are represented by this company, who I might add, it's owned by my second cousin but I didn't know that at the time of short listing"

"This company is in the UK" Joshua says pointing at the screen.

"Sorry Joshua, I forgot to mention. I sent Billy to England to find a property for me that will become Skye's anniversary present" now it's my turn to look smug as Joshua's jaw unhinges in astonishment, then he starts to laugh "so Billy show me what you've found"

Billy looks at me then Joshua with a lost bewildered look then seems to collect himself "Okay, I found three properties as I mentioned but it's the last one I came across that I think will really appeal to Skye"

I trust Billy and his instincts as to what Skye will like; he's worked for her long enough "Show me that one first then"

Billy's face splits into a wide grin as he brings up the property details "This is Dove Mill Hall; it's situated on the outskirts of Dove Mill village. The nearest town being Henley-on-Thames about five miles away and it's just over thirty-seven miles north of London" Billy says proudly sitting back so Joshua and I get a better view of the building.

"But it's a derelict shell of a building" splutters Joshua in shock.

"Skye will love it" Billy and I say together.

Billy blushes making me laugh; he really does know Skye and her taste in property "Well done, tell me more about it." I know he will have found out as much as he possibly could about the place.

"The Hall was destroyed by fire over twenty years ago and the family couldn't afford to rebuild due to the insurance refusing to pay out. It's believed the fire was started deliberately in order to claim on the insurance, allegedly" Billy adds grinning at Joshua "the ensuing legal battles left the family completely broke. Due to various covenants on the property and land that comes with it meant the family couldn't sell to the developers that came forward over the years plus it made finding a buyer willing to deal with all the restrictions extremely difficult. In a nutshell the property has to be restored to its former glory" Billy riffles through the papers he put on my desk "I managed to find some old photographs of the place, here" he hands them over to me.

The pictures are grainy black and while but it doesn't detract from the fact the house was once a very grand and imposing Gothic looking building. Multiple chimneys and what look like Corinthian columns, huge double doors, floor to ceiling arched windows over two floors, it also has what appears to be circular turrets at either end of the sprawling building.

"From what I could find out the Hall was originally built in seventeen twenty and had many extensions added over the eighteen and nineteen hundred's. I was also told that it's rumoured Henry Holland had a hand in designing parts of it but I couldn't find any concrete evidence" Billy pauses, I must look as clueless as Joshua, who in the hell is Henry Holland? "He was an architect to the English nobility. Those pictures are from the nineteen fifties unfortunately I wasn't able to get any later photographs. Just before I left I found out there is a surviving relative who still lives in the village it's possible they may have more recent pictures"

"You're right Billy, Skye will absolutely love this" I say as I hand the photographs over to Joshua "what else do I need to know?"

"The property sits in one hundred and twenty acres. It also comes with woodland and three cottages situated in the village along with a fifty-hectare farm that has working tenants" Billy clears his throat and shifts in his seat "I took the liberty of contacting the English Heritage to get information about the Hall and restoring it" Billy pats the pile of papers "this is what they gave me, also through my cousin I got a list of companies that specialize in this kind of restoration project"

"Excellent, as usual Billy you have gone above and beyond the call of duty. So, how much do they want?"

"I got them down to eight and a half million pounds, sterling"

"Cash" I ask, Billy nods.

"Are you mad?" Joshua bursts out "for a derelict shell of a building"

"Plus a farm, three cottages, woodland and a load of land. To see the smile and joy on my beautiful wife's face when I give it to her" I pause imagining Skye's reaction "it's worth it, so yes, I am mad" Joshua rolls his eyes at me. I look at Billy "go ahead and confirm. How quickly can they get the papers to me?"

Billy opens his satchel and hands me a manila envelope "Is that quick enough sir" Billy smiles at my stunned face "another liberty I took when I was in the area was paying a visit to the law firm that is handling the family's estate"

"Ha!" I bark out a laugh "Billy you are too good"

Billy blushes again at the praise "Although I do need to confirm" he says waving his phone.

"Go ahead"

Billy rises and moves to the other end of the office to make his call. I hand the envelope to Joshua "I want the deeds in Skye's name"

"Okay, why England?" I can hear the puzzled curiosity in his voice.

"In about eighteen month's Skye has to go over there with work, so I thought why not make it so she has somewhere nice to stay and a place we can call home whilst we're there"

Skye knows her work commitments well in advance due to the two year waiting list she has for private commissions; she'll be working in England for at least nine months with a strong possibility it could be longer.

"We, does that mean you are going with her?" Joshua says shocked. It puzzles me that he's so shocked, everyone knows that I go with Skye when she works away and in the five years of being together there has only been one instance when I couldn't join her, that was the longest and most miserable fortnight of my life and I vowed never to be apart from her ever again.

"Yes and no I haven't told Mom yet so don't go blabbing to her" I threaten pointing my finger at him.

Joshua holds his hands up in surrender "She won't hear a peep out of me. Only promise me I can have a front row seat when you tell her" Joshua's smile is positively wicked as we both know mother will go thermonuclear when I tell her. Skye suggested we take her with us, I soon squashed that idea. However, I will tell her she can come and visit whenever she wants.

"All confirmed" Billy says coming back to my desk "you have the solicitors contact details in the envelope, my cousin is more than happy to help should you need it or you can use me to liaise with him, whichever you prefer"

Billy glances at his watch and bends to pick up his satchel, I stand "Thank you for all you've done Billy" I shake his hand "we'll see you at the party"

"Looking forward to it" Billy smiles, then shakes Joshua's hand "nice meeting you, sir"

Joshua is looking through the papers when I return from showing Billy out "At first glance it all looks straight forward enough. I'll take this with me and double check on these covenants Billy mentioned and call you early evening with my findings. All being well you should be able to sign tomorrow" he says putting the papers back in the envelope.

"Excellent" I say picking up the English Heritage stack of papers and flick through them. Skye will get a real kick out reading through all this; I'll get a fancy box and wrap them up as part of her present I decide.

"Well baby bro you certainly took the wind out my sails for being a smug bastard and here I was thinking I would enjoy seeing you fret over what to buy Skye" Joshua huffs at himself "any idea what Skye is getting you?"

"None and I don't know whether to be shit scared or excited with anticipation"

"Be afraid, be very afraid baby bro" Joshua says gleefully rubbing his hands together "I can't wait to see what she's got you this year"

For our first wedding anniversary Skye booked me motorcycle lessons and my test. She did it because I had been horrified to learn she could ride and I foolishly tried to forbid her from getting on a motorcycle ever again. When I passed my test Skye then presented me with tickets for the Daytona Bike Week and a trip along Route 66. Needless to say I thoroughly enjoyed myself and the experience, now we regularly go out on rides together. Then there was the year Skye took me on a tour of theme parks where we rode the scariest roller coasters she could find—Sheikra in Tampa Florida, Stratosphere X-scream in Vegas, Kingda Ka in Jackson New Jersey, The Intimidator 305 in Doswell Virgina all spring to mind—she did that after I admitted I had never been on a roller coaster. "You've never lived until you've scared the crap out of yourself having fun" is what she said to me to justify going on the rides, and as much as I hate to admit it she's right.

Skye is an adrenaline junkie, over the last five years I have bungee jumped from a bridge one hundred and sixty feet above the Cheakamus River in Canada. Paragliding when we vacationed with Mr C on his yacht and we went soaring because Skye happened to see it on a TV programme and wondered what it would be like. I also made the mistake of mentioning I'd never been to a concert or gig; Skye does no more than drag me along to see one of her favourite rock bands. I swear to god it was three days before I could hear properly and my ears stopped making a hissing noise, now I make sure I wear ear plugs whenever we go to see a band play.

"That woman sure knows how to keep you on your toes" Joshua smirks at me as he gathers up his things, my family think it's hilarious all the things Skye has gotten me doing.

"Tell me about it" I grumble "I've learnt to keep my mouth shut, the hard way"

"Hey, have you met Andrew's new girlfriend?" Joshua says excitedly. I shake my head "he brought her to dinner at Mom's on Monday, shame you and Skye couldn't make it. Alicia, she's called, seems nice enough. I'm assuming he'll be bringing her to the party."

"Is she any improvement on the last four girlfriends?"

Joshua laughs "You mean is she going to get your seal of approval since Mandy?"

"Fuck off Joshua. I still haven't forgiven that bitch."

"I know" Joshua pats my shoulder trying hard to stifle his amusement "even after five years the minute one of Andrew's girlfriends has made a snide comment, and it's not even about Skye, your hackles go up and the girlfriend in question is out the door before you can blink. It's like watching a porcupine lift its spikes only I can see your hair stand up on end. Poor Andrew doesn't stand a chance finding the one."

"I'm that bad?" I sigh "really?" Joshua nods "Christ, Andrew must hate me."

"Actually he doesn't. In fact, he uses you as a gage and judge of character. He says since you never liked Mandy he trusts your judgement on sussing out how genuine the women in his life are" I'm stunned, gobsmacked as Skye would say "he trusts you" Joshua reiterates, his hand tightening on my shoulder "and I must admit as much as it pains me, I think he's right."

"Huh, I wish he'd told me" I say a tad sulkily.

"And if he had then he wouldn't see your honest reaction. You'll be too conscious of your behaviour and you'll over adapt or compensate. Look forget I said anything and just be your usual bullish self when you meet her" Joshua looks at his watch "got to go, speak to you later"

"Yeah sure" I say distractedly as I open the office door. I'm not sure I can forget what he's just said. Fuck! I don't want to be responsible for whether Andrew's relationship succeeds or fails. What the hell can I say to Andrew to convince him to stop using my reactions to make his decisions? I need to speak to Skye; she's good at putting this kind of thing into perspective. 'Love Walked In' starts playing from my phone — Skye's ring tone — brings me out of my thoughts.

My heart surges with overwhelming love every time it plays and I'm instantly taken back to our wedding day. We had gone onto the dance floor to do the first dance, instead Skye shocked the shit out of me by making me sit in a chair that Bruce had placed in front of the stage and taking the microphone from Paul she proceeded to tell our guests she was doing away with tradition and the following song was dedicated to me. Then she sang, the music and words of the song resonating so deeply it brought tears to my eyes and I wasn't the only one, I don't think there was a dry eye in the house when she finished.

"Skye, baby I was just thinking about you" I purr down the phone. Her knowing husky, throaty laugh sends tingles of desire hurtling around my body and straight to my cock, never fails.

DOVE MILL VILLAGE

"Lady Farringdon, yoo hoo, Lady Farringdon"

Marjorie Brennan the village busy body rushes out of the mini supermarket shop calling out at the top of her voice causing those walking home from a hard days' work to turn and watch the elderly plump woman waddle up the high street as fast as her short legs would take her.

Lady Farringdon continues walking, her beloved Labradors playfully dance around her as she debates whether to stop or not, she could pretend she hadn't heard someone calling out but her conscious and propriety won out. Her upbringing made it difficult for her to be outright rude to people, so reluctantly slowing her steps it was enough to allow a huffing and puffing Marjorie Brennan to catch up.

"Lady Farringdon, have you heard the news" Marjorie pants out, bending over putting her hands on her knees trying to get much needed air into her lungs.

"Marjorie please, I've told you enough times to call me Joyce and what news is so urgent you nearly give yourself a coronary to tell me?" Joyce says trying to hide her irritation by adjusting her head scarf against the bitter autumn wind.

"Dove Mill Hall, it's been sold" Marjorie gasps between gulping in air, standing upright and taking great delight in seeing Lady Joyce Farringdon's reaction to the news that her childhood home is finally, after twenty-two years of being an eyesore and a blot on the landscape, off the market.

Trying hard Lady Joyce Farringdon struggles to hide her emotions as relief floods through her. At last she will be rid of the speculation that surrounds the ruination of a once beautiful building. "Sold, how do you know?" As much as she disliked Marjorie for being one of the village's biggest gossips she couldn't help herself from asking.

"Well, I was just in the mini supermarket shop buying a few bits and pieces when I overheard Sally, you know she's one of Caleb Raven's grooms, she was talking to Eddie the estate agent. Apparently there was an American over here a few days ago representing a potential buyer and confirmation of the sale came over late yesterday afternoon" Marjorie paused to take a breath.

"Thank you for letting me know" Lady Farringdon gave Marjorie a smile she hoped came across as pleasant and not as a grimace as she turned to walk away, she didn't care if she appeared rude not now she had a call to make.

Lady Joyce Farringdon, although she wouldn't gain anything from the sale of Dove Mill Hall is curious enough to contact her uncle to find out more. Joyce had been fortunate enough to have married well so she hadn't suffered from the financial hardship her mother's brother had when the insurance company refused to pay out as they suspected arson. Joyce knew it was true because her uncle had told her his father, her grandfather, started the fire deliberately because he'd gambled away the family fortune, although the latter wasn't common knowledge. Three months after the fire her grandfather died of a heart attack and her uncle inherited a shell of a building and huge debts. Due to so many covenants on the property and surrounding land he was in a no win situation. After failing to overturn the insurance company's decision and a costly legal battle her uncle moved to London permanently where he worked in the City, as far as she knew it had taken him years to pay off all the debt he had been saddled with, so if he had finally sold the place and he was making some money in the process she was pleased for him, he deserved every penny.

"I'm sick to death of being bloody skint, any spare cash we do get goes on those fucking horses" Gabrielle Raven screams at her husband.

"Those fucking horses, as you so delicately put it, are our livelihood. We are skint because of you and your excessive spending you stupid bitch" Caleb growls back through gritted teeth, deliberately keeping his voice low so his grooms wouldn't hear, the last thing he wanted was his staff worrying about losing their jobs.

"Oh that's right, blame me!" Gabrielle screeches and jabs her finger at her husband "you will only be happy if I'm walking around in shitty clothes with holes in"

"Don't be fucking ridiculous" Caleb hisses, his jaw was beginning to ache as he clenches his teeth tighter together to stop himself from saying anything else as he riffles through the paperwork, all bills, cluttering his desk "how the fuck can you justify spending six hundred pounds on a pair of shoes and eight hundred on a dress" he points at the credit card bill and glares at his wife.

That money alone would pay the staff wages for this week and buy horse feed for the month. Christ, Gabrielle really is a selfish bitch. 'Why the fuck did I marry her? All I've had is eight years of bloody misery' Caleb thinks to himself as he runs his hands through his wild unruly wavy black hair.

"So you're saying when we get invited to one of Lord Baxter's dinner parties you want me to turn up in last year's fashion? Oh! Or better yet, how about I go naked?" spittle flew from Gabrielle's mouth, her red face twisting with hate.

What did I ever see in her? He wondered. A thought suddenly occurs to Caleb. Gabrielle wouldn't make this kind of effort for him; she had long stopped making herself look pretty for him.

"Who is he?" Caleb's voice is low and soft, it totally threw Gabrielle and guilt flashes across her face, an expression Caleb caught, confirming his suspicion, she was being unfaithful… having an affair… another one… yet again.

"Just because I decide to make myself presentable for a dinner party all of a sudden I'm having an affair!" Gabrielle shouts defensively.

"So who is he?" Caleb turns to face his wife making sure to see her reaction to his words, his emerald green eyes flashing dangerously, daring her to deny it "if you're not having an affair then you have your sights on someone, so who is he?"

"You're fucking unbelievable" Gabrielle screams in his face "how dare you!"

"I dare because I know you Gabrielle" Caleb's voice is ice cold, matching his hard cold set handsome face "so I'll ask you again, who's the poor bastard you've got your claws into ready to bleed dry?"

Gabrielle stills; her clenching hands and the pounding pulse at the base of her throat are the only sign of her anxiety. Caleb has rumbled her there is no point in trying to deny it anymore "I'm not telling you" she says defiantly lifting her chin, challenging him to push her for more information.

"Fair enough, pack your bags and get the fuck out. I want a divorce" Caleb says impassively, dismissing her he turns back to the paperwork on his desk, wondering how in the hell he is going to find the money to pay all the bills.

Gabrielle couldn't believe he was dismissing her like one of his employees. There was a time he would have fallen to his knees and begged her not to leave, swearing his undying love for her. Cold reality and dread settles in her stomach, she no longer had a hold over Caleb; his feelings for her were gone.

"You fucking bastard" Gabrielle screeches in retaliation and slams the door behind her.

Caleb leans back in his chair listening to Gabrielle's footsteps stomping up the stairs, not long after sounds of draws being roughly opened and closed filter down. Caleb let a breath out in relief. A tentative knock on the door startles him "Yes, come in" he snaps.

Sally, one of his longest serving grooms pokes her head round the door "Got a minute?"

Caleb nods and waves for her to come in. He notices her nerves as she enters which is unusual for her, dread settles in his gut. Whatever it is she has to say his instincts were telling him he wasn't going to like it.

"Promise not to shoot the messenger?" Sally says with a nervous laugh entering the room.

Caleb's anxiety climbs up a notch, his expression is impassive and makes Sally shift nervously from one foot to the other "Go on" Caleb says softly.

Sally takes a deep breath "Dove Mill Hall has been sold" she blurts out in a rush. Oh that's just fucking great, that's all I need Caleb's mind shouts "confirmation of the sale came through late yesterday afternoon, apparently an American has bought the estate"

Sally's words hang heavy in the air between them, she watches Caleb closely trying to read his expression but gets nowhere, not the slightest indication of what he's thinking or feeling. His face is still impassive, an emotionless mask.

"Thanks for telling me. How did you find out?" Caleb asks after a few minutes.

"I saw Dodgy Eddie in the mini supermarket shop, you know the estate agent" she adds when Caleb looks at her clueless "Marjorie Brennan was in there eavesdropping, she couldn't get out of the shop fast enough when she saw Lady Farringdon passing. No doubt the whole village will know by closing time" Sally snorts a derisive laugh. Caleb remains quiet, his eyes looking out the window but not seeing the yard or any of the activity taking place "what do we do about using the field?" Sally asks in a small voice.

What do we do? Caleb asks himself. Fuck, this is all I need. Looking back at Sally he smiles, hoping it's reassuring "We keep using it until we are told otherwise by the new owner" hopefully it will be a long time before that happens he adds silently.

Sally perks up and smiles, her blue eyes sparkling "Okay with any luck they love horses and let us continue using it" her optimism makes Caleb return her smile "I'll get back to work and let the others know"

"Thank you Sally; I appreciate that"

Caleb watches Sally's plump womanly form disappear through the door, he admired her ability to find a positive in everything. Many times over the years when he despaired, usually over money, Sally had the knack of seeing the silver lining and brought him out of his depression. He had been using the top field that was next to his land for years with the permission of Anthony Cookson, Lady Farringdon's uncle and now former owner of Dove Mill Hall.

Caleb Raven inherited the stables and training yard at the age of twenty from his Uncle Michael, he had lived with his uncle since the age of three after his mother had died. Caleb knew nothing of his father, he had walked out on his mother before he was born and all his uncle would say when questioned was his father was a free spirit who broke his mother's heart. His jet black wavy hair and emerald green eyes are the only features he inherited from his father, according to his uncle his good looks came from his mother.

The yard and horses were Caleb's life, it's all he knew and over the years he had built a good reputation for being an excellent trainer, especially with difficult horses and turning them into winners. The only problem was since marrying Gabrielle it seemed he was always on the verge of bankruptcy. The yard and buildings desperately needed updating and a lot of repair and maintenance work doing. For the last twelve months he had been losing owners to better equipped and luxurious training yards, being an outstanding trainer producing winners was no longer enough for many owners. Caleb put his head in his hands, gripping and pulling his unruly wavy hair in despair, muttering a prayer asking for divine intervention.

"You'll be hearing from my solicitor" Gabrielle's high pitched spiteful voice intrudes on his thoughts and nerves.

Slowly Caleb stood and drew himself up to his full six foot four height, he could be quite intimidating when he wanted to be and right now he wanted nothing more than to scare the shit out of his soon to be ex-wife, giving her a smile that flashed all of his straight white teeth—a shark's smile, he lent forward slightly into Gabrielle's personal space "I look forward to it" he says sardonically. Gabrielle, unnerved, takes a step back and stumbles over one of the suitcases she placed in the hallway "Let me help you take them to the car" Caleb laced his words with sickening politeness.

Before Gabrielle can respond Caleb steps forward, picks up her cases and strides outside before she realised what is happening. A shocked Gabrielle meekly follows, she really thought by packing her things she would call Caleb's bluff, that he would back down and beg her to stay once he saw her cases. "He's toying with me, well two can play at this game" she mutters to herself stepping out into the yard.

The grooms in the yard all stop what they are doing and watch Gabrielle, on her six inch heels, totter out of the house trying and failing to look nonchalant as Caleb practically threw the cases into the boot of the car then went to the driver's door and held it open.

"Ever the gentleman" says Gabrielle smiling sweetly getting in.

"No just making sure you fucking leave. Don't bother coming back, ever" Caleb slams the door in Gabrielle's startled face and walks back to the house without turning round at the sound of the engine starting and tyres screeching as the car leaves the yard at high speed.

"Thank fuck Boomerang has finally left" Marty mutters under his breath to Sally.

"Yeah, but for how long?" she whispers back feeling pangs of relief, happiness and sadness.

Relief that her wonderful, devastatingly good looking boss will finally have peace now that the selfish, conceited bitch has gone. Happiness that the mood and everyone's spirits in the yard will be lifted and positive. Sadness because she knew deep down that one day, at some point in the future, the bitch will be back and Caleb like every other time will welcome her with open arms. Hence the reason Gabrielle is nicknamed Boomerang by the grooms... she always came back.

Later that night in The Coach House, Chris the landlord is ecstatic. The pub is full to capacity and doing a roaring trade, people are packed in like sardines in a tin. He racked his brains, as he served customer after customer, trying to remember the last time the place was so full and couldn't, the place hadn't been this full last New Year's Eve. Everyone was talking and speculating about the same thing – who the new owner of Dove Mill Hall was and more importantly how rich.

Eddie the estate agent, or Dodgy Eddie as he is called behind his back, was holding court. He revelled in all the attention and free drinks he was getting "The American that came over is my second cousin from my father's side. Billy was representing the buyer. He couldn't give me any details because he had signed an NDA" he said for the umpteenth time whilst snatching the double Jack Daniels out of Chris's hand before it could be taken away. The fact his cousin had said no such thing and he hadn't even bothered to ask for details on the buyer didn't deter Eddie from telling a few white lies. He was making a shit load of money in commission on this deal, even if his cousin had screwed the price down by two million.

"What's one of them" Marjorie Brennan slurs, she'd been in the pub since speaking with Lady Farringdon earlier in the afternoon.

"Non-disclosure agreement" Chris the landlord supplies as he cleared empty glasses off the bar.

"So you don't know the name of the buyer or where they are from?" Marjorie asks not hiding her disappointment at the lack of juicy gossip as she looks blurry eyed at Eddie.

Eddie opens his mouth to answer but a cultured female voice says "His name is Mr Blake. He has bought the property as a gift for his wife and he lives in New York"

The whole pub went quiet and turned to the source. All eyes bulged at the sight of Lord and Lady Farringdon standing in the door way. Taking a deep breath Lady Farringdon walked up to the bar "I believe Mr Blake bought Dove Mill Hall as an anniversary present. Good evening Chris I'll have a glass of white wine please" she turned to look at her husband.

"I'll have a pint of bitter Chris. Oh and I believe Mr Blake is a billionaire" Lord Farringdon added smiling at his wife.

The stunned silence was now complete. The villagers were used to having wealthy neighbours. They had their fair share of titled gentry, millionaires and minor celebrities but they didn't have a billionaire… until now.

"How did you find this out?" Caleb Raven's deep raspy voice came from behind them and broke the spell of stunned silence, prompting a cacophony of noise that almost shook the pub's foundations. Locals shouted out questions.

"When are they arriving?"

"Is it true they will be restoring the Hall?"

"How much did they pay for it?"

Lord Farringdon held up his hand to stop the barrage of questions and moved to his wife's side, by rights this was her moment and he loved her dearly. He had agreed to come with her tonight so she could give out the information she had gotten from her uncle. Lord Farringdon hoped it would help his wife get over the stigma that had plagued her for all of their married life and put a stop to the locals making her the topic of wild speculations. In a rare public show of affection Lord Farringdon put his arm around his wife's waist and squeezed her to him and placed a kiss on her temple.

With a slight flush to her cheeks and drawing strength from her husband Lady Farringdon continued "After speaking with Mrs Brennan this afternoon" Marjorie blushed at being singled out by her ladyship "I rang my uncle. He confirmed Dove Mill Hall had been sold for an undisclosed sum and the exchange happened early this evening" Lady Farringdon knew the amount her uncle got and she wasn't about to share it with the locals, she hoped Dodgy Eddie hadn't told any of them and she gave him a meaningful look as she spoke "As most of you are aware the estate has various restrictions due to the covenants, I am pleased therefore to announce that the Hall will be restored to its former glory. I understand it has been bought for that purpose alone. We have no idea and nor does my uncle know when Mr Blake will be coming over here or when they intend to start work on the Hall, we are not in contact with him so please don't ask"

At that news the locals all started talking at once, again the noise rose to ear splitting levels, speculating between themselves who would get what work on the restoration and how much money could be screwed out of the unsuspecting American billionaire.

"Well done my dear" Lord Farringdon murmurs in his wife's ear, his hand slips down and cups her bottom giving it a squeeze as he leans over to pick up his pint of bitter off the bar. Lady Farringdon blushes and a shiver of desire jolts through her, after almost twenty-five years of marriage her Lord and Master could still elicit sexual cravings from her body with the simplest of touches.

"The usual Caleb?" Marie the barmaid calls out breathlessly thrusting her chest out and giving him her best 'come and get me' alluring smile as Caleb muscles his way over to the bar. Only ten minutes ago Marie heard the good news of Caleb kicking out his bitch of a wife and by all accounts is back on the market. Tonight Marie planned on doing her damnedest to get a roll in the sack with this fine specimen of a man.

Caleb ran his assessing green eyes up and down her body, then holding her gaze gives her a slow nod and a lazy smile as he points to the optics. Marie felt the twang of her knicker elastic snapping and squirms under his intense stare as her heart rate increases tenfold making her light headed.

"I'll have another as well sweetheart" Rex Davies slaps his empty glass down on the bar and turns to Caleb, clapping his hand on Caleb's shoulder "hey my man, sorry to hear the news"

Rex ignores the scowl Marie gives him for ruining the moment she was having with Caleb. There definitely had been a moment, she was sure of it. Marie set about getting the drinks when Caleb turned his attention to his friend Rex.

"Bullshit you are!" Caleb says on a derisive laugh.

"You're right my friend, I'm not" Rex barks out a laugh picking up his drink and raises his glass to Caleb "good riddance to the bitch" they clink glasses.

"Here, here" mutters Caleb and downs his scotch in one go, wincing as he welcomed the burn of the liquor sliding down his throat, handing his glass back to Marie he indicates for another round.

"Any idea who he is?" Rex murmurs in a low voice, leaning on the bar looking sideways at Caleb's hard set face.

"No" Caleb says paying for the drinks and winks at Marie causing her to blush and flutter her eyelashes at him "take one for yourself Marie" her come hither smile widens.

"You're in there mate" Rex nods in Marie's direction as she moves away.

"I've told her I want a divorce" Caleb says quietly.

Rex splutters and chokes on his drink, his friend has just uttered the words he thought he would never hear. Caleb frowns and pats Rex on the back looking at him in concern.

"Seriously?" Rex squeaks around a bout of coughing. From the solemn look Caleb gives him he knew his childhood friend is deadly serious "And you've no idea who he is?"

Caleb sighs and shakes his head "Whoever he is, he'll be at Baxter's dinner party and he's welcome to the bitch. I've had nothing but eight years of fucking misery and being sucked dry of every penny. I've had enough. You know what, I don't even care who the fucker is. I'm done"

"Jesus Christ" Rex whispers in stunned awe "it's finally over. I mean well and truly over"

"Yeah, you could say I've finally seen the light" Caleb knocks his drink back, he's determined to get drunk tonight, steaming drunk, falling down drunk and maybe have a drunken fumble with Marie.

From all accounts according to Rex she gave good head. Remington Davies, Rex to his friends should know as he is the village and surrounding town's serial womaniser or man whore depending on who you spoke to. There wasn't a woman who he hadn't gotten in to the sack once he decided he wanted them. They all succumbed to the tall blonde haired, blue eyed, model good looks at one point or another the fact that he was filthy rich just added to the attraction. Even his wife, ex-wife Caleb reminded himself, had succumbed.

At least that had been before they got married. Rex warned him what a bitch and slut Gabrielle was but he refused to listen, back then Caleb was infatuated and in lust with her. Eight years on he was seriously wishing he could turn the clock back and regain those lost years. He finally realised the last time she left him that all she cared about was herself and money. When she came back four months later with her tail between her legs begging forgiveness and promises she would change he had given in – again. Caleb knew he didn't love her anymore but pride got the better of him. He wanted to prove the doubters and gossips wrong. Over the course of their married life Gabrielle had left him four times, today being the fifth. Each time it was to a man who she perceived had more money than he did. It lasted anything from a couple of weeks to a few months. When the money didn't materialise or she got wind that Caleb was doing well and the horses were winning she would hot foot it back to him giving the same sob story and promising to try harder. Gabrielle would do her bit in the yard and help run the business for a week or two but inevitably she always, always went back to her selfish, whining ways. Well enough was enough, no longer was he being taken for a fool and made to look a stupid twat.

When word got out about his impending divorce Caleb knew 'The Goats' would run a book on him, taking bets on anything from if the divorce went ahead to how long it would be before he took Gabrielle back, or Boomerang as she was locally called behind his back. A nickname he knew originated from his own staff, he roared laughing to himself when he overheard his grooms first use the name, it was then that he realised he no longer loved her if he found the nickname so funny.

Caleb spied The Goats sat in the far corner huddled around a table in deep discussion. The three men were all named William, to differentiate them they were called Will, Bill and Billy. They notoriously bet on anything and everything, roping in as many people as they possibly could to bet on the potential outcome of the current scandal or gossip. It was all made legal by Will, who ran the local betting shop in town, as village residents Chris the landlord turned a blind eye to The Goats activity of taking bets off people in the pub purely because they were his best customers. Caleb debated going over and asking if they had started the book on him yet.

"Listen Caleb, why don't we go to the club" Rex says excitedly bringing Caleb out of his thoughts "come on mate, it's been years since you last went. You can poke her any time" Rex subtly nods in Marie's direction "come with me and work over some decent girls, what do you say?"

Caleb glances sideways to see Rex waggle his eyebrows suggestively making him smile. "Sure, why the hell not" Caleb started in surprise hearing the words slip from his mouth "Fuck it, let's go and have some fun and meaningless sex to celebrate my new found freedom. I might even see if I can get my own private room back"

"That's my boy" Rex claps his hand on Caleb's shoulder as they head out of the pub "I also hear a rumour the place has a new owner, perfect excuse to see how true it is don't you think?"

Marie sighs wistfully as she watches Caleb walk out the pub with Rex. Fantasising about the rippling muscles she knew he had hiding under his clothes. Last year one day during the summer she had seen first-hand the gorgeous fit body he possessed as he had worked the horses unaware he was being watched. Caleb's retreating back covered in a heavy leather coat did little to stop her lusting over his broad shoulders, slim waist, narrow hips and tight arse.

CHAPTER TWO

SKYE

"Bollocks" I mutter under my breath as I rip up the piece of paper in frustration "this isn't working, go to bed and get some sleep" I admonish then laugh at myself as I reach for yet another piece of paper and start drawing.

My mind won't settle; it keeps jumping from one thing to the next. If it's not running through the check list of things for tomorrow, I look at the clock, okay today's party then it's thinking ahead to the commissions I've got coming up over the next six months. Hell, my thoughts even stretch to the next twelve months. I have a lot of work coming up, a huge chunk of it overseas, which means I'll be spending a lot of time in the UK and other parts of Europe but predominantly in the UK.

I feel excited and nervous at the same time. It will be the first time I've been to England in nearly six years, well it will be by the time I get there. I know my nerves or more accurately my anxiety is to do with seeing my relations. Since my grandfather passed and made me the main beneficiary of his Will I haven't heard anything from them, not that I expected to and nor have I made any effort to get in touch. But part of me wonders, no hopes, they might reach out when they learn I'm back in the country.

God I'm pathetic! Who am I kidding? They didn't care about me when I lived with them and never bothered when I left home at eighteen, actually I got kicked out and disowned by my grandfather but let's not split hairs over minor details. And I would definitely be kidding myself if I believed for one minute if they did get in touch it was because they wanted a family reunion, it would be more about manipulating me into giving them money.

"Manipulate my arse, blackmail more like" my snide side says making a rare appearance, in my mind's eye I always see a rake thin, mean pinch faced woman, arms crossed over a non-existent chest, hair scraped back in a severe bun "don't forget your cousin already tried that, so take off those rose tinted glasses as the rest of them are no better" she reminds me.

A wave of sadness washes over me as I remember Alfie's betrayal. On my eighteenth birthday he attacked me – brutally raping and beating me – as I headed home from a night out celebrating with my friends. I didn't know it was Alfie at the time, I found out five years ago he was my attacker and his best friend Pete stood by and did nothing to stop him.

Alfie thought I overheard his conversation arranging a shipment of drugs and subsequently he convinced himself I told our grandfather. Alfie's vicious attack was to try and establish what I knew and what information I had passed to grandfather. All he achieved was putting me in hospital dangerously close to death.

Alfie and Pete devised a plan to blackmail me, using the rape and the fact that I changed my identity as leverage. The plan failed thanks to Pete's piss poor attempts to get information out of me and his psycho bunny boiler of a girlfriend who stalked and shot at Clayton only to be killed by the police when she turned on them.

The last I heard, thanks to Nessa and Detective Sanders, Pete is now in witness protection somewhere in the world since he helped various drug enforcement agencies around the globe arrest and prosecute a number of drug barons and cartels. If Pete is still alive, he seriously is the epitome of a dead man walking. Thanks to Pete squealing, Alfie is serving time at Her Majesty's pleasure for his part in an international drugs ring. The case made headline news in England due to the scale of the operation, the millions of pounds' worth of drugs seized and the fact he was the grandson of a much respected business tycoon – all juicy stuff. Nessa had avidly followed the case mainly because it involved someone she indirectly knew and had kept me informed. Alfie is serving a life sentence because the dumb idiot stashed all his drugs in his house along with his ill-gotten gains. The police recovered five hundred thousand pounds in cash along with twenty bricks of un-cut cocaine. Good riddance to the pair of them, they deserve everything they get.

I look at the drawing in front of me, then tear it up. I'm just not in the mood to produce erotic works of art. Mr Dario Benenati will have to wait a bit longer for his rough sketch ideas for his new club. As I clear up the mess I've made I think back over all the work I've done for him in the last five years. The first commission was five paintings for The Gentlemen's Club here in New York, since then he's opened in Las Vegas, LA, Miami, Moscow, Milan, Paris and he informed me this morning he has bought a club somewhere on the outskirts of London. I've produced work for all his American clubs plus he's on the waiting list for his other clubs. I'm currently working on ideas for Moscow.

The clubs cater for those who have certain sexual needs and like to live an alternative lifestyle, outside of what society generally considers normal. When Mr Benenati first commissioned me, the series of five paintings were a futuristic take on pole dancing – I was led to believe the club was a high-end strip club. However, about twelve months later by pure chance Mr Benenati happened to see some fantasy erotic paintings I had done a few years previously for another client, the next day he got in touch and came clean about the nature of his clubs and promptly commissioned ten paintings for the New York club and each club he opened there after.

The good thing is I have free reign on what I produce, my only directive is that each painting must be tasteful, sensuous, erotic and inspire, following the BDSM theme – of course. Over the last three years I have produced some of my best pieces of work. I have to admit I thoroughly enjoy painting them plus it gives me an excuse to try out some of my ideas with Clayton, not that we need one anyway. I shiver as desire and lust flushes through my body, muscles clench in my lower abdomen and between my legs as I remember our playing although, it has been quite a while since we last played. No wonder I'm feeling horny!

I pull my robe around me, my breasts and nipples tingle as the soft silk fabric brushes across my sensitive skin. Time to go to bed I decide switching off the desk lamp. I don't have to worry about blindly making my way out of the studio in the dark as the room is lit by the brightness of the full moon coming in through the large picture windows, these windows run throughout the whole of our apartment making it easy for me to creep back to our bedroom.

As I enter I hear Clayton's soft snores. I stand at the foot of the bed and admire the view of his perfectly sculpted body. Five years on and I still go into a gooey wet puddle at the sight of him. He makes my heart flutter with just a look that tells me what he wants to do to me when he gets the first opportunity. I shrug off my robe and climb on to the bed and smile down at him as I remember our wedding day.

I had finally agreed to go to Vegas and get married but when it came to the crunch Clayton bottled it. We got as far as the airport when he finally said he couldn't face disappointing his mother or the grief she'd give him if we went ahead. I suggested we call his Mom, brothers, Simon, Shelley and Phil and take them all with us. He seriously considered this but in the end he stuck to his decision, so we came home instead and got married as planned on his birthday. I supress the snort of laughter threatening to explode from me, it damn near killed him waiting those four weeks.

Stephanie insisted we spent the night before the wedding apart. Clayton had an apoplectic hissy fit at this and to his shocked horror I sided with her. In the beginning I did it purely to see what his reaction would be, but as time went on the more Clayton did his damnedest to persuade me otherwise the more I stuck to my guns and stayed at Don and Brenda's house – they lived a few miles away from Stephanie – along with Phil, Shelley, Simon, David, Macy and Paul. We arranged to get ready there and I would arrive by car in time for the ceremony.

Much to everyone's amusement Brenda kicked Clayton out of the house at midnight, Alan and Bruce had to prize him away from me and literally threw him into the back of the car. They hadn't got half way down the drive when Clayton, the soppy git, rang me to say he loved me and was missing me already.

On the morning of the wedding, I had just finished putting on my underwear and pulling on my bathrobe when a light tapping at the window scared the crap out of me. Shaking with nerves I tentatively pulled back the curtains to come face to face with Clayton leaning precariously out of a tree that happened to be at the side of the house. I've never opened a window so fast in my life. I didn't know whether to laugh with joy at seeing him or shout at him for being so bloody reckless.

Clayton's face was so full of mischief and love as he climbed in through the window "I can't bear another second of not seeing you and I certainly can't wait another five fucking hours" he grumbled scooping me into his arms and hungrily attacking my lips.

"Where are Bruce and Alan?" I mumble against his lips between kisses.

"Gave them the slip, said I was going for a run around the grounds" Clayton grins impishly at his own cleverness making me laugh because I know they will have tracked him and it won't be long before they arrive knocking at the door to take him back. "What are you wearing under this" Clayton tugs at the belt of my bathrobe.

Stepping back out of Clayton's grasp I slowly undo the knot "Look and no touching" I smile salaciously.

Clayton's eyes flash with hunger and lust as he remembers I said something similar to him on Shelley's and Phil's wedding day. I slowly open my robe, push it off my shoulders and let it drop to the floor. Clayton's eyes greedily trawl up and down my body. I feel the heat of his appreciative gaze prickle my skin, his hands clench and unclench at his sides.

"I see you like what you see" I purr as my eyes linger on his crotch, watching his ever growing erection tent his running shorts.

"Oh yes baby, I like very much" his voice a thick raspy whisper as his eyes work their way slowly from my white silk covered high heels, white stockings, delicate white lace French knickers, up to the silk and lace corset. The lace cups showing off my breasts and tight erect nipples. "I like very much indeed" Clayton cups and adjusts himself. He takes

a step forward. I hold still as he leans forward his lips millimetres from mine "I look forward to peeling you out of this as soon as the ceremony is over" he growls.

"In the meantime, all you will be thinking about as I walk down the aisle is what I've got on underneath my dress" again my words echo what I said to him six weeks ago.

Clayton's eyes sparkle with lust and amusement, his chuckle is full of dark promises as his lips close the distance and he kisses the life out of me. The only part of our bodies touching is our lips and tongues as they dip and weave in the all too familiar dance of seduction. A knock on the door brings a halt to our dancing mouths.

"Miss Darcy please let Mr Blake know that Bruce is waiting outside to take him back to his mother's" Paul calls out. We both burst out laughing.

"Busted" Clayton grins as he bends to pick up my bathrobe and holds it out so I can put it back on "and here's me thinking I'd have time to fuck you against the wall one last time before you make an honest man of me" he whispers low in my ear sending shivers of lust racing through me as images flash in my mind, he kisses and grazes his teeth against my neck, grinding his hips into my bum so I can feel his arousal. My French knickers are saturated "wet for me baby?"

I don't need to answer him; the bastard knows what he's doing to me "Go" I groan "before I hold you to your word" gathering all of the little self-control I have left I push him towards the door.

I open the door before he has the opportunity to man handle me. Shelley, Phil, Simon, Macy and Paul are all stood there grinning like loons. Brenda is scowling.

"How did you know he was here?" Brenda asks no-one in particular.

"Come on Brenda you must know by now that Clayton can't bear to be apart from Skye too long, he gets withdrawal symptoms" Simon says cheekily and winks at us.

Brenda rolls her eyes and huffs "Well its bad luck to see the bride before the ceremony. I'm going to ring Stephanie and let her know you've been found" she stalks down the hallway muttering to herself about how ridiculous love struck men are.

Clayton grasps my hands and brings them to his lips, keeping his dark blue eyes on mine "I'll meet you at the altar in a few hours my love" he breathes in deeply taking in my scent and makes an appreciative hum at the back of his throat "look after her for me" he says to Paul, who nods. Paul is so used to Clayton saying that to him he doesn't take offense or react.

I watch Clayton as he walks to the end of the hallway, it takes everything I have not to run after him, jump on his back and beg him to stay. At the top of the stairs he turns and blows me a kiss. I pretend to catch it and hold my hand to my heart, then he's gone.

"God that was so romantic" Shelley sighs heavily.

"How did he get in?" Macy asks, puzzled curiosity written all over her face, the others grin at me looking expectant.

"The silly sod climbed up the tree that's at the side of the house and knocked on the window to get my attention so I would let him in"

We all look at each other and burst out laughing.

"That man has got you bad" Phil says shaking his head in wonder.

"What's so funny?" David asks arriving with all his hair styling equipment, I step aside so he can enter my room.

"Clayton has just been caught with Skye. He climbed up the tree and came in through the window" Simon says a tad too gleeful.

"Seriously!" David looks at me with surprised wide eyes for confirmation.

I nod "Like a love struck teenager"

"Aww that's so sweet" gushes David clutching his chest.

"I'm off to make a few last minute amendments to my speech" Simon says jumping up and down on the spot and clapping his hands with a huge wicked grin on his face "this is too good an opportunity not to pass up. Taking the piss out of Clayton and embarrassing him in front of his family, and I'll get away with it!" he literally skips down the hallway chuckling to himself.

Shelley and Macy, also in their bathrobes, join me and David in my room speculating on what Simon is likely to say. I'm cringing on the inside as I know he won't hold back but then again I can't wait because I also know he'll be funny as hell, Simon is a natural comedian, if he wasn't a marketing and PR guru I'm sure he would have made it as a successful stand-up comedian. We sit down on the bed and watch David as he sets up his things. Shelley winces and rubs the side of her belly.

"You okay" I ask, concern evident in my voice and I rub her back.

"Yes, she's woken up and is playing football with my insides, here" Shelley takes hold of my hand and places it on the side of her belly where she was rubbing. I feel a powerful thump against my hand.

"Wow!" I look at her in wonder "now I understand why you're wincing. Better sign her up for martial arts with a kick like that"

Shelley and Phil know they're having a girl. I went with them the week before when they finally decided they did want to know the sex of the baby and had one of those three dimensional scans done. I shed a few tears at the sight of the baby on the monitor, it was a beautiful moment.

"Okay ladies who's first" David says wielding his brush like a sword at us. Shelley and Macy point at me.

Time seemed to fast forward then because I was soon in my dress and stood in front of the full length mirror looking at my reflection. My hair piled up on my head in a loose up do and held in place by an elaborate… head dress is the only word I can think of to describe it. It most definitely isn't a tiara.

Matthew designed and made it for me. It was made of finely spun platinum so it was hardly noticeable against my hair at a distance. The design was almost in the Art Nouveau style or kind of like the Elves wore in Lord of the Rings. The whole piece threaded throughout my hair, at the front and sides and scattered throughout the twisting knots and loops were sapphires, diamonds and moonstones. Matthew and Gerrard had presented it to me the day before saying it was my something new and blue. The crafty buggers aided by Simon had got in touch with David to find out how he was styling my hair in order to make it. I was so touched by their thoughtfulness and gift I cried.

"Skye you look absolutely stunning" Shelley's soft whispered voice came from behind me.

I lifted my eyes to meet her gaze in the mirror "All thanks to you" I smile at her. A gasp has both of us turning round to see Macy, her eyes filled with tears.

"You look..." she takes a deep breath "you look... I don't have the words" she half laughs and sobs.

"Well you look fabulous" I look at her fondly.

The light and dark blue silk gown suited her light caramel skin tone. I'd asked Macy to be my bridesmaid after Nessa was banned from travelling by her doctor. I kicked myself for not asking her sooner, it just didn't occur to me.

"Here" Macy holds up a blue garter as she dabs her eyes "this is your something blue and borrowed. I want it back" laughing I lift my dress as she bends to put it on my leg. As Macy straightens the skirt of my dress a knock on the door makes me jump, god my nerves are worse than I thought.

"I'm coming in" Simon calls as he opens the door, he pulls in a sharp breath when he sees the three of us "just look at my girls, beautiful, all of you. But Skye, you..." smiling he sighs holding his hands over his heart "Mr Moneybags will be on his knees the second he lays eyes on you" Simon puts his hand in his pocket "and he asked me to give you this" he holds up a delicate diamond bracelet "it's your something old. Apparently it belonged to Clayton's great grandmother"

"It's beautiful" the three of us whisper in unison. I lift my arm as Simon steps forward fastening it around my wrist. I know one of his grandmother's will have given it to him and I have a feeling it may well be Granny Blake, she's my favourite although I would never tell anyone that. I really hope that I'm like her when I get to her age. Wicked sense of humour, strong zest for living and on occasion cantankerous.

"The perfect finishing touch" Shelley beams at me "ready?"

Butterflies start somersaulting in my stomach and my legs have gone to jelly, suddenly my dress feels two sizes too small and my vision seems to have gone fuzzy.

"Breathe, come on big deep breath in" Macy is standing in front of me "breathe with me Skye, in through the nose and slowly out the mouth" I follow her instructions "that's it girl, and again"

"Feeling better" Shelley rubs my back, I nod giving her a weak smile, I don't trust myself to speak for fear of throwing up and try to swallow the excess saliva in my mouth "let's get going before we have Clayton turning up here again, only this time all in a panic" a bark of laughter escapes me as I picture a frenzied Clayton hurtling through the door with a pissed off Bruce hot on his heels, that alone gets my feet moving.

At the bottom of the stairs Don, Brenda and the rest of Phil's family all look up at me, I can't help but smile as they all have the same speechless wonder expression on their faces, as I descend the stairs. Every one of them will be joining us later for the reception, I express my thanks for letting me and my party stay the night and get nods of acknowledgement in return. Paul and Alan both do a poor job of hiding their amazement or should that be appreciation, their usual stoic persona's disintegrating before me as we approach the cars.

Shelley, Phil, Macy and David get into the first car with Alan, whilst Simon and I get in the second car with Paul. The closer we get to Stephanie's my nerves really start to kick in. I have nightmare visions of falling flat on my face getting out of the car, stumbling and tripping over my dress as I walk up the aisle, tripping up the steps to the altar.

"Breathe" murmurs Simon, he picks up my hand and rubs warmth into it "Breathe in and out, in and out" I follow his softly spoken instructions, funny how something so simple can help "that's it baby girl" he gives my hand a gentle reassuring squeeze. The car slows down to a crawl as we near the lane that takes us to Stephanie's estate.

"Why are we slowing down?" I ask Paul leaning over to look through the windscreen in between the front seats, what I see makes my stomach drop to the floor "holy shit!" I whisper as I slowly sit back.

"What?" Simon says alarmed and moves to look himself "bloody hell, where did they all come from?"

People, everywhere, so many bodies blocked the road and entrance. Paparazzi, news crews and fans, many holding placards of congratulations surged forward, surrounding both cars. Shouts from the photographers and news crews clash with the cheers of the fans, I can hear the constant shutters of the cameras, the flashes muted by the tinted windows. I am so glad Paul talked me into travelling by SUV rather than a vintage car that Stephanie had pushed for. Relief washes through me after the initial shock and panic at seeing the crowd, at least we are high up. Memories of the last time Clayton and I got mobbed flash through my mind, we had attended a charity function as we left *and got in the limo the paparazzi had surrounded us. It was weird how vulnerable and claustrophobic I felt being low down.*

"Did you know about this Paul?" my voice is barely audible over the noise intruding from outside.

"Yes ma'am" Paul remains looking straight ahead. Simon starts to laugh, I couldn't see anything funny about this situation and the look on my face obviously tells him the same thing. He does his best to control himself.

"I was just thinking, I bet Bruce nearly had kittens earlier when Clayton did his disappearing act if this lot was around then" Simon gestures to the crowd and starts laughing again "oh I am so going to use this later"

Now that did make me smile, it certainly explained his naughty school boy, aren't I clever attitude and look when he climbed in through the bedroom window "I bet this has sent Stephanie in to melt down" I sigh.

Paul caught my gaze in the rear view mirror "We took care of everything when they started to show up this morning" I roll my eyes, of course he did.

I shouldn't be surprised. The media has been following us around since the engagement was announced. The news and gossip columns have been full of speculation about my dress and of course the inevitable baby bump watch. The gates to Stephanie's estate open and a stream of security guards come out forming a line either side allowing our vehicles to go through and keep the crowd at bay. Luckily Stephanie has a long driveway that is shielded by trees and shrubbery so the media will be hard pushed to get a decent picture of me. Driving up to the house I spot guards with dogs patrolling the grounds.

"How many have they caught sneaking over the wall?" Simon says jokingly to Paul.

"Five so far and three posing as catering staff" Paul says in his matter of fact tone, I catch his eyes in the rear view mirror and I see the subtle lift of his shoulder, his silent apology for not telling me sooner, I nod letting him know it's okay, if he had told me earlier I would be heading for a nervous breakdown round about now.

"Bloody hell! That is some seriously scary shit" Simon says in amazement and reflecting my very thoughts. Neither of us say anything else as we approach the house.

I'm greeted by Clayton's over excited twin nephew's Lucas and Samuel, who are page boys, and Marilyn the wedding planner as I enter the house. We all walk through to the living room and the French doors that leads to the marquee, Marilyn gives everyone final reminder instructions on the what, where and when. My mind tries to pay attention and grasp the instructions but no sooner has her words hit my gray matter the meaning doesn't register and disappears. At the mouth of the marquee Shelley and Macy fuss over me, straightening my dress and train. Shelley hands me my bouquet, it's made up of my favourite flowers Blue Moon Roses and white Calla Lilies, the girls carry a smaller version of my bouquet. The men have Blue Moon Roses in their button holes and Macy fastens one to each of Simon, Paul and Alan.

"Right is everyone ready?" Marilyn says smiling brightly at each of us. I bite my tongue to stop myself from saying no. The butterflies are having one hell of a party in my stomach. Marilyn ushers Lucas and Samuel in to place, both look adorable in their dark blue three piece suits. I smile fondly at the pair of them, they really are mini duplicates of Joshua. Stephanie had shown me pictures of all her boys as children and I remember seeing one of Joshua at the age of three, held next to the pictures of his sons you would swear blind they were triplets.

"Ladies, if you will" Marilyn's polite instruction to Macy and Shelley stops them from fussing with my dress and hair and they move into position. Paul and Alan stand discretely behind me and Simon as we take up our places.

The stringed music that had been filtering through to us changed and at the first chords of 'Here comes the Bride' the boys step through in to the marquee followed by Shelley and Macey. I pause and take a deep breath, the butterflies are now doing flip flops in my stomach.

"Ready honey?" Simon whispers holding out his arm. Threading my hand through I look at him and try to smile but my mouth doesn't seem to want to cooperate, instead I nod and take another deep breath as we step through the floral archway in to the marquee.

Gasps of ooh's and ah's greet us, plus I swear to god I hear wolf whistles. Simon's chuckle confirms I'm not mistaken. I see Clayton stood at the altar looking magnificent in his slate gray suit, dark blue silk vest and pale blue cravat. His dark brown wavy hair is brushed back off his face displaying his devastating good looks. He's looking down the aisle and I know he can't yet see me but I do see Stephanie gesturing to him to turn round and face the altar but he blatantly ignores her. Shelley and Macy reach the top and move to the side revealing me and Simon.

The frozen, shocked wide eyed and open mouthed wonder on his face makes me smile and all of my nerves disappear. I feel more confident and I know with all my heart I am doing the right thing with each step I take towards the man I love on a soul deep level. I can feel my cheeks aching with the size of the smile on my face. We're halfway down the aisle when Clayton seems to come to his senses and physically shakes himself and starts to walk towards me, actually stalk is more apt. I hear Stephanie hiss "Clayton! What are you doing?" that makes me laugh, Simon joins me and so do some of our guests, no doubt it's those that know how Clayton is with me.

Simon and I stop walking; I wait for him to reach me. Simon dutifully hands me over. Clayton brings my hand to his lips, his smouldering dark blue eyes never leaving mine. My knees go weak and my heart thuds painfully in my chest seeing the depth of his love, lust and need for me. Clayton lifts my arm around his neck and leans in to kiss me, our lips meet tenderly then I'm swept off my feet as he scoops me up in to his arms and carries me to the altar all the while kissing me. Those that know us well and are used to Clayton's show of affection all laugh, cheer and clap.

Clayton lowers me to my feet, reluctantly. No sooner had I handed my bouquet over to Shelley, Clayton wraps his arms around me and we stay like that whilst we say our vows, neither of us looked at the Officiate or anyone else for that matter. I lose myself in the unconditional love shining from Clayton's beautiful face, it had me rooted to the spot. The second it was pronounced we were man and wife Clayton kisses me senseless to cheers, clapping and whistles then he picked me up.

"Now I'm going to fuck you senseless Mrs Blake" he growls low in my ear, every muscle in my body tightens as he set off down the aisle, out of the marquee and towards the house, no-one dared stop him. Clayton kicked the bedroom door shut and locked it before setting me on my feet in the centre of the room.

"You look absolutely stunning. My heart stopped and I couldn't breathe when I saw you walking down the aisle" Clayton ran his fingers down my cheek, lightly kissed my lips then turned me around and started undoing the buttons at the back of my dress "When I got over my shock I couldn't keep away from you" Clayton's warm lips press against my skin at the base of my neck and slowly move across my shoulders then down my back as he revealed more skin. His lips leave a trail of blazing tingles in their wake, I could feel the start of a fine sheen of perspiration breaking out all over my body as my heart rate increased with each kiss descending down my spine until he reached my corset and worked his way back up.

Slowly and carefully he removed my dress "I don't want Shelley after my blood for ripping the delicate lace before anyone gets a chance to see the dress properly" he chuckles as he helps me step out of it.

I laugh with him "And don't forget the photos" I remind him.

"Of course, how could I forget" he smiles salaciously at me as he lays the dress carefully over the chair in the corner of the room. His eyes rake my body from head to toe and back again, the heat of his desire for me makes my whole body thrum. Clayton reaches down and cups himself, adjusting, making room in his pants. Christ I want to rip his clothes off and drop to my knees taking him deep in my mouth. A knowing smile spreads across his face.

"I like the blue garter" his deep voice rasps, betraying his desire and lust "I'm looking forward to peeling it off with my teeth later in front of our guests"

"It's my something borrowed and blue from Macy" I move to the bed and sit to watch Clayton strip out of his clothes. He puts on a show for me and doesn't disappoint, I'm wet and raring to go. For no other reason but to try and keep some decorum I lift my wrist to show the diamond bracelet "this is beautiful, which of your grandmother's lent it to you?"

"Granny Blake and it's yours to keep" Clayton says stalking towards me gloriously naked, his erection jutting out thick and very proud, a bead of pre-cum glistens on the end.

Instinctively my tongue darts out and runs around my lips as I remember the delicious tangy taste of him. With an effort I drag my greedy eyes up his hard muscular torso to his face "Seriously?" I breathe heavily.

Clayton nods his head and gracefully drops to his knees before me, placing his hands on my knees he spreads them apart and moves his way in between them "Her exact words were "I know you both want for nothing, however I doubt Skye will have something old to wear on her big day. Give her this gift with my love and blessing" and it does look stunning on you" Clayton dips his head and kisses my wrist. I gasp at the generosity. Clayton's hands snake round and cup my bum, pulling me closer to him "what can I say, you're her favourite daughter-in-law, no sorry grand daughter-in-law" Clayton frowns and shakes his head "never mind we can discuss the semantics later, now I want to devour my wife" Clayton tugs at my French knickers and I lift my bum so he can pull them down "now Mrs Blake I get to do to you what I desperately wanted to do before" he grins wickedly at me as he pushes my legs further apart, opening me up, exposing my sex "hmm, Mrs Blake my beautiful naughty wife, your pussy is so wet and ready for me"

Clayton dips his head and places kisses on the inside of each thigh, then nips and grazes his teeth as he works his way up. My sex is quivering in anticipation. My fingers thread through his soft dark wavy hair and drag my nails across his scalp. A deep groan rumbles out of Clayton. I fight the urge to pull his head closer to my sex where I desperately want his mouth, my whole body is shivering in expectation of the boundless pleasure he is about to bestow on it. Need is pulsing heavy in my lower abdomen making my hips rock forward.

"Oh god" I moan low at the back of my throat as Clayton's tongue lightly traces my slit then flicks over my clit. I feel my juices flow as desire cascades through me.

"Mrs Blake you taste divine" Clayton murmurs "I'm desperate to be inside you, tell me you're ready for me Mrs Blake" he slides me off the bed and on to his lap, lifting me to position his cock at my entrance.

"I'm ready Mr Blake" my voice is barely a whisper.

As I drape my arms over his shoulders, my hands and fingers cup the back of his head, sinking and twisting in to his silky soft hair. Clayton thrusts upwards at the same time pulling my hips down, he penetrates me to the hilt in one swift move. I cry out at the sudden feeling of fullness, my internal muscles spasm and contract greedily around his thick cock. I can feel every glorious inch of him pulsing and twitching deep inside me. I rock my hips and clench my muscles, hard.

"Fuck" Clayton roars throwing his head back and clenches his jaw making the veins in his neck stand out under the strain. He drops his head forward resting his forehead against mine, his eyes clenched shut. Deep gusts of warm minty breath hit my face as he fights for control.

I run my tongue lightly over his lips and tentatively kiss him, he responds matching my light movements. Our mouths start the familiar seductive erotic dance of exploration. Our tongues join the tantalising dance of dipping and weaving in and out, licking, tasting. My hips start to move and gyrate mirroring the movement of our lips and tongues. I feel my orgasm rushing head long towards me. I move faster, Clayton thrusts upwards making me gasp at the deeper penetration. His hands release my hips and snake around me. One hand moves and cradles the back of my head, the other at the base of my spine. He pulls me closer to him, leaving no space. I continue to move my hips as Clayton holds still. Pleasure sensations hurtle around my body.

"I going to come" Clayton's words come out as an animalistic growl further heightening my need for him "make me come Mrs Blake" he thrusts his hips upwards as I bear down on him "fuck, you feel so good, shit I'm coming Mrs Blake"

I feel his cock thicken inside me, I clench my muscles around him as I bear down and grind my hips. He gives a powerful thrust upward and I feel his release explode inside me.

"I love you Mrs Blake" Clayton roars his declaration; I feel it reverberate around the room. I continue to gyrate and grind as I hold his shuddering body to me, helping to prolong his orgasm as I run head long and swan dive off the precipice in to the welcoming waves of pleasure as they crash around my body. Clayton's arms tighten around my juddering body, his lips trailing kisses up the column of my exposed throat.

"I love you so very much" my voice is husky; my throat feels raw as if I'd screamed. If I did, I have no recollection of it. We hold onto each other as our breathing slows down.

"Today is the happiest day of my life. You make me extremely happy Mrs Blake, you complete me. I love you" Clayton kisses me tenderly.

"Me too" I smile feeling shy for some reason.

A loud bang on the door makes both of us jump "If you two have finished in there, you have a marquee full of guests waiting for you and Mom said the photographer can't take anymore pictures without you" Joshua's amused voice filters through the door.

"Duty calls" Clayton grumbles as he lifts me effortlessly off him and sits me on the end of the bed "tell Mom we'll be five minutes" he calls out.

"Yeah right. I'll tell her ten" he chuckles "no, better make it fifteen"

Clayton winks at me as I listen to Joshua's fading laugh, I blush. Blimey what is wrong with me! Clayton comes out of the bathroom with a cloth in his hand, he kneels down and spreads my legs, gently wiping the cloth between my thighs cleaning me up. Then it hits me. I have to go back down stairs to a marquee full of people who will know exactly what we've been up to. My cheeks are on fire, oh sweet lord! How am I going to face them? Clayton's fingers trailing down my cheeks brings me out of my embarrassed thoughts. He leans forward and gently kisses each burning cheek. He doesn't say anything he doesn't have to; he knows exactly where my head is.

Without a word he helps me back into my French knickers and dress, kissing up my spine and across my shoulders as he fastens the buttons. I help him back into his clothes. We constantly touch, feel, smooth, and caress each other. His touch reassures me, gives me confidence to face our guests.

"I must say you look very dapper and extremely handsome in this get up" I say breaking the silence as I smooth out his cravat and run my hands down his chest enjoying the feel of silk under my fingers.

Clayton places his hands over mine, I look up to his beautiful face, eyes sparkling with love and a lascivious smile on his perfectly sculpted lips. He brings my hands to his mouth and kisses my fingers then the backs of my hands, turning them over and kissing each palm. "Come my love if we stay here a second longer we won't be attending our reception"

I laugh "Yes, you're right my dear husband. I would hate to get on the wrong side of my mother-in-law so early on in our married life" I can't hide the sarcasm in my voice.

"Say that again" Clayton looks at me earnestly.

"What? I'd hate to get on the wrong side of my mother-in-law" I sound and look puzzled at Clayton.

"No, the beginning part" he's almost bashful and lightly squeezes my fingers.

It dawns on me then, it's the first time I've said it "My dear husband" I whisper lifting my hand to cup and caress his cheek. Clayton gives a contented sigh, his smile knocks me for six, my heart swells with so much love for him.

We are three quarters of the way down the stairs when Stephanie appears at the bottom "There you both are. How could you Clayton?" she admonishes "I have never been so embarrassed in all my life!"

"Oh give it a rest Stephanie" a waspish old voice cuts in before she can get in her stride "it's blatantly obvious the boy is madly in love and who can blame him with such a stunning bride" Granny Blake appears holding out her hand to me as I reach the last step. I take it. She has a surprisingly strong grip for such a frail looking old lady. Her arthritic gnarled hands clasp mine and she winks at me. I can't help but smile at her. I bend and kiss her cheek.

"Thank you for your gift Granny Blake. It's beautiful and very thoughtful of you"

Granny Blake waves away my thanks and takes hold of my wrist with the bracelet on, the light dances off the diamonds as she gently moves my wrist from side to side "It's my pleasure and it suits you. My father gave it to my mother when I was born. They were deeply in love and it's only fitting it goes to you. I see Clayton look at you as my father looked at my mother and you return his love as she did. I wish you both as many years of happiness as they had"

I feel privileged and a little daunted, the bracelet carried such sentimental value for her. Plus, I now know the bracelet is at least eighty-five years old, assuming her father bought it from new.

We enter the marquee to loud cheers, clapping and whistles. My earlier embarrassment returns full force. I'm certain an egg could be fried on my cheeks; hell a whole barbeque could be cooked on them they're burning that much. Clayton on the other hand is unaffected and unapologetic for his actions. He didn't apologise to his own mother; hell would freeze over before he uttered the word sorry to anyone in this room for disappearing on them as soon as the ceremony was over. Sensing my discomfort Clayton sweeps me up in to his arms, causing the cheering to get louder and carries me in to the room. Camera flashes go crazy, blinding me temporarily. We pose for photographs for the next half an hour when Marilyn calls a halt instructing everyone to make their way to the next marquee for dinner.

The speeches are as entertaining as expected. Simon stole the show, much to Clayton's family's delight he is merciless in taking the piss out of Clayton. True to his word he started off by telling everyone what Clayton had done this morning, then he started on me and he said because he had a new audience he re-hashed the stories he told at Shelley and Phil's wedding, throwing in some new ones for good measure. I cried laughing along with everyone else, although the end of his speech really did bring a tear to my eye.

"I wish you both a long and happy life together. Now Clayton a word of warning" Simon turns to face Clayton "I may have handed over my baby girl to you but I will never let her go. So if you ever hurt her, I'll bitch slap you so hard it'll make my hand hurt" Simon waits for the laughing to stop "then I'll set Paul on you" Simon points to Paul who is stood discretely at the back of the room. Everyone turns in their seat to see who Simon is referring to, an eerie silence came over the room when they see the fierce imposing figure that screams potential violence. Paul inclines his head to Clayton. Clayton nods acknowledging the message in return then stood up.

"Thank you Simon, considering I have already experienced one of your bitch slaps it's not something I intend to repeat, ever" Clayton dramatically shudders "he bloody hurts, don't let his size deceive you" Clayton says playing for the sympathy vote to the room at large, this broke the tension *"and besides, my beautiful wife kicks Paul's ass every day"* chuckles of laughter fill the room *"I'm not kidding. I'm more scared of her than I am of him"*

"He's right, Skye spars with her body guards every day" Andrew shouts out, the room erupts in laughter. I raise my glass to Andrew then look over to Paul, Alan and Bruce and raise it to them. Smiling with pride each of them salute me. Clayton smiles adoringly at me and winks, leaving our guests to chat and speculate how true it is.

After a few minutes Clayton picks up a knife and taps it against his glass, the ringing sound brings everyone's attention back to him, the room falls quiet. Clayton thanks everyone for coming and various people for pulling the day together and gives out gifts. He gives a special mention to Bruce, Paul and Alan and thanks them for their forward thinking and fast actions that averted a media frenzy that could have spoilt our special day. This got a round of applause as he raised his glass to them.

Clayton stuns me completely when he turns towards me and pulls me to my feet, wrapping me in his arms he looks deep into my eyes, my knees go weak and I'm thankful he's holding me so tight otherwise I'd be a messy puddle on the floor. *"Most of all I want to thank you for making me the happiest man alive. I was nothing but a hallow shell before I met you. All I knew was work but you have shown me how to live, to feel and made my heart beat. I love you Mrs Blake"* he kisses me with so much passion the top of my head blew off.

When it came to the part in the evening to do the first dance, I had a surprise in store for everyone. For the reception we agreed to have a live band play for the first couple of hours then a DJ for the remainder of the night. As soon as we hired the band I contacted them with a special request, which they readily agreed to. So for the past three weeks, swearing Paul, Bruce and Alan to secrecy, I'd been sneaking off to practise with them. No-one bar those three knew what I was about to do.

As we approach the dance floor Bruce places a chair in front of the stage. *"Sit down"* I point at the chair, the surprise and confusion on Clayton's face makes me smile mischievously.

"Mrs Blake what are you up to?" he complies and sits anyway. My smile gets wider when Paul hands me a microphone. The room is buzzing with confused conversation, I can hear people ask what's going on and see the puzzled expressions on my friend's faces.

"Ladies and gentlemen" I say into the microphone; the room immediately falls silent *"tonight we are not going to do the first dance. Instead I've have a surprise for my loving husband and all of you. My darling beautiful husband, as many of you know and those that didn't, have witnessed today he doesn't hold back on showing how much he loves me"* the room erupts with cheers, laughter and whistles. As I wait for the noise to die down I pick up Clayton's hand *"when we first met I worried that I didn't reciprocate in showing*

my feelings for him to those around us. So I'm going to sing a song it's called Love Walked In, this is for you my love" I squeeze his hand, he returns the gentle pressure.

The band start to play, the song is one of my favourites it's by an English rock band called Thunder and I never thought I would ever sing it to someone who meant so much to me, the lyrics of the song sum up how I feel and the experience I've been through. I sing my heart out, I lose myself in the music, the meaning of the words and the shear love and adoration on Clayton's face, his cheeks wet with tears. As the song nears the end Clayton slides off the chair to his knees and wraps his arms around my thighs, his chin resting on my stomach. His upturned face and eyes never leave mine. With the dying chords of the song I bend down and kiss him "I love you Mr Blake" I whisper against his lips.

A cacophony of noise explodes around us. Clayton stands and people descend on us from all sides. Stephanie is weeping buckets, so are Simon, Shelley and Macy as they all wrap their arms around us.

"Oh you sweet, sweet girl" *Stephanie wails down my ear.*

"Baby girl after that no-one will ever doubt you don't love him" *Simon blubbers.*

"That was so romantic, beautiful" *Shelley sobs.*

"Ditto and I can't believe you kept it so quiet" *Macy cries.*

And on, and on the compliments came.

Now five years on my beautiful husband still takes my breath away. Clayton stirs in his sleep, his arm stretches out to my side of the bed his hand flexes and searches for me. Before he comes fully awake I shift so he can find me and I snuggle in to his hard warm body. He hisses and wraps himself around me "You're cold" he grumbles in his sleep tightening his arms around me. I absorb his warmth and hardness, breathing in deep his musky male scent "you've been up drawing" he mumbles then sighs drifting back to a deep sleep. I place a kiss in the centre of his chest, he makes a contented hum at the back of his throat. I fall asleep happy and content listening to his deep breathing and the rock music playing in the background.

CHAPTER THREE

CLAYTON

I will never tire of watching Skye sleep. She looks relaxed and so young, much younger than her thirty-one years. Lying on her front with her arms under her pillow, her long white blonde curly hair spread around her like a blanket of finely spun silk shimmering in the morning sun light. Carefully I move it off her so I can see her delicate porcelain skin and the curve of her back to the swell of her buttocks. And Christ, what a fantastic ass she's got. Peachy, tight and pert. Kept in shape by all the daily exercise and sparring she does with Paul, Bruce and Alan, not to mention her weekly session with Phillipee our personal trainer.

Unable to stop myself I trail my fingers down her spine, the satin smoothness of her skin making my fingertips tingle, a sensation that continues up my arm and through the rest of my body joining the dull ache and throb between my legs. I cup and adjust myself. Big mistake, my cock twitches and demands more attention. I ignore it and concentrate on the feel of Skye beneath my palm as I gently cup and caress her ass alternating the pressure of the squeezes and my fingers across each cheek as I stroke back on forth. Skye's hips circle and lift pushing into my hand. Fuck, I love how her body responds to my touch even when she's asleep. I continue the caressing pattern, increasing and decreasing pressure all the while her pelvis moves with the rhythm of my hand, swirling and grinding into the mattress.

A low deep moan emanates from her, the sound going straight to my already straining rock hard cock. Lengthening and thickening me even more, the dull ache in the pit of my stomach intensifies. Fuck! I need to be inside her, like balls deep inside. Before my mind has registered what my body is doing I find myself moving over her pushing the bed sheet out of the way.

Starting at her ankle, I place my lips and slowly kiss, nip and taste my way up her leg when I reach her butt I start again with the other leg. As my mouth reaches her butt Skye lets out a sexy low moan and pushes her hips up into my touch. I swirl my tongue, graze my teeth and nip her fleshy cheeks, with feather light flicks of my tongue I follow the seam of her butt. Skye lifts and spreads her legs further apart, her body silently telling me to taste her further. I can smell her arousal and I know if I plunge my fingers into her she'll be swollen, wet and so, so ready for me.

"Mr Blake, you really need to stick your dick inside me, like right now" Skye's sleep filled husky voice demands as she flexes and lifts her hips higher.

Taking advantage of the raised position of her hips I dip my head between her thighs, thrusting my tongue inside her hot wetness, Skye gasps. I swirl my tongue then pull away and crawl up her body continuing with the licking, nips and kisses. I blanket her. I adjust the position of my cock so it slides against her pussy, coating my sensitive head and shaft in her heat and arousal. I bite back the groan as pleasure shoots from my dick straight up my spine. I flex my hips and slide along her sex as I drag my teeth along the fleshy part where her neck and shoulder meet. Skye buries her face in the pillow muffling her moans.

I nibble her ear lobe "Good morning my beautiful Mrs Blake" I whisper in her ear.

Skye circles and lifts her hips ensuring my cock strokes every inch of her sex with my slow thrust "Morning, it'll be even better when my darling husband fucks me" I chuckle when she pushes up against me by arching her back and raising to her knees.

"Does my beautiful wife want me to take her from behind?" I tease her ass with my cock.

"Yes please" Skye groans, it's deep and throaty causing my cock to pulse and weep.

I swivel my hips, the head of my cock has no trouble finding and breaching her entrance, feeling her hot wet heat against my tip triggers the primal need to mate and I have to force myself to hold still, fighting the urge to slam into her. Skye lifts her body and pushes back onto me, my cock slips inside effortlessly. The feel of her grasping, clenching muscles along with the hot moistness surrounding me is my undoing. A groan rumbles deep in my chest and I feel it claw its way up the back of my throat. I rear up onto my knees, my hands grasping where her waist and hips join, getting a good grip as I flex my hips pulling back so only the tip of my cock is in her.

"Ready baby" I pant; my control is slipping.

"Oh yes" Skye takes in a deep breath and lifts onto her forearms, bracing herself. I slam into her. Skye screams out her pleasure.

I start a rhythm of swivelling my hips and slow withdrawal, revelling in her greedy muscles pulsing and grabbing around my cock, then pulling her hips back onto me as I thrust forward, hard. I feel my balls slap against her with the force. Losing myself in the feel of her, the sounds of satisfaction she makes filling my ears. I want more of it, of her. My blood is pounding in my veins, my heart clattering in my chest, pleasure builds heavy in the base of my back and lower abdomen. My cock thickens and pulses, my orgasm is close, so close.

"Faster... harder... please... faster" Skye pants out, her muscles flutter madly around me. I am so glad she's with me.

I adjust my grip on her sweat covered hips and let go of my control. I pound into her over, and over again. Hard, fast, deep with each strike. Skye screams as her orgasm rips through her. She collapses back down onto the mattress her body shuddering as pleasure ripples through her. The grasping muscles of her tight cunt clamp down hard on my cock triggering my own orgasm. My body locks, I roar my release as I shoot my load into her, those delectable muscles milk me of everything I have. I collapse on top of Skye as my body shudders riding out the last of my orgasm.

Gasping for air I lift myself, just enough to ensure I don't crush her under my weight. I can't move off her just yet. I don't have the energy or the coordination, my muscles are like jelly. My head is buried in the crook of Skye's neck. My lips automatically kiss her, my tongue snakes out, tasting her slightly salty yet sweet skin. Hmm delicious. Skye twists her head to the side and kisses my temple. I raise my head and find her lips, kissing her, tasting her. I love the concentrated morning taste of her. People talk about morning breath or their mouth being stale and don't want to kiss their partner for fear of putting them off but I couldn't care less and I've never had that problem with Skye and she doesn't seem bothered about it either. In fact, I crave her taste as much as I crave her. This craving I have for her has only got stronger with each passing day over the last five years.

"Happy birthday my love" Skye's husky voice stirs my blood; my hips flex in response.

"Happy anniversary baby" I kiss her deeply as I pull out of her, moving on to my side I pull her to me.

Skye wraps her arms around me and kisses me tenderly "Happy anniversary" she whispers against my lips "I love you"

My heart feels fit to burst with happiness. Those three little words get me every time. It took a while for Skye to say the words when we first got together but since we married she tells me at least once a day. I on the other hand tell her about twenty times a day, at least. I squeeze her tighter to me. Skye makes a 'humph' kind of sound as I push the air out of her lungs, she doesn't complain. I relax my hold, but only a little. We stay wrapped around each other enjoying the peaceful silence and feel of our bodies against one another, Skye's soft curves moulding and fitting perfectly around the hard muscular contours of mine. Our hands draw slow lazy patterns over the surface of our backs, sides, hips and anywhere else they can reach. My stomach gurgles and growls loudly breaking the tranquil peace. Skye snorts a laugh.

"I was just thinking about what to have for breakfast and asking you" Skye lifts her head and leans back to look at me "what would birthday boy like to eat?" A lascivious smile spreads across my face as I think of sitting Skye on the breakfast bar, spreading her thighs and devouring her pussy "You can have me later, what food do you want?"

Christ, this woman can read me like a book. I scowl and pout at the thought which makes Skye laugh. Her sensual throaty laugh has a direct line straight to my dick and it immediately jumps back to life. I'm about to flip her onto her back when the phone rings. I decide to ignore it and pounce on her.

"Down boy" Skye squeals with laughter "you better answer that, it'll be your Mom and she'll keep ringing until you pick up"

"Fuck, you're right" I grumble, giving her a chaste kiss. As I lean over and grab my phone Skye gets out of bed. I'm distracted by her luscious figure and watch the sway of her hips as she heads for the bathroom. I look down at my phone and see it is my Mom. I'm sorely tempted to still ignore it and follow Skye. The phone stops ringing, gleefully I get out of bed and head to the bathroom, half way across the room my phone starts ringing again. Shit, Mom just doesn't know when to give up. Sighing I answer "Good morning Mom"

"Oh good Clayton you're up" in more ways than one I think wryly looking at my dick "happy birthday and anniversary darling"

"Thank you and yes I've only just got up. What can I do for you?"

"What makes you think I need anything, can't a mother call her son and wish him happy birthday?" she says defensively.

Her felicitations could wait a couple more hours or until I saw her this evening, I know my mother and calling me this early in the morning only amounts to one thing, she's after something. "Of course Mom, now tell me what it is you want"

Mom sighs heavily, so heavily is rattles down the phone line. I don't like the sound of that "Oh Clayton!" I can hear the despair in her voice, my stomach knots and I go cold "I… I don't… I…"

"Mom, whatever it is you can tell me" I say softly. I actually want to shout it at her but I know that won't get her to talk.

"Andrew has a new girlfriend" Mom blurts out.

"Yes I know. Joshua told me the other day, said something about meeting her at yours last Monday. He did tell me her name but I can't for the life of me remember it. He also said he thought Andrew would be bringing her to the party. If that's what you're calling about I'm okay with it and so will Skye" I keep my voice level, why in the hell is she calling me to tell me this.

"Yes, her name's Alicia… Alicia Adamson" Mom pauses, she's waiting for me to acknowledge the name.

I'm fucked if I'm supposed to know it. "So?" I prompt.

"You dated her" translation I fucked her… maybe.

"I don't recall the name, when did I date her?" I say quietly and move away from the bathroom. I can hear the shower so I doubt Skye can hear me, still I don't want to have to explain myself.

"It was just before you started seeing Skye. When Andrew brought her to dinner I thought she seemed familiar but it wasn't until yesterday when I was at dinner with Marcia Chapman and she mentioned it. Alicia is her niece" I can hear the panic in Mom's voice.

"Does Andrew know?" I'm racking my brain trying to drag up any memory of this Alicia and come up with zilch.

"No, oh Clayton I don't know what to do!" Mom wails.

"Nothing"

"Nothing?" it's barely a whisper.

"Yes, nothing. Absolutely nothing. Don't say anything. Leave things as they are. If Alicia wants Andrew to know we dated, then it's up to her to tell him. I don't remember her, and I'll tell him as and when he says something plus I'll tell her the same if she brings it up" I pause giving Mom time to absorb my instructions "do you think you can do that?"

"Yes, yes I can do that" she says happily, relieved "thank you darling. I'll see you tonight. Happy birthday, enjoy your day"

"I'll see you later" I hang up and throw my phone at the wall in a sudden fit of frustrated anger. It hits the cushioned headboard, bounces off and lands in the middle of the bed. Shit, just what I need.

I shove any more thoughts about ex-girlfriends — ex-shags are a more apt description — to the back of my mind and head for the bathroom, if I'm lucky I can scrub Skye's back for her.

I grab Skye's plate as soon as she finishes eating and load everything into the sink. I'm feeling nervous and excited about giving her my anniversary present.

"Whoa! Slow down Speedy Gonzales what's the rush?" Skye laughs when I grab her hands, pull her to her feet and push her out of the kitchen with my hands on her shoulders, she's not moving fast enough so I scoop her up into my arms "Clayton!" she squeals in delight and shock.

"Present time" I grin and wink.

"Oooh, goody. What did you get me?" it's my turn to laugh as she claps her hands and kicks her legs in excitement. Skye has never made any secret about her joy in receiving gifts from me.

"You're about to find out Mrs Blake"

I carry Skye in to our home office and sit her in the big leather chair. In the centre of the huge wooden desk is a large box with the biggest and most ridiculous bright pink bow wrapped around it. Helena helped me wrap it and went overboard with the bow. "Trust me Mrs Blake will love it, plus it'll make her all the more curious" she said as she pulled a pair of scissors over the ribbon making the ends spring into spirals. I remember my heart fluttering in my chest at hearing Helena call Skye, Mrs Blake. So few people did as she kept Darcy as her professional name, even the press referred to her as Darcy. It didn't bother me that she kept her name. I can fully appreciate and understand her reasons why. Skye's agony at bringing the subject up for discussion is still fresh in my mind as if it was yesterday. It had taken her a week to finally come out with it, I knew something was weighing heavily on her mind and every time I tried to get her to talk she changed the subject. In the end I dropped to my knees and begged her to tell me, she and the suspense was killing me, I couldn't take it anymore. The relief I felt left me feeling weak and light headed because I convinced myself she didn't love me anymore and wanted to call the wedding off. Now, Skye jokes that when she wants to go anywhere or travel incognito she uses Mrs Blake.

"What is it?" Skye's curiosity is definitely piqued; she reaches for the box. I lightly slap her hands away.

"Not just yet" I admonish with a laugh. Skye sticks her bottom lip out in a sulk "I need you to close your eyes, no peaking" I warn as she dutifully closes them.

I lean over and bring the computer to life, I glance sideways at Skye and see her squinting at me "I said no peaking, do you want me to blind fold you" I say sternly.

"Oh yes please" Skye says with enthusiasm and lifts her hands, wrists together and waggles them in front of my face. My cock stirs. It's been a very long time since we played like that.

"Mrs Blake you are incorrigible" I laugh and adjust my pants. Skye's eyes darken, the tip of her tongue pokes out and runs across her luscious full lips. I lean in and kiss her slowly "close your eyes and if you behave yourself I'll give you what you want later"

"Promise" Skye purrs. The sexual energy emanating from her has my skin sizzling and I can feel it bouncing around the room.

"Promise" I growl back.

Skye settles back in the chair, eyes closed, her hands folded on her lap. Complete submission. My body thrums with need for her, my cock aches painfully. Fuck it! I'm going to play with her straight after this. Working quickly, I bring the website up I need. I alter the angle of the chair so Skye will be looking directly at the screen when she opens her eyes.

"Open your eyes" I watch as her eyes slowly open and continue to widen as she takes in what she sees "happy anniversary Mrs Blake"

Skye's mouth drops open, her eyes snap to mine then back at the screen, she leans forward to get a better look "You bought me a ruin of a house" she looks at me again, I can't read her expression and anxiety is settling in the pit of my stomach. I nod "I love it" she suddenly squeals making me jump. Throwing her arms around my neck she peppers my face with little kisses "I love it, love it, love it" Skye lets go of me, returning to the screen "where is it?"

"England" Skye gasps, looking at me in wide eyed shock "as in England, UK" I reiterate.

Skye opens and closes her mouth, looks back at the screen then back at me. Her eyes are bright and I can see tears forming in them. I kneel down next to her, she turns in the chair so I can fit between her legs. Skye grabs me into a fierce hug "Thank you. It's beautiful. I am so lucky to have you.

I love you so much" she squeezes me tighter "and it's also very thoughtful of you"

Skye gets me on so many levels. I knew I wouldn't have to explain my present, she gets it, she gets me and how my mind works and I love every delectable inch of her for it "Glad you like it" I absorb her warmth and soft curves as I nibble at her neck.

"So what's in the box?" Skye says after a few minutes. I chuckle because curiosity is getting the better of her.

"Open it" I say moving out of the way so she can get to it.

Skye pulls carefully at the ribbon "Helena did a good job with this" she laughs at my shocked expression "come on, did you really expect me to believe you wrapped it"

"Okay you've got a point" I concede as she lifts the box lid.

"Paper" Skye looks at me questioningly.

"Take a closer look" I indicate to the box.

I sit back on my heels as I watch Skye take out the reams of paper Billy got from the English Heritage. Her expression goes from one of confusion to understanding to absorbed interest as she reads through the random pages as she flicks through. I reach into the box and pull out a manila envelope.

"Here, open this"

Skye puts the papers back in the box and takes the envelope, ripping it open and pulls out the document. Her eyes dart across the front page, the frown and curious expression on her face suddenly changes to shock as she realises what it is she's holding, her eyes snap to mine "This is the deeds to the house... the property and it's solely in my name" the document quivers as her hands tremble. In fact, I notice she's trembling all over.

"That's correct, it's all yours to do with as you wish... well within the restrictions that are set out in the covenants" I turn back to the computer and pull up my email account, finding Billy's email I open the attachments which show the house in its former glory "this is what the house looked like back in the fifties"

"Wow" Skye gasps "it's magnificent" she took the mouse from me, enlarging and clicking through the images. Billy had worked his usual magic by managing to find some more pictures rather than the grainy one he'd shown me in my office.

"It's called Dove Mill Hall and it's situated about a mile outside Dove Mill village. It was destroyed by fire over twenty years ago. The nearest town is a place called Henley-on-Thames and it's about thirty-seven miles away from London. The property sits in a hundred and twenty acres of land, comes with a fifty hectare working farm and three cottages situated in the village" Skye's smile dazzles and blinds me, momentarily frying my brain "oh! And a woodland as well, according to Billy a relative of the previous owner lives in the village, so it's possible they may have more recent pictures than the ones he sent me"

"I'm blown away. Thank you. I can't believe you've done all this. God, my head is hurting with all the possibilities that are bouncing around in it. We are going to have a fabulous house and home to live in when we move to England next year" Skye throws her arms around my neck and squeezes tight, effectively choking me.

"I have no doubt whatsoever with you at the helm Mrs Blake" I turn in her arms, Skye kisses me passionately in the way that she does to show me through touch how much it means to her, how much I mean to her, actions speak louder than words – that is most definitely true in Skye's case. I lose myself in her.

"As much as I would like to spend the day kissing you, it's time to give you my presents" Skye mumbles between kisses, reluctantly I let go of her and move back so she can stand "your turn to sit in the chair"

I sit down and watch her as she moves to the studio side of our office. The day when we bought the apartment, and building, Skye ear marked this room to be her studio. I told her I was okay with it so long as I could have a corner for a desk, we're both workaholics and if we are going to be working in an evening I at least want to be able to see her, be near her.

Skye reaches the cabinet where she keeps all her art materials, bending down from her waist to open the bottom draw. Her pose is pure provocative pin-up. My semi flaccid cock springs back to life. I enjoy the view as she rummages. Skye is a petite five foot four but she has long slender legs and the short shorts she's wearing show them off beautifully. Her perfectly round ass jutting out is begging to be spanked and fucked. Her long white blonde hair falls like a curly curtain around her hiding the luscious upper part of her body, abruptly Skye flicks her hair over her shoulder in annoyance revealing her fantastic tits as they strain against the confines of her tee shirt. She makes an 'ah ha' sound when she finds what she's looking for. Turning to face me I can't help but drag my eyes slowly up and down her body as she walks back to me. My throbbing cock is tenting my sweat pants. I'm one lucky bastard I think to myself, having a wife built like a Playboy bunny and she's all natural, women pay a fucking fortune to have hair, lips and body like hers.

"Like what you see Mr Blake" Skye's husky voice purrs. The sound tightens my balls, a tingling sensation runs up my shaft, I feel the spurt of pre-cum release.

"Fuck yes!"

Skye places what she has in her hand on the desk. I don't see what it is I'm too intent looking at her. Skye drops to her knees, pushes mine apart and settles in between my thighs. I know what's coming and I'm not going to stop her. Instead I grip the arms of the chair as Skye reaches for the waist band of my sweats, releasing my cock and balls. Her small delicate hands are cool against the heat of my raging hard on. I shift to move the elastic of the waist band to a more comfortable position, instead Skye releases me and removes my sweats completely. From her kneeling position she looks up my body, pure lust and hunger in her beautiful yellow green eyes. I want and need her just as much as she wants and needs me. It's a heady mix.

Skye reaches for me, wrapping one hand around my cock, the other on my balls. She massages my balls and starts to stroke my cock in slow long hard pulls, just the way I like it. Closing my eyes, my head falls back against the chair, I groan as I absorb the pleasure sensations.

I hiss in a breath as hot wetness suddenly surrounds my cock and gentle suction intensifies the pleasure thrumming around my body. I open my eyes. I love to watch Skye suck me off, she has one hell of a wicked tongue and naughty mouth. My cock pulses and throbs as she traces the veins with the tip of her tongue, then wraps her lips around my glans and sucks hard and deep as she pulls back. My hips thrust upwards my cock wanting all of her mouth around it. Skye adjusts her position so she can deep throat me. My hands automatically cup her head, I stroke her hair then fist it in my hand partly so I can still watch her work my cock but also I know she likes the sensation and the control I'm about to exert over her movements.

I start to move to the rhythm Skye sets, my hips moving in a slow thrust and grind as her hand moves up and down my shaft, her tongue and mouth teasing and sucking. I can hear the rush of blood in my ears as pleasure pounds through my body and the thumping of my heart in my chest and ears. I feel the heat radiating out of me, sweat breaking out and mixing with the cool air dancing over my sensitive skin. My control is slipping, it gets harder and harder not to thrust up and drive deep into Skye's mouth. I drag in air through my nostrils filling my lungs and blow out slowly through my mouth in an attempt to regain some modicum of control. Skye drags her nails over my balls, my control snaps. I take over and fuck her mouth. I'm on a mindless mission as I chase my orgasm. Sensing I'm close Skye tightens her grip and pumps faster. I hold her head still as I power into her greedy, tight hot mouth. She increases the suction by hollowing her cheeks, her teeth lightly scrape my shaft. Her other hand squeeze my balls the immense pleasure sensations tip me over the edge.

"Skye" I roar as my release starts "fuck" my back arches, my head pushes back into the chair. My body locks as I pump into her waiting mouth, the shudders take over as my orgasm rolls through me, leaving me gasping for air. Skye laps, licks and sucks prolonging my stay in the land of pleasure and ecstasy.

"Ready for your presents now" Skye's husky voice brings me back to earth.

Lifting my head, I shake it to get rid of the fuzziness and bring my brain back on line "You mean that wasn't one of them?"

Skye laughs "Happy birthday" she kisses me deeply. I dip my tongue into her mouth, tasting the last remnants of myself then I get a blast of pure unadulterated Skye, hmm delicious. Skye moves out of my reach before I can pull her in to me "present time" she reminds me.

Skye turns to the computer, closes down the email and opens up the internet. After a few seconds of tapping she moves out of the way so I can see the screen. On it is an image of a helicopter, a Bell 505 Jet Ranger X to be precise. Skye hands me an envelope.

"This is your birthday present" she's grinning from ear to ear.

Cautiously I open it and pull out the folded piece of paper. At the top of the page is the name of a flying school. Skye has booked me helicopter flying lessons. I look at her open mouthed.

"This is your anniversary present" she points at the screen "you get that when you pass your test" she points to the paper in my hand "your first lesson is in" she looks at her watch "half an hour"

I'm at a loss for words. I'm too stunned to even form a sentence, how the fuck did she know I was thinking of buying a helicopter. I had told no-one. Skye watched me with a huge smug smile on her face as I looked back and forth between her, the screen and the flying school's instructions.

"How did you know" I eventually croak out.

Skye chuckles, taps her nose and leans forward "I'm not revealing my sources" she places a light kiss on my lips "happy birthday and anniversary my love"

I am so going to get that information out of her. I try to deepen the kiss but Skye stops me "You need to get ready for your lesson. Bruce is waiting for you downstairs and I have a date with Shelley, Macy and Simon at the Spa"

"I will find out" I give Skye my best stern look as I pull my sweat pants on, it doesn't work as she looks back nonchalantly "you will tell me" I smack her backside making her yelp.

"Oh no I won't!" Skye shrieks and runs out of the room laughing as I give chase.

Skye deftly moves around Lisa, our housekeeper, as she steps out of the laundry room. I'm not so lucky and collide with her, neatly folded clothes are launched in to the air but I manage to catch Lisa, twist and land on my back with Lisa on top of me. All the air is knocked out of me. The clothes rain down on and around us. Skye's laughter fills the narrow space of the corridor.

"Oh Lisa, are you okay" Skye manages to get out between splutters of laughter "I'm so sorry. It's Clayton's fault for being such a randy bugger"

Lisa chuckles as Skye helps her up "I'm okay Mrs Blake. It's not often that I get a good looking man tackling me to the ground but I appear to have squashed your husband" both women look down at me, smiling, not one ounce of concern on their faces.

"I'm fine thanks for asking" I say sardonically and lift myself off the floor.

Skye starts picking up the clothes and I follow suit "Leave those. I'll do it" Lisa admonishes taking the items from us "you two need to get going. Paul and Bruce are waiting for you. Go on, go" she shoos us away.

Skye and I head to our bedroom like naughty school kids sniggering, pushing and shoving each other. I'm just thankful that our housekeeper is used to us. Lisa Pryor has been with us since we moved into the apartment, luckily Skye has known her for years since Lisa used to work for one of her LA clients. Over the years Lisa has caught Skye and I in a fair few compromising positions in various rooms around the apartment and I have to salute the woman, she's not phased one bit. When she first started working for us she often said "I've worked in LA for thirty years and there isn't anything you two can do that I haven't seen already, so don't be embarrassed because I'm not"

Skye loves to get Lisa telling stories of her time in LA, the things she's witnessed or heard about and often tells her to write them down saying "You can be the next Jackie Collins" but Lisa laughs and says she's signed too many non-disclosures' to be able to get away with it.

As we head down to the garage where Bruce and Paul wait with the cars we discuss plans for the rest of the day. We'll be heading to my mother's mid-afternoon to help with any last minute things and get ready for the party. Each year we hold it on mother's estate, with the exception of the Halloween theme and costumes, we replicate everything on our wedding day. Retaking our vows, the speeches, cutting the cake, I even get Skye to sing 'Love Walked In' with the same band. I've never told Skye this but that is the best present money can't buy and I'm the lucky son of a bitch who gets it every year.

SKYE

"Breathe in" Shelley says as she pulls on the corset ties.

"Bloody hell, if I breathe in anymore I'm going to pass out" I complain.

"I need you to breathe in so, you'll have room to breathe and not pass out" Shelley states in her matter of fact don't mess with me tone. I do as I'm told "there, done" she says satisfied stepping back to look at me.

I turn and look at myself in the full length mirror "Holy shit Clayton's going to have a heart attack when he sees me in this get up"

"Well you did say you wanted sexy scary fairy" Shelley says distractedly as she messes with the corset and skirt. Ha! What skirt, it's that short it just covers my bum.

Shelley and I are in the bedroom that she and Phil use when they stay at Don and Brenda's, it's actually the same room we got ready in for both our weddings only this time Shelley is helping me get dressed in my Halloween costume. The corset is covered in rich burgundy velvet, on the right side of my waist is a silver star with trails of silver thread shooting out from it that swirls and spirals across the rest of the bodice. The skirt is full but currently it hangs in folds all the way round, when I get back to Stephanie's I'll put on the underskirt which has loads of layers of netting so the skirt will stick out, almost like a ballerina's tutu. I'll be wearing multi coloured striped stockings that have a lacy frill around the top with a fantastic pair of six-inch killer heel ankle boots. I have my wings, my hair is done, once I do my makeup and put in my teeth I'll have the 'scary' part of my fairy costume.

"It's brilliant, thank you Shelley" I hug my best friend.

"As always it's my pleasure" she pulls back and runs her fingers through one of my coloured curls "what was Clayton's reaction when he saw your hair?" Shelley says with an evil grin on her face.

"He freaked, just as you predicted" I roll my eyes "I let him think that I had actually dyed my hair for half an hour before I put him out of his misery"

"Skye you are wicked" Shelley burst out laughing

"When I told him they were coloured hair extensions he didn't believe me; he was all for me taking one out. I told him to bugger off, I wasn't sitting in a chair for two bloody hours whilst David worked wonders with my hair to undo it just to prove to him I hadn't permanently coloured it. Then I told him I was going to dye the whole bloody lot bright pink because he doubted me, that was even funnier"

Shelley is rolling around on the bed crying laughing "The poor man, you don't half give him some grief"

"Serves him bloody right…" I'm cut off mid-sentence as the bedroom door bangs open.

"Aunty Skye" Abby's, or Abs for short, excited high pitched voice shatters the peace of the room.

"Abs" I turn and open my arms ready to catch the bundle of joy that is my four almost five-year-old god daughter. Abby runs and launches herself at me.

"Oh no you don't" Shelley calls out and catches Abby in mid-flight "you are covered in chocolate and you're not getting those sticky fingers all over Aunty Skye"

Just then Phil appears at the door red faced, out of breath and holding a squirming two-year-old Nathan on his hip "Sorry love" he apologies to Shelley "Mom let slip Skye was here and she moves bloody fast. She was off Dad's knee and out the door in the blink of an eye" he nods at Abby.

"Don't worry we were finished anyway" Shelley says holding Abby's hands away from me as I lean in to give her a kiss.

"Hmm chocolate, delicious" I make Abby squeal with laughter as I pretend to go to eat her.

Shelley put the wriggling, squealing Abby down on the floor and steers her in the direction of Phil "Go with Daddy whilst Mommy finishes off with Aunty Skye… go on you'll see Aunty Skye at the party later" Shelley says a bit more forcefully, I wave bye to the kids as the door closes. I give Shelley a puzzled look it's not like her to be short with them. Seeing the look on my face Shelley gives me an apologetic smile and shrug "there's something I need to tell you"

"Oh" I look more closely at Shelley. She looks washed out, she has really pale skin anyway but now she looks paper white and the shadows under her eyes are darker. The reason why dawns on me as I sit next to her on the end of the bed, I place my hand over hers "when are you due?"

Shelley half sobs and laughs "I should have known you'd guess right away. If you ever fancy a change from being an artist you'd make a good living at being a psychic" we both chuckle "I don't know, we only found out yesterday but I think I'm about six weeks gone"

"How do you feel about it?" I ask tentatively, she had a really rough time with Nathan the whole pregnancy and delivery, so much so both of them said they weren't going to have any more children.

"Oh Skye, I'm so happy" Shelley wails breaking down in floods of tears.

"I take it these are tears of joy" I say softly wrapping my arms around her. She nods and I let her cry, after a few minutes she sits up straight.

"We're not telling anyone else until the doctor gives me the okay" she sighs heavily "not even Simon or Phil's parents" she adds reading my mind.

"I'm honoured that you've told me" I squeeze her shoulders "let me know if you need anything or if there's anything I can do"

A light knock on the door has both of us cursing softly. I stand to answer it "It's probably Paul letting me know I'm being summoned back to HQ" I open the door but it's Phil.

"Next best thing" he grins at me "and yes you have been summonsed"

As I grab my things and put my coat on Phil comes in and stands with Shelley, lovingly wrapping her in his arms and kisses her. I walk up to them and put my arms around both of them "Congratulations" I whisper "I can't believe I'm going to be an aunty again"

Leaving them to enjoy a few minutes of tranquil bliss I head downstairs. I shout bye to Don and Brenda, and let the kids climb all over me—now that I'm protected by my coat from sticky fingers—and smother them with kisses and hugs.

In the car I think about Shelley and Phil. They had been to hell and back with the last pregnancy. Phil in particular had been devastated by what Shelley had gone through, thank the heavens Shelley and Nathan came through okay and both are strong and healthy but at one point it looked like we would lose both through the various complications Shelley suffered. I lived every painful anguished second of the pregnancy with them, as Phil is fond of saying "There's three of us in this" he said it throughout the first and the second was no different. When Shelley was diagnosed with pre-eclampsia we got her the best medical attention available then eight weeks before her due date Shelley collapsed and had a seizure. Doctor's said she'd developed eclampsia and they had to perform an emergency Caesarean section. The following forty-eight hours were sheer hell. I'm not religious but during those hours I prayed to every god and goddess I could think of, praying and willing them to pull through.

It was heart breaking to hear Shelley and Phil say they weren't going to have any more children because I knew they both wanted a big family. Phil is the youngest of five and had what seemed like millions of aunts, uncles and cousins whereas Shelley had no family having been made an orphan aged eight.

I love their kids as my own, since I can't have children I borrow theirs from time to time although I gladly hand them back. My thoughts turn to Clayton, I know he enjoys having them around and sometimes when I watch him with them I get filled with so much grief it's crippling that I can't give him his own because he will make a great Dad. I've never been maternal but at times it doesn't sit well with me that even though my choice to have children or not, was taken away from me. I shouldn't be, or, I don't want to be the one to take that decision or choice away from someone else simply because of my misfortune. I rub my temples with my fingertips, all this is making my head hurt.

"Are you okay Skye?" Paul's softly spoken question interrupts my internal babble.

"Yeah" I sigh "just got too much bouncing around in my head" I look out the window, we're not far from Stephanie's "how is Jack doing?" I ask to get my mind off Shelley and Phil.

"He's doing well" Paul says with pride "getting good grades at school, says he still wants to work with horses, hates his Mom's new boyfriend with a passion and keeps asking to move in with me and Macy" Paul chuckles to himself.

Jack is Paul's twelve-year-old son. His ex-wife will never remarry as long as Paul is in my employ due to all the benefits she gets courtesy of me, although these benefits come with strings attached one of them being Paul has full access to his son as and when he wants. Over the ten years Paul's been with me this has worked well for all concerned. Jack has never liked any of his Mom's boyfriends but I'm the guilty party for his ambition to work with horses.

Two years ago we had gone to stay with our friends Mike and Penny Holstead for a few weeks at their ranch in Tennessee whilst I worked on Mike's commission. Since it was the school holidays I had suggested to Paul he take Jack with us. During those two weeks Jack had learnt to ride plus everything needed to care for a horse, he even mastered how to lasso and he became an honorary stable hand. One-night Jack and I took a walk; he was educating me on each of the different breeds when we came across one of the stables in which a pregnant mare had gone into labour. Keeping out of everyone's way we stayed to watch only Jack and I ended up helping deliver the foal when complications set in and there wasn't enough time to get extra help. It is one of the most exhilarating and frightening things I've ever done.

Mike offered Jack a job saying it was open until he was old enough to decide what he wanted to do and providing he did well at school, what a great incentive to get good grades. I bought the foal and called him Dark Moon. I get regular updates on his progress which I share with Jack.

"You know we can always remodel your apartment to accommodate him, just say the word"

Paul barks out a laugh "Don't tell him that, he'll be packed and moved in before you take your next breath… and thanks for the offer. I think its best he stays with his Mom for now"

In other words, he doesn't want the grief and agro Jack moving in will cause with his mother, I let it go rather than challenge Paul on it "Well the offer stands, anytime he wants or needs to move in"

"Thanks… I really appreciate it" Paul says as he brings the car to a stop and gets out, he helps me with my bags up to the house.

Inside the house is a hive of activity, at first glance it appears to be pandemonium with catering staff rushing about, teams of people carrying armfuls of Halloween decorations but in the distance I can hear Stephanie's voice shouting instructions. I look at Paul and incline my head to the stairs, he grins at me knowing full well I'm going to attempt to sneak up to mine and Clayton's room without being spotted. We get a quarter of the way up when I hear Joshua behind me.

"Finally, there's the little lady" I turn and look down at Joshua's huge grin "your husband has been a real pain in the ass for the last few hours whilst you've been gone" he reaches me on the stairs and gives me a hug.

"And that's my fault how?"

Joshua takes the bags off Paul and continues up the stairs with me "He's absolutely buzzing about the presents you've got him, hasn't shut up about it" Joshua laughs "actually what's more entertaining is the fact that you little lady have got him something he has told no-one of what he was thinking of getting for himself, he's flummoxed as to how you knew"

"And I'm not revealing my source" I laugh at the look of disappointment on Joshua's face "so I take it he enjoyed his first lesson?"

"That's a bit on an understatement" Joshua chuckles "I don't know how you do it. Each year you come up with something that either scares the crap out of him or he's so stoked about it he's annoying. I should be pissed because I'm his brother and known him a damn sight longer than you" Joshua says trying to sound indignant and failing miserably.

"I pay attention, that's how I do it" I wink at Joshua as I take my bags off him and I let myself into the bedroom "thanks for your help. Time to finish getting ready"

"And on that note I need to go and get ready myself" Joshua kisses my cheek and walks down the corridor to his room "Love the hair by the way" he calls out over his shoulder.

In the bedroom I grab the things I need and went into the bathroom, locking the door behind me. I didn't want Clayton seeing me before I had all of my outfit on and as soon as he heard I was back he'll be making a bee line for me. Sure enough within ten minutes he's pounding on the bathroom door.

"Why didn't you ring or text me saying you were back" his muffled voice doesn't hide the fact he's pissed at me "open the door baby, please"

"No, I'm getting ready and you're not seeing me until I'm finished" I retort. I smile at my reflection because it's going to irritate the hell out of him. I'm so close yet he can't reach me "tell me about your lesson, how did it go?"

"Baby, it was amazing" I listen to the wonder and excitement flowing out of him as he explains everything he had done and seen, I even get caught up in his enthusiasm for the experience he had "I've booked another lesson for tomorrow afternoon, I couldn't wait another week for the next one"

I mentally pat myself on the back for giving the flying school the heads up because I knew that if he enjoyed the first lesson there was no way he would be patient enough to wait a week for the second lesson. At the time of booking I informed — no warned more like — the instructor to have availability the following day, just in case.

"But my darling wife you knew that already didn't you" Clayton's voice is low and gravelly. My body reacts instantly; an involuntary shiver runs from my head to my toes as warm desire unfurls in my stomach.

"Of course, I know you" I try for nonchalance but the huskiness of my voice makes me sound seductive. I shake my head and continue putting on my make up

"Yes, you do" Clayton sighs "I haven't told a soul and I've only been toying with the idea about buying a helicopter and getting lessons for the last three weeks and the instructor told me the lessons had been booked for the last two months so tell me, how did you know about the helicopter?"

He tugs at my heart strings when I hear the plea in his voice and I relent "You butt dialled me... or should that be tit dialled... no wait... pectoral dialled since you would have had your phone in your breast pocket"

"What on earth are you on about?" his voice is louder, he's back at the door. I picture him frowning at the door with his arms braced on either side of the frame.

"About three months ago you were on your way back from an out of town meeting, somehow your phone rang mine. I could hear you complaining about how bad the traffic was, I listened to you bitch about it non-stop for ten minutes before I hung up. I felt sorry for poor Bruce, he was the one doing the driving" I pause as I put black lipstick on and apply Lipcote lipstick sealer "anyway, listening to you moan it gave me the idea. Later that night I collared Bruce told him what I heard and asked for his help in choosing a helicopter"

"Why ask Bruce?"

"Because he can fly them" I hear Clayton's huffed sound of disbelief. I clip in my false teeth and look at my reflection. My hair with its multi coloured curly hair extensions is piled in a loose mess on my head. I'm wearing the head dress piece I wore for my wedding. My eyes are heavily shadowed in smoky gray and black eye-liner, black lips, very pale foundation and glitter over my face and chest. I smile revealing a row of sharp teeth and fangs, the cosmetic dentist has done a brilliant job at making the set. I look sinister when I smile, just the look I'm after "and it was Bruce's idea to book you flying lessons. It's his friend that runs the school" I say opening the door.

I'm almost bowled over backwards. Clayton is leaning on the door frame with his arms braced either side, he has also changed into his Halloween costume and it's that along with the blast of pure raw masculinity that has my legs giving way. Clayton is going as one of the characters out of his favourite TV series Sons of Anarchy, he's wearing a tight black t-shirt and the leather vest with authentic patches plus he's wearing his leather trousers, an added bonus. His dark brown wavy hair is messed up and he's not shaved so he has two days-worth of stubble. He really rocks the bad boy biker image, his eyes darken as they rake my body up and down. Lust burns out of him, his tongue runs across his bottom lip. Heat is pooling in my lower stomach and it's heading straight between my thighs, my internal muscles spasm in response to him.

"You are one sexy fucking fairy baby" Clayton drawls as his eyes do their circuit of my body again "not seeing the scary though" I smile at him, revealing my teeth "fucking hell" he shouts stumbling back in shock.

Smiling even wider I step out of the bathroom "Scary enough for you?" I say in my most sinister voice but it sounds more of a purr, damn I'm turned on.

"Jesus, baby" Clayton clutches his heart bending over "I wasn't expecting that... come here" he says straightening and reaches for me "let me have a closer look"

I dutifully open my mouth, pulling my lips back to reveal as much as I can. His finger traces each tooth, lingering on the canines "These are real" he sounds surprised, before I can stop myself I bite down on his finger "shit... they really are real"

"Of course they are, what were you expecting, plastic?"

"I guess so, yes. Fuck these are turning me on" Clayton grabs my butt and grinds in to me, he really is turned on. He releases me suddenly making me stumble. He moves fast locking the bedroom door then removes his leather vest and t-shirt dropping them to the floor as he walks over to the chaise lounge that sits by the window. He lies down "come here" he commands.

The simmering lust I was feeling as I came out of the bathroom turns to boiling instantly. I devour the vision before me. I can see the huge bulge of his erection through the leather trousers as they hug every delectable inch of his hips and thighs. For a man of thirty-five Clayton has a better body than any guy ten years younger than him. He has the kind of muscle definition that renders intelligent women stupid and I'm more than happy to be in that mix every time I look at him naked. It's a wonder I'm not a dribbling mess. I squeeze my thighs together as I walk over to him, a shiver runs through me as the anticipation of pleasure shoots upwards from my sex to my aching breasts and tingling nipples.

Clayton catches my hand, pulls me on top of him. His hands run down my back and cups my butt firmly then slides me up his body so our faces are level "Bite me baby, I need to feel those teeth on me" Clayton's gruff voice tells me all I need to know.

It's not often that Clayton asks or allows pain to be inflicted on him, I can count on one hand the number of instances that's happened. When he's in the mood to play he's more of a sadist than a masochist, but on those very rare occasions it happens I gladly deliver it. Leaning forward I gently kiss him, using the fangs to nip his bottom lip, he groans. His hands move down, under my skirt and lacy boy knickers. His warm hands knead and caress my cheeks slowly. I move my lips to his jaw scraping my teeth and tongue against the stumble and work my way down his throat, a low groan rumbles out of his chest. His reaction causes thrilling excitement to flutter in my stomach and desire pools lower down.

Clayton moves the angle of his head as I work my way round to the side of his neck. I run my tongue over his jugular and kiss lightly feeling the throbbing pulse beat rapidly. I bear my teeth and drag them across the skin of his neck, then I bite down.

"Oh fuck, yes" Clayton hisses, his hips jerk up catching me in just the right spot. I moan as I continue dragging my teeth and nipping at his neck. My hips gently rotate against his erection starting the slow build of pleasure to my orgasm.

I move down his chest with swirls of my tongue, tasting the saltiness of his skin, followed by digging my teeth in and dragging down until I reach the knub of his nipple. I suck hard and bite. Clayton thrusts upward, hard, jolting and misplacing me "Sorry baby" he pants "do that again"

I repeat the move on the opposite nipple only this time the one I previously teased I pinch between my thumb and forefinger at the same time "Holy fuck!" Clayton calls out, thrusting hard again "I need to be inside you, now" he lifts me effortlessly.

I stand straddling his legs and watch as he quickly undoes his trousers, lifts his hips and shoves them down far enough to release his glorious cock. Clayton is commando underneath which means only one thing – during the course of the evening he plans to fuck me whenever and wherever he can. My whole body tightens at the thought. Quite early on in our relationship I discovered that I'm a closet exhibitionist and I get off on almost being caught, Clayton has no problem fulfilling my... fetish, fantasy, whatever.

Clayton lies back down, leaning over I run my tongue up his shaft to the angry purple head. I lick the pre-cum pooling on the end of the tip. Hmmm, delicious. I surround the tip and suck, then open my mouth and throat taking him as deep as I can. Closing my lips around him I pull back sucking hard, lightly scraping my teeth over the hot soft velvet skin of his shaft.

"Jesus fucking Christ! That feels amazing" I go down on him again only this time I apply pressure and do small bites on the way back up "stop baby you're making me come. I want to be inside you" I go down on him again "please" Clayton begs only he grabs my arms and pulls me up his body. He kisses me hard, running his tongue over my mouth and teeth as his hand is between my legs. His fingers hook into the leg of my knickers, roughly shoving them aside, feeling me "baby you're soaking... always ready for me"

Clayton positions me over his cock, he thrusts breaching my entrance. His hands grip my hips. I know he's going to hold me still whilst he regains his control. I don't wait and push down, taking him to the hilt in one swift move.

"Fuck!" Clayton shouts throwing his head back, his whole body locks and tenses.

I take a moment to relish the fullness of his penetration. I run my hands over the taut muscles of his stomach and chest. I hone in on one nipple with my teeth and mouth, the other I twist and pinch with my fingers. At the same time, I clench my muscles around Clayton and grind my hips. Clayton's orgasm is immediate and so intense I feel him release into me. He curses like mad, I even get called a 'fucking bitch'. I continue sucking and biting as I ride him hard. Clayton jerks and shudders beneath me for what seems like eternity.

Suddenly Clayton is on the move, the next thing I know I'm on my back and he's looming over me, still buried deep inside. Sweat runs down his forehead and cheeks. I lift my hands to his chest, loving the feel of his hot wet skin under my fingers as I run them all over him. I trace the bite and scratch marks I've made all the way up to his neck until my fingers find their way into his damp hair. Clayton is still gasping for breath, I can see the pulse in his throat and at the side of his temples beating rapidly. I lower one hand and place it over his heart, the frantic clattering beat travels up my arm it's thumping that hard.

I circle my hips; the friction rekindles my ebbing orgasm. Clayton circles his hips and gently thrusts forward, he hasn't even softened "I should deny you your orgasm as punishment" he growls.

"But you won't" I sigh as the pressure of pleasure builds with each stroke and circle of his hips. My head tilts back and my lips part to draw more air into my lungs.

"You look so fucking hot and sexy like that" Clayton's thrusts harder, I whimper as I grab hold of the sensations hurtling around my body trying to delay my orgasm a little longer. I want to savour Clayton's brute force and passion, it's not often he loses it and really, really fucks me "you're right I won't deny you, although I will think of a suitable punishment for later" his words and hard thrusts tip me over and I let go as pleasure explodes through me, my mind full of images of being spanked and whipped.

As I regain awareness I realise Clayton is shuddering against me as he rides out his second orgasm. I absorb his weight and hold him to me, stroking his shoulders, spine and the back of his head pulling gently on his hair. I breathe in deeply taking the mix of the light cologne of his body wash and his natural musky male scent. I'm in heaven.

Clayton takes a deep shuddering breath, the warmth brushes over my neck and shoulder, raising his head he looks deep into my eyes "I love you Mrs Blake" he whispers and kisses me tenderly as he pulls out. I feel the rush of seamen leak out over my thighs, Clayton frowns "I seem to have made rather a mess of you. Christ, those orgasms were intense. Stay there"

I do as he instructs, enjoying my post orgasmic state a little longer and feeling quiet smug that I can make my husband loose his mind with intense orgasms. I open my eyes when I feel the light brush of a cloth between my thighs, my heart swells with love as I watch Clayton clean me up. Once he's done he helps me stand, reaching up I kiss him.

"I love you Mr Blake" I whisper. His arms tighten round me and he deepens the kiss.

"Let's skip the party" Clayton murmurs, it's tempting to say yes and I'm about to when a loud banging and the rattling of the door handle rudely interrupts us "guess not" he sighs dramatically as the banging continues.

Clayton picks up his t-shirt as he makes his way over to the door, I nip into the bathroom to check on my makeup and hair, both look fine then I quickly put my wings on. As I come out Clayton is closing the door.

"Who was it?" I ask as I straighten my corset and fluff my skirt out.

"Mom, she was worried you weren't here" Clayton says not looking at me, he's paying too much attention to straightening his t-shirt and leather vest. My bullshit meter goes off the scale, something isn't right I can sense it. I know there's more to it, he's keeping something from me. Bide your time, I tell myself. I will find out – I always do.

"How do I look?" I ask instead giving a twirl.

"Like a very fuckable sexy scary fairy. I'm getting hard again just looking at you"

"So this is another costume to add to the collection"

"Damn right" Clayton adjusts himself "come on let's go before I can't control the urge to nail you again"

"I give you half an hour" I laugh as Clayton smacks my bum as I walk out the door.

CHAPTER FOUR

SKYE

The marquee is already three quarters full and it looks fantastic dressed out in the Halloween theme. Stephanie and the party planner have really excelled themselves this year. I smile as I remember Stephanie's shock when I first suggested the Halloween theme, she tried to talk me out of it and reluctantly gave in when Clayton said we would hire a room if she didn't want to go with our plans. When the first party was a huge success and it got mentioned in all the gossip columns and blogs she was beside herself with glee. Ever since then she starts planning the party in July.

On entering the marquee, we are immediately surrounded by family, friends and well-wishers. Each year we invite those who attended our wedding and reception, however as time has gone on other people have been invited. I don't know any of these people as they are either Stephanie's friends or business associates of Clayton's and his brothers. I'm not bothered that our special day has been high jacked as a business networking opportunity and I'm not daft to believe that this wouldn't have happened on the actual day itself if Clayton hadn't culled his side of the guest list, mind you it would be hypocritical of me to complain considering I have invited a few business associates. I play my part of dutiful wife as I'm introduced to these strangers and when that's over I surround myself with my friends and family members.

Each year we retake our vows. At first I couldn't get my head around the fact why we should. I didn't buy the 'its romantic' crap line everyone was intent on feeding me, yes we love each other deeply but why retake our vows to prove it. What eventually swayed me was seeing how much it meant to Clayton. I couldn't say no. However, I did put my foot down I was not doing the whole ceremony thing so instead we stand in the middle of the dance floor, repeat our vows to each other in front of everyone then Clayton gets me to sing 'Love Walked In' just like I did at our wedding, only this time he spends the whole song on his knees with his arms wrapped around my thighs.

One thing I did insist on when we started recreating our wedding was we had 'official' photographs taken of everyone who attended the original day. We have some great photographs of everyone stood in the same position as the original only this time in their Halloween costumes.

We have pictures of me as a vampire and Clayton as a werewolf, me as a Zombie and Clayton as Dracula. One year Clayton and I dressed as Gomez and Morticia Adams. I wore a black wig and convinced Clayton that I had dyed my hair black, he was not a happy bunny. I can still feel the tingling sting across my buttocks left by the strap he'd used to punish me 'for putting him through unnecessary mental anguish'. That was the day I realised how much Clayton liked the colour of my white blonde hair and the only time he really punished me. The following year Clayton went as the Mad Hatter so I dressed up as Alice. I had my hair straightened, Clayton freaked when I said I was going to keep it straight from now on. I ran like hell when I finally admitted I was winding him up, he still caught me. So now I know it's not just the colour of my hair he loves. Hence the reason Shelley nearly wet herself laughing earlier when she asked what Clayton's response was to seeing my hair today. Everyone in the family finds Clayton's reaction hysterical, guess that's why I do it all the more.

"Wow Skye, you look amazing" I turn to see a zombie Andrew making his way towards me, he has a woman dressed as, I'm guessing, Pocahontas behind him. He puts his arm around her waist "I'd like you to meet my new girlfriend. Alicia" I hold out my hand "this is my sister-in-law Skye, the one I told you about"

"Pleased to meet you" we both say together.

She has naturally dark long straight hair tied in a loose plait that falls over her shoulder. She's tall and slender, big doe brown eyes with a long thin nose and thin lips set in a heart shaped face. She's the complete opposite of me. Before I can say anything else two large hands land on my waist. I don't have to turn round to see who it is, I know its Clayton.

"And this mountain of a man is her husband and my baby brother Clayton" Andrew says laughing at his own joke. I feel Clayton stiffen, his hands clench tighter on my waist. He knows this woman "Clayton, meet Alicia, my new girlfriend"

Clayton puts out a hand to shake hers "Pleased to meet you" Clayton's tone and face give no indication that he recognises her, I watch Alicia's face and her reaction tells me otherwise and everything I need to know. For a brief second she recoils as if Clayton had slapped her in the face. Andrew misses it, so does Clayton.

"Pleased to me you" Alicia says politely, she looks him directly in the eye and I can see she's willing him to recognise her or to say something else. Clayton does but it's not what she is expecting.

"If you'll excuse us, I need to whisk away my beautiful wife. Enjoy the party" with one hand gripping my waist and the other at the back of my neck Clayton steers me away towards the dance floor "time to get this party started Mrs Blake"

I shelve everything that I've witnessed to the back of my mind. I know without a shadow of doubt that Alicia is an ex of Clayton's. How long of an ex before we met is a question I intend to ask. Over the years I have met numerous women who have introduced themselves as an ex-girlfriend, some blatantly let me know not in so many words that they intend to get him back now that they know he is the marrying kind.

I love challenges and I know I don't have to fight to keep Clayton, so I simply sit back and let the women make complete fools of themselves. That's not to say I don't have a jealous streak, I do. Early on in our relationship if we attended a function and any of these overzealous women were fawning all over Clayton and he did nothing to stop them all I had to do was find a man — any man, it didn't matter what he looked like he just had to be male — and start talking to him. Clayton would be at my side in a flash, possessively putting his arms around me, claiming me.

For a couple of months after this kept happening I came to realise that our behaviour was having a detrimental effect on our relationship, we were playing a very destructive game. One evening taking the bull by the horns I sat Clayton down and pointed this out, the lethal patterns that we played to. I told him I didn't want to continue. This is the only time I have seen Clayton go into a complete panic, he honestly thought I was going to tell him I wanted a divorce after only four months of marriage. He broke down, he admitted he knew what he was doing and he did it to get a rise out of me. I hit the roof and lost it big time. I screamed at him. I hit him and I walked out telling him he could find someone else, preferably one of his multitude of ex's to play mind games with. I had enough of that shit growing up, I certainly didn't need it in my adult life or marriage. I camped out at Simon's for two days refusing to see or speak to Clayton or anyone else for that matter.

It was Paul of all people that brought us back together. He engineered the whole meeting, it was in the underground car park of our apartment building. Paul claimed he had to call in to get some fresh clothes, he had refused to leave me on my own at Simon's. Not long after he had left me alone in the car the passenger door opened. Clayton had gotten in the car and before we realised what was happening the car had been locked, from the outside. Neither of us could get out because Paul the crafty devil had put the child locks on plus he had done something to the front doors as we couldn't open them either. An ingenious and novel way to get us to talk.

It broke my heart seeing Clayton a complete wreck, he was on his knees crying and begging me to forgive him. All I could ask was why? Why would he do such a thing knowing what I had been through growing up? Why manipulate me in such a way? Why did he feel the need to make me feel jealous? Why did he want me to feel insecure? Why do this to us?

At first Clayton said he didn't know but I pushed him until he finally admitted that he wanted to test that I still loved him, wanted him and I would fight for him. Apparently, marrying him wasn't enough and rather than tell me what he needed he resorted to stupid mind games, something he bitterly regrets. Even five years on he still carries that regret. Comprehension suddenly hits me then, like a lightning bolt.

As I stand before Clayton saying his vows to me I realise why repeating them to each other is so important to him. It's the reaffirmation of our love and commitment to each other. No matter what we or others put us through, together we are strong enough to fight for each other, for us. This simple act gives Clayton the reassurance that he needs, my love for him is as strong as ever. In that moment I decide to change the words of my vows.

"I love you Clayton Blake" his eyes widen in surprise as I start speaking "with all of my heart, my body and my soul. When we first met I was broken, hollow, a shell, I merely existed. Then you came into my life and showed me what it is to love, to truly love. To live a full meaningful life with those that love you as much as you love them" Clayton's eyes are filled with so much love, and tears. I reach up and cup his face. Clayton drops to his knees. I place both my hands on his face and wipe the tears as they fall. The words I'm speaking he's heard before, but our three hundred plus guests haven't "I never knew what it was like or meant to love someone so much it hurts until you showed me, helped me and because of you I am a stronger person, a better person. You love me for me, just as I love you for being you. I love you on so many levels it makes my head hurt just thinking about it. You complete me. I thank the heavens every day for making our paths cross, for bringing you to me and I'm never going to let you go my love, my soul mate" I lean forward and kiss him.

Clayton wraps his arms around me, buries his head in my stomach and cries. I wrap myself around him. We're oblivious to our cheering guests.

After a few minutes I look towards the band and gesture for them to start playing. I sing my heart out. The lyrics take on a new meaning for me, for Clayton. He remains on his knees, his arms vice like around me. As soon as I finish singing Clayton stands and carries me out of the marquee to more cheers and whistles.

CLAYTON

I can't breathe, my lungs are screaming for oxygen. I gulp in much needed air. My body carries on shuddering as my orgasm rolls through me. Fuck, I can't get enough of Skye tonight, she's killing me. I only just made it to the downstairs bathroom in time before I lost control and unleashed the beast raging inside of me, eager to get at her.

My undoing? It was the words she spoke to me instead of her vows. Said with so much love, feeling, passion it crippled me… no, shattered me into a million pieces. I dropped to my knees because I couldn't stand up right any more with the weight of what she was saying in front of all our guests. Yes, I've heard the words before but she has never declared her love for me in the way that she has tonight, I lost it. Crying like a fucking baby in front of everyone but I don't give a toss what they think. Then she sang my song like a fucking angel, it finished me off. I had to have her. I would've taken her to the floor and rutted like the animal I am if it hadn't been for the fact that we had kids attending the party. Instead I fucked my wife up against the wall of the downstairs bathroom in my mother's house.

Another shudder rolls through me as Skye's muscles squeeze my dick and I feel her lips then those fucking amazing teeth at my neck. Earlier when Skye smiled revealing them I can't believe the overwhelming urge I had to feel them biting all over my body and dragging across my skin. Scared the shit out of me at first but when she bit my finger my already achingly hard cock nearly exploded with the thrill and my mind went into overdrive at the images flashing through it. Christ, when she took me in her mouth I felt the top of my head blow off, the following orgasms ripped me apart I came that hard. Even now I can barely stand. I'm aware my weight is flattening Skye against the wall but that's the only thing keeping me upright.

"You okay?" Skye's husky whisper tickles my ear.

I nod. I can't raise my head it feels too heavy to lift, so I stay buried in the crook of her neck. The cool tiles of the wall are a welcome relief against my hot sweaty forehead "Just need a minute" I mumble and kiss her neck.

Skye chuckles "Take all the time you need" her arms tighten around my neck.

I find the energy to shift, turning so my back is against the wall and slide to the floor with Skye sitting in my lap. I can't let go of her. "Thank you for making me the happiest man alive"

Skye pulls back, lifting my head off her shoulder. She cups my face with both hands, her fingers flex and stroke my cheeks. Her beautiful yellow green eyes sparkle like the diamonds in her ears. I can see the love she has for me shine just as strongly "Thank you for making me the happiest woman alive" she says earnestly repeating my words back "I love you" she kisses me slowly and tenderly. I follow her lead and absorb everything she gives me.

Suddenly Skye stops, her eyes dart to the door and she tilts her head to the side, listening. Then I hear it.

"Aunty Skye, Uncle Clayton. Where are you?" children's voices call out.

"They're not upstairs" a little girl's voice I identify as Abby says exasperated.

"And we've looked everywhere down here and can't find them" a boy's voice adds, that's either Lucas or Sam. As twins they don't just look alike they sound alike as well.

"What's the betting the adults have sent the kids to come and find us" Skye whispers. I nod my agreement as little feet run past the door.

"Hey, have you tried in here?" Abby's voice is close to the door. I move fast, shifting my body and Skye against the door as the handle starts to turn.

In my haste to fuck Skye I hadn't locked it. Skye lets out a startled yelp, then starts laughing. I slap my hand over her mouth which only makes her worse.

"The door is stuck" Abby calls out.

"You mean locked" Lucas or Sam's voice is outside the door. Skye snorts. "Did you hear that?"

It goes quiet. I imagine the kids pressing their ears to the door, listening hard. Skye is hysterical, she's shaking with laughter, tears rolling down her face. I grin widely at her and bite the inside of my cheek to stop myself joining her in the hysterics that have gripped her.

"No-one's in there, let's go find Granny Stephanie and get the key" Lucas or Sam says.

We stay still and silent for a few minutes, ears straining for any small sound. When I think it's safe I remove my hand from Skye's mouth, she gulps in air.

"Time to get back" I say reluctantly.

Skye eases herself off me then helps me to stand. We help each other clean up and straighten our clothes. Skye does a quick check on her makeup which is still perfect. My face and clothes however are covered in glitter, much to Skye's amusement. I stick my head out the door to check the coast is clear then we sneak out of the bathroom.

"Well you lasted twenty-five minutes Mr Blake" Skye says cheekily as we cut through the living room to the French doors to get to the marquee. We don't get far in to the living room before we are spotted.

"Aunty Skye, Uncle Clayton. There you are" Abby shouts as she runs up and launches herself at me. I catch her and throw her up into the air, making her giggle and squeal in delight, before settling her on my hip. Lucas and Sam come charging in and tackle Skye nearly taking her off her feet.

"Whoa! Guys easy" I call out alarmed. Skye laughs and hugs the boys as they fight each other to wrap their arms around her.

"Sorry" the boys chorus but don't let go of her "come and dance with us Aunty Skye" says Lucas "you can't say no because we're Uncle Clayton" Sam adds. Both of them are dressed in three piece suits, their blonde hair has been darkened to brown and they have stubble on their faces. The effect is quiet disturbing. They really look like a mini me.

"Well aren't I the lucky one to have two younger versions of you" Skye winks at me as the boys lead her out to the marquee. The boys start pulling on her hands so she has to jog to keep up with them as they drag her towards the dance floor.

"That's the last you'll see of Skye for a while" Shelley says from behind me, she holds her hands out to Abby. I go to hand her over but Abby has other ideas and clings to me like a limpet.

"No. I'm staying with Uncle Clayton" Abby says stubbornly, shaking her head and tightens her arms around my neck.

"I'm sure Uncle Clayton doesn't want you climbing all over him" Shelley says attempting to peel her off me. Abby's grip gets tighter, almost cutting off my airwaves.

"It's okay" I assure Shelley "in fact little lady would you do me the honour of dancing with me?"

"Yes" squeals Abby in delight down my ear making me wince and my ears ring.

For the next hour Skye and I dance with our niece and nephews along with anyone else that cares to join us. It was highly entertaining to watch the boys keep any men wanting to dance with Skye at bay, the only exceptions were Simon and David. Lucas and Sam seem to sense those two weren't a threat. They even stopped their own father and uncle from dancing with Skye much to my amusement and through it all Skye was oblivious, she was enjoying herself too much.

"I'm going to get a drink" Skye declares, the boys protest and try to stop her from leaving the dance floor by holding on to her "come on guys I'm sure you both can do with a drink also" she tries to cajole them into going with her. It doesn't work. After a few more minutes I can see Skye starting to lose her patience with them, it's very rare for her to lose it with the kids but the boys are overwhelming her. I step in.

"That's enough" I say picking up Sam under one arm. Lucas is shocked and let's go of Skye immediately. I pick up Lucas in my other arm. Skye mouth's 'thank you' I wink at her and follow her off the dance floor carrying each of the boys under my arms.

As we near the tables where our family and friends are sat they all turn to see what people are laughing at. Elizabeth jumps up out of her seat when she sees me "What have they been up to now?" she says glaring at the twins, the boys protest their innocence as I put them down.

"They wouldn't let Skye leave the dance floor when she wanted to get a drink. I had to intervene" I pat each of the boys on the shoulder, I feel them sag under the force of my pat.

"I told you both to behave yourself and to leave Aunty Skye alone..."

I leave Elizabeth to berate the boys and go to get some beers. On my return I see Skye sitting down next to Shelley. Her butt hasn't connected with the seat when Nathan is scrambling off Phil's knee to sit on Skye's. She laughs and brushes Shelley's reaching hands out of the way as she lifts Nathan up. He snuggles into her and by the time I reach Skye with the beer Nathan is fast asleep.

"Would you look at that" Phil says to me as I hand Skye her drink "we've been trying to get him to sleep for the past two hours. He sits on Skye's knee for all of two seconds and he's out like a light"

"What can I say, it's the effect I have on kids" Skye chuckles.

I lean down and kiss her temple "I'm going to mingle" Skye nods and offers her lips for a kiss which I oblige. I leave her with our good friends as I set out to say hello to my business associates and other branches of my family I only ever see at weddings, christenings, funerals and the occasional anniversary party. Plus, I want to stay the fuck away from Alicia. If she and Andrew hadn't been sat at the table, I would be snuggling up to Skye instead of Nathan.

As I work my way around the room I watch Skye. She's great with the kids, never turning them away, smothering them with love and affection not to mention spoiling them rotten. Yet I can't help wondering why she's never brought up the subject of us adopting our own. I've always maintained that it will be Skye's decision if we ever go down that road and I don't know why but I'm surprised she's not brought it up for discussion especially since Skye has been Shelley's birthing partner along with Phil for both pregnancies.

The kids absolutely adore her, to prove the point as soon as Phil has lifted the sleeping Nathan off her knee Abby climbs up and snuggles in. Skye wraps her arms around Abby and tenderly kisses the top of her head. Skye rocks gently and from where I'm stood I can see Abby's eye grow heavy within minutes the child is fast asleep. I look at my family watching Skye as she chats with Simon, David, Macy, Shelley and Phil whilst holding Abby in her arms. I can tell from my Mom's face she longs to have another grandchild.

I'm thankful since the awful night Andrew's bitch of an ex-girlfriend forced my hand and I had to tell my family about Skye not being able to have children then weeks later they learnt the truth first hand from Skye as to why she couldn't. None of my immediate family have brought the subject up around her. That doesn't stop them from saying anything to me, namely my mother and grandparents.

When are we going to adopt?

Did I not want children?

Those are the two favourite questions.

From time to time the press question why we haven't started a family yet, or speculation that Skye is finally pregnant circulates when she is seen attending clinic appointments with Shelley. I realise I need to talk to Skye about this, find out her thoughts and feelings. We haven't talked about this since I asked her to marry me in Vegas. My stance hasn't changed, I love my niece and nephews but I'm always glad to hand them back. I don't feel the need to have our own kids, not yet anyway.

Movement at the table shifts my focus. Andrew is leading Alicia to the dance floor. Christ what a fucking mess that conversation is going to be as and when Andrew decides to get my opinion. I'm hoping I haven't given Skye any reason to be suspicious. I patted myself on the back when Andrew introduced us, feigning that I didn't know her and I'm certain Alicia realised that I didn't remember her even though we went on two dates. One was before I met Skye the other after, I'm thankful and relieved that I didn't fuck her on either occasion, if I had… a shudder goes through me, that is a conversation I really, really didn't want to have with Skye. At least I can stand in front of her with a clear conscience.

Phil takes a sleeping Abby off Skye and not long after she stands and moves away from the table. Joshua grabs hold of Lucas and Sam as they make a beeline for her. He shakes his head and points to the chairs, both boys sit down scowling and looking mutinous at their father crossing their arms showing how disgruntled they are. I watch Skye move around the room, chatting to her few business associates and other friends. I lose sight of her as she gets swallowed up when they all surround her.

It's a shame Boris Cheremisinova, or Mr C as Skye calls him, couldn't make it this year. He's almost like a grandfather to Skye; he certainly treats her as one of his family. Every year we vacation with him on his yacht along with everyone else — with the exception, thank Christ, of Maxine and Brett — who were on the very first trip Skye and I took together. Those couples have become good friends especially Mike and Penny who we see at least three times a year. Mike still has Skye on pedestal and hero worships the ground she walks on, at least he's no longer star struck around her.

After I have done my duty I head back to our table, there's no sign of Skye. I can't see her as I look around the marquee, even with three hundred plus guests I would find her easily. I look around the perimeter there's no Paul either. I find Bruce stood by the entrance.

"Mrs Blake's gone into the main house sir" Bruce says before I open my mouth, he talks into his sleeve "she's on the library veranda" I nod my thanks and head into the house to find her.

The library is in darkness; I don't need to switch the light on as the French doors are open letting the external lights outside flood the room with enough light so I don't collide with any of the furniture as I make my way across. I step out and see Paul stood at a discreet distance to my left, he nods in the direction where I will find Skye, as I turn to look for her Paul retreats into the library. I know he won't go far and Bruce or Alan, or both will be coming to join him in a matter of minutes.

Skye is stood at the far end of the veranda, leaning against the post looking out across the garden towards the pond. She sighs heavily lifting her head to face the bright shining waning moon, stars flicker as dark clouds move across in the ink black sky.

"That was a heavy sigh" I say slipping my hands around her waist, pulling her back in to me. I kiss the side of her neck. Skye doesn't even flinch; she knew I was near "you okay?"

Skye turns to face me. Lifting on to her tip toes her arms circling my neck I dip my head to meet her lips "Hmm, I am now" she murmurs. Skye turns back to face the garden and pond "I love this view, I always find it calming, soothing. I could stand for hours looking at it"

I pull her tighter to me and enjoy the view with her for a while, listening to the distant noise of the music and our guests enjoying themselves. I can sense her melancholy; I instinctively know Skye is working up to discuss something serious. Give her time and space, she'll talk when she's ready I tell myself. After another ten minutes I can't stand it anymore.

"Talk to me. What's bothering you?" I turn her back round to face me. I need to see her face if it's as serious as I think it's going to be "and don't say nothing because I can tell something is, especially since we should be over there enjoying ourselves" I incline my head in the direction of the marquee.

Skye gives me a sad smile, closes her eyes and takes a deep breath. She opens her eyes slowly and I can see infinite sadness in them. My heart plummets to the ground. I know I'm not going to like what she's going to say… at all.

"I don't know where to start" she sighs "so much is going round my head I can't process it all"

Cold sweat breaks out all over my body, panic is rising from the pit of my stomach making it clench and twist painfully. Thoughts hurtle through my mind each one getting worse finishing with she wants a divorce or has an incurable illness and hasn't long to live. My hands are trembling as I raise them to cup her face "Give me one word that sums up what has you feeling like this" my voice is barely a whisper.

"Children" Skye whispers back. That one word has my knees buckling with relief. I sag to the floor taking her with me. I wrap my arms around her holding on for dear life. Of all the things that raced through my mind that wasn't one of them. Skye runs her hands through my hair and back in soothing motions. I realise my whole body is trembling.

"Thank fuck for that" I gasp out; my pounding heart makes it difficult to breath. Skye doesn't say anything; in fact, she's gone very still. I move Skye so I can see her, lifting her face "look at me" her eyes are still full of sorrow "whenever you want to adopt then we will, just say the word" I say with as much sincerity as possible.

"That's just it. I don't" Skye's eyes fill with tears "I'm sorry but I don't want children. I know it's selfish of me and to deny you that choice is killing me. I don't want to be responsible for withholding something that you want"

"What makes you think I want children?"

Skye gives a pitiful shrug "You've been watching me all night with the kids I just… I just thought" she takes a deep breath "and I know your Mom would love for us to adopt"

"What has she said to you?" anger mars my words. I'll drag my mother over fucking hot coals if she's upset my beautiful wife.

"She doesn't have to say anything, I can see it on her face" Skye looks down at her lap, she moves her arms from around me. I feel the absence as if someone has surgically removed my own. I take her hands and place her arms back around my neck, surprise flits across her face.

"I've watched you tonight in awe. For your patience, boundless energy and love that you shower on our niece and nephews. I will admit that not having kids of our own has crossed my mind. However, it was more to do with why you haven't brought the subject up sooner and would it help ease your conscious if I said I don't want kids either"

"You're just saying that to make me feel better" Skye says despondently dropping her head.

"Look at me" I say sharply. Skye's head snaps back up, her eyes wide in shock "I. Don't. Want. Kids. Understand" I say each word clear and succinct "that's not to say that one day I may change my mind, just like one day you might. When that happens we will sit down and discuss it. As it is, at this moment in time I'm too selfish. I want you all to myself. I am not prepared to share you; it's been bad enough having to do that with the four of them this evening"

Skye sags against me "Thank god for that" the relief evident in her muffled voice "actually it'll be more than four in about seven or eight months' time" Skye sits back up smiling "but I haven't told you that"

"Shelley?" Skye nods "when did she tell you?"

"Earlier when I was at Don and Brenda's. I'm the only one that knows, they're not telling anyone until she's got the okay from the doctor"

"How does she feel about it? You know after everything she went through with Nathan, I thought they said they weren't going to have anymore"

"She's over the moon, although I think this will be the last. As you know they both want a big family and this will get them part way there at least" Skye stands, holding out her hand to me "come on we best head back"

I stand and move towards the French doors. Skye stays where she is looking out into the garden. "What are you looking at now?" I look across the garden curious, Skye points towards the bushes that are half way down running alongside the lawn.

"Someone is stood over there. They're watching something or someone" Skye leans over the balcony trying to get a better look "it's a man" her voice has gone to a loud whisper "he's… oh my lord" Skye gasps in shock then laughs "he's… let's say pleasuring himself"

I can't see anyone from where I'm stood so I move next to Skye and hunker down to her height, then I see him "Fuck me, you're right. I thought you were winding me up"

There is no mistaking what the tall shadowy figure is doing. I can make out his fast pumping arm as he masturbates. His attention is fixed on whatever is happening in the bushes. Both of us lean further over the balcony, ears straining.

"Did you hear that?" Skye whispers, I shake my head I can only hear the music "he's watching a couple have sex. I can make out a female groaning" just then there's a lull in the music and distinct groans of pleasure drift in our direction. Skye sniggers, which sets me off. I grab her hand and indicate to the door. Skye shakes her head "sod that! I want to find out who the randy buggers are that are squashing your Mom's plants"

We don't have to wait long and both of us get the biggest shock of our lives when the self-pleasuring shadowy figure and the couple having sex emerge out of the garden passing the side of the house to head back to the marquee.

"Holy shit!" Skye exclaims "did you know they…"

"No" I cut Skye off.

"Well at least Alicia can claim a hat trick now"

"What the fuck is that supposed to mean?" I shout rounding on Skye, she takes a step back but holds my glare, defiantly.

"That she has fucked all three Blake brothers" Skye replies acerbically and I hear the challenge in her voice daring me to deny it and I do.

"She hasn't scored a hat trick" I say defensively.

Skye raises a sceptical eyebrow "Clayton, I'm not stupid and don't insult my intelligence. I know she is an ex-whatever of yours. You know her and dated her" Skye is getting angry; she doesn't lose her temper very often. I certainly don't want to be on the receiving end it.

"Okay, I'm sorry" I sigh reaching out for Skye. I need to hold her but she resists my attempts to pull her close "I went on two dates with her. The first one was a few weeks before we met. The second was when you went to Russia"

"Oh my god, she's one of the four" Skye gasps.

"Yes. I didn't remember her when Mom fixed up the second one. I remembered more about the function we attended than I did her, that's how much of an impression she made on me. I didn't fuck her on either occasion. The second date was horrendous. I already knew by then that I wanted to be with you and she came on so strong, all night she was relentless. Anyway she's the reason why I lost it with Mom and her meddling ways" I look into Skye's eyes. I see sympathy "this morning Mom rang to say that when she first met Andrew's girlfriend she couldn't help feeling Alicia seemed familiar, then yesterday she realised why. Alicia is the niece of a friend of hers and that I had dated her. She was worried it would cause a problem between me and Andrew. I told her I didn't remember the name, I couldn't recall a face either and I would tell Andrew and Alicia as much if either of them said anything"

"But you did recognise her when Andrew introduced us and that's why you've kept your distance all night from both of them"

Damn! My wife is very observant and astute, something I am forever underestimating. "What gave me away?" I can't help but smile at her.

"Your body language. I must say you are a very good actor because you fooled Andrew and Alicia" Skye says smugly.

"Forgive me, I should have said something sooner. I just didn't want to spoil our special day" I pull my best contrite and puppy dog eyed face, it works. I see Skye relent as she steps in to me, her arms circling my waist.

"You're forgiven" we stand for a few minutes just holding each other "I would never have guessed Joshua and Andrew are into… what are they into? Wife swapping?" Skye looks up at me puzzled.

"I don't know" I pull Skye towards the library "all I know is that Joshua and Elizabeth have some sort of 'open relationship' whatever that means" I shrug "I've known Joshua to have one night stands over the years but he's never had an affair. I did tackle him about it years ago, that's when he explained about their relationship. I've never said anything to Elizabeth and I'm guessing she's had her fair share if Joshua is telling the truth"

"Do you think all of them are into swinging?" Skye is curious.

"It's not something I really want to think about or find out about" I smack Skye's backside "and don't you be getting any ideas; I'm not sharing you with anyone. I am clear" I smack her again, slightly harder.

"Message received loud and clear" Skye half yelps and laughs as she tries to dodge my hand coming in for another smack "but I have to admit, I am curious as hell about their relationship. Maybe I can get Elizabeth to spill" I can practically hear the cogs whirling in her brain "mind you, I don't think I can look at Joshua or Andrew again without smirking or laughing" Skye adds mischievously as we enter the marquee and what do you know the first fucking people we see are my brothers. I look at Skye and we burst out laughing.

"What's so funny?" Joshua asks.

Skye becomes hysterical, shaking my head I guide her away as fast as possible leaving both my brothers looking bemused.

CHAPTER FIVE

CLAYTON

Hot water pounds my body from three different directions as I angle the shower heads to work their magic on my neck and back muscles. I stretch in different positions and directions trying to work out all the kinks. I love having our party at my mother's house but I hate sleeping in my old bed. I'm buying a new bed for this room, a snort escapes me I say that every year and I've not done it yet. I grab the shampoo and start to lather some in my hair. A small pair of hands trail over my stomach, up my chest and back down. I can't open my eyes for the soap but I don't need to. I enjoy the feel of Skye's hands exploring my body as I rinse the shampoo out of my hair and face.

"Morning baby" I bend down and kiss her gently "how's your head and did you sleep well?"

Skye smiles sleepily at me, her voice is raspy "My head is fine. I didn't drink that much and yes, I slept very well thank you. How about you?"

"Let's just say I'm definitely buying a new bed" Skye chuckles as she reaches for the shampoo, it's the kind that says yeah right, I'll believe it when I see it "you and Elizabeth seemed to be thick as thieves last night. What did you talk about?"

Skye grins impishly "Guess"

I turn Skye around and help wash her hair "I have no idea. I'm not at all familiar…" I pause as I start to consider a possibility, something Skye had mentioned "you didn't" I say in drawn out disbelief.

"I did" Skye smugly chuckles.

She doesn't volunteer any more information. After we have rinsed her hair Skye applies conditioner and I get the body wash. We enjoy soaping each other. I love the feel of Skye's soft silky body under my hands, she is so responsive to my touch. Her body arches into my caresses and my mind keeps flitting back to what we witnessed last night in the garden. I said I didn't want to know, but now… damn curiosity.

"Okay, I give in. What did you find out?" I sound resigned, Skye is gleeful and I know instantly she's been dying to tell me.

"We're not the only kinky ones in the family, only we don't share each other" Skye's says with a huge grin.

"How in god's name did you get that out of her?" I'm stunned "and what did you tell her about us?"

"She started it by asking did I mind you making such a public display of carting me out so you could have your wicked way with me"

A jolt shoots through me and my hands stop caressing her body. I've never considered that before, how did Skye feel about that? She's never said anything so I've assumed she doesn't have a problem with it.

"I love it, so don't beat yourself up about it" Skye says answering my thoughts. She steps into the spray of water, rinsing the conditioner out of her hair. Her raised arms show off her glorious jiggling tits as she works her hands through her hair.

Unable to resist I lean forward and latch onto a nipple. I suck deep drawing it into my mouth. Skye gasps. "Tell me more" I murmur as I bring my hands up and massage both fleshy globes, my mouth going back to work her nipple.

"I told her I didn't mind... Macy said I was so used to it happening it would be unusual if it didn't happen..." Skye's breathing is getting heavy "then I asked her did Joshua do anything like that to her... let's just say once she started talking... it was difficult to shut her up" Skye moans as I trail my fingers down her taut stomach and between her legs "gave us all a laugh with some of the stories she was telling us" Skye's fingers tangle in my hair, her hips circle and thrust in to the rhythm of my hand and fingers "when no-one was listening... she told me she's Joshua's sub" Skye sighs "she told me... she told me about the things they get up to"

"Enough" I say picking Skye up; her legs automatically wrap around me. Reaching between us I position my cock at her entrance and thrust forward gently. Skye's head falls back on a low groan "I really don't want to know about my brother's sexual antics, last night was bad enough"

"But if it had been someone else we'd seen..." Skye opens her eyes and bites her bottom lip. I see excitement, lust and mischief in them. Her muscles clench and grip me tightly, her body telling me she finds the whole thing erotic. The very thought makes my control slip. I take her to the wall, one hand slaps on the tiles as the other arm wraps around her waist, greedily taking her mouth as I start to pound into her. Skye tightens around me. I can tell a fantasy is playing out in her head.

"Tell me what you're thinking" I demand.

"Just as we saw last night, but we can see the couple having sex and you... you..." Skye groans as I thrust deep and hard at the image that's now in my head "you are fucking me at the same time" she finishes in a rush. Her muscles are gripping and milking me. I picture us on the veranda, I'm taking her from behind, hard.

My orgasm hits me unexpectedly "Fuck" I shout and thrust powerfully into Skye as I empty into her, my hips and back locking as pleasure rolls through me. Skye joins me. I hold her shuddering body close. I circle and thrust my hips gently, drawing in and out of her at a leisurely pace dragging out our orgasms, bringing us gently down. I rest my forehead against the cool tiles as I get my breath back to normal. Skye's lips move across my chest, kissing her way up my throat and under my chin. She hums contentedly. I pull back and look into her beautiful satiated face "who would have guessed my naughty wife has a voyeurism streak" I tease then kiss her soundly.

"You like the idea of it" Skye retorts as I ease out of her. She had me there, I do.

"I'll admit it does so let's discuss it when we get home" I slap her butt as I direct her out of the shower "right now I have a flying lesson to get ready for"

As is our usual ritual when we bathe together, we take great delight in drying each other and I love helping Skye apply moisturiser all over her body. I leave Skye to sort her hair out and get dressed.

"What are you going to do whilst I'm having my lesson" I call.

"I was just thinking of going for a bike ride if the weather is good" Skye walks in to the bedroom. I watch her gloriously naked figure as she goes over to the window, poking her head between the closed curtains "it's sunny out, clear blue sky"

"So that means it could be icy" I add; anxiety is building in my stomach. I reach Skye and pull her round to face me "please don't go out if it's icy"

Skye's eyes soften, reaching up she runs her fingers down my cheek then cups my face. I turn my head and kiss her palm "Okay, I won't if it'll stop you from worrying and having a panic attack. I need you to concentrate on your flying lesson and not me when you're god knows how many hundreds if not thousands of feet up in the air"

"Thank you" I whisper, letting my gratitude sound in my voice. Skye smiles, giving me her brain frying megawatt smile.

A knock on the door stops me from giving her a kiss "Yes" I call out irritated at being disturbed.

"Excuse me sir" Bruce's muffled voice filters through the door "we need to be leaving in the next fifteen minutes for you to get to your flying lesson on time"

"Thanks Bruce I'll be a few minutes"

Skye gives me a kiss and moves out of my arms "I suggest you take Macy with you" Skye says putting on her underwear. I can watch her all day putting her clothes on, it's as much a turn on as watching her strip. Skye snaps her fingers "earth to Clayton" she chuckles. I drag my eyes up her body to her amused face "I said I suggest you take Macy with you. She has brought her tablet and has access to your diary if you decide to go ahead for your Private Pilot Licence. I know the legal requirement is forty hours plus you have tests to do so she'll be able to plan it straight into your schedule, saves any messing around"

"Good idea and as always you're right" I plant a kiss on her forehead "I better get going" I grab my jacket and head out of the door, only to turn round and give Skye a long lingering kiss goodbye.

"Go" Skye says giggling and shoving at my shoulders with little effect to move me "go on, or you'll be late" with a sigh I leave her.

My whole body is thrumming with adrenaline, still. My lesson finished thirty minutes ago and I haven't come down from the exhilarating high of actually flying the helicopter, okay so it was aided, but I still flew it myself for a short time. I can't believe I flew it. I've definitely been bitten by the flying bug. It is so much more exciting being at the controls than sitting in the back as a passenger. Skye was spot on about me going for my Private Pilot Licence, she knew before I did that I would go for my licence. Macy admitted to me that Skye had told her to bring her tablet and forewarned her that she will be coming with me to the second lesson.

Christ! Skye knows me so well, better than I do myself. I smile in wonder as I look out the window and see the countryside whizzing past. I can't wait to see her to tell her about the lesson, thankfully she didn't go on the bike ride as the roads are icy instead she went into town for a mooch as she put it and that's where we're heading now to meet her, Paul and Alan.

I listen to Macy, sat in the front talking to Bruce as she runs through the list of things Skye and I will be doing over the next couple of days. Macy really is meticulous, she certainly makes my life easier and Helena's job for that matter. I suddenly realise that in the five years of being with

Skye we have never once discussed the extra work load I put on Macy. I feel ashamed of myself for taking her for granted.

"Macy"

Macy stops talking and shifts in her seat so her head appears in between the gap. Her large chocolate brown eyes look at me expectantly "Yes, Clayton" I smile, she rarely calls me Mr Blake.

"I just want to say thank you for everything you do for me" a look of surprise crosses her face "I realise that I don't say it often but I really appreciate what you do in organising me when it's not really in your remit"

Macy smiles broadly "Oh don't worry Clayton, organising you is in my remit and thank you anyway"

Now it's my turn to look surprised "Since when?"

Macy chuckles "Just over five years ago" Bruce joins her laughter, he's clocked the expression on my face in the rear view mirror "Skye and I sat down and reworked my job description. Skye got in touch with Helena and explained what I would be doing since there was going to be overlap in some of the things we do. Between the three of us we worked out the best way of working that would give the least disruption to what we were doing at the time. Over the years we've changed or tweaked things as and when necessary"

"Huh" I'm flummoxed; I don't know what to say.

"And by the look on your face it's obvious Skye never told you"

I shake my head "I shall be having words with my wife when I see her" I say in mock sternness.

"Well if you're having words" Bruce adds "she changed mine and Paul's job descriptions as well at the same time as doing Macy's"

"You know in the last twenty-four hours I'm learning just how good my wife is at keeping things from me. What else is she keeping from me?"

Macy and Bruce both laugh "You can ask her yourself in a few minutes" Bruce says pointing in front of him.

Across the junction we are approaching I see Skye, Paul and Alan stood on the side walk waiting for us. My heart does its usual flip flop at seeing her. Bruce follows the flow of traffic through the junction. Suddenly I hear screeching tyres, muffled shouts of alarm then a horrendous bang… the world blanks out.

SKYE

"Christ! It's bloody freezing" I say through chattering teeth. I stamp my feet and rub my gloved hands together trying to get some warmth in them.

What in the hell possessed me to come for a walk around the shops in this weather? Joshua and Andrew my mind throws up. Oh yeah. I didn't want to be stuck in the house with them, not after last night seeing them in the garden. I know I'll collapse in hysterical laughter again just as I did when we got back to the marquee and I have absolutely no intention of letting them know they were seen.

"A couple more minutes and you'll be in the warmth" Paul says pointing behind me.

I turn towards the junction and see our SUV approaching, the lights change to green and the cars in front move off.

A high pitched screeching sound fills the air, everyone on the street stops and looks around trying to locate the source. Shouts of alarm go up; people start running towards the junction waving their arms at the moving traffic.

A garbage truck suddenly appears and ploughs through the junction, pushing stationary cars out of its path and into the moving traffic. I can see the driver frantically fighting for control of the vehicle, it turns sideways then swings back straightening before it collides, with an earth shattering bang, with the passenger side of our SUV. The truck carries the SUV across the street smashing it into a post. The truck side winds still moving taking the SUV with it and comes to rest when it hits a shop front. The sickening sounds of grating, crunching metal and shattering glass are replaced with screams and shouts to call nine one one.

The screaming is so loud... I realise it's me... my throat is raw... my brain won't accept what my eyes are seeing. It can't be happening. I'm trapped in a horror movie. It's just like something out of Final Destination only this is real, very real.

Other high pitched sounds fill the air. Sirens, lots of them. I lurch forward to get to Clayton, something is stopping me. I fight against it. The steel bands tighten. I fight harder.

"Skye, stop!" a man's voice is gruff in my ear. Alan is holding on to me. Oh god! Macy, Bruce. I double my efforts to get free. I see Paul running across the street towards the SUV. The driver of the garbage truck stumbles out of the cab.

"Please, we've got to help them" I beg frantically wriggling in his arms to get free.

"Okay but stay close and don't do anything rash" Alan says softly.

His arms loosen and I fly, literally, across the street. I'm at Paul's side in seconds. He spins round and grabs me "Don't look" he holds my head to his chest. I struggle, I need to get to Clayton, to all of them "Skye please, you don't want to look" the strain of his voice stops me, it's filled with emotion. Tears.

"Oh god! Macy" I whisper.

"She's gone" his voice cracks.

"No, no, no" comes out in agonised moans "Clayton?"

"I don't... I don't know. It's hard to tell"

The police and ambulances arrive then and everything happens quickly, highly organised chaos. I'm numb as I watch the whole process. Clayton is barely alive, there's so much blood. The paramedics frantically work on him. Bruce has to be cut out. Macy is the only fatality.

I don't remember getting to the hospital. I just remember holding onto Paul, even in the waiting room. I couldn't let go of him. The feeling of numbness is still with me. My whole body and brain seem to have switched off. The arrival of Clayton's family doesn't jump start any kind of emotion or feelings in me. I'm empty.

My mind throws up the memory of the last time I sat in a hospital waiting room for news on Clayton, only this time it's far worse. I know how badly injured he is. The image of the paramedic pumping on Clayton's chest as they loaded the gurney into the ambulance doesn't bode well.

Simon and Shelley arrive. They prize my hands off Paul, both wrap me in a hug. No words are spoken. There are no words to speak whilst we wait for news. Joshua and Andrew pace the small room. Stephanie's restrained sobs fill the silence whilst Elizabeth comforts her. Her own cheeks wet with silent tears.

Hours pass. Alan brought in drinks and sandwiches for everyone. I sip at the flavoured water he gave me; the sandwich remains untouched. I couldn't eat. Paul left the room for a while, he had to go to the morgue to formerly identify Macy's body. When he came back, grim faced, I went to him and held him. He buried his head in my shoulder, his arms tight around my waist, we both finally broke down. Mourning our loss. Paul his beloved wife, me a beloved friend. Other arms came around us, joining and sharing our grief.

Eventually a surgeon came into the room with news on Bruce. Relief made me light headed and my knees give way when I heard he was going to be okay. His injuries were bad, but they had every expectation he was going to pull through. He had a skull fracture, broken ribs, arm and leg. I wanted to go and see him but the doctor said they had put him into an induced coma because of brain swelling. He was being taken to the ICU once he was settled I could go then. Someone would come for me. There was no news on Clayton, he was still in surgery.

The numbness of earlier was wearing off. I start feeling anxious, agitated. I can't keep still. The greyness of the room is depressing. The plastic chairs too hard. I pace the room, with all the people in here it feels too small, claustrophobic almost. Eyes follow my every step. I shut them all out as I fight the urge to scream 'get the fuck out of here. Let me cope with all of this in my own way'

Joshua joins me pacing the room. I glance over to the other side to a grim faced Andrew comforting Stephanie. Elizabeth is sat the other side of him, holding his free hand. She gives me a weak smile. Bizarre images flick through my mind of Andrew, Joshua and Elizabeth… together. I shove the sex scenes out of my head, they have no place being there at a time like this. Any other time I would have enjoyed speculating with Clayton what they got up to. It would gross him out like it did last night and this morning. As I remember his reaction an involuntary snort of laughter escapes me. I quickly turn it into a cough when Joshua gives me a puzzled curious look. Before he can ask me if I'm okay I take my seat in between Shelley and Simon.

"Listen, you two head home. I'll call you when there's any news" I say picking up their hands in mine and squeeze "I appreciate you both being here, but Shelley you have the kids and a husband to think of. And you Simon have David to spend time with before he heads back to Vegas"

"We're not going anywhere" Simon say adamantly "besides David has already left for Vegas"

"And Phil is more than capable of looking after the kids" Shelley adds.

I open my mouth to give a counter argument when the door opens "Mrs Blake" the surgeon calls as he steps into the room.

"Yes" I say along with two other voices. The surgeon looks momentarily taken aback "is it about Clayton?" I ask walking towards him, he nods "I'm his wife, this is his mother and sister in law" I point to Stephanie and Elizabeth as they approach "these are his brothers" I indicate to Joshua and Andrew.

The surgeon closes the door behind him, he looks exhausted. I'm guessing he's come straight from the theatre as he's still got his cap on and face mask under his chin. He stands in front of me as everyone else gathers behind me.

"Mr Blake sustained substantial internal injuries along with a fractured skull, broken ribs which punctured his lung and a number of superficial lacerations. We stopped all the internal bleeding but unfortunately he went into cardiac arrest during surgery. We have managed to stabilize him but he is in a coma and we have no way of knowing the extent of his injuries until he comes round. He's being taken to the ICU and you can see him shortly" the surgeon pauses, his eyes flit to those behind me before coming back to me "Mrs Blake, I need you to understand that we have and will do everything we can for him" fear trickles through me.

"What are his chances?" Stephanie whispers, putting a voice to my fear.

"He's young, extremely fit and healthy. He has that on his side, other than that we have to wait and see. I'm afraid I can't be any more specific"

"Thank you doctor" I manage to say around the huge lump wedged in my throat "can I… we go up and see him now?" I look at the doctor pleadingly. If Clayton's, chances are uncertain I don't want to waste any more time being away from him.

The doctor smiles sympathetically "Yes of course, follow me"

On the way up, no matter how much I mentally prepared myself to seeing Clayton wired up to machines and tubes everywhere it is still a shock seeing him lying there so still, bruised and broken. The numbness returns, I can't cry or speak. Stephanie all but throws herself on him, hysterical. I stand at the end of the bed like a marble statue, cold, unmoving, unfeeling.

Someone guides me to a chair at the side of his bed. I lower myself to the soft comfy leather seat. Carefully, so I don't dislodge the sensors on his fingers, I lift his hand in mine. His large, lifeless hand is surprisingly warm and I realise how cold mine are. Clayton's beautiful face is obscured by the ventilator tubes coming out of his mouth. In between the butterfly stitches and wound dressing on the side of his head I can see bruises forming on his forehead and cheek. I reach a shaking hand out and stroke his hair away from his face. The click, bleeps and hiss of the machines seem too loud.

"I'm sorry but only two visitors at a time are allowed"

I turn to see a middle aged nurse in pale pink scrubs stood in the doorway. No-one makes a move. I see her take a deep breath preparing for a fight to empty the room.

"Excuse me is Bruce Jackson close by?" I ask.

"He's next door ma'am" she smiles kindly at me, almost motherly.

I look at Clayton's family "I'll go and see Bruce" no-one tries to object. I lean over, mindful of the wires and tubes, and kiss Clayton's forehead "I'll be back soon my love. Get well and heal. I love you" I say in a low voice in his ear. I've heard that hearing still functions when patients are in this state. I hope with all my heart he hears me. Andrew and Elizabeth follow me out of the room. After a brief word with Simon and Shelley, I go straight to Bruce. Paul is with him, so is a nurse.

"How's he doing?" I say as I enter.

The nurse looks up from the clipboard she's noting readings on from the machines "I'm sorry, only family are allowed" she says with an apologetic smile.

"Bruce doesn't have family. He works for me and my husband, who is in the bed next door. We are his family" I look back at Bruce. His head is bandaged, his left arm and leg are in plaster. There aren't as many tubes and wires on him as Clayton but he's still surrounded by clicking and beeping machines.

"Mrs Blake" the surprise in the nurse's voice has my eyes snapping back to her. She looks to be in her late thirties, pretty with short spikey dark blonde hair. Her tall slim figure hidden by her pale pink scrubs "Mr Jackson is in an induced coma, he has swelling of the brain and so far he is responding to treatment. The doctors will make an assessment tomorrow and decide when to bring him out of it.

"Why's he in an induced coma?" I go to stand by Paul. He starts to rise from the seat, I put my hand on his shoulder and push him back down.

"Mr Jackson has suffered brain trauma and head injuries. The induced coma shuts down the brain function giving it and his body time to heal and the swelling goes down as a result" I nod to show my understanding "Mr Jackson's arm is broken in two places" she indicates on her arm where the breaks are, the humerus and radius "and his leg has a fractured femur and broken tibia. He also has two broken ribs on the same side. Mr Jackson is extremely fit and healthy for a man his age" I smile as her words repeat that of the surgeon. I catch the admiring look she gives Bruce.

The sheets do little to hide Bruce's muscular physique and for a man in his late forties he does have the body any man half his age would be jealous of. I instantly know she's going to make sure he gets the best care and so is my husband. I bet the nurses are beside themselves at having two fine specimens in their care. They'll be fighting each other in the corridor as who gets to give them a bed bath.

"We'll take good care him Mrs Blake" the nurse reassures me.

"Thank you nurse. I know you will"

The nurse finishes off taking her notes and leaves Paul and me alone. I reach over and take Paul's hand "How are you holding up?" I tentatively ask.

Paul looks at me, his grief surfacing briefly. The heart rendering sadness flashes through his hazel eyes before he shuts down the emotion. He gives a shrug and a heavy sigh "I'll survive. Why are you not sat with Clayton?"

"Two visitors at a time" it's my turn to shrug "Stephanie's gone to pieces so I thought let her and his brothers spend some time with him as I don't plan on going home"

"Thought as much" Paul gave a humourless laugh "I sent Alan to go and get some things for you from the apartment and I've spoken to the nursing staff"

I kiss Paul's cheek "Thank you"

We sit in silence for a while. Every now and again Paul squeezes my hand and I allow myself to think of Macy. I can't believe she's gone and I'll never hear her raucous laughter or her sassy comebacks ever again. I feel a huge hole ripping open in my chest at the sense of loss for my friend, my sister – because that is what she became to me. A big sister in my makeshift family.

"Skye" I look up to see a puffy red eyed Stephanie barely holding it together. I go to her, we embrace "I don't want to go home" her watery whispering voice tickles my ear "I don't want to leave him, please don't make me go. I need to stay with my boy. Please" she begs me, her whole body shakes as she fights to hold back the tears.

"Stephanie you don't need my permission to stay. I'm not going home either and if the hospital staff don't like it — tough, they can go and get lost" I whisper, my hands rub her back in a soothing motion. Her whole body sags against me in relief.

"Thank you, thank you" she squeezes me "come, it was selfish of me and my family to be with him so long" Stephanie takes my hand and pulls me out of Bruce's room.

The next forty-eight hours pass in a sleep deprived haze. During the night Stephanie and I take turns to sit with Clayton whilst the other grabs a few hours' sleep but invariably I go and sit with Bruce. During the day when Joshua or Andrew turn up I leave and go to Bruce taking over from Paul or Alan to give them a break. Paul takes a couple of hours off to go and see Jack and break the news to him since the accident is all over the news. The poor boy is devastated, he loved Macy and called her Mom. Jack insisted coming to the hospital to see me, the second he lay eyes on me he broke down. He is inconsolable, even though he is now twelve and his growth spurt only just happening he still manages to sit on my lap and cry his heart out.

On the second day the doctors bring Bruce out of his induced coma as his brain is back to normal size. And so the waiting starts for him to wake up. We all take turns to read the newspapers to Clayton and Bruce. The business and financial pages for Clayton and the news and sports pages for Bruce. The doctors wouldn't give me a time frame of when Bruce will wake up which I find irritating as hell. "He will wake up when he's good and ready" was all the doctors and nurses say.

On the morning of the third day whilst I read out a report speculating about a football club looking to sign some hot shot quarter back Bruce came round.

"You have absolutely no idea what it is you are reading do you?" a rough raspy voice cut through my monotonous drivel. Bruce's eyes are still closed but there is a grin on his battered face.

"Not a frigging clue" I agree. I'm grinning like a loon. I'm so happy he's come round "can you open your eyes?"

"I'm working on it… too bright"

"Stay there, I'll get the nurse" I jump up and realise what I've just said is stupid "not that you can go anywhere" I add laughing. Bruce laughs with me then grimaces in agony. I hot foot it to the door.

"Nurse" I yell, three of them come running out of different rooms "Bruce is awake" I'm so happy my voice sounds shrill in the relative quiet of the ward.

Nurse Janice is the only one to continue towards me, the other two smile but turn back to where they were. Paul and Alan materialise out of nowhere, I can see the relief I feel reflected in their faces. The three of us crowd into the room. Nurse Janice is chatting to Bruce as she makes notes on his chart part way through the doctor turns up and Nurse Janice turfs us out.

In a mixed daze of relief and anxiety I make my way to Clayton's room. Stephanie is reading the business news out to him, she looks up as I enter "Bruce is awake" I sit down in the chair opposite and pick up Clayton's hand and press my lips to the back of it. I run my other over his arm, my fingers tracing the prominent veins from the back of his hand and up his forearm.

"Oh that's fantastic news, do you hear that Clayton? Bruce is awake, now it's your turn" Stephanie says with joy in her voice, although I detect desperation as well. Stephanie stands and leans over kissing Clayton's forehead "I'm going to take a quick shower. I won't be long" she says to me gathering her wash things.

I smile and nod, suddenly I don't have the energy to converse but then Stephanie and I have an unspoken understanding, she pats and squeezes my shoulder to prove it. We don't need words because if there is any change even the slightest of slight changes in Clayton's condition whoever was with him would get the other immediately.

I lift Clayton's hand and kiss the back of it again, feeling the warmth of his skin against my lips. I would give anything to kiss his lips, instead I rest my head on his thigh and look up his torso to his face only the ventilator obscures his bruised handsome face. I watch his chest rise and fall in time to the click and hiss of the machine "Please wake up" I whisper to him.

Something brushes across my hair, a feather light touch. My eyes snap open. I must have dozed off. I look around the room. No-one is with me. My hand moves to my head, stroking my hair where I felt the soft touch. I look at Clayton but I can't see any change in him. His hand is still in mine, his other is motionless at his side.

"I'm imagining things" I mutter to myself. The cool feather light touch caresses the side of my face running from my temple, down my cheek to my jaw. I freeze. It's too light to be a breeze, there is no breeze. In fact, the room is stiflingly hot "I didn't imagine that" confused I look around the room then back at Clayton. Still no change in him. The touch comes again "Clayton" I gasp.

"I'm sorry"

The words whisper through my mind, the most overwhelming sense of love surrounds me and my heart feels fit to burst with happiness. Then it's gone... snuffed out... leaving me feeling desolate... lost... alone... empty.

Clayton has gone, left me.

I stand and place a kiss on his cheek "Good bye my love, my soul mate" I whisper.

The machines start to scream then. The alarms hurt my ears. Nurses and doctors are everywhere. Gentle hands guide me out of the room. Other arms embrace me but I watch through the window as the doctor's fight to save my beloved Clayton in vain.

"He's gone" I say through numb lips.

"Shh, you don't know that yet" its Alan holding me I realise as his deep voice rumbles in my ear.

"He's gone" I repeat in the same flat voice.

The sound of running feet slapping against the tiled floor from both directions fills the corridor.

"What's happening" Stephanie's panicked voice breaks through some of the fog filled numbness that surrounds me. I lift my head off Alan's chest and drag my eyes away from the frantically working doctors. The look on my face says it all "no, no, no" Stephanie wails.

Joshua and Andrew catch her before she hits the floor. Stephanie's agonised groans of grief and sobbing fill the corridor, yet I feel nothing. I turn back to watch the doctor's. After what seems like forever they finally stop working on him. I don't pay attention to the doctor when he comes out of the room to break the news to the family. Instead I watch the nurses as they quickly and efficiently remove all the wires and tubes from Clayton's body. Once they've finished we're allowed to go in and say goodbye. I lean over and kiss Clayton's cooling lips.

"Good bye my love, my soul mate" I whisper my farewell again, yet the tears still don't come.

I take a deep breath, it's been five days since Clayton's and Macy's funeral and this is the first time I've been back to our apartment since the morning of our anniversary. I have no recollection of the last ten days;

each day seems to have merged with another. There is no distinction of passing time for me it's all a blur. A numb hazy blur. I've not shed one tear. Not even at the funeral. I cried all my tears for Macy at the hospital and strangely I have no tears for Clayton. I'm empty… a hollow shell of the person I used to be. I've lost interest in the world. All I need is rotting flesh and I'll have the zombie look as well as the persona. I know my friends are worried about me. I hear them whispering. I know Clayton is gone, but I can't believe that he is truly gone. I'm torturing myself as I keep ringing his phone so I can hear his lovely raspy voice when the voice message kicks in and the hole in my chest rips a little more each time I do it.

I haven't told a soul about the paranormal experience I had in the hospital, if I did they would think me certifiable but I know deep down and with all my heart that it was Clayton saying sorry and good bye to me. For some strange reason that doesn't give me any comfort. I can feel everyone watching me, waiting for me to snap or break down and give in to the grief but it's still not happening. Is something wrong with me?

"Are you sure you are ready to do this?" Paul's gentle question pulls me out of my melancholic thoughts. I nod not taking my eyes off the dark wooden double doors leading to our, there is no more 'our' anymore I remind myself it's 'my', my apartment "just say the word if at any time you want to leave" Paul says moving forward and opening the doors.

I take a few more deep breaths and convince my feet and legs to get moving. I walk into the vast living room. Memories flood my mind, everywhere I look memories flash before my eyes. I stagger under the weight of them. Paul steadies me "I'm okay" I murmur.

I move towards the pool table. I smile at the fond memories of the amount of times we tried to play a normal game of pool and failed miserably as we always ended up having sex on it. The smile on my face widens even more at the memories of when we 'played' and tormented the hell out of each other whilst the other tried to take their shot. I look over at the sofa, boy has that seen some action. Then the memories of when we just cuddled and snuggled as we watched a film or talked about our plans whether it was business related or leisure.

Slowly I work my way through each room. At each turn I keep expecting to see Clayton coming to greet me with his arms open wide, a heart stopping smile and a mischievous glint twinkling in his eyes. My broken heart grows heavier and heavier with each step. Finally, I find myself stood in front of our bedroom door. This is going to be the most painful. I realise, the hole in my chest I felt tearing open in hospital for Macy has gotten bigger with each step I've taken throughout the apartment. I can feel the jagged edges flapping around the open wound.

I push the door open. My eyes fall straight to the huge bed that dominates the room — the hole in my chest tears open a little more — standing out against the white sheets a small square box wrapped in bright pink wrapping paper sits in the centre of the bed. Curiosity has me moving further into the room, I kick my boots off and climb onto the bed. The box is bigger than I first thought. With trembling hands, I reach out to pick the box up.

It's light.

I shake it, something rattles inside.

Tentatively I peel open the wrapping paper.

My heart is in my mouth and my stomach is doing somersaults.

I know this is a present from Clayton, another anniversary present.

I lift the lid and peer inside.

There is a key, it's a vehicle key, and a folded piece of paper.

I frown pulling out the paper, what on earth has he got me I wonder as I open it up. There are two pieces of paper folded together.

On one is a picture of a motorcycle, a Ducati Monster S4R. The frame is pink and the tank a deep purple – my two favourite colours. The other is a letter in Clayton's large looping scrawl. The words jumble as the paper shakes in my hands. I lay the letter flat on the bed so I can read it, my arms wrap around my middle. I'm holding on… barely.

To Skye, my dearest darling wife.
To Mrs Blake, my beautiful wife.
To the love of my life, my soul mate.
I couldn't decide how to start so take your pick from any of the above, but knowing you… you'll call me a soppy git and choose all three (greedy).

A choked sound, a mix between a sob and laugh escapes me. I smile at the letter as I hear Clayton saying these words.

Inside this box is another present, yes another one. Now I know you are really smiling but my beautiful darling wife you know I love to spoil you so delete where applicable. Is it to be another anniversary present or an early birthday or Christmas present? Again the choice is yours.

I really am smiling; my cheeks are aching so much. It's so typical of him to do something like this. A splodge of water hits the paper. I look at it confused, another one joins it. I put my hand to my face, it's wet. Tears are rolling freely down my cheeks. Taking a deep shaky breath, I carry on reading.

This beautiful beast of a motorcycle awaits your arrival in England. Nessa has it in her garage, the key as you will have seen is in the box. I can't wait to join you riding through those twisting country lanes that you so fondly talk about and I definitely can't wait to see you again in your leathers, hmmm...

Come and find me and show me how much you love your present. I'm waiting.
C x

Without a second thought I jump off the bed. I have to find him. Clayton will be hiding and I know he'll be somewhere where he can watch me as I opened the present. I rush over to the closet and yank the doors open ready to shout "found you" — it's empty. Huh! Where else can he be, the bathroom? I run to the opposite side of the room and fling the door open, empty. Disappointment hits me as I slowly shut the door, think... where else... the office, yes that's where he'll be. I snatch the letter, picture and key off the bed and run through the apartment to his office and my studio.

I burst in through the door ready to gleefully and triumphantly shout "found you" – but he's not there. There's no grinning, eye twinkling, devilishly good looking Clayton coming to greet me with open arms. Momentarily confusion muddles my mind, I frown looking at the letter, he said come and find me, he's waiting for me.

But he'll never be waiting for you ever again.

He's left you all alone even when he promised he would never leave.

The realisation hits me like a thunderbolt.

I drop to my knees choking... retching... a high pitched keening sound fills the room. My arms fold tight around my stomach as I rock back and forth trying to ease the pain.

The hole in my chest rips wide open, the broken pieces of my heart... shatter.

The brightness of the room dims.

Darkness wraps me in his cold embrace.

CHAPTER SIX

DOVE MILL VILLAGE

"Guys, tell me what do you think?" Harry Davies spread his arms wide to encompass the lavish lounge bar.

"Not bad cousin" Rex Davies smiles impressed leaning back against the bar taking in the luxurious fixtures and fittings around the room "very impressive. What do you think Caleb?"

It looked more like someone's sitting room with its large comfy white, beige and gold pattern sofas and oversized armchairs big enough to seat two people. The crackling flames of the log fire dancing in the huge grate surrounded by a massive ornate stone fireplace. The large ivory and taupe rugs complimenting the highly polished oak floor and the subtle lighting from the modern chandeliers hanging over head. The only give away it wasn't someone's sitting room is the mahogany and white marble topped bar that runs the length of the room. Behind the bar along the wall, interspersing the mirrors are shelves of bottles, every conceivable alcoholic and soft drink gives the wall a multi-coloured mosaic look.

Caleb picks up his bottle of beer and leans an elbow on the bar "Very plush" his keen green eyes scanning the room taking in the well-heeled patrons sitting around talking in muted tones "the new owner obviously spared no expense"

"You have no idea" Harry shakes his head remembering all the invoices "I'm telling you I thought the guy was nuts when he told me the refurbishment would be completed in eight weeks, but look at the place" Harry gestures again to make his point.

"You could have called me to say the place was shutting down for the refurbishments. Month's ago Caleb and I came all the way out here for nothing" Rex admonishes his cousin "who is the new owner anyway?"

"Sorry about that, but we did have notices around the place so the more active members knew about the temporary closure" Harry looks contrite and shrugs sheepishly "the new owner is Mr Dario Benenati" Rex and Caleb look at Harry with sceptical raised eyebrows "I know what you're thinking and no he isn't Italian. He's American, although he does have Italian relations"

"So you didn't sell out to the mob" Rex says jokingly.

Harry snorts a laugh "My measly five percent stake is still mine, so theoretically I didn't sell out"

"But you kept your job though" marvels Caleb.

Harry raises his bottle and taps Caleb's "I did that my man" he gloats.

"You're a lucky bastard" Rex says enviously "how many people can say they are a shareholder and manager of a high end exclusive sex club?"

"Not many" Harry laughs "but I have to have something going for me since you're the twat that nicked all the good looks in our family's gene pool"

All three laugh good naturedly at the banter. The only thing that Harry and Rex share is their age and blue eye colour. Both are blonde although Harry's hair line had long ago disappeared and he now favoured the skull crop look. Rex stood six-foot-tall whilst Harry only just tipped five eight. Rex is broad shouldered and muscular but not as big as Caleb, Harry is stocky with a good physique. And even though Harry couldn't compete with Rex in the model looks department it didn't stop him from getting the ladies.

"So what's with the name change?" Caleb asks shifting his stance and getting the bar tenders attention for another round of drinks.

"Mr Benenati owns, including this place, nine clubs around the world"

"Fucking hell" Rex and Caleb whisper in amazement.

"All of them are called The Gentlemen's Club. But as you can see" Harry nods to the wealthy men and women around the room "women are more than welcome" all three chuckle.

"When's the party? You know to celebrate the new look and ownership" Rex asks eagerly.

Harry shakes his head and laughs at Rex's crestfallen pouting face, he knew too well how his cousin loved a good party "There's no need. In the six weeks since we re-opened membership has been on the increase, it's doubled in the last week alone. And" Harry inclines his head in the direction of two new arrivals entering the lounge bar "old members are coming back in droves. Welcome Lord and Lady Farringdon. Good to see you again" Harry calls out as he went to greet them.

"Well wonders never cease" Rex speculates as he watches his cousin shake hands with Lord Farringdon and kisses Lady Farringdon's cheek.

"Come off it Rex" Caleb scoffs "you know those two live the lifestyle"

"Well, yes" Rex shrugs "but I just thought they'd stopped because they didn't come here anymore"

"Are you telling me you never got invited to one of their toga parties?" Caleb raises a quizzical eyebrow then roars laughing at Rex's shocked face "you didn't know!" Caleb splutters. God it feels good to laugh he thought.

"I had no idea. I mean, yes I got the invites but I thought they were for a lame fancy dress party that would be full of stuffy gits who are full of their own self-importance" Rex grumbles, miffed at the thought of all the orgies on his own doorstep he had missed "come on let's get some food. I need to eat"

"Good idea" Caleb agrees following Rex in the direction of the restaurant.

Women's eyes, and a few men's, follow the two men as they walk towards the restaurant entrance. As different as the two are in hair colouring, height and physical build — Caleb being the bigger of the two — both are striking figures and ooze the kind of sexual animal magnetism that has women dropping their knickers at just one look in their direction. Of the two Rex knew this and took advantage at every conceivable opportunity whereas Caleb is oblivious to his charm and pull, making him all the more appealing.

Taking their seats in one of the many semi-circular booths that run the length of the room Caleb takes in the royal blue opulence of the restaurant whilst Rex eyes the waitress as she hands over the menus.

"Good evening gentlemen, my name is Lyndsey. What can I get you to drink?" Lyndsey couldn't believe her luck at having two gorgeous fit as fuck men sitting in her area, her appreciative eyes didn't know which one to ogle first.

"Bring us a bottle of Krug" Rex winks at her. Lyndsey's cheeks flush, her stomach flutters with excitement.

"Not for me" Caleb cut in quickly "I'll stick to beer, bring me another one of these please" he says tapping the bottle of Corona.

Lyndsey felt her knicker elastic snap as a direct result of the devastating smile the tall, dark and ridiculously handsome guy gave her.

"Aw come on mate, let's celebrate your new found freedom in style" Rex cajoles "and besides, neither of us has to worry about driving tonight"

Caleb sighs "As much as I'd love to, I still have to be up early"

"That's a load of bollocks and you know it" Rex laughs at Caleb's scowl "your staff are more than capable of running the yard in fact they can do it with their eyes closed whilst standing on their heads"

Caleb rolls his eyes at his best friend but he couldn't argue with his assessment, Rex is right his staff probably ran the yard better than he did "Okay, but I'm not getting wasted" Caleb concedes reluctantly.

"Bottle of Krug?" Lyndsey asks just to make sure. Rex gives her a knock out smile and winks again causing her blush to deepen.

As the waitress moves away both men study the menu. Rex hums a tune to himself, his fingers lightly tap out a beat on the table as he makes his choice. Caleb remains quiet. After a few minutes Rex snaps the menu shut. Caleb looks up at the sound of the forced action to find his friend studying him closely, a deep frown creases his brow as his eyebrows pull together. Caleb knew this look all too well. Rex has something on his mind and he was working out how to broach a sensitive subject, only Rex didn't do sensitive. Rex is as delicate and sensitive as a bull in a china shop.

Rex sighs heavily and leans forward resting his forearms on the table "Look, I know you didn't want me to do any digging" he says in a heavily resigned voice "but I couldn't help myself"

Caleb felt his heart miss a beat, he knew exactly what Rex was referring to. A couple of weeks ago they had attended Lord Baxter's dinner party. Gabrielle had been there in her new dress and shoes courtesy of the now shredded credit card. At the party there were two men, either one of them could be Gabrielle's new fling as she flirted outrageously with both making it difficult for the gossips to say which man was her lover. Caleb didn't care and ignored his wife — soon to be ex-wife he mentally added with glee — the whole night, which infuriated Gabrielle so she flirted all the more trying to make Caleb jealous. It didn't work.

"And now you have an overwhelming need to tell me" Caleb glares, not hiding his annoyance. Rex with a sheepish grin lifts one shoulder in an apologetic shrug "fuck it, let's hear it then"

"The guy Gabrielle has shacked up with is Tobias Belling"

A jolt of surprise went through Caleb as he recalled the man from the dinner party "The balding short fat bloke who liked the sound of his own voice" Rex nods exultantly "fucking hell, she's obviously gone after the money in his case. He's got to be more than twenty years older than us"

Rex threw his head back and laughs at his friends' accurate appraisal "Mate, you are absolutely spot on. I believe he is fifty-eight. Although he's not as rich as he could have been. Rumour has it that when his old man the late Lord Matthew Belling died he left the bulk of his fortune to one person, the identity of whom has never been revealed"

"But he's still stinking rich compared to me" Caleb says sourly "well he's welcome to her. No doubt she'll bleed him dry and in return he's got himself arm candy"

"I don't think she'll get her hands that easily on his millions. Apparently he's a tight fisted bastard plus as far as I know he's married"

"Ha! Thanks for the tip. I better give my solicitor a call and tell him to push through the divorce ASAP"

"Ah, perfect timing sweetheart" Rex smiles warmly at Lyndsey as she places the ice bucket stand holding the champagne next to the table. Rex picks up the bottle and deftly opens it, the cork makes a satisfying pop as he twists it free "to new beginnings" Rex raises his glass to Caleb.

"And good riddance to money grabbing bitches" Caleb clinks his glass against Rex's.

"Bring another glass please Lyndsey" Harry says as he slides into the booth next to Rex "have you ordered yet" he indicates to the menu on the table.

"Just about to" Rex grumbles as he shuffles over making more room for Harry.

Lyndsey places another glass in front of Harry, then stood with her pad and pen at the ready "What would you like to order sir?" she says addressing Caleb.

"I'll have the steak, medium and all the trimmings" Caleb hands the menu to her.

"I'll have the same" Rex and Harry say together "bring another bottle of Krug" adds Harry.

"Here, I forgot to give you these earlier" Harry says reaching into his inside jacket pocket. He hands a black wrist band to each of them "you need to wear these at all times when you're here"

"What are they for?" Rex looks at his dubiously.

"It's so each member can identify what your preference is. New ruling brought in by the new owner, does it in all of his clubs. I must admit it's a bloody good idea. Black is for Dom's. Blue is for Sub's. Green is for Switch's. All the staff wear a different band. If they're wearing a plain white band, it means they're off limits. If they have a striped white and a colour showing their preference band, it indicates they are staff and willing to play but that refers to only playing in the Play Restaurant and Bar area"

"What in the hell is that and more importantly where is it?" Rex asks intrigued.

"I'll show you later when I give you the grand tour" Harry grins.

"Take mine back" Caleb holds the black wrist band out to Harry, who declines by shaking his head "look, I'm only here tonight because he dragged me out and besides I can't afford the membership fee. Even if I wasn't going through a costly divorce I still couldn't afford it"

Harry looks furtively around him to make sure no-one is eavesdropping, leaning across Rex he whispers "Keep it and don't worry about paying the membership fee. It's on the house, my treat"

Caleb inhales sharply "That's very generous of you but I can't accept it"

"Yes, you can and you will" Harry says insistently "okay I'll admit I do have an ulterior motive and it's a win, win situation for both of us"

"Go on" Caleb says cautiously, if not somewhat guarded.

"When word gets round that you're single and back frequenting this place the female membership is going to go through the roof. I know it's been a fair few years since you were last here, and believe me when I say your reputation as a Dom is still talked about. In the lounge bar I saw how all the women lusted after the pair of you as you walked across the room to the restaurant, so" Harry leans back placing his arm along the back of the seat, looking highly confident Caleb will accept his offer "you get as much action as you want, when you want and I get an increase in memberships. What do you say?"

Caleb looks down at the black band, rolling it between his fingers. It's tempting, a very tempting offer. He'll be a fool to turn down something like this "I get the use of a private room?"

"Whatever you want, it's yours" Harry resists the urge to smile, he could taste victory "also that band gives you free entry in to any of the clubs around the world"

"Okay, you've got yourself a deal" Caleb says holding out his hand, the two men shake on it.

"What about me? Do I get my membership free?" Rex says feeling put out.

"My dear cousin, you have never paid for your membership" Harry and Caleb laugh at the stupefied look on Rex's face as he realises his cousin is correct.

Lyndsey arrives with their food on a large tray balanced on her shoulder, her eyes widen as she spy's the black wrist bands on the two drool worthy men. They hadn't been wearing them before of that she is certain. Deftly shaking her right wrist to loosen her staff band from under the cuff of her blouse — today she wore her white and blue band — before placing the plates on the table. She very much wanted to make sure her wrist band was highly visible, because seeing those black bands was a trigger to unleashing her submissive lust. Tonight, she is more than willing to play, hell she'd spread herself naked on their table right now without being asked or commanded even though it is against the rules in this restaurant and sod the fact they're sitting with the boss. She has no qualms about unleashing her inner slut.

From the corner of her eye she catches a glimpse of the blonde with the Calvin Klein model worthy looks noticing the band and a lustful gleam flash in his eyes but for some reason she is disappointed, as she walks away from the table she couldn't help but look back at the dark haired man with the amazing emerald green eyes. It's him I want she realises. For the rest of her shift her imagination runs riot with fantasy after fantasy of submitting to him, of being his sex slave to do whatever he pleased.

As they eat Harry fills them in on the latest news and gossip he's heard from different club members. 'Christ, I've missed this' Caleb thinks to himself. It made him realise just how much of his life he put on hold or sacrificed for his ex-wife. 'What a fucking idiot I've been denying my own sexual needs to keep a faithless bitch happy'

When he first met Gabrielle she had been into the scene, not so much living it as a lifestyle but more of a dabbler, experimenting. He honestly thought she was someone exploring her sexuality and he firmly believed he was the person to help her make new discoveries about herself. In the beginning she was a willing participant, he had brought her to the club, she had enjoyed herself or so he thought. Caleb fell head over heels in love, although now he questioned if it wasn't just lust. After a few short months of being together he asked Gabrielle to marry him. Refusing to listen and against the advice of his friends Caleb went ahead and married her six weeks later.

Caleb wasn't prepared for the almost instant changes in Gabrielle, he chose to ignore them instead making excuses for her. She stopped all play saying she didn't get off on it anymore, so their sex life became strictly vanilla. It had to be missionary and in bed, dull as fucking dish water.

The first time she left him he had been devastated and gladly welcomed her back after a few months. The second time it didn't hurt so much and Rex dragged him to the club, that night he realised he needed to embrace everything he had given up. Gabrielle came back and he continued to visit the club at least once a month. Gabrielle went ballistic when she found out. It turned into the nastiest fight they ever had, she didn't like the fact that Caleb pointed out she was a hypocrite because it was okay for her to have extra marital affairs only he wasn't having an affair, all he simply was doing was getting something she refused to give him – sexual gratification. Gabrielle recoiled as if he had slapped her, she left him again. After a few days she came back, they sat down and talked, agreeing to give their marriage another go only this time they would both work at it. Gabrielle gave up her affairs and Caleb gave up the club, a year later Gabrielle left only to come back five weeks later.

Contrary to popular belief Caleb didn't welcome her back with open arms. He did it out of pity, he knew he no longer loved her, he hadn't for a long, long time but he also knew she had nowhere else to go and he couldn't see her homeless. He insisted on separate bedrooms and told her to be discreet when she embarks on any affair. It took Gabrielle three months to get back in Caleb's bed. To everyone around Gabrielle appeared to be the perfect supportive wife, she really seemed to be trying to make their marriage a success, she even started talking about starting a family. Caleb wasn't fooled.

Eighteen months later Gabrielle started to make hints about visiting the doctor to find out why they hadn't conceived. Caleb refused to go, he already knew why. He had known for months, ever since Gabrielle started to make noises about having kids he took himself to the doctors to be tested. When they had first got married neither of them had used protection but as the years progressed and with Gabrielle's infidelity he had insisted on using condoms until she could produce proof she was clean, so that he wouldn't appear to be an uncaring cold hearted bastard he too got tested, even though he knew he was clean thanks to the one rule everyone followed at the club – condoms must be worn. No questions, no argument, no condom, no penetrative sex. It was that simple. Only this time he asked the doctor to do a fertility test to satisfy a niggling suspicion. Caleb's results confirmed his niggling suspicion… he was firing blanks.

Strangely this news didn't upset Caleb, neither did he question his masculinity. He knew this had no impact on his virility or his sexual performance, adding in the fact he never once in his life craved for a family of his own being sterile didn't bother him in the least. Yet, for reasons he couldn't quite pin down he was loathed to share this news with his wife.

"Can I get you anything else... sir?"

The sound of the waitress's voice with the added emphasis on Sir brings Caleb out of his thoughts, looking up from his empty plate he notices the white and green band on her wrist before seeing her warm smiling face, on making eye contact she immediately cast her eyes down. Oh she wants to play. Shame he wasn't in the mood tonight.

"No thank you" for the life of him he couldn't remember her name.

"That will be all, you can clear the table Lyndsey" Rex commanded, he was game to play even if Caleb wasn't.

Harry glances at his watch "Come on you two, I've just enough time to give you the grand tour and sort out your passes for the gates and private rooms"

A small gasp escapes Lyndsey in response to Harry's words. Caleb hears her and he can feel a smile tug at his lips "No doubt we'll see you again" he murmurs as he passes her. On seeing her blush his knowing smile gets bigger. She has definitely been fantasising about serving Rex, or me, or both of us he thinks to himself as he follows Harry out of the restaurant.

Harry takes great pleasure in showing them around the place. The improvements to the property are astounding. Over the years the manor house has gone through major renovations, structurally the building is in excellent condition unfortunately it left little money to improve the interior so it always had that neglected seedy feel to it. Now the place screams opulence, the private rooms and the communal play room are decorated in rich sensuous fabrics and thick plush carpets. The new owner added a huge conservatory which now houses a state of the art gym and spa, along with two of the biggest hot tubs Caleb had ever seen sitting outside on the decking by the outdoor pool.

"There's a couple more additions to show you, also some new rules that have been implemented since you last visited" Harry informs Rex and Caleb as he heads towards the grand staircase, instead of heading up the stairs he walks down the left hand side, stopping at the hidden door in the recess of the wall "welcome to the dungeon gentlemen" Harry smiles as he pushes open the door.

Stone steps lead down into darkness. Harry leans in flicking a switch. Muted light fills the narrow stairway, at intervals along the wall torches sit in sconces. As the men descend the stairs, the sound of their feet echoing around them all add to the feel of actually entering a dungeon. A few paces from the stairs the room opens up into a cavernous room with a low ceiling. Caleb reaches up, his fingers brush the smooth black painted plaster.

Throughout, square brick pillars join together forming arches, on the far side of the room three arched shaped wooden doors stand open, showing a smaller room within. Caleb notices something attached to one of the pillars, he walks over for a closer look. Shackles are attached to a large metal ring at the top and base.

"This used to be a wine cellar back in the day" Harry's voice echo's around the room "you'll see various types of restraints attached to the pillars. At the far end are the private rooms, however for safety reasons the doors have hatches which have to be left open when the room is in use. No-one is allowed to come down here on their own, a Dungeon Master has to be present at all times"

"Dungeon Master" Rex says laughing "how do you get to be one of them"

"Usually it's a member of the staff and before you ask yes, they dress up for the part. However, word is getting out that we now have the dungeon and quite a few BDSM groups are booking this room out to hold their own parties and they bring along their own Dungeon Master" Harry made his way over to Caleb who is inspecting the rows of canes, whips and floggers "as you can see we even provide all the equipment. There's more, come on"

Harry led them through another door way that Caleb had mistaken for an alcove. This room truly did look like a medieval torture chamber.

"Fucking hell" Rex whispers as Caleb makes a low whistling sound through his teeth.

In the centre of the room is a large rectangular wooden frame, holding a wooden roller at each end, chains and rope ran the length of the frame. It's a rack Caleb realises as his eyes fall on the four large hanging cages — big enough to hold a man, or woman — around the room, the ceiling in here is higher than the previous room. A metal free standing Saint Andrew's cross takes up most of the far wall, on the adjacent wall at an angle to it is a metal frame with lattice work in the centre.

"Christ, I don't know whether to be scared shitless or to have a raging hard on" Rex says looking around in amazement "is this real?" he reaches out to stroke the smooth wood of the handle and ratchet on the rack.

"Yes and it's proving to be very popular, so much so we've commissioned another one to be made"

"No wonder you insist on having a Dungeon Master present at all times. This shit can do some serious damage" Caleb says inspecting the metal frame "electrocution, seriously?"

Harry nods "This room is for the hard core only but we're not stupid, the rack and this beauty are set to a specific limit so no serious damage can be done. Even if someone begs for more it can't be changed, as yet we haven't had anyone go to the maximum setting" Harry gives a snort "we had this guy in last week and he wanted his sub to go on the rack, she refused. So Matt, who was Dungeon Master that night tells the Dom to get on it and experience it for himself before he can make any demands on his sub. The guy didn't make it past the first setting"

"So what are the other new rules you mentioned" Caleb asks.

Harry indicates for them to follow him, as he makes his way back towards the exit Caleb notices the free standing candelabra's holding large church candles placed around the room, a shiver went down his spine. He liked pain pleasure play but something about this room made it seem sinister.

"The old rules of wearing condoms and providing monthly proof of cleanliness still apply. The only other new rule to tell you about is with the exception of the play restaurant and bar area the whole of ground floor, including the spa, gym and outdoor pool area there is no play or sex or nudity and appropriate clothing is to be worn at all times. You can wear whatever you want just no 'bits' being shown"

"Far enough" Rex says "what I'd really like to know is how do you make sure no-one from the play restaurant accidently walks into a no go area, plus can we go and see it now"

Harry chuckles at his cousin's impatience "I'll show you" he says leading them back into the foyer "the play restaurant is accessed from the lounge bar"

The lounge bar is a lot busier, Caleb glances at his watch and is surprised to see that it's nearly ten. The atmosphere is relaxed and happy, the occasional burst of laughter breaks the quiet ambiance of the room. All three acknowledge those who call out a welcome to them but they don't stop. Harry leads them to a door on the far side of the bar.

"This is the way in. The code is fourteen twenty-three, remember it" Harry punched in the numbers on the keypad at the side of the door "this is the only way in, once the door closes behind you, you can't get out this way" Harry held the door open and gestured for the two of them to walk through. Caleb and Rex enter a short corridor with another door at the end. Opening the second door reveals another corridor, this time it is longer and ends in a dead end, halfway down on the left is a single door, directly opposite is a set of double doors.

"That door on the left takes you into the changing room, the double doors take you into the bar and restaurant" Harry pushes open the double doors.

Immediately in front of them stood a dark wood podium, behind which stood a buxom blonde, her hair pulled back into a high ponytail, her eyes heavily lined black with false eyelashes and bright red lipstick. Caleb fleetingly wonders how she would look with softer makeup.

"Mr Davies" the woman says in surprise and quickly recovers "will it be a table for three?"

"No Diana, I'm giving these two a tour" Harry slaps Rex and Caleb's shoulders.

Diana's eyes snap down to their wrists, her eyes widen at the sight of the black bands and a salacious smile spreads across her face "Please let me know if there is anything I can assist you with" she purrs and keeps her eyes down.

"I'm liking this place already" chuckles Rex as Harry leads the way into the bar.

The play bar is an identical layout and colour scheme as the lounge bar only the majority of the patrons are dressed differently, in fact very few have clothes on and those leave little to the imagination.

"I feel overdressed" Caleb murmurs under his breath causing Rex to snigger "how does this work" Caleb gestures to the room in general taking in several scenes already in play.

"Members who have a sub, or a sub willing to play can bring them in here and the sub acts as their own personal waitress, waiter, slave or whatever" Harry gestures to a group of six men sitting around the fire whilst two women dressed in white diaphanous robes, each wearing a gold collar round their neck and gold cuffs around their wrists stand close by with their heads bowed "Some ask staff members to play, in this instance they are playing slaves. If you engage a staff member there is no penetrative sex, you can titillate as much as you want and use other means to bring them to orgasm. If the staff member is off duty and comes here to play, then that's a different matter. All staff get free use of the facilities"

"What happens if you find the staff breaking the rules or a member talks the staff into breaking them" asks Rex, curiosity clearly evident in his voice.

"Instant dismissal, as for the member they're barred for life and escorted off the premises immediately" Harry says gravely "I had to terminate someone's membership yesterday. He kept offering money to the staff to play on the condition they broke the cardinal rule, one girl came forward and reported him. When I interviewed other staff four more admitted the guy had approached them as well over the last couple of weeks. Luckily they didn't take up his offer. Turns out the bastard is an undercover reporter, trying to do an expose on this place"

"Jesus, how did you get that out of him?" says Rex.

"I did a little digging of my own. When he showed up last night I had him escorted directly to my office. We searched him and found a digital recorder, which I confiscated. The idiot says he hasn't downloaded any of the material from it but to be on the safe side we scared the crap out of him and I pulled out his membership form which also doubles as a signed non-disclosure agreement. I reminded him that if he published one word or if any report about this place or any of our members and the lifestyle they're into appears in print or online that he will be in direct violation of his agreement and we would ruin him. Of course he tried to tell me we couldn't do that, I asked him if he was willing to find out. That shut the fucker up"

"Bloody hell cousin remind me not to get on your bad side. You can be a scary little shit when you want to be" Rex mock shudders "come on show us the restaurant"

Rex and Caleb take in the various scenes as they follow Harry through the bar, from the naked male submissive on his hands and knees being used as foot stool by his Mistress to the female submissive crawling to the bar to order drinks.

Entering the restaurant, they are greeted by the maître de "Good evening gentlemen. Mr Davies, I'm sorry but we don't have any tables available at the moment. I wasn't aware you planned on dining in here tonight" the discombobulated impeccably dressed man spoke with a highly cultured accent.

"Don't worry George I'm not" Harry smiles warmly "I'm giving these two the tour. You remember my cousin Rex"

"Of course, Mr Davies good to see you again" George greets Rex shaking his hand.

"This is our mutual friend Caleb Raven, who after many years spent in the wilderness is coming back as a member" Harry slaps Caleb's shoulder. George jolts in surprise at Caleb's name, then what appears to be a star struck look crosses his face.

"The Caleb Raven" George askes Harry who nods with a smug smile, George turns back to a puzzled looking Caleb and shakes his hand "Mr Raven I'm honoured to meet you. I've heard so much about you. Please don't think me presumptuous but I would love the opportunity to be mentored by you"

Harry and Rex both laugh at Caleb's dumb struck expression "See I told you, your reputation precedes you, even after all these years" Harry says gleefully "let Caleb get settled in as a member first" he says to George "but I do like the idea of starting a mentoring programme, let me give it some thought"

"Please forgive me. It was presumptuous of me to think you would want to be a mentor, I meant no offense" George says apologetically to Caleb.

"That's okay and none taken" Caleb says finally getting over his shock "you just took me by surprise. I mean it's one thing having Harry telling me people still remember and talk about me" Caleb smiles cheekily at Harry "but I always take what he says with a pinch of salt"

Before Harry can respond they're interrupted by a group of men, Caleb recognises them as the ones sat by the fire in the bar, walking in with the two women. George ushers them in, as he shows them to their table Harry, Rex and Caleb follow behind the women.

The play restaurant is decorated in shades of deep reds and burgundy with gold trimmings. Running the full length of the room on both sides are semi-circular booths, at the top end is a large bay window with heavy draped burgundy and gold velvet curtains. In the centre of the room are square tables, the majority are set for two places. Tonight though some of the tables have been put together to allow for a large party including the six men. Every table is occupied.

"That group" Harry says in a low voice indicating to another large party that consisted of men and women "are all members of one of the

BDSM clubs I was telling you about earlier, they'll move down to the dungeon once they've finished in here"

"Jesus, have they got… tell me you see a naked woman lying on the table covered in food?" Rex splutters.

"Yes and they're eating it off of her" Caleb laughs.

"They wanted to do Nyotaimori, that's when you eat sushi off a naked person" Harry explains "but our chef refused to do it on hygiene grounds plus he pointed out the body warms up the raw fish so salmonella could be a problem. As you know we cater for all needs… well within reason, so we came to a compromise all food is cooked and is eaten within seconds if not a couple of minutes of it being placed on the body. And being the cautious soul that I am" Harry places his hand over his heart "I got them to sign a waiver so if any of them get food poisoning it has nothing to do with us and the restaurant"

"Good thinking" Caleb praises "but I see the traditional chocolate sauce and ice cream you have no problem with" he inclines his head towards a couple in one to the booths.

A naked woman is sat on the table, her feet tucked into her bottom, knees angled out wards, resting back on her elbows as the man pours sauce over her breasts and down her stomach then adds ice cream. The woman's head falls back with a hiss and low moan in response to the cold ice cream, giving them a clear view of their faces – Lord and Lady Farringdon.

Lord Farringdon looks up and winks, he murmurs something to his wife, she nods and a smile spreads across her face as she slowly opens her eyes taking in their watching audience but her attention is quickly diverted as her Master sets to work eating his desert and her.

"Christ, I'll never look at Lady Farringdon again in the same way after watching that" Rex says as he adjusts himself "I mean that was hot and who knew she has such a good body under all those dreary tweed clothes she wears and for a woman her age"

"At least you had the decency to wait to say that" Caleb laughs as they walk into Harry's office "Joyce Farringdon is forty-eight you make her sound as if she's nearly sixty"

"How do you know that?" Rex says surprised.

"Joyce is eleven years older than me, as a kid growing up she used to come to the stables to help out and exercise the horses"

"You had a crush on her" teases Rex.

Caleb held his hands up in surrender "I was a skinny, snotty nosed hormonal boy can you blame me. She had a fucking fantastic body that I had many a wet dream about. And before you start getting any ideas" Caleb's voice drops in warning as he recognises the scheming lustful look in Rex's eyes "Bertie Farringdon does not share. He catches you sniffing around his wife he'll have your balls served to you on a silver platter"

"I'll second that my dear cousin" Harry chips in "the Farringdon's are exhibitionists and as you saw they enjoy an audience. I've seen Bertie nearly rip a guy's throat out when he touched Joyce on the arm, he's very possessive of her. I know you like a challenge but just don't go there"

"Okay I get it, no touching" Rex says resigned, then he perks up as a thought occurs to him "but that doesn't mean I can't flirt with her" Rex rubs his hands together in anticipation "just think of the fun I can have there!"

Caleb and Harry roll their eyes at Rex knowing full well that he wouldn't stop there, it's not in his nature to.

"Come on, spill the beans what's on your mind" Rex says looking at his friend in concern. Caleb has been quiet for most of the journey home, quieter than normal. Rex presses the button on the side panel to raise the privacy screen "what did Harry say that has you so deep in thought"

After they filled out the necessary paperwork Rex left Caleb in the office with Harry whilst he went to find someone willing to play. He had seriously been turned on watching the Farringdon's in the restaurant and didn't fancy going home with a boner.

Caleb drew in a deep breath "We discussed the mentoring role idea, plus a few other things. He wanted to know if I still practised with the bull whip and would I be willing to give lessons, well more demonstration and talks really on the do's and don'ts of its use"

Rex's mouth pops open in surprise "Do you? I mean do you still practise and why did he ask if you'd give demonstrations if you did"

"I never stopped" Caleb's voice is soft "aside from the fact that I use it in training the horses, actually it's a lunge whip I use with the horses but I do practise with the bull whip. Apparently Harry's been asked by one of the BDSM groups if he knew of anyone that would be willing to give a talk at their monthly meeting. I'm the first person he thought of" Caleb shrugs "I said I'd think about it"

"But that's not all that's on your mind is it?"

Caleb sighs heavily "No, you're right"

"Want to talk about it?"

Caleb shifts in his seat and faces his friend, seeing the concern on Rex's face and in his eyes, he smiles "It's not that bad" Rex relaxes and returns Caleb's smile "I was thinking about Bertie and Joyce Farringdon. Did you know that next year they celebrate their silver wedding anniversary?"

"Wow, I didn't know" Rex says in surprise "bloody hell, can you imagine being with someone that long?"

"I know" Caleb agrees "seeing them together tonight got me thinking. I wonder if it's like that for everyone, you know if you find someone who's compatible with you in every way"

"What like a soul mate kind of thing" Rex says sceptically.

"Does that kind of thing even exist?"

"Fuck if I know" Rex barks out a laugh "I do know that I've never connected with a woman where the earth moved for me. So are you saying it wasn't like that for you and Gabrielle, ever?"

Caleb nods "There was a time in the beginning I would've convinced myself it was the real deal, but seeing the way Bertie and Joyce looked at each other… Bertie absolutely adores and worships Joyce. It's the same for her as well. Tonight I've realised just how fucking much I want that too, I want what they have" Caleb says enviously "I'm not ashamed to admit to you I want, no I crave that soul deep connection they have. And I'll slap you in to tomorrow if you tell anyone I said that"

Rex holds his hands up in surrender "I won't breathe a word, cross my heart" Rex makes the slashing cross mark over his heart to emphasise his point, seeing how serious his friend is he genuinely wouldn't "so my man, tell me what your ideal woman looks like and the kind of personality she'll have"

Caleb puffs his cheeks out as he thinks then exhales slowly "She'll be blonde and petite"

"With big tits" Rex cut in smiling wickedly.

"And an amazing tight arse" Caleb laughs holding up and cupping his large hands as he imagines caressing his fictitious woman's bum "big eyes that are an unusual colour, full lips and cheek bones, porcelain white skin. None of that spray tan shit for my woman"

"Christ, I'm feeling horny just thinking about her" Rex says squirming in his seat.

"She'll be small in height" Caleb adds.

"Anyone is small compared to you" Rex snorts.

Caleb ignores the dig "You'd want to protect her, keep her safe but she's tough, independent. Highly motivated, knows what she wants and goes out and gets it. She's a free spirit and you'll piss her off if you try to smother her or curb her freedom. She'll be intelligent and solvent, doesn't need a man to support her… financially I mean" Caleb becomes more animated as he builds the picture of his ideal woman "the tough independent image she projects hides the sexual submissive inside her and she's feisty making her a crap sub in the obedience and subjugation sense but she's willing to experiment and explore her sexuality"

"You have got to introduce me to this woman if you ever meet her" Rex says eagerly.

"If such a woman does exist you are the last person I would introduce her to" Caleb laughs heartily.

"Spoil sport" sulks Rex "you'd let me play with the two of you, wouldn't you?" he asks hopefully. Caleb laughs harder in response "I can't help but notice this fictional woman is the complete opposite of Gabrielle"

That sobers Caleb up quickly "Can you blame me?"

"No my friend, that I can't" agrees Rex "hey, you up for going back to the club next Saturday?"

Caleb shakes his head "No can do I'm afraid. I'm out of the country for a few of weeks" he adds quickly seeing the disappoint on Rex's face "I leave on Tuesday"

"Don't tell me you're finally taking a well-deserved holiday for once in your miserable life" Rex says in mock shock and clutches his chest.

"Okay I won't tell you it's a holiday because it's not. What I will say is that it's a horse buying trip"

"I should have known" Caleb chuckles as Rex rolls his eyes at him "all expenses paid I take it" Rex wiggles his eyebrows.

"Of course" Caleb laughs at his friends' insinuation "but I'm going on my own, sorry to burst your bubble"

"Who you buying for and more importantly where are they sending you?" Rex's curiosity is peaked.

"The syndicate that's headed up by The Goats, Bertie Farringdon and a polo playing friend of his. Baxter was making noises of buying for him as well but that's not going to happen. Between you and me he's skinter than I am"

"I knew Baxter was struggling but didn't realise it was that bad. How did you find out about his financial situation?"

"Will the bookie told me. He overheard me and Bertie discussing and arranging the buying trip when we were in The Coach House, he wanted me to buy a couple of horses for the syndicate. Bertie happened to mention Baxter was talking about getting into racing horses and he might be interested in getting me to buy some horses for him. Bertie went to the bar to get a round of drinks and Will said not to touch Baxter even with a barge pole" Caleb chuckles "apparently Baxter owes Will big time, personally and as a bookie. Months ago they kicked him out of the syndicate because he was borrowing money off the members. I don't know how but Will also found out that Baxter owes god knows how many thousands to more than one bank, he believes it's only a matter of time before they foreclose on him"

"Jesus fucking Christ. I'm glad you told me. I was about to lend the bastard fifty grand" Rex felt sick, he trusted his friend and Caleb wasn't one to gossip or fabricate the truth "thanks you've just saved me a bloody fortune"

Caleb left Rex to his thoughts and looks out the window, not that he can see much in the pitch black night "Where are you going?" Rex says after a few minutes "you didn't say where you're going to buy the horses" he adds seeing the puzzled look on Caleb's face.

"First stop is Argentina, I'm there for four days. Then America for three days split between Dallas and Tennessee. Then over to Italy for three days. I'm waiting on confirmation for France but my last stop is Fort William in Scotland"

"That's one hellva horse buying trip" Rex whistles low "you'll be knackered and in need of a holiday when you get back"

"Hopefully since I'll be travelling most of the time it won't be too bad. Actually if I'm honest, I'm looking forward to it. Getting away, change of scenery" Caleb shrugs his shoulders he didn't need to finish the sentence as he could see Rex got it.

"Well don't forget to enjoy yourself and have some fun" Rex winks salaciously.

"Oh, I plan to" Caleb chuckles.

CHAPTER SEVEN

SKYE

"It's been nearly five months" I hear Shelley say in a low voice "I'm worried about her"

"I know sweetie. I know" Simon replies trying to keep his voice low and not quite succeeding "so am I, so am I sweetie"

Neither of them realise the bedroom door is a jar and I can hear them. They think I'm asleep. I've spent the night at Simon's apartment. He insisted on dragging me along to a dinner party at one of his friends and staying over. Shelley and Simon mean well, six weeks after the funeral they started their 'Get Skye out and about' campaign, unsuccessfully I might add. I don't begrudge them and I understand why they're doing it. I would be doing the same thing if it was one of them in my situation but sometimes I just can't help wishing they'd leave me alone.

I threw myself into my work, plus I had Clayton's business to run. After he had taken care of his family Clayton left everything else to me, including his company. Although Clayton involved me in his business and I helped out from time to time, usually giving my opinion on the various deals he was considering or as a translator, I have no interest, inclination or intention to lead the company, so I offered the business to Joshua and Andrew, both declined.

Last month, within days of each other, two competitors approached me with very generous offers to buy me out and last week I called a meeting with all the senior executives and heads of departments along with Joshua and his team. I made sure everyone who needed to be present was, if they couldn't make it in to the office they were conferenced in. My news came as no surprise to the staff when I told them about the offers and the fact I was seriously considering them, however they surprised me by asking for time to put together a management buyout bid, to which I agreed.

Telling Stephanie, I was going to be selling her favourite son's business, the one her beloved husband started, was going to be a barrel of laughs – not! At least I didn't have to broach the subject for a couple of months yet, unless Joshua had already told her. I can feel irritation stir, it used to really piss me off that Joshua would tell the family all about my business affairs, including Clayton's. Whenever I brought it up with Clayton he would laugh and say "It's what family members do when there's good news to be shared" and because I have no points of reference on that score I let it go, but it still riled me. I never should have moved my business affairs to Joshua's firm.

"I spoke to Paul yesterday and he said as far as he knew she hasn't cried" Shelley sighs "I know everyone grieves differently but to bottle it up isn't healthy. Have you tried to get her to talk?"

"Yes, but she changes the subject or just doesn't answer"

No-one witnessed my melt down the day I returned to my apartment. I exhausted myself of all tears, letting loss and grief consume me as I lay curled up on the studio-office floor. I eventually fell asleep only to wake up when the early winter morning sun shone through the windows. I dragged my stiff aching body back to the bedroom. Fresh tears rolled down my cheeks again as I lay soaking in the hot steamy bath. But there was no sobbing, no sense of feeling helpless or loss. I was numb. I have been ever since. I'm operating on auto pilot, not even taking one day at a time. I'm barely existing as a human being.

"I saw Matthew the other day" Simon continues "he told me that Skye had come by the shop with a load of new jewellery designs. He was blown away by them, said she's given him enough material to keep him and his team busy for the next two years"

"That doesn't surprise me, she's working too hard. I suggested to Phil…" Shelley stops talking as my phone rings.

In my mind's eye I picture both of them holding their breath as they look towards the bedroom door. I let it ring and dance around the top of the bedside cabinet a little longer just so my friends wouldn't suspect I overheard them. I answer without looking at the screen.

"Hello" my voice breaks partway through.

"Skye, I'm sorry did I wake you?"

I recognise the southern drawl but still pull the phone away to check the name on the screen to make sure "Morning Penny, don't worry I was partly awake. How are you and Mike?"

"We're both good. How are you?" I hear the well-intended sympathy in her voice.

"Not bad. I was out last night with Simon and his friends. It was good fun" I fake enthusiasm as I know he'll be listening.

"How tender is your head?" chuckles Penny.

"Don't know it's still nailed to the pillow" I dead pan making Penny laugh more.

"Well I'll get to the point of my call and let you get back to sleep. I want you to come and spend some time with me and Mike at the ranch, at least a week. I'm not taking no for an answer" she adds sternly.

I instantly like the idea. It will do me good, a different environment and besides Penny and Mike no-one will know me so I can get away from the wary sympathy looks and people treating me like I'm about to breakdown in hysterics at any moment if they say the wrong thing to me. Plus, I get to see Dark Moon, my horse. I feel a spark of excitement ignite and take hold, something that I haven't felt in a long time it feels… strange.

"Sure, why not. When are you thinking?"

"Seriously? You're definitely coming?" Penny says shocked, now it's my turn to laugh.

"Yes. You did just say you weren't taking no for an answer" I mock scold her.

"I know but I didn't think you'd take me seriously" she retorts defensively "how are you fixed for coming out next week?"

I didn't need to check my diary. I have no social engagements booked, I haven't since the funeral and work wise I'm so far ahead I could bum around for the next six months and I'll still be ahead, that was the reason why I'd been able to give Matthew two years' worth of designs.

"That's fine with me, what day are you thinking of?"

"How about Wednesday? Mike will be in New York on Tuesday for a meeting and will be flying back on the Wednesday morning so I was thinking why not hitch a ride with him"

The first genuine happy smile in months' spreads across my face "Sounds like a plan. Email me times and tell him I'll meet him at the airport"

"Yay!" Penny squeals, I pull the phone away from my ear and wince "I'm so excited, see you next week"

We chat for a few more minutes finalising some details, mainly who will be coming with me. Paul and Alan definitely. Bruce is still recuperating with the aid of the lovely Nurse Janice. I can't help smiling as I recall watching the blossoming relationship unfold during the weeks Bruce spent in hospital. Now Nurse Janice is a regular fixture in Bruce's apartment. I keep teasing him about giving me plenty of notice to go and buy a hat for the wedding. As I end the call there's a knock on the door, Shelley and Simon walk in.

"Morning honey, who was that?" Simon asks sitting down at the foot of the bed. I scoot over making room for Shelley.

"It was Penny inviting me to the ranch. I'm going out on Wednesday for a week" I can see the relief in their faces. Shelley practically sags against me.

"That's great. It'll do you the world of good" Simon says reaching out to grasp my hand. Shelley puts her arms around me and hugs tightly.

"Yeah, I think so too" I sigh, I decide there and then to own up to over hearing them "look, know you're both worried about me. I heard you" I add quickly to cut off their protests "I understand why you think I'm bottling everything up but I'm not. I've cried my tears. I've already had the melt down you keep waiting for me to have. No one was around to see it. And before you ask it happened the day I went back to the apartment. I miss Clayton every single second of the day and no doubt I will do for a long, long time to come. I work as hard as I do because if I don't my grip on reality will slip" I look at my two best friends to see if they understand "I'm barely holding on by the tips of my fingers as it is" I whisper.

Simon moves up the bed to sit the other side of me and wraps his arms around me and Shelley "I don't talk about it because I have nothing to say. Something happened at the hospital seconds before Clayton died" I feel both of them start in surprise "I'm not going to tell you what it was because I don't want it picked over or analysed to death or a logical explanation found or told it's a figment of my imagination. Maybe one day I'll share but not right now"

"I get it" Shelley whispers "I really do" the compassion in her voice brings a lump to my throat and my eyes sting with unshed tears.

"Thank you" I whisper back.

We sit holding each other in comfortable silence for a while, each lost in our own thoughts.

"Can I come with you to Penny's?" Simon asks tentatively "I'll stay out of your way, I promise"

"Of course you can" I say puzzled as to why he'd want to come with me "and you don't have to stay out my way"

"I'd love to come with you too, but I can't" Shelley says rubbing her very pregnant belly. At seven months she looks to be closer to full term.

"Doctor's orders" the three of us chorus, then laugh "how are you feeling?" I add.

"Good, apart from the swollen ankles and occasional back ache. This pregnancy is a doddle compared to the last one"

"And that's with two babies in there" Simon says leaning across me to rub Shelley's belly.

Four weeks after the funeral Shelley and Phil announced the pregnancy, well they had to since they found out Shelley is expecting twins and the doctors are keeping a closer eye on her even more so. They couldn't keep coming up with new excuses as to why Shelley had so many doctor's appointments. Shock, surprise and genuinely being over the moon for them was a roller coaster of emotions I'd gone through for them at the news. God only knows what they felt. Don and Brenda are the proudest grandparents anyone could possibly wish for. There's no history of twins on Phil's side and Shelley has absolutely no clue about her family as she's the only surviving member of hers, since her parents and grandparents were killed in a car crash when she was eight. The doctor has said they'll have to wait until the babies are born to see if they are fraternal or identical twins.

"Shelley, I've been thinking"

"Uh oh, waddle for the hills that's not a good thing when Skye says that" Simon laughs. I slap his leg in retaliation.

"As I was saying" I say pompously "a few weeks back you were saying Phil was on about looking to build a new family home rather than get a bigger apartment" Shelley slowly nods her head "well how about you move into my apartment, no hear me out" I hold up my hand to stop her "as you know I'm going to be spending a lot of time in England. I'm way ahead in my schedule workwise and I've decided to go over there earlier than originally planned. I just haven't decided when but now I'm going to Penny's I think I'll go straight from there. By moving into my apartment it means you can sell yours at your own convenience without any added stress and it will give you and Phil breathing space and all the time you need to find and buy a decent plot of land and build your dream home without the pressure of a deadline"

At the time I offered to finance the project for them — even though they can afford to do it themselves — but Shelley refused saying it was only an idea but I think it was more to do with not wanting to take money from me in my vulnerable state. Shelley looks at me absolutely stunned.

"Have a think about it and discuss it with Phil, the offers there. I'll probably spend a couple of weeks in England so you could move in whilst

I'm away. Then I'll be back to finalise and make plans for a more semi-permanent move to the UK" I frown "does that make sense?"

"Yes" Shelley laughs "I understand, but are you sure?"

"Why not?" I throw back "I'm not going to be there, you'll need somewhere to live whilst your new dream home is being built and you need more room especially when the babies arrive" I tenderly stroke her belly "this way it will take a huge amount of stress and worry away keeping you safe as well as my nieces or nephews in here" I gently pat her tummy "I won't be offended if you decide no, like I said the offers there"

"You'll be stupid if you don't take up her offer" says Simon "if I was you I'll be snatching her arm off right about now"

"Okay I'll talk to Phil about it, and thank you for your very generous offer"

"My pleasure. Right I need to get up, things to do, places to go and all that crap" I say disentangling myself from Shelley and Simon. I feel invigorated now that I have a clear sense of purpose.

It's been a mad four days. Since Penny's phone call on Saturday morning I haven't stopped. I'm surprised I haven't met myself coming back. It's made me realise even more how desperately I need to get a new PA. Right on cue the familiar pang of guilt follows those thoughts – every time. I delegated the travel and vehicle arrangements to Paul and Alan but I also realise how much crap Macy actually shielded me from and I send a silent thank you up to her. God, I miss her.

Simon and Alan have gone ahead to the airport with our luggage whilst Paul and I go to collect Jack. When I rang Paul from Simon's on Saturday he had been driving with Jack in the car, on hearing we were going to Tennessee Jack begged to come with us. I said yes so long as Paul and his mom were okay with it, naturally he is allowed to come if the boss says so.

Jack is waiting for us on the sidewalk outside his apartment building, his excitement palpable as he bounces up and down when he sees us approaching. He has the door open and is climbing inside before Paul has brought the SUV to a stop.

"Hello Jack" I laugh, his bright shining blue eyes glow with happiness matching the smile on his face.

"Ms Darcy, thank you, thank you so much for letting me come" he bounces in the seat as he scrambles to close the door.

"Don't you have any luggage son?" Paul asks him.

"Oh shoot!" he stumbles back out and runs up the steps of his apartment building — he seems so uncoordinated, all gangly arms and legs — only to be met by his mother coming out with his suitcase. Paul gets out and closes the door Jack left open, stopping the cold spring air rushing into the car.

I watch Paul take the suitcase from his ex-wife. She waves to me in the car, not that she can see me through the tinted windows. Jack gives her a brief hug. He towers over his mother. Jack appears to have doubled in size since I last saw him and his growth spurt is the reason for his awkward movements, it's as if he's getting used to his new height. In the blink of an eye Jack turns and runs back down the stairs, he's in the car with his seat belt fastened before Paul has the trunk open to put his case inside.

"How long were you stood outside in the cold waiting for us" I smile at Jack as he looks at me sheepishly.

"Dad rang me as you left your place"

"You must be frozen" I exclaim, normally it takes ten minutes but we got stuck in traffic so it took twice as long.

"Nah" he grins back cheekily "Dad texted me saying traffic was bad so I waited in the vestibule, nipping out every few minutes to look for you"

"So you're just a tad excited about this trip" I tease.

"Are you kidding me? I'm so stoked" he jigs in his seat "I can't wait to see the horses. My mates are so jealous. I get to spend a week out of school to ride horses" he gloats.

"If I'd known you would be missing school I wouldn't have agreed to you coming" I say sternly, raising an eyebrow at Paul as he gets in the driver's seat. Jack's face falls, crestfallen.

"Good job he's a straight A student and ahead in his course work isn't it" Paul smirks at me and doesn't hide how proud he is of his son.

"Plus I have homework, well it's a project about my week at the ranch and how it's going to help me in my chosen career" Jack adds earnestly.

"So we're good to go" Paul says nonchalantly pulling into the flow of traffic.

"Okay, I concede" I laugh holding up my hands.

"Besides you pay my school fees and as a main benefactor to the school they could hardly say no" Jack informs me boldly. That really makes me laugh, he's right and he knows it – the little sod, well not so little anymore.

On the way to the airport I listen to Jack update Paul on his studies and what has happened in his life since they last saw each other on Saturday. They chat easily and freely, it's almost as if they've forgotten I'm in the car with them.

"Mom's boyfriend is still a total flake, louse and smartass"

"Jack" Paul's voice is full of warning.

Jack's eyes flick to me "Sorry Ms Darcy" he mumbles in apology.

I have absolutely no clue what he's apologising for "You're forgiven so long as you explain flake and louse. Smartass I get but I have no idea what the other two mean"

"Flake is someone who says they're going to do something but doesn't. Louse is a nasty person" Jack says in a low voice; he picks at his cuticles not wanting to meet my eyes or the hard stern disapproving look from his father. He's tense waiting to be rebuked. Poor lad, my heart constricts for him.

"Wow! Unreliable, unpleasant and a know it all. What a winning personality combination that is" I say sardonically. Jack sniggers giving me a sideways look. I wink at him and he relaxes.

I notice the warning look Paul flashes Jack, he obviously doesn't want his son to say anything else and I bite my tongue to stop the question that I'm about to ask. Jack flushes and busies himself picking at his finger nails. I decide to bide my time and I'll ask my questions when I spot the opportune moment.

"So Jack, tell me everything you hope to do and get out of this week" I say instead, the tension in the car eases as Jack launches into everything he wants to achieve.

We arrive at the private airfield side of the airport. Paul drives the SUV straight into the hanger where a gleaming Lear Jet waits for us. The cold wind pulls at my hair and I tighten my coat around me as I get out the car.

"Don't be too hard on the boy" I say under my breath to Paul as we make our way to the Jet.

"Yes ma'am" Paul's rumbling chuckle brings a smile to my face, we both know he'll be having words with Jack.

Mike appears in the doorway as we ascend the stairs "Good to see y'all, right on time" he calls out smiling warmly "well look at how much you've grown Jack" he slaps Jack on the shoulder making his knees buckle "ready to work with the horses?"

"Yes sir" Jack replies full of enthusiasm.

"Call me Mike. Sir is my father" Mike chuckles as he ruffles Jack's hair.

"Skye, lovely to see you" he kisses my cheek "Paul" he nods "come and get settled, we'll be taking off in fifteen minutes"

Three hours later we are driving towards Pikeville. Mike's ranch is situated not far from the town. The nearest airport is Chattanooga, normally Mike would have taken his helicopter from the airport to the ranch but because of the size of our party we're driving. Mike and his driver Marco, Paul and I are in one vehicle. I thought Simon would sulk when Mike said he wanted to ride with me but he seems more than happy to travel with Alan and Jack. Hmm, something occurs to me. I know Simon has always fancied Alan and flirts with him at every opportunity. As far as I know Alan is heterosexual but he doesn't seem to mind Simon hitting on him. Maybe Alan is bi-sexual or a closet gay I speculate. What the hell does it matter if he is? I scold myself. I'm not bothered about his sexual orientation so long as Simon doesn't distract Alan from doing his job I don't care what they get up to. Still I'll keep an eye on Simon, the last thing I want is a sexual harassment case on my hands.

I settle back into the plush leather seat of the huge truck we're travelling in and take in the Tennessee scenery as we hurtle down the highway. I love the area Mike and Penny have their ranch, you can see the mountain ranges in the distance, there's lots of greenery with the surrounding woods and forests that have trails to hike and explore. The weather is a damn sight warmer too. The afternoon sun shines brightly in the clear blue sky with only a few wispy clouds.

Mike is filling me in on Dark Moon's progress and how he is responding to his training, the good news is he now stands quietly whilst being groomed as well for the vet and farrier – at least he's stopped biting people. Mike said they were still working on his obedience and the short lunge line sessions appeared to be working.

"As you know six months ago we introduced him to the saddle"

"I can't help thinking that was too soon"

Mike nods "I understand but it was only the saddle, he didn't carry any weight until he turned two and we waited until he was used to it before we put anyone on his back. And he still promptly bucks them off" Mike pauses then chuckles "I suppose I should tell you Dark Moon has been nicknamed Goliath by the grooms and stable hands"

"Don't tell me they've given him a stable mate named David as well" I laugh.

Mike's eyes crinkle as his smile broadens "Actually they have, a Falabella, it's a miniature pony" he cracks up laughing "Dark Moon is huge. I think he'll be nineteen hands when he stops growing. He's already touching eighteen now" he says wiping his eyes.

"Wow" I'm stunned, all I can see is the weak little foal from when Jack and I helped deliver him "he must have had a tremendous growth spurt since I last saw him" I quickly work it out "nine months ago"

"He's literally tripled in size"

"Blimey, I can't wait to see him" I feel excited and daunted at the same time as images of a humongous horse flash through my mind.

Mike clears his throat "There's something else I should tell you as well" I raise my eyebrows as Mike shifts and looks uncomfortable "we had an old friend who's a horse trainer over from the UK on a buying trip. He came to see us on Monday and he took a real interest in Dark Moon and wanted to buy him. He offered big money, I hope you don't mind but I took the liberty and told him the owner wouldn't sell"

I can't stop the broad smile breaking out on my face "I don't mind at all and you said the right thing. I'll never sell him" Mike looks relieved "at least you know money is never going to be an incentive to sell him" we both laugh at my lame joke, but it's true "since you're in confession mode is there anything else I should know about before we get to your place?" I eye him speculatively.

"Penny has organised lots of activities" he says cringing.

"Should I be afraid?" I screw my face up in anticipation of his answer.

"Hell yes, be very afraid. Mwahahaha!" he finishes with an over the top sinister laugh.

Sitting out on the patio eating breakfast enjoying a rare solitude moment along with the peace and tranquillity of my surroundings I marvel at how fast the week has gone. Even though Penny had organised lots of activities as Mike warned I found myself thoroughly enjoying each one. My favourite by far is the day trip we took to the Great Smoky Mountains and the Cherokee reservation, we even managed to tempt Jack away from the horses for that one.

With each passing day I began to feel more and more… human. Has my slow journey to recovery begun? I wonder. I've definitely had fun with my close friends and I've laughed a lot but I still get those pangs of loneliness and sadness mainly because I will never be able to share these new experiences and memories with Clayton. I take a deep breath bringing the aroma of flowers, fresh grass and the distant smell of horses into my lungs. I slowly release through my mouth as I admire the different shades of green from the surrounding trees and how they complement the pale blueness of the sky, the warm morning promises a lovely day ahead.

Picking up my mug of tea, I descend the steps to walk around the garden and down to the stream that runs through the property. I turn to look back at the house. It's magnificent, a three story sprawling predominantly wooden structure with a peaked roof. Balconies run around each of the floors and the supporting pillars give it a real colonial feel. The ranch isn't anything I expected it to be like when Penny first invited me and Clayton to stay. The images I had in my head were based on the old TV programme Dallas, I snort at my own naivety, the house is huge that's the only similarity. I slowly walk back towards the imposing house, the gardeners start to work on the already perfectly manicured lawn and flower beds.

Mike and Penny are surrounded by staff who are genuinely happy to work for them. None more so than the grooms and stable hands. I'm pleased that they have taken Jack under their wing again, especially Waya. Mike was keen to introduce me to him as soon as we arrived, I didn't get chance to say hello to Penny first. Waya is Cherokee and started working for Mike six months ago. Mike speaks very highly of Waya and puts a lot of Dark Moon's progress down to him. I must admit I am impressed particularly with how patient he is with Jack, never tiring to answer his endless questions and taking time to teach Jack at the same time as training Dark Moon and the other horses. Jack's ambition to work with horses has well and truly been cemented now.

"Skye"

My name being called snaps me out of my reverie. I look towards the house and see Penny waving, beckoning me to her. I mustn't be walking fast enough for her because she comes to meet me partway.

"We have a visitor wanting to see you, actually he's insisting on it" she says linking her arm through mine.

"Oh, who?" I'm intrigued, no-one knows me out here.

"Waya has brought his father Atohi with him today. Apparently his father is insisting on speaking with the lady who has hair the colour of the full moon" my mouth unhinges "Waya will have to translate as his father doesn't speak English or refuses to, I don't know which" Penny waves a hand dismissively as she steers me through the house and out of the front door where Simon, Paul and Alan stand on the veranda along with Mike and Waya.

An elderly gentleman with dark olive deeply wrinkled skin is sitting on one of the many wicker chairs that grace the veranda. His steel grey and white long hair is braided, falling over his shoulder. He's dressed casually in a plaid shirt and jeans. I mentally slap myself for thinking he'd be in traditional Native American dress, that's for the tourists you moron. As soon as he sees me he stands, unsteadily, leaning heavily on his walking stick. He speaks to me, his voice is deep and rich making his words sound musical, hypnotic. I don't understand a word but I couldn't care less I could listen to him all day.

"Ms Darcy, may I introduce my father, Atohi. He says he must speak with you. I will interpret" Waya looks at his father "he has instructed me to and I will translate faithfully. Will you permit him your time and listen to what he has to say?"

I look at the old man and can't help but smile, my fingers itch to pick up my pencils and sketchbook to draw him "Of course. It's a pleasure to meet you Atohi, my name is Skye" I gesture to the chair "please take a seat"

Waya finishes talking and Atohi smiles warmly at me, his dark eyes sparkling as he sits back down. I sit in the chair next to him. Waya hunches down whilst everyone else remains standing, open curiosity and intrigue on their faces reflects my own.

Atohi starts speaking, Waya immediately starts to translate. I keep my focus on Atohi "I thank you for allowing me to speak with you. I am solely responsible my son had no choice in bringing me today" a hint of a wry smile plays across Waya's lips and he rolls his eyes obviously remembering some earlier argument "he wouldn't get out of my truck" Waya adds and winks making me laugh. Atohi gives his son an affectionate look and starts talking again.

"I receive messages from the spirit world and sometimes I am shown things" I suck in a sharp breath as do some of the others. My eyes are glued to Atohi's face so I don't see who else reacts to this news. My palms become clammy, my heart starts to thump painfully in my chest "last night I was shown you, the woman with hair the colour of the full moon" he lifts a gnarled arthritic hand and touches my hair "then a horse, black as a moonless and starless night. This morning I asked my son the colour of the horse he is training, then I asked the owners hair colour, when he told me I knew the message I received is for you"

My heart is in my throat now; I feel as if I'm about to hyperventilate. Someone taking hold of my hands startles me. I tear my eyes from Atohi to look into Simon's concern filled eyes. I realise I'm shaking.

"Skye, you don't have to hear this. Who knows how genuine this guy is, he could be a very skilled charlatan" Simon's eyes are pleading now. I know he's thinking of my fragile mental state and well-being.

"It's okay. I want to hear what he has to say" Waya is murmuring to Atohi "please carry on" I say to him.

The wise old man nods, smiling kindly "You have been touched by a spirit and heard their message just before they passed on" tears instantly spring to my eyes, rolling freely down my cheeks.

"Oh my god" Simon whispers, his hands tightening on mine.

"The message I have been given is to tell you they were your shadow soul mate. You will soon meet your true half, in a different land. You will be drawn to this soul. They are your destiny. Trust and follow your instincts in all matters of the heart" Atohi reaches out and takes one of my hands, I'm surprised by the power and strength in his grip "your shadow soul mate wishes for you to be happy and to love again"

Freeing my other hand out of Simon's grip I wipe away my tears "Thank you for coming all this way and giving me the message" my voice sounds watery and rough. I lean forward and kiss the old man's cheek.

"Thank you for listening" Atohi smiles kindly at me then stands and speaks directly to his son.

Waya looks to Mike "My father wishes to go home. I will come straight back"

Mike nods, too stunned to say anything. We all watch Waya help his father into the truck. I wave goodbye to them. It remains quiet as we watch the truck disappear down the driveway.

"Skye, I don't mean to pry but what did Atohi mean when he said you have been touched by a spirit and heard their message" Penny asks timidly, her wide eyes burn with curiosity.

I see the same look in Paul, Alan and Mike's faces. Simon has already deciphered the meaning of Atohi's message and just wants confirmation for the conclusion he's reached.

"A few minutes before Clayton passed away I felt someone touch my head. I'd fallen asleep with my head resting on his bed. I woke up thinking he'd come round but he hadn't. I looked around the room to see if someone else had come in but it was empty. The touch came again, only this time it ran down the side of my face" I trail my fingers down my cheek "I heard the words "I'm sorry" and I felt surrounded by so much love, it was so strong I could hardly breathe... then it was gone. I knew it was Clayton saying goodbye. I leant over and kissed him, whispered my goodbye and seconds later he flat lined" every face has the same open mouthed and shocked expression "I've never told anyone about that, so Atohi, in my book is the genuine article" I look Simon straight in the eye, challenging him to say otherwise.

Simon wraps his arms around me "I get it" he whispers "I totally get why you never wanted to share something so precious. I'm sorry to say I would have tried to find a logical explanation and convince you otherwise, but you knew that already" he pulls away holding me at arms-length, a wicked smile spreads across his face "I wonder what your true soul mate will look like. I mean Clayton was sex on legs. Does that mean your new man is going to be a sex god?"

I burst out laughing, trust Simon to be twenty steps ahead of me.

CHAPTER EIGHT

SKYE

I sprint down the platform following Paul, Alan is beside me. The guard holds the carriage door open gesturing us to run faster, the sound of a whistle blasting out makes the three of us kick harder. Paul throws the luggage in through the door and follows it. Alan picks me up and literally throws me in. I manage to pant out a thank you to the guard before the door slams shut behind Alan.

"Talk about cutting it fine" I wheeze. The three of us are bent double gasping for breath "just our bloody lousy luck to pick a time to come to Scotland when one of the worst storms in history hits" I grumble.

"Thank your lucky stars we were able to get booked on this train last minute, otherwise you'll be still stuck here tomorrow" Alan grins as he stands "come on let's find our cabins"

Paul and Alan pick up our luggage leaving me to lead the way down the corridor looking for our sleeper cabins. It doesn't take long.

"We'll give you a knock in five minutes to go and get something to eat" Paul says handing me my bag, I acquiesce whole heartedly, I'm starving.

Surprisingly the cabin is quite roomy, compact but roomy. Then I imagine Paul and Alan in this space and change my mind. Two big strapping blokes will dwarf this space. Along one side are bunk beds, directly in front of me under the small window is a cabinet. I dump my case on top and open it. I take off my coat and dig out a thick woollen cardigan. The cabin is warm but I'm still acclimatising to the British weather and its bloody freezing especially with the howling wind and torrential rain that's now battering the train as it picks up momentum leaving the station.

I'm grateful that Alan had the hindsight to keep tabs on the developing storm during the day whilst I was in meetings, by three this afternoon he interrupted me saying if the pattern continues he could see our flight to London being cancelled. I have a very important meeting first thing with Dario Benenati so contingency plans were made, sure enough two hours later Alan's prediction came true. Fortunately, my last client didn't live too far from Fort William where we picked up the overnight sleeper train to Euston.

We find the Lounge Car easily enough and get a table as it's not very busy. The waiter is with us instantly, we place our food and drinks order straightaway, no-one wanted to wait. Paul and Alan update me on various business calls that have come in during the day and I make a 'to do' list. I feel guilty because taking my business calls and messages really isn't in their job description. It's time I took the bull by the horns and get a new assistant.

"There's a couple of things I need to share with you" Paul and Alan look at me expectantly; I look down at my folded hands on the table because I can't bring myself to look Paul in the eye as I say "I've been thinking about appointing a PA"

"Thank god, about time" my head snaps up in shock at Paul's words, he smiles and in one of his rare moments of showing affection he places his large hand over my clasped ones, gently squeezing "I love my job but I can do without all the other shit you've been dumping on us"

"Here, here" Alan mutters.

Both men laugh at my stupefied face, their reaction – well more Paul's reaction is not what I was expecting at all.

"You're okay with that?" I still have to ask even though it's blatantly obvious he is.

"Skye, it makes sense. It was okay when you were working from one place and everyone came to you but now you're out and about it's a logistical nightmare. You need a PA" his voice softens "I appreciate your concern and consideration it means a lot, but life moves on and we both need to catch up" I feel my eyes filling up, he gives my hands one final squeeze "so what are the other things you need to share"

The waiter arrives with our food and drinks; it gives me time to compose myself. I take a few bites out of my Aberdeen Angus Cheeseburger before I speak again just to stop my stomach from protesting how empty it is. I let out a groan as the flavour assaults my taste buds.

"Once I've done everything I need to do in London I was thinking about taking a ride out to Dove Mill Village to see the property. It's under forty miles from London"

"I can't help but notice you said ride and not drive" Alan says grinning at me.

"Well if the weather clears up I thought I might try out my new motorcycle" I give Paul a sideways glance to gage his reaction "seems criminal for it to be gathering dust in Nessa's garage" then a brilliant idea strikes me "you two could hire Harley's and we can show Alan the English countryside" I add smiling innocently.

Paul rolls his eyes at me. He knows that I know he's not going to say no or put up an argument as why riding is a bad idea, especially when I dangle the prospect of riding his beloved Harley.

"I'm sold even if he isn't" Alan laughs. Paul grunts in response.

"That's settled then. Now the other thing I was thinking is rather than travelling back and to from Nessa's I thought we could check into a hotel or bed and breakfast in the area and use that as a base instead. I plan on spending maybe a week there, gives me chance to look over the other properties to see what needs doing. What are your thoughts?"

"Good plan and it makes sense" Paul says wiping his mouth on his napkin "we just need to consider the usual potential threats and risks then plan security accordingly"

During the next hour and a half, we thrash out all possible scenarios and agree the security procedure for each. I take this very seriously as it's the first time I've surfaced in public since Clayton's funeral. As one of the richest women in the world I'm an easy target. Even without Clayton's wealth I would still be one of the richest women in the world thanks to my own business interests, all Clayton's wealth did was push me further up the rich list. Once Paul and Alan are satisfied we call it a night and head back to our cabins.

CALEB

The sound of a fog horn and buzzing wakes me up. It's my phone, I realise belatedly as it rings off only to start again immediately after. Disorientated I try to locate it in the darkness, the shaking movement of the train makes it difficult to lay my hand on it. It rings off again just as I pick it up. Cursing under my breath I blearily look at the screen. It lights up and rings again. Rex.

"Yeah" my voice rasps thick with sleep.

"Hey my man, where are you?" his cheerful voice makes me want to punch him.

"On the overnight train to Euston" I growl at him instead.

"Jesus sorry man. I thought you were back today"

"I should have been but all flights out of Scotland are cancelled due to the fucking storm. I managed to get a last minute booking on the train, this was the earliest one out of Fort William" I sit up, remembering at the last second to duck my head and narrowly miss bashing it on the top bunk. I rub my face "what time is it?"

"Just after ten thirty" Christ I've been asleep for three solid hours, just shows how tired I am "listen will you be able to get to the club around eleven tomorrow morning?" Rex says in a rush, piquing my curiosity.

"Yeah, the train gets in just before eight. Why? What's going on?"

"Harry has some big meeting tomorrow with the new owner. I'm not a hundred percent certain but I think he wants to pitch the mentoring programme to him. Whilst you've been away Harry has canvassed members' opinion on the idea and it's proving to be very popular, he's got a list as long as his arm of people who want to sign up to it. It's only a hunch but I think Harry wants us around so he can introduce us as two possible mentors for Dom's. I'm assuming he'll have someone for the Sub's mentor"

"Tell Harry I'll be there about nine to nine thirty and I'll be using my room to shower and change" I look critically round the tiny cabin. If I'm lucky I might snatch an hour's kip on a comfortable bed because I sure as hell won't get it sleeping in here, my back and legs are already protesting at the cramped conditions.

"Will do. I'll catch up with you tomorrow for all the gossip about your trip and the fun you've had with the ladies"

I snort a laugh "I'll see you tomorrow" and hang up.

I stand and stretch, my muscles and joints pop satisfactorily. I'm wide awake now. 'Go get a drink', I decide snatching up my phone and wallet. I stop at the basin to wash my face to freshen up. I run my fingers through my hair. It needs cutting, its touching my shoulders now. The usual unruly curls have dropped with the weight now I have jet black wavy hair. I quite like this length. I only kept it short because Gabrielle preferred it that way. I'm definitely keeping it long. I run my hand over the two-day old stubble on my chin, the shave can wait until tomorrow. My skin has that healthy sun kissed glow to it thanks to the good weather in the countries I've been in.

The Lounge Car is relatively quiet only a handful of people, all men, sit around either working on laptops or flicking through their phones. I order a double scotch and take a seat not far from the bar, grateful that the chairs are not those ones that are attached to the fucking floor. Instead they are comfortable blue cushioned chairs with chrome legs and side arms, I revel in the fact I can stretch my legs out.

The conversation I had with Rex comes to mind and I start to think about what I'll be telling him tomorrow. He'll want all the dirty details about the women I've fucked, that's nothing to shout about. Pretty bland vanilla stuff, he's not going to be interested in any of that and the women were pretty bland too. Not one of them stands out, I can't remember any of them not that I had many. I do a quick mental tot up, four over the two weeks. I only remember by thinking of where I was at the time of picking them up or rather they hit on me. Each one was a quick fuck either in the toilet cubicle or round the back of the bar, I had one woman in her boyfriend's truck whilst he played pool with his buddies.

Now the horses that's a completely different story. I managed to procure Bertie and his polo friend the twelve horses they wanted and I got three horses for the consortium. The only downer was I didn't procure the one horse I really wanted. A jet black Friesian Sport horse, he was a fucking monster of a colt called Dark Moon. I couldn't believe it when Mike said he was almost two and a half years old. The beast was nearly eighteen hands and Mike reckons he'll be nineteen once he's fully grown. I watched the Cherokee guy working with him, I was dying to get into the ring and take over. As I was leaving the ranch I saw Dark Moon again in the field and that horse can bloody run. I offered silly money to buy him but Mike turned me down flat. I managed to convince him to put my offer to the owner when he let slip he would be seeing them. I rang Mike when I arrived in Italy to see if the owner accepted my offer. I couldn't believe it when the answer came back no.

"Money isn't an incentive for them to sell" Mike informed me.

"They must to stinking rich to turn down that kind of money" I grumbled.

"You have no idea my friend" Mike laughed.

Damn, I really wish I could've bought that horse. I could see him winning the Grand National in years to come. I wasn't going to give up. I'll get in touch with Mike again in a couple of months and renew my offer.

"Well, hello sweetheart"

A man's nasally voice drawls as the door to the Lounge Car opens. I look up and frown at the leering creep, that's what he sounds like. Men like him give us guys a bad rep by weirding out women with their freaky come on and the delusional bastards think they're god's gift. The guys' hair is thinning, slicked back dark blonde and it looks greasy with all the crap that's in it. He has a thin face, beady eyes and a long pointy nose he reminds me of a rat. The idiot tries to pull in his paunch with zero effect. I look down the car to the woman he's fixated on... my heart lurches to a stop.

Holy fucking shit, I can't believe my eyes. In looks and appearance she is everything I mentioned to Rex over two weeks ago when I described my ideal woman. She has masses of long white blonde hair; the curls spiral to her waist. She's tiny — if I stood next to her the top of her head would probably just reach chest level on me — and petite, big tits. Large eyes, full lips, defined cheek bones and no fake tan in sight. Her eyes sweep the car as she approaches the bar, she completely ignores the creep. I pull my legs in so she can pass, a small smile plays on her lips and her eyes lock with mine. Everything goes blurry except for her, I see every detail with crystal clarity. Her eyes are a pale yellow green, like the colour of autumn leaves when they start to turn from green to yellow before falling off the branch, those beautiful eyes are also filled with so much sadness. Long dark lashes surround her almond shaped eyes, her dark blonde eyebrows have a natural arch and there's a faint rose colouring on her cheeks. She is absolutely stunning and a natural beauty, her face is clear of makeup.

She reaches the bar, as she rests her elbows on the counter the cardigan she's wearing rides up revealing her perfect tight arse. I become aware of my dick throbbing painfully, discreetly I adjust myself but it doesn't alleviate the pressure in my groin.

"Do you have any Southern Comfort?" her low throaty voice sends tingles all over my skin and a shiver down my spine.

"No, I'm sorry we don't" the barman says "plenty of scotch... not a fan I take it" she shakes her head "we have Bailey's"

"Yes please, make it a double" again tingles ripple over my skin.

The barman sets about getting her drink. Creepy guy sidles up beside her, he picks up a lock of her hair and pulls it through his fingers "Tell me darlin' is this natural" he sneers, his eyes undress her as they run down her body "I'd love to find out for myself" he runs his tongue over his lips, trying pitifully to be seductive.

I'm up out of my chair before I know it, she's mine and I'll rip his fucking arms out of their sockets if he touches her again then I'll pull out his fucking tongue and shove it down his throat. I place my empty glass on the bar. Creepy guy grabs hold of her wrist, before I can do anything her stance shifts slightly and she's free of his grip, he's face planted on the bar with his arm and hand twisted at a painful angle in the blink of an eye. Nice, this woman can take care of herself.

"Touch me again and I'll break your arms" I hear her murmur in his ear, she releases him. Creepy guy is badly shaken and stumbles away from her rubbing his shoulder.

"Smooth moves, have this on me" the barman says in admiration handing over her drink.

"Thanks" she smiles at the barman and takes a seat at the table opposite from me.

I get a fresh drink and sit back down. I angle myself so I can watch her without being obtrusive. She takes a small sip and places the glass on the table. For a long while she stares out of the window, the blackness of the night makes the window a mirror and I can see the sad expression on her beautiful face. I feel an overwhelming urge to comfort her, to take away the pain she's feeling. She sighs heavily then looks down at her hands. She plays with the huge diamond ring on her left hand, damn it she's married, and my heart sinks. She slides the ring off her finger and places it on her middle finger of her right hand… or maybe not. She goes back to looking out the window, massaging her ring finger on her left hand absent minded.

Does that mean she's separated? Getting divorced? Has her husband cheated on her? Who in their right mind would cheat on such a beautiful woman like her? What a fucking idiot if he has.

"Cheer up love, it might never happen" an elderly man with a hint of a laugh in his voice says to her on his way to the bar.

"Too late, it already has" she replies with a sad smile. Christ I want to wrap her in my arms and hold her tight.

"Well you know what they say, once you've hit rock bottom the only way is up"

She snorts a humourless laugh and raises her glass to him in salute before taking a drink. The old guy leaves her alone after that. Ten minutes pass I signal to the barman for another drink and get one for her as well. Feeling bold I put the drink down in front of her and sit down. She looks me in the eye then down at the drink then back in my eyes, her expression never changes, she'll be good to play poker with I mentally note. I notice a dark blue circle surrounding the pale yellow green iris of her eyes. I lose myself in them for a while, her pupils dilate and her lips part, I observe the shallow rise and fall of her chest as she breathes… she's affected by me. A thrill shoots through me at that realisation. I hold myself perfectly still as her eyes travel up and down my body, she's blatantly checking me out. I resist the urge to strip all my clothes off so she can have a better look. I can't stop the smile tugging at my lips.

"Another thing they say is talking to a complete stranger about something that is on your mind can help" I say softly.

Her full lips twitch in an almost smile "And what makes you think I want to talk about it?" she challenges.

I shrug "Just offering my ears, I'm a good listener. No names need be exchanged, whatever you choose to talk about I will take to my grave" I place my hand over my heart to show my sincerity "and chances are after tonight we will never see each other again"

That almost smile appears again as she looks down at her ring and twiddles it.

"Tell you what, how about I take an educated guess to get the ball rolling. Please feel free to correct me if I'm wrong" still she doesn't say anything but the look in her eyes challenges me to take my best shot "Okay, here goes. Your husband has recently left you" her eyes widen; I've hit the bulls eye "you found out that he was having an affair with your best friend"

She smiles and shakes her head "Almost right" she takes a mouthful of her drink. I wait as she contemplates something, focusing on the liquid swirling in the glass she whispers "you were right about my husband leaving me but he didn't have an affair" she looks up and holds my gaze, I stop breathing. Her beautiful eyes shimmer with unshed tears "he died"

Fuck! I wasn't expecting her to say that "I'm sorry for your loss" I murmur. She takes a deep breath and her eyes drift to the window again, she's seeing images from the past and not her reflection. Her pain and sadness is from a broken heart "tell me what happened"

Again I wait, giving her all the time she needs. I'm a patient man. She surprises me by talking a lot sooner than I expected.

"The day after our fifth wedding anniversary he was in a car accident with two of our... friends. My husband and the person driving were badly injured. My other friend wasn't so lucky" her voice is quieter than a whisper "I saw the whole thing" she looks at me then with hollow, haunted eyes "my husband suffered complications during surgery and slipped into a coma... he died a couple of days later" she drains her glass then went back to looking out the window.

Christ, she's been through some heavy shit and I have a sneaking suspicion based on the rawness of her sadness it happened not long ago, certainly within the last six months – I'd put money on it.

"Tell me about your husband, what was he like?"

The sad almost smile turns up the corners of her luscious full lips. I so want to kiss and bite those lips. I shove the inappropriate thought out of my head and fail as my eyes are drawn to them.

"He was the same height as you" that surprises me, I didn't think she paid any attention to me when she first walked in, my eyes find hers and I see a brief appraising sparkle "you're six four right?" I nod, her smile widens but it still doesn't reach her eyes "you're bigger than he is, in build I mean" she raises her shoulders and holds her arms in a muscle man pose to emphasis her meaning. It makes me smile "don't get me wrong he was muscular, very fit and athletic" she pauses chewing her bottom lip, I so want to do that "dark brown hair a bit shorter than yours and not as wavy, his eyes were dark blue. He was very driven, focused. Excelled in his business, he could be a tyrant one minute then a mushy soppy git the next" she snorts a laugh at some memory that's come to mind "he used to drive me bat shit crazy with his over protectiveness and he'd laugh at himself because he always underestimated me. He was supportive, loving, generous… he was my soul mate"

"Sounds like he was a great guy to know"

"Yeah, he was" she looks down at her ring and twiddles it again. I leave her to her thoughts. It's my turn to look out the window only to see my own distorted face reflected back "your turn now" I turn to look at her puzzled "tell me what happened to your wife?" she points to my left hand. I look down and see the clear white mark left by my wedding ring "actually let me take an educated guess to get the ball rolling" she grins at me; mischief is written all over her face "please feel free to correct me if I'm wrong"

I throw my head back and laugh as she repeats my own words back to me "Go ahead, by all means it's only fair"

Her glorious eyes bore into me. I feel as if she's mentally stripping layer upon layer away to truly see me, to see into the deepest depths of my soul. Such intense scrutiny would normally have me squirming and feeling uncomfortable but not with her… I welcome it… want it.

"Your wife left you… no that's not right" she frowns "you threw her out after you had enough of her infidelity. In the past she left you but you always took her back, only this time…" she pauses looking at me concerned "are you okay? You look like you've seen a ghost"

"What, yes I'm fine" I splutter out "you just shocked the shit out of me" I take a couple of deep breaths, a poor attempt to soothe my jack knifing heart.

"I'm sorry for upsetting you and for being way off. I shouldn't have said that" she says contritely, her pale small slender hand reaches out towards me, at the last second she curls her fingers in making a fist to stop herself from touching me. I feel the loss acutely, how strange!

"No, don't be sorry. In fact, you are absolutely spot on in everything you said. You'd make a good living as a psychic" I wink and grin at her.

"Ha! That's what my friends keep saying to me" she snorts "tell me about your ex-wife" she raises an eyebrow, challenging me.

"I warn you now that it's going to make me sound bitter and twisted" I place my hand over my heart "but I swear on my honour it's the truth" she giggles; it is such a beautiful musical sound "my ex-wife is taller than you"

"Everyone's taller than me" she mutters reaching for her drink.

"Beautiful things come in small packages" I wink at her. She blushes and rolls her eyes at me "she's a brunette with short bobbed hair" I indicate the length by holding my hands to my ears "dark brown eyes and has a penchant for fake tan, so more often than not she looked like an Umpa Lumpa" that gets another giggle "she is skinny on the point of being anorexic" I shudder "when we first met she had a good body but she became obsessed with being thin. Everything you said about your husband being loving, supportive and generous well my ex-wife is the opposite" her eyes widen in surprise "self-centred, selfish, mean and money grabbing. See I told you I'd sound bitter and twisted" I grin at her.

"I'm curious, why did you take her back when she first left you?"

"That my dear lady is a very good question" I say grimly as I take a sip of my scotch "not only did I take her back once but four times"

"Four" she splutters in shock.

I nod holding up four fingers and mouthing four "What can I say in my defence, hmm… I'm a glutton for punishment" I hold my hands up.

"You must have really loved her" she whispers.

"I thought I did but by the third time I knew I didn't. I only took her back the fourth time because she had nowhere else to go and I couldn't see her homeless but she seemed determined to make our marriage work so I agreed to try. It seemed to work for a while and she appeared to have changed for the better, but" I sigh and play with my glass "as they say a leopard can't change its spots. As soon as her old behaviours resurfaced I knew she was up to her old tricks and I called it a day"

I can see sympathy in her eyes and I'm grateful when she doesn't say anything "You know the irony is when I threw her out she wasn't actually having an affair. Don't get me wrong it was about to happen I took action before she could and I believe she's with the guy now" I let out a humourless laugh "another thing, where I live they're taking bets on how long it'll be before I take her back. Even my own staff have nicknamed her Boomerang"

"Oh my god! Because she keeps coming back" my beautiful mystery lady laughs, the rich throaty sound resonates deep inside me. I can't help myself but smile with her.

"Only this time there's a difference. I filed for divorce, by the end of the month I'll have the Decree Absolute" I feel quite smug, I'm sure my face shows it as well.

"I propose a toast" she picks up the drink I bought her, raises her glass to me. My smile gets broader as I raise my glass "to a new beginning and happier future" we clink glasses.

"For both of us" I add, she smiles shyly and nods her head in acknowledgement, we both down the contents of our glasses.

I look at my watch, it's one in the morning "Well I'm calling it a night, it was lovely talking to you" I stand and hold out my hand, she surprises me by standing as well.

"I need to call it a night as well" she takes my hand, there's an audible crackling sound and pain shoots from my hand up my arm. What the hell, my mystery lady yelps and quickly drops my hand "what the bloody hell was that?" she says scowling, rubbing her hand and arm.

"You felt it too" I mimic her action of rubbing my arm "we must have a lot of static inside us to zap each other like that" we both laugh nervously as we make our way out of the Lounge Car.

We arrive at my cabin first "This is me" I gesture to the door "it was lovely talking with you" I repeat my earlier sentiment, I haven't got a fucking clue what else to say and I desperately rack my brain to find something that isn't pathetic or lame.

"Yeah, same here" she seems to hesitate then boldly steps into my personal space, she raises to her tip toes. I dip my head closing the distance, the thrumming in my body intensifies as I get a lungful of her unique feminine scent. She kisses my cheek; her soft lips linger longer than necessary. My skin ignites at her close proximity. Her body heat scorches me making my nerve endings jump and twitch as the building pleasure acts like electricity lighting my whole body up. My arms automatically slip around her, holding her in place. She's a perfect fit "thank you for listening. It really helped me" her warm breath tickles my neck.

"My pleasure" I murmur and before common sense kicks in, I kiss her.

Her lips mold to mine flawlessly. What the fuck are you doing my mind shouts, I slam the door shut on my internal voice and common sense. Any minute now I'm expecting to get my face slapped so I might as well enjoy the moment. To my utmost elation she responds. Her lips move against mine as her hands slide up my arms and twist into my hair. That's all I need. With both hands I grab her arse and pull her up my body. I groan at the exquisite feel of her against me. Her tongue dips tentatively into my mouth, her legs wrap around my hips. In one step I have her back against the carriage wall and I deepen the kiss. Greedy for more of her sweet taste.

I'm as hard as iron, the longer and deeper the kiss gets the harder I become. My body instinctively takes over and my hips start to thrust, my aching dick craving friction, preferably deep inside her. She breaks the kiss with a deep moan, I trail kisses along her jaw and down her neck. Her body responds to mine by arching in to me.

"Tell me to stop and I will" I murmur between kisses – yeah like hell you will "tell me what you want" her low moans and soft whimpers are her only answer and her body is telling me to continue, so I do.

I need to regain control of my raging lust. If I continue this way, I'll be fucking her in no time at all. I need to be able to stop if she utters the words. I pray to god she doesn't. I have my ideal dream woman in my arms and I want to make this last as long as I possibly can. Reaching round I take hold of her legs and apply slight pressure, a silent command. Instantly she unlocks and straightens them. I lower her to the floor and gently turn her around so she's facing the window. I place her hands on the glass at either side of her head. I move her hair to one side, revealing multiple small diamond hoops in her ear. I put my mouth close to her ear, my hands on her waist slide under her t-shirt, I move them across the soft silky skin of her stomach and back, she arches in to me pushing her lower back against my groin. I dip my knees and I let her feel me, the full hard length of me.

"Tell me what you want" I whisper, again she doesn't answer. I run my tongue over her ear tracing the outline, taking the lobe into my mouth, the earrings make a delicate clinking sound against my teeth as I gently bite. At the same time my hands find her glorious breasts. I cup and kneed them, dragging my finger nails over the lace material of her bra, tweaking her erect nipples. She whimpers "do you want me to stop? Answer me" I command.

"No… don't stop" her breathy moan doesn't hide the urgency in her voice.

Music to my ears.

SKYE

Did I just say that, seriously? Have you lost your mind? You're in the middle of a corridor behaving like a brazen slut with a totally hot guy at least get in the cabin, my conscious tries to reason. My body however has other ideas. Mystery Man's touch has me on fire!

His hands are rough — I can feel the calluses — but his touch is gentle. It's a mind blowing combination. As he moves them over my skin his touch leaves a trailing blaze. I find myself pushing into his hands to get more from his touch. I rest my forehead on the cool glass, my breath coming in short gasps fogs up the window. My hands are clammy causing them to slip from their original position. His hands move back to my breasts.

"Oh god" I moan; my head falls back against his shoulder. His lips press into the hollow below my ear and work their way down my neck, the light prickling from his stubble mixes with the sensations of his tongue and gentle scrapes of his teeth. Sweet lord he's going to make me come if he keeps this up. One of his hands moves south, my heart clatters against my rib cage in anticipation. His fingers circle the waist band of my yoga pants, then slip inside. His fingers gently move from hip to hip.

"Tell me to stop and I will" he whispers in my ear. Hell no, keep going my inner slut yells. A low moan escapes me "do you want me to stop? Answer me" there's that command again, the authoritative bite to his words is a huge turn on, lust rolls through me. Mystery Man is a Dominant and a practising one, of that I have no doubt.

"No… don't stop" I whisper. Are you for real? My mind screams at me as his hand moves down into my knickers, his large warm hand cupping my sex shuts up all internal voices "Oh god!" with a soft thud my forehead hits the window as his fingers tease my clit and pleasure explodes through me.

My legs move of their own accord, widening my stance to give him better access. Mystery Man adjusts his position behind me. He spreads his legs so they are on the outside of mine, his hand slips further down between my legs, inserting a finger inside me. My internal muscles clench, welcoming the penetration. His chest against my back pushes me forward against the window so my front is flat against it. I can feel his erection against my bum. With his other hand he lifts my t-shirt up so it's only my lacy bra protecting my breasts from the coldness of the window. I realise that the vibration of the train teases my nipples making them harder. Mystery Man thrusts his hips against my bum, pushing his finger deeper inside me at the same time I feel the vibrations through his hand and in to me. My eyes roll to the back of my head.

Pure unadulterated pleasure, that I've not felt for a long time hurtles around my body. Every cell and nerve ending light up as the long forgotten sensations make their presence known, intuitively my body takes command and moves to the rhythm set by Mystery Man. I no longer care if we get caught, I'm too far gone. I open my eyes, through the window I see multiple lights flash by, then it's dark again. We've just gone through a train station. Would someone have seen me, pressed up against the window with a man behind me with his hand buried in my pants? Who cares? I certainly don't!

The quickening feeling in my lower stomach and between my legs has me thrusting against his hand "I'm coming" I whimper. Mystery Man grinds his hips against mine pushing them further against the window, the vibrations become more intense against my sensitive nipples, his fingers move faster in and out, in and out. My breathing becomes more ragged as the quickening pleasure sensation builds and builds, suddenly I'm on the edge of the precipice.

"Come for me... quietly... now" Mystery Man's deep rich voice commands, his fingers thrust deeply, stroking the spot that pushes me over the edge.

I let go.

Free falling into what feels like a raging fire as pleasure burns through me. I know I make some noise; I can't help it. Mystery Man holds me tight as my body shudders through my orgasm. His fingers continue to move in and out gradually slowing down, drawing every dying ember of pleasure out of me. Leaving me in a state of spaced out bliss.

He turns me round slowly; I force my eyes open to look at him. His green eyes sparkle like emeralds, he dips his head and I meet his kiss. My arms automatically wrap around his neck. I feel one of his large hands cup the back of my head. He breaks the kiss; his lips move to my ear.

"I want to continue what we've started, will you let me?" his smooth rumbling voice sends shivers down my spine.

"Yes" I say without hesitation.

Mystery Man gives me a beautiful, knicker elastic busting smile as he steps back, clasping my hand and pulls me towards his cabin.

Standing in the centre of the cabin I'm uncertain of what to do, should I strip or let him remove my clothes. With Clayton it was so easy I didn't have to second guess. A sudden bout of nerves hits me, for Christ sake you've just let this guy, this complete stranger finger fuck you in the corridor, get a grip. I'm not nervous about what he'll do, I honestly feel safe around him. I just, ah hell I don't know, what if I don't…

"Come here" Mystery Man's rich soft voice cuts through my internal babble. I step into him, he cups my face with his big hands "I want you to enjoy this as much as I am, I want you to tell me to stop if there is anything I do that you don't like. I promise I will stop immediately, understand?" I nod "good girl, now I want you to strip for me"

Now that I can do.

CALEB

I step back and lean against the door, folding my arms cross my chest and wait patiently for my gorgeous mystery lady to start stripping. I'm acutely aware, plus I'm assuming the last man she slept with was her late husband and I'm determined to help her to reconnect with her sexuality, what had just happened in the corridor surpassed my wildest expectations. Figuratively speaking, now the door is open I want to see how far she'll take it, or rather let me take her.

I feel the burning of her gaze as her eyes travel up and down my body, she doesn't hide the fact she likes what she sees. Christ, I feel stripped naked. My body responds to her, I fight to keep myself still. She slips off her shoes, then slowly peels off her cardigan, her t-shirt follows just as slowly. When she peels off her pants and thrusts her arse out I know she's done this before. I feel a twinge of jealousy, it's strange how you can feel jealous of a dead guy. Only now it's me she's putting the show on for. Hell yeah! And what a show, feeling my dick pulse and throb I put my hand inside my jeans to adjust my cock at the same time letting her know the effect she's having on me. A sly smile plays on her lips; the little minx knows exactly what she's doing to me.

Her body is magnificent. She's toned, not one ounce of fat. There's muscle definition but it's not sinewy as she has her feminine curves. A tiny waist, gloriously big tits and a bare smooth pussy, just how I like it. I soak in her nakedness; I could spend days just looking at her. Without prompting she turns round, moving her hair over her shoulder giving me a better view of her back, oh Jesus I am so going to fuck her pert tight little arse.

"Get up onto the cabinet and kneel" I instruct her.

Without a word she climbs up. Fuck me! I hiss in a breath when she assumes the submissive waiting pose. The cabinet is just wide enough for her to do it. Back straight, knees apart, hands face down on her thighs, head down. In two paces I'm stood in front of her.

"You know what I am?" my voice is a hoarse whisper. My fingers curl into my palms, if I touch her I won't be able to stop myself.

She lifts her head "Yes… Master" my cock pulses, I'm almost about to come "and I'm a crap sub" she grins at me.

Holy fucking shit! Her words knock me sideways. Another piece of my ideal woman falls into place. There is a god after all "But you like to play?" her smile gets wider as she nods.

Without thinking I pick her up placing her on the top bunk, in between the two leather straps that run from the roof to the bed frame. I assume the straps are there to stop the person sleeping on the top bunk falling out of bed, however they are also ideal for spreading her and keeping her legs open.

"Lean back"

She rests back on her elbows as I lift her legs in the air, unable to resist I run my tongue along her crack from anus to clit. She gasps then moans as I swirl my tongue and suck her clit as I separate her legs wide, her arousal tastes like nectar, mmm I'm going to enjoy feasting on her. I adjust her legs so she's more comfortable.

"Can you sit up?"

Without a word she does just that. I adjust the leather straps so I have full access to her tits.

"Raise your arms and hold on to the leather straps. You can drop them if it gets too uncomfortable. You okay?"

"Yes" she whispers; her body is trembling with excitement.

"Yes, what?" I say in my best stern Dom voice; I give her the look as well that usually has subs quailing. However, my minx gives me a heart stopping smile.

"Yes Master" her low husky voice sends my heart rate through the roof.

I step back and admire my improvised handy work. Her pussy glistens she is so turned on. I strip out of my clothes leaving my boxer briefs on. I can feel her eyes boring in to me as she savours every inch of my body. I'm often asked by men how I keep the physique of a body builder without going to the gym. I tell them working with the horses, shifting bales of hay and other manual work around the yard keeps me physically fit. I'm not ashamed to say I'm proud of my body and I look after myself and yes I know women like what they see and want to devour me but none have made me feel so desired like the beautiful creature before me has.

I run my hands from her ankles up her calf and thighs and back down. Her legs flex and move with my touch, she is so responsive and I know she will have a hard time keeping still. I smile as my sadistic side kicks in.

"You are to remain still and quiet at all times. You are not to come until I say so" her head drops back and a low groan escapes her "the walls are very thin and as much as I would love to hear you I don't think our neighbours will appreciate your screaming" she brings her head back down; her eyes are sparkling. I kiss her "I will gag you if you can't keep quiet" her eyes briefly widen.

Moving back, I pick up one of her legs and starting with her toes I nip, lick and kiss my way up the inside of her leg until I reach the leather strap, then I start on the other one. On the second circuit as I work my way up her inside leg she starts to squirm. I make a mental note of her misdemeanours for her punishment later. Once I've finished with her legs I set to work on her hands and arms by the time I get to her breasts and stomach she's mewling like a kitten. When I eventually pay attention to her pussy she is soaking wet. I clamp my mouth over her sex and suck… hard, she comes instantly. Her juices hit my tongue, the divine taste ignites a hunger for more. I know I could eat her for eternity and never tire of her taste.

"Oh god. Fuck" she cries out, her grip on the leather straps slips she's shuddering so much. I wrap my arms around her, supporting her weight. I love the feel of her body against mine as she comes. I work her down slowly.

"Oh dear, you came without permission" I murmur in her ear "now I'm going to punish you for all of your disobediences"

She snorts a laugh "I did warn you I'm a crap submissive"

"That just means your last Dom was too soft on you and wasn't very good at making you learn. That doesn't get you out of your punishment" I help her down off the bunk bed "get up on the cabinet. Kneel facing the wall with your hands placed at shoulder height" she complies without complaint "knees further apart, push your beautiful arse out a bit more… perfect"

I move her long hair over her shoulder. I run my hands down her back and over her arse several times. She moans and lifts her body to my touch. Christ she's addictive. I slap her arse without giving her any warning and she yelps followed by a deep groan.

"Shh, keep quiet" I reprimand her and slap her again. I work a pattern on her arse and she's soon lifting for more "my naughty girl, likes being spanked. Tell me, what did your husband use on you?"

"His hand, paddle, flogger and riding crop" she sighs heavily.

I lean over her, my hands finding her breasts. I roll and pull her nipples, her head drops back against my shoulder "Which is your favourite?" I bite her ear lobe at the same time I tweak her nipples hard.

"Oh yes" she gives a throaty moan, her breathing is heavy "flogger and riding crop" she finally answers.

"Well my beautiful wanton girl, you're in luck. Stay as you are" I command softly.

I cannot believe my luck, tonight is turning up one surprise after another, all thanks to my mystery lady. I rummage through my case until I find what I'm looking for. I walk slowly back admiring the pink glow of her arse. It's about to get a damn sight pinker. I run my hand down her back and rub her arse, slipping my hand between her legs. I massage her sex dragging her wetness up to her anus, my fingers probe but I don't penetrate.

"Did your husband fuck your arse often?" I ask as I keep running my fingers over her sphincter, preparing her.

"Depends on what your interpretation of often is"

I push my little finger inside her arse, she gasps. I hold still letting her get used to the feeling. Her anal muscles contract I gently and slowly thrust my finger in and out "How many times in the month would he fuck your arse?"

"Sometimes none, others once" she pants out.

"Do you like your arse being fucked" I slap her arse as I thrust my finger in.

"Oh god, yes" she calls out.

"Shh" I warn her "have you ever had two cocks at once? One here" I replace my little finger for my middle one and push into her arse, her groans get louder "and one here" I reach round the front of her palming her sex and insert a finger deep inside her. I start to move my fingers in and out. She swallows a strangled scream. Her muscles grip my fingers greedily, her body is telling me she likes the idea of two cocks buried deep inside her "answer me, have you ever had two cocks at once?" I work her harder.

"No" she whimpers, her body is trembling, her head rocks from side to side with the effort she's making to stave off her impending orgasm.

"Would you like to be fucked by two men?" in and out my fingers trust, she's pulsing inside "answer me"

"I don't know… oh god… you're making me come" her breathing is erratic, sweat trickles between her heaving breasts. I don't let up.

"Answer me truthfully. Your body is telling me it does, what do you want?" I thrust faster. I can feel her muscles quivering.

"Yes" she throws her head back, her eyes clenched shut, her jaw and lips lock tight as she screams out her orgasm from the back of her throat. She sags forward resting her forehead against the wall, her body quivering as she tries to bring her breathing under control. I continue to pump my fingers in and out of her.

"Oh dear, you came again without permission" I admonish, I think I succeed in keeping the glee out of my voice.

"You're a sadistic bastard" she mutters under her breath.

I kiss her shoulder and run my nose along her skin breathing her heavenly heady scent deep into my lungs "And you're loving every minute of it" I whisper in her ear as I remove my fingers. Running my hands over her back, hips and thighs, lightly massaging her muscles I marvel at the perfection of her body "now I have to really punish you" I murmur, not in the least regretful "lift your head and open your eyes" she does as she's told. I bend down and pick up the riding crop bringing it in front of her so she can see it, she gasps when she realises what I'm holding.

"Where the fuck did you get that?" she whispers "don't tell me you have a Dom travelling kit"

"That's a very good idea" I laugh, in fact it's a bloody good idea "but no, I don't. I use this my dear lady in my job"

"You work with horses"

"I do and you are about to find out how proficient I am with this" I hold up a pillow "you'll want to bite down on this. I'm going to give you six strikes, normally I would do more but I want to fuck you for quite some time yet"

She takes the pillow off me, removes the pillow case and rolls it length ways. She uses it as a gag. I help tie it behind her head. She takes a couple of deep breaths and places her hands back on the wall, she keeps breathing deeply. Christ, I'm in danger of falling for this beautiful woman, she just keeps giving. Her trust leaves me feeling humble.

I run my hand over her back and arse "Ready?" she nods. I swing my arm and flick my wrist. The thwack of the leather striking flesh bounces around the room. Her body arches beautifully, her muffled scream has me wanting to hear her properly. Instinctively her hands go to her arse.

"Oh no, this will not do" I mock exasperation "I'm going to have to secure your hands. Stay as you are"

In my case I find my dressing gown and pull the belt free. Thankfully it's long enough for what I have in mind.

"Get off the cabinet and stand facing the beds" I wait patiently and watch her glorious body as she follows my commands "raise your arms and grasp the leather straps as far up as you can"

Christ this woman is perfect, she's a better sub than she realises. I stand behind her and adjust her arms slightly, bringing them lower down. The last thing I want is her accidently dislocating any of her joints. I make quick work of securing her wrists to the leather straps but make it so she can easily free herself if it gets too much.

I step back to admire her, if only we were at the club, oh the fun I would have playing with her. The cheeky minx adjusts her position and thrusts her arse out, giving a little wiggle. She's deliberately baiting me!

With lightning speed, I strike, she pulls against the restraints, her back arching and this time she doesn't make a sound. On the third strike a short muffled cry is the only noise she makes. The fourth, fifth and sixth strikes follow in quick succession, I make each one harder than the rest. Her muffled cries go straight to my cock. I'm impossibly hard, it hurts. I have never in my life experienced anything like this.

I can't stand it anymore I need to be inside her. I drop the crop and push my boxer briefs down far enough to release my cock. I grasp her hips and push slowly inside her.

"Oh fuck, you are so tight" I groan as I ease slowly into her hot wet pussy. Her muscles grip me "oh yes" my head falls back.

I hold still and breathe deeply getting used to the feeling of her muscle spasms and heat surrounding my cock. I feel as if I've died and gone to heaven, it's exquisite. I couldn't find the words even if I tried to explain the sensations that are bursting from my dick and racing around my body. I fight the urge to fuck her hard. I want to savour this.

Once I've regained my control, I start to move slowly in and out of her. It's not long when she starts to push back onto me, taking me deeper. My control slips, I grip her waist and hips tighter and start to move faster and harder, she pushes back meeting my thrusts. She wants it harder. I groan loudly as pleasure spikes with each thrust, her muscles grip me tighter. My groin grows heavy as the pressure builds, my cock gets thicker and harder. I've never been this thick and hard before. I pump faster, her muffled groans spur me on. I feel her muscles quickening, she's ready. My own orgasm starts to peak.

"Come now" I bark out. I thrust forward bringing her hips down onto me, my hips slapping her arse. Three more thrusts and she's coming hard, her screaming muffled. I follow her. I'm buried deep inside her, my cock jerking as I empty myself in her. My lower back and hips lock, my teeth are clenched as I fight to hold back my own scream of release. My body shudders violently as I ride out the remains of my orgasm. My hips circle and move slowly back and forth bringing us both down. My arms are wrapped around her, holding her close to my chest. Our erratic breathing and pounding hearts are in sync. I reach up and loosen the knots so she can free her hands. I remove the gag from her mouth and drop to my knees taking her with me. She slumps forward on the bed, I follow her.

I can still feel her muscles twitch and spasm around my dick, she came as hard as I did. Gradually our hearts and breathing returns to normal.

"Are you okay?" I murmur kissing along her shoulders and back as I ease out of her.

"Hmm, yes" her voice is croaky.

After a few more minutes I lift her and stand. I gently rub her arms and shoulders then I kneel and work over her legs and knees. Her fingers play with my hair as I take care of her. When I finish she bends down and tenderly kisses me.

"Now it's my turn to give you pleasure and explore your body" she says against my lips.

SKYE

Mystery Man gives me a sweet sexy smile "You already have; you've given me so much pleasure by letting me do those things"

"That maybe so" I smile back "but you're so intent on pleasuring a woman you neglect yourself. You need to receive as well to keep you balanced" he gives me a puzzled look. I need to show him what I mean.

I look at the bunk beds, there is no way we'll fit on either of them comfortably. The only option is the floor, inspiration hits me. I move out of Mystery Man's hands – I really need to come up with another name for him – I pick up our clothes putting them on the top bunk, he watches me with open curiosity.

"Take the mattress off the lower bed and place it on the floor" I instruct; he raises an eyebrow at me. Oh! He's still in Dom mode "please Master" I add smiling sweetly.

He chuckles as he pulls the mattress off the bed. I move out of the way so he can lay it on the floor. I put the duvet back on the bed.

"Lie face down" I say pointing at the mattress. I look up at him when he doesn't move. I can see uncertainty in his eyes and he's nervously chewing his bottom lip. He's never surrendered control before I realise, this is new to him "if it pleases you Master, I'm going to give you a massage"

"Huh!" is the only sound he makes as his whole body relaxes. He kneels and lies down, I admire the flex and ripple of his huge shoulders and muscles as he moves into position. The narrowness of the cabin doesn't give much room to manoeuvre but there is just enough room for me to straddle him.

I press my thumbs either side of his spine at his lower back and push upwards towards his shoulders. He lets out a low moan as I work the tense knots in the muscles at his shoulders. His skin has a healthy golden tan glow, as if he's been abroad recently. I'm surprised for a guy who is so dark he has very little body hair, it makes giving him a massage easier without the use of lotion or oil. I work every inch of his neck and back and the parts of his arms I can reach, his legs and of course his gorgeous tight arse. Then I use my mouth, teeth and tongue as I suck, nip, scrape and lick every inch of his fabulous body. He smells and tastes incredible. I noticed his scent earlier but now the heat of his skin and the light sheen of perspiration intensify and assault my senses. He's addictive, my very own version of catnip.

"Oh fucking hell that feels amazing" his muffled voice praises.

When I've finished with his back I get him to turn over. My eyes nearly pop out of my head at the size of him. I'm amazed he fit inside me. Unable to resist I lightly run my fingers over the length of his cock. He hisses in a breath as his hips jerk and thrust upwards a silent demand for more. I smile he's going to have to wait.

I start the whole massage process again followed by my mouth. His body is flawless, I marvel at the hardness of his chest, stomach and arms the definition would make any male underwear model green with envy. My hands look tiny against his huge biceps; this is a man who is no stranger to manual work.

I slowly work my way all over his body following the contours of his muscles, I touch everywhere except his cock. Apart from his groans and occasional jerks of his hips Mystery Man is still. He watches everything I do, his eyes burn with desire and need. When I finally take him in my mouth a long deep moan rumbles from his chest. It's one of the sexiest sounds I've ever heard. I want to make him make that sound again… a lot.

I open my mouth, taking as much of him as I can. I grasp the base of his cock with one hand and cup his balls with the other. I start with soft sucks, slowing increasing the pressure to sucking him harder as I work his shaft whilst I scrape my nails over his balls.

"Jesus fucking Christ" he hisses through clenched teeth. His arms fly out to the sides. One pushes against the wall the other grips the bed frame "do that again" he commands; he braces his legs.

He immobilises himself as I do exactly as he wants. I don't let up as I swirl my tongue around the head of his cock, I tighten my grip on his shaft and balls as I pump. The muscles of his six pack, pectorals and arms strain, the veins in his arms and neck stand out prominently all in the effort to keep himself still. Sweat trickles down his strikingly handsome face, chest and stomach.

"Fuck… I don't… Jesus… fuck… want to…. fuck… please stop" he eventually gets out. I look at his sweat drench face, his chest heaving as he gulps in air "I want to be inside you"

I move swiftly, straddling him. I hold his cock at my entrance and slowly lower myself down. My head falls back as the breath taking stretch and fullness sensations invade my body once again. I move up and down a couple of times taking him deeper. I feel my internal muscles greedily grip and milk him. His hands rest on my hips and he easily lifts me, the slow withdrawal of his cock makes my eyes roll to the back of my head. He thrusts upwards as he brings me back down onto him all the way to the root.

Oh sweet lord the fullness feels wonderful, mind blowing. I grind my hips and rotate them making us both groan. He lifts me again and thrusts up as he brings me back down, I grind and rotate.

Lift, thrust, grind and rotate.

The pattern gets faster and harder.

The incredibly intense pleasure he's eliciting from me is scrambling my mind. I can't contain this… this… feeling. I want to scream and shout with joy.

Suddenly Mystery Man sits up. His mouth is on mine, claiming me. His tongue licks and tastes, his teeth nip and pull at my bottom lip. We're moving positions, the next thing I know I'm on my back and he's pressing down on me, pushing me into the mattress. I can feel the thrumming vibration of the train. My hands tangle in his long hair. I pull and tug. He makes that sexy rumbling growl sound. He powerfully thrusts in to me. I raise my hips to meet them. The now familiar quickening feeling in my lower stomach and the fluttering and clenching of my internal muscles has me urging him to move faster, harder. I may have said those words because he does just that. My hands move down his back to his arse. I push him trying to get him deeper. It works…. my nails dig in, he yells and thrusts powerfully, I see stars and fireworks as my orgasm explodes through me. I come so hard I blackout… again.

When I come to I'm lying on top of Mystery Man, I have no recollection of being moved. His rough callused hands lightly stroke my back. I take a deep breath drawing in his heady masculine scent, god I want to bottle it. I place a kiss on his chest and lift my head to see amused green sparkling eyes.

"Welcome back" he grins; I feel giddy inside "how are you feeling?"

I do an internal check, my bum is sore from the spanking but it's a nice warm glow and I know it will be tender in the morning. My vagina is tender but not uncomfortable. All my bones feel as if they've turned to mush. My skin and nerve endings are singing. I'm relaxed, sated and extremely tired.

"I feel good, how about you?"

"I feel fantastic, never have I been scratched and bitten so much in my entire life. You're like a wild cat only you play like a kitten. I shall forever remember you as my wild kitten" he laughs.

I like the sound of that, wild kitten… I laugh with him.

I rest my head back on his chest and listen to the steady strong beat of his heart as he gently strokes my hair and back. Every so often I feel his lips press against the crown of my head. It's not long before the gentle rock of the train has him drifting off to sleep.

This stranger will never know just how much he has helped me tonight. He has given me four very intense and pleasurable orgasms, two so intense that I blacked out. It wasn't unusual for me to briefly space out with the intense orgasms Clayton had given me but I have never blacked out before, that took things to a whole new level all of its own. He pushed me further into the realms of pleasure pain play than Clayton ever did. He knew things about me and my body that I didn't even know and he got me to admit it.

How the hell did I end up here anyway?

You couldn't sleep, remember! And went to the Lounge Car to get a drink.

Oh yes.

After I'd scared the crap out of the creep at the bar I sat down with my drink ignoring all the leering and ogling looks the men in the place gave me, only Mystery Man was subtle about it. I could see from the reflection in the window he was looking in my direction.

Staring at the horizontal rain running across the glass I let my thoughts wander, events from my recent stay with Penny and Mike flit through my mind until one memory brought me up short. It was from the day we had spent at the Cherokee reservation. There was a plaque in one of the shops, a Cherokee proverb written on it and for some reason I committed it to memory.

It read: There is a battle of two wolves inside us all. One is evil. It is anger, jealousy, greed, resentment, lies, inferiority and ego. The other is good. It is joy, peace, hope, humility, kindness, empathy and truth. The wolf that wins? The one you feed.

Running the proverb through my mind I realise why it struck a chord with me. Unknowingly I've been feeding the evil wolf. Anger and resentment in particular, I've been angry at Clayton for leaving me, resenting the promise he made to always stay with me. Angry at the injustice of him being snatched away from me, resenting the fact we had shared so little of our lives and we'd never have the opportunity to grow old together. Lies, the lies I had told myself, friends and family that I was okay when I clearly wasn't. The biggest lie of all was working flat out in order to convince myself I was living and getting on with my life when I was barely existing and functioning as a human being, at least I admitted to that one, eventually. But now it's time to stop the lie and actually live again.

I'll never stop loving Clayton; my shattered heart is proof of that. Looking down at my rings, twisting them around my finger I remember the day in Vegas when he proposed, I slipped them off before I could give it any more thought. Holding them between my fingers, they're unique beautifully made rings, I knew I didn't want to stop wearing them. I slid them onto the middle finger of my right hand. Perfect fit. Moving my rings was the physical display, to me at least, I've made my commitment to start living again. I looked out of the window, only to watch the horizontal rain create crazy patterns on the glass, each time my conscious tried to throw up an argument about my actions, I slapped it down.

When Mystery Man sat down at my table I thought I was having a heart attack, my heart beat so erratically it gave me palpations. He was hell of a lot bigger close up, I passed him when I went to the bar. I know I smiled a thanks to him when he moved his incredibly long legs, other than that I hadn't paid much attention to his looks or physique.

The guy looks like Jason Momoa for heaven's sake, how in the hell did I miss that. He even has the same kind of scar that cut through the perfect arch shape of his left eyebrow. Jet black shoulder length wavy hair. A strong straight nose, a couple of days' worth of stubble over his jaw and incredibly intense green eyes framed with thick black lashes. Then he spoke… oh my good lord… his voice made my skin tingle and the hairs on my arms and head stand on end. Deep, rich and gruff. I was shocked by how turned on it made me, he made me.

And he got me talking about Clayton, I realise now the true healing process started for me at that point. He was easy to talk to; he's right about talking to a complete stranger helps. Even when he asked me about things Clayton did during sex, the weirdness should have freaked me out but bizarrely it helped. It helped me have the most amazing orgasms of my life. I frown at that thought, why don't I feel guilty? I should be riddled with angst at betraying Clayton's memory. Then I remember Atohi's message.

When we reached Mystery Man's cabin the words 'trust and follow your instincts in all matters of the heart' floated through my mind. I also felt drawn to this man, my instinct was to kiss him… so I did. I was powerless to stop it; I didn't want to stop it. I felt a connection, something inside me clicked into place. I realise now that it's been happening all night. The gaping hole that has been in my chest for so long is no longer there, the broken pieces of my shattered heart are back together.

Is it possible that this stranger, my Mystery Man is my true soul mate, my other half? Don't be silly, I scoff at myself. A couple of hours of lust filled fantastic kinky sex doesn't make him your soul mate. It's like he said we'll probably never see each other again. Our paths crossed at this juncture only to go our separate ways when we get off the train. A soft snore breaks my reverie. I lift my head to look at my handsome stranger, he looks peaceful. His long lashes brush the tops of his cheekbones, his perfectly carved lips part slightly as he breathes. I look out the window, it's still dark but in the distance I can see the sky lightening.

Slowly and carefully I move out of his arms and lift myself off him. I cover him with the duvet and collect my clothes off the top bunk. I dress quickly not bothering with my underwear, only because I can't find my knickers, and slip out of the door, closing it quietly behind me.

CHAPTER NINE

CALEB

The loud blaring of a fog horn startles me awake. I sit up in a rush, my bleary eyes and sleep addled brain take in my strange surroundings.

Where the fuck am I?

The shake and thrumming vibrations I feel answer that question, train.

Why the fuck am I on the floor?

I look around me trying to find some sort of answer, I come up with nothing. I rub my face attempting to rid my mind of its grogginess. My phone alarm goes off again. I look at the cabinet behind me, it's not there. Images of my mystery woman, my wild cat, no… my wild kitten submitting to me flood my mind. The deluge of memories as I look around the cabin has my body reacting in an instant. The fog horn sounds again. I get up to find my phone, it's the best alarm ever, my dick juts out from my hips, he has other ideas. I ignore it.

I locate my jeans on the top bunk and dig the phone out of my pocket. It's seven thirty, the train will be getting into Euston shortly. I look out the window, buildings flash by. I put the mattress back on the lower bunk, on the floor I spot a pair of lacy knickers. I pick them up and put them to my nose, breathing in her unique fragrance. So what, I am a kinky pervert at least this is evidence she is real and not some figment of my imagination. Everywhere I look images of my stunningly beautiful ideal woman in different poses come to me. I wish she hadn't sneaked out, right now I could be banging the shit out of her. No you wouldn't, you'd be going slow savouring every second of her my mind corrects me.

Those few hours with her have been the best of my life. We truly connected sexually. I've never come so hard, shooting my load like a fucking rocket launcher going off. I've heard people talk about having an orgasm so intense that they saw stars, now I know what they're talking about. My only regret is not getting her name and number.

"Oh fucking hell… shit" I slam my palm in to the bed frame "you fucking idiot" I didn't use a condom. Never in my entire life have I been so wrapped up in the moment that I completely forgot to suit up, only I did it twice.

The train starts to slow down and I look out the window, a few more minutes and we'll be in Euston. I start getting dressed. At least I don't have any worries about her getting pregnant, still best make an appointment at the doctors to get checked out for any STD's besides I'll need to produce a certificate for the club but somehow I know I'll come back clear. I look around the cabin to make sure I've got everything. I smile fondly and finger the riding crop before putting it in my case.

Disembarking the train and walking down the platform with all the other bleary eyed travellers I keep a look out for her, she can't be that easy to miss with her distinctive long curly white blonde hair but I don't spot her. There's no chance of me finding her when I get to the concourse it'll be like looking for a needle in a haystack, yet somehow I know I will find her anywhere. Dejectedly, I make my way to the taxi rank and join the very long morning rush hour queue, further disappointment sweeps through me when I realise she's not here either.

It takes forever to get to The Gentlemen's Club. It's situated on the outskirts of Windsor making it easily accessible for the majority of its members. By the time I arrive its closer to ten. Harry meets me on the steps as I get out of the taxi.

"Thank god you're here" he says in greeting.

"Hi Harry good to see you too" I say sarcastically as I lug my case up the steps.

"Sorry, it's good to see you" he laughs shaking my hand and slaps my back "I've got a lot on my mind right now. Did you have a good trip?"

"Yes, thanks. Rex said you've got some big meeting with the new owner. He also seems to think you're pitching the mentoring programme to him that's why you want us here"

Harry nods "Yes, I thought it would be a good idea if he met the person the majority of the members named as their ideal mentor"

"You're shitting me!" I'm stunned.

"Afraid not my man. You are Mr Popular, not only with the ladies but the men as well" Harry laughs heartily. The sound of a car coming down the driveway draws both our attention "shit, he's here. Your room's ready, its number three. Go and get yourself cleaned up and have a shave" he says pushing me through the door.

The private room I've been allocated is very spacious. I put my case on the huge four poster bed and take a look around. The colour scheme is various shades of burgundy, gold and cream. At the far end of the room is a large bay window, a deep burgundy chaise lounge sits in front of it along with a two seater sofa and coffee table. Fixed to the wall to right of the window is a St Andrews cross. Directly opposite is a large cabinet. I walk over and open the doors. Inside is an assortment of whips, floggers and canes. Underneath the doors are three draws, I don't open them as I know they will be filled with various toys, restraints, gags and masks. Along the left hand wall about four foot apart are two doors, the rest of the wall is bare. I know one of the doors will lead to the bathroom, curiosity has me opening the doors to find out what's behind the other. It's a closet, only it also stores a swing and whipping bench.

I go into the bathroom, it's a good size. Black, white and gold tiles cover the walls and floor. There's a large walk-in shower along the far wall, a free standing modern bath on the right. His and her marble vanity unit and sinks opposite, toilet and bidet just behind the door. Back in the bedroom I open my case, grab my toiletry bag strip out of my clothes and head back to get a shave and shower.

Scolding hot water pounds my shoulders, slowly I bend forward so the powerful spray works down my spine, getting my muscles at the same time, it's a great way to iron out the kinks in my back from sleeping on the floor although I have to admit I did have the best couple of hours sleep I've had in weeks. But this technique is nothing compared to the massage my wild kitten had given me. Right on cue my dick springs to life as I remember how her small delicate hands felt, sure and confident as they worked my muscles, she really knew what she was doing. And her mouth... fucking hell what a mouth.

I turn the dial to cool the water down, grab the shower gel and start to wash my body. My skin tingles as I remember the feel of her lips moving across it with soft kisses, then the warm suction as she pulled it into her mouth, the light grazing of her teeth and the gentle nips all set my nerve endings on fire, sensitising my skin all over my body.

She was right about getting pleasure by receiving it. No woman has ever done that to me or for me before. Yes, they sucked my dick which most women thought was obligatory or something they had to offer in return for the mind blowing sex I'd given them. So for me blow jobs fell into two categories. Group one: they wanted to get it over with as soon as possible and they thought the best way to do that is to suck hard right from the get go. Most of them can suck chrome off a tail pipe which is good if you like that kind of thing, I don't. Group two: faked it. Faked the enthusiasm, faked the noises, faked they liked it. They gave up after a few minutes claiming they were so hot for you, you had to fuck them.

Wild kitten didn't belong in either of these categories, she is in a league of her own. She enjoyed it, I would go as far to say she loved it. It blew my mind as she started off soft and gentle gradually building the pressure. My hand wraps around my cock, I start long slow even pulls recreating what she did to me. I purposely kept still so I wouldn't take control. I wanted to watch her work and fully appreciate the experience of her... worshipping me. That's exactly what she did starting with the massage right the way through to fellatio.

I groan as my mind re-enacts everything. I widen my stance and pump harder, my dick remembers the feel of her hot mouth and wicked tongue trailing up and down my shaft. The feel of her nails dragging across my balls, her hand pulling and squeezing them. My hand moves faster, my breathing is harsh as my heart accelerates, my hips thrust forward. A heaviness in my groin builds and builds, my cock thickens. Remembering the feel of her tits brushing against my dick sets off my orgasms. I collapse against the cool tiles as I ride out my release. When my legs feel steady enough I straighten, soap myself down again and wash my hair.

I just finish getting dressed when I hear voices outside the door. The handle jiggles as if someone's trying to get in. I move to the door and listen.

"Are you sure this is the right one?" I hear a muffled female voice say, I can hear the tones of a man's voice but not the words "number three... yes this is it... okay... can you get the tape measure I left it in my other case... thanks, see you in a bit" the door handle moves downwards. I release the lock and open the door.

"Whoa, shit!" the woman squeals and falls backwards into the room "ouch" she shouts as she lands hard on her backside. I see a mass of white blonde curly hair... it can't be, can it?

"Christ, I'm sorry. Are you hurt?" without hesitating I lift her up off the floor.

"Only my bum and pride other than that I'm okay" she straightens her skirt and jacket then looks up "holy cow it's you!"

"Kitten!"

She looks as taken aback and shocked as I feel.

"Is everything okay?" a well-built suited man with short blonde hair appears in the doorway, he eyes me suspiciously. Even though he is a couple of inches shorter than me I wouldn't want to get into any tangle with him. I get the distinct impression I would be the one coming worse off.

"Yes I'm fine, just fell over" Kitten says rolling her eyes to him "have you got the tape measure already?"

"No I heard you shout and came back to see if you needed help" his eyes never leave my face "I won't be long"

"See you in a few minutes" Kitten bends down and picks up a large bag from the floor "I'm sorry I didn't mean to disturb you, Mr Davies told me this room would be free" she starts backing out of the room.

"Don't go" I reach out catching her hand and pull her back, the next thing I know I've got her pinned up against the door and I'm kissing her. My hand buried in her soft hair holding the back of her head, my other hand resting at the small of her back moving down to cup her arse. She moans and opens her mouth. I claim her.

There's a dull thud, she's dropped the bag. Her hands run up my arms and around my neck. Her fingers tangle in the back of my wet hair. Our lips slip and slide in perfect synchronicity. My mind and body revels in the taste and feel of her against me. I can feel the air around us thrumming and crackling, talk about sparks flying. My blood is boiling and my body is aching for more. I have no idea what the hell is going on but one thing I'm certain of… my wild kitten… she is mine.

Someone knocks on the door; I growl at the intrusion. The knock comes a second time. Kitten breaks the kiss, breathing heavily her yellow green eyes shimmer and her smile dazzles me. Placing her hands on my chest she gently pushes me. A silent instruction to back off.

"I need to answer that, otherwise they'll be breaking the door down" she whispers. I step back putting a fair bit of distance between us. Kitten composes herself by taking a couple of deep breaths, straightens her jacket, picks up her bag and opens the door.

Harry and another man stood next to him smile widely at Kitten. This new guy is quite rotund, medium height with short slicked back greying hair. I'm no fashion guru but I know an expensive suit when I see one and this guy is wearing the best money can buy tailor made. Kitten steps back opening the door wider and both men walk in. Harry's eyes widen when he sees me, then he grimaces, he's obviously realised he gave Kitten the wrong room number, lucky for me. Just as the door is closing the blonde guy from earlier magically appears.

"Oh good you've got it" Kitten says and takes something out of his out stretched hand. She moves over to the wall in between the bathroom and closet. Blonde guy shadows her.

Harry and the new guy, after both of them give me a quizzical look that I ignore, silently watch Kitten. I stand with them and watch, admiring Kitten as she measures the width of the wall between the doors.

"Do you want the whole space covering?" Kitten says without looking up as she makes a note in a pad. She then starts pushing the tape measure up the wall towards the ceiling.

"About three quarters on the length, but definitely take up the full width" the new guy says. He's American, new owner maybe? I look at Harry, who subtly nods his head in answer to my unspoken question. I suddenly realise that blonde guy has an American accent as well.

"Will you be getting them framed?" Kitten asks as she crouches down to read the measurement whilst blonde guy holds the tape measure in place, a feat to behold considering the height of the heels she's wearing. It makes me wonder if he's some sort of assistant because he's definitely done this with her before but the size of him and the vibes from him aren't congruous with his current actions.

The new owner looks at Harry for the answer "I don't know. What do you think?" he throws back. I notice beads of sweat across Harry's forehead, he's nervous. It surprises me because I've always found him to be so confident and self-assured.

Kitten stands and looks around the room. Her eyes, when they land on the St Andrews Cross, flick to mine and I see that almost smile touch her lips.

"Without" she says turning to Harry. I have no clue what they are discussing "are all the rooms the same as this?" Harry nods "and the space is the same as well" she points to the wall.

"Yes, all ten rooms are identical" Harry confirms.

Kitten nods and makes a note "Right, I've got what I need here. Show me the restaurants and bars" with that everyone files out. No doubt about it, she is calling the shots.

"Oh, Caleb" Harry calls back to me, I step out into the hallway. Kitten turns back and looks at me with that almost smile on her lips. My cock pulses at the thought of having those same lips wrapped around my dick again.

"Yes Harry" I smile broadly, in response to her full blown dazzling gleeful smile. She now knows my name and I don't know hers.

"Can you meet me in my office in about ten minutes?"

"Sure" I nod.

Harry turns and leads the way back down towards the stairs. I watch Kitten, her spiral curls swish from side to side in the opposite direction of her hips. I admire the shape of her arse in the tight black skirt — I kick myself for wasting time kissing her when I could have been attending to her arse checking for bruises —her long slim legs down to the six inch stilettos. I absently wonder if she's wearing tights or stockings. At the top of the stairs she turns and winks at me. Then she's gone.

My jaw cracks as my yawn gets to its peak and I let out a huge gust of air. I rub my face trying to wake myself up a bit, caffeine is no longer working. It's been a long day and I can't wait to crawl into bed, even though it's only four in the afternoon.

"Let's get you home, you look dead on your feet" Rex says sympathetically "we can finish this off another day"

"We'll clear up, you two get going" Barney says pointing at himself and Sasha. I look at the desk littered with paper and gladly get up.

"Thanks" I mumble "and thanks for your input, it's appreciated and a great help" both smile broadly at me.

Harry got Mr Benenati's approval for the mentoring programme and appointed me as project leader, team leader, head honcho… I don't know what to call myself but I'm in charge and have the final say. Big responsibility. I was pleasantly surprised by Mr Benenati, I had thought he would be loud and brash with an 'it's my way or the highway' kind of attitude. He was loud but he was attentive, open, welcomed new ideas along with being one of the most astute businessmen I have ever met. I was disappointed that Kitten wasn't in the meeting.

I pumped Harry for information about her but he was useless. All he could tell me was Benenati hired her to provide all the artwork in his clubs. Apparently she arrived about twenty minutes into their meeting and Benenati didn't introduce them. I laughed when Harry realised she hadn't given her name when he introduced himself. "She's fucking gorgeous. I'm surprised I even managed to get my name out I was a blubbering, dribbling idiot" he said laughing with me.

I say bye to Barney and Sasha, who are going to be the Sub mentors, grab my case and follow Rex out to the car park. The cold wind whips around me, blasting away my weariness and rudely waking me up.

"What do you think?" says Rex with an indulgent tone to his voice.

"To what?" I look at him quizzically.

"The car" he points as we approach a bright orange Porsche.

"Nice" I drag the word out sardonically "what made you decide to get a new toy?"

"Toy!" Rex exclaims indignant "I'll have you know this beauty is a Porsche Carrera GT" Rex runs his hand over the bright orange paintwork in complete rapture.

"It's ostentatious, couldn't you have got it in black or red even" I grin at the glowering scowl Rex gives me. I love winding him up.

"You can fucking walk home" he snaps petulantly.

"Don't ask for my opinion in future if you're going to act like a spoilt brat because you don't like what you hear" I laugh "besides I thought you wanted all the juicy gossip about my trip" I throw a playful jab at his shoulder.

"Get in before I change my mind" he grumbles taking my case off me.

"I thought you were happy with the Audi R8, what made you change to this one?" I'm intrigued because Rex loved the R8, best babe magnet car he ever had according to him so I'm surprised he got rid of it.

"To wind up that prick of a minor celebrity Miles Cunningham" Rex says turning the engine on "just listen to that" he revs the engine "five point seven litre V10 engine, top speed two hundred and five miles an hour, nought to sixty in just over three seconds" Rex lovingly runs his hands over the leather steering wheel.

"Okay, stop before you have an orgasm" I chuckle. Rex grinning wickedly pulls out of the parking space at top speed "so what has Miles done now to piss you off?"

Rex and Miles have a love hate relationship - they love to hate each other. Miles for some reason copies everything Rex has and does, try telling Rex to take it as a compliment and you're likely to get a smack in the mouth for your effort. Miles is one of the village's celebrities, a minor TV one at that. He's a presenter on the local news channel and has a house in the village he uses at weekends, in my opinion Miles is jealous of Rex and his lifestyle including all the women he attracts. Although Miles uses his minor celebrity status unashamedly to pull women he isn't much to look at, so I've heard various women in the village say. Rex could have made a fortune modelling; Miles wouldn't have gotten through the model agents door – not even a foot to have the door slammed on it.

"The twat finally got enough money to buy one or he's leased it" snorts Rex disdainfully "he was driving around in it, posing, last weekend. The prick even got in his car to go from his house to the mini supermarket" we both laugh, Miles would have got there quicker by walking "and as you have probably guessed, yes in retaliation I did go out and buy this beauty but enough of talking about him, tell me about your trip"

I sigh settling in to the comfy leather bucket seat deciding to tell him everything about my trip up until leaving Fort William, what happened on the train between me and my wild kitten will stay my secret… forever.

CHAPTER TEN

SKYE

The cold early evening wind tugs at my hair and coat as I walk around the garden. I pull my coat tighter round me and don't attempt to restrain my hair, there's no point trying to fight a losing battle. I make one more circuit around the lawn watching the daffodils and crocuses bob and bend in the wind, the bare swaying branches of the trees are filled with buds, spring is definitely making its presence known in Nessa's garden. Sounds of voices and laughter drift over to me, I glance back at the house and see people stood around in small groups drinking and chatting. I can't bring myself to go in and fake a smile or pleasantries just at the moment.

I've been in a funny niggling mood all day and I have no idea why. I can't pinpoint anything that's causing me to feel the way I do. The slightest thing has irritated me, I've been frustrated with people's lack of indecision and action. If I had been behaving like this yesterday I could understand and put it down to the lack of sleep, all thanks to my Mystery Man – who I now know is called Caleb. I can't help smiling nor stop the warm shiver running through me as I touch my tingling lips remembering the way he hungrily claimed my mouth when we saw each other again at the club.

Christ that had been one hell of a bloody shock to my system. You could have pushed me over with a feather, never did I ever expect to see him again. If Dario and Harry hadn't knocked on the door when they did I have no doubt in my mind we would have been fucking the life out of each other within minutes, no in seconds, not surfacing again until many hours later... if at all. And when he growled at the intrusion, oh my god that sound, so animalistic, went straight to my core. I was wet instantly. I wanted to lie down on the floor, spread my legs and beg him to fuck me.

I'm horny... desperately. Oh sweet lord is that what's wrong with me! Is that why I'm in such a foul mood? I have an itch and it needs scratching. A chuckle escapes me, after all these months of feeling numb my body is so alive I could cry with joy and frustration. Now, the question is: Do I go inside and pick up any man to scratch the itch? An involuntary shudder rolls through me and I know the answer, I want my Mystery Man... I want Caleb.

"Skye" Nessa voice calling me has me stepping out of the shadows of the trees "there you are. Come on in, it's freezing out here" as I walk up the patio steps she comes out to meet me "what's wrong?" the concern in her eyes and voice makes me feel guilty about my shitty behaviour.

"Nothing, I'm fine"

"No you're not" she takes hold of my shoulders and looks me straight in the eye with a steely determination that makes my heart sink "after the guests have gone you and me are sitting down to talk. Something's happened to get you like this and I don't like it. It's screwing with your head"

That surprises me, I didn't think my night of wild sex was affecting me so much but then I can't see what other people are seeing in me. I relent "Yes something did happen, but it wasn't a bad thing, I think"

"You still need to talk about it, this…" Nessa waves her hand up and down in front of me "needs sorting out" Nessa links her arm through mine and leads the way back inside "when was the last time you talked? I mean really talked like you would in your monthly group session with Shelley and Simon, you still do those don't you?"

"Yeah we do" I sigh "but not since before the accident" I murmur.

"Well it's long overdue" Nessa states, I can only nod my agreement as I take my coat off "come on and I'll introduce you to everyone"

Nessa and I make our way through the huge kitchen, dodging out of the way of the hired catering staff. Since my last visit, Nessa and Chuck have moved to a larger house. They now have three beautiful children, all of whom are my god children. Ella is now seven and the image of her mother. Frankie is five and Chuck Junior just turned two, take after their father. I couldn't believe how much they've all grown in the twelve months since I last saw them, you don't really get an indication of growth spurts via Skype.

Both Nessa and Chuck are doing incredibly well in their careers. Last year, Nessa was appointed Managing Director of the TV station she left New York for eight years ago. Chuck is a born entrepreneur, he has so many business interests it makes my head spin. Their success has enabled them to buy this fabulous seven-bedroom property in the heart of Chelsea.

Entering the drawing room, I ignore the squinty eyed scrutiny from the women and the lecherous leers from the men that look our way. Instead I focus on the décor.

"Your interior designer has done a fantastic job" I murmur to Nessa as I take in the rich fabrics of the curtains, cushions, chairs and sofas all are in varying tones of cream and beige. The walls are painted white with the exception of one which is papered with a swirling rich copper colour pattern.

"Let me introduce you" Shelley takes my elbow and steers me towards a group of three men "Elliot, how are you?" Nessa interrupts their conversation.

"Nessa, darling. Looking fabulous as ever" he kisses her cheeks, then he spots me "please introduce me to this gorgeous divine creature next to you" he flamboyantly flutters his hands in my direction. The guy is camper than Simon and any of his friends put together. I take an instant liking to him.

"This is one of my oldest and best friend Skye Darcy" Nessa says fondly putting her arm around me. Elliot gasps his hands flying to his cheeks.

"Skye Darcy, as in Skye Darcy the artist" he says hopefully, his wide eyes flicking back and forth between Nessa and me.

"The very one" I grin holding out my hand "pleased to meet you Elliot"

Elliot squeals and flaps his hands "Oh... my... god. I can't believe it. I'm a huge fan of your work" he grasps my hand in both of his "ohmigod, ohmigod" I look startled at Nessa as Elliot appears to be hyperventilating.

"Calm down Elliot" Nessa grins at his reaction "this is Sean and Chris, they work for Elliot and helped decorate the house" I awkwardly shake their hands with my free one as Elliot is still super glued to my other.

"I was just saying to Nessa you've done a fantastic job. I really like what you've done to all the rooms. You'll have to give me your card as I'll be in need of your talent in a few months" Elliot lets out a strangled squeak.

"Really" Nessa says surprised then something dawns on her "of course, Dove Mill you're going out there tomorrow, I forgot"

"Do you take jobs on outside of London?" I throw the question out to the three men, I'm not sure Elliot has got the capacity to speak as he's still looking at me dumbstruck.

"Yes we do" Sean replies giving Elliot a frown "you'll have to forgive Elliot; he really is a huge fan"

"Where is the property?" Chris says handing me a business card.

"Dove Mill Village, it's roughly five miles from Henley-on-Thames and there will be several properties. The main one being Dove Mill Hall at the moment it's derelict, destroyed by fire over twenty years ago and

I have no idea what kind of condition it's in. That would be the biggest project and the one that will take the longest I imagine. I'm going over there tomorrow for a preliminary look. How much notice do you need if I wanted to make an appointment?"

"For you Ms Darcy I would drop everything at five minute's notice even if it meant there was just a smidgeon of a possibility of working with you" Elliot has finally found his voice and let go of my hand to clutch at his chest "it will be a dream come true" he gushes.

"Please call me Skye" I lift up the business card "and thanks for this, I'll be in touch"

Nessa and I leave the three men talking excitedly, the last thing I hear is Elliot saying "I have got to call Charles, he will not believe me when I tell him who I've just met. Shoot, do you think I can get a picture with her"

I head back to them, taking Elliot's phone out of his hand I give it to Sean "Do the honours" I say as I stand beside Elliot linking arms. Five minutes later I leave them to gloat to their friends and post the pictures.

"You've really made their night, thank you" Nessa chuckles.

For the next half an hour I'm introduced to various friends and business associates of Nessa's and Chuck's there are a couple of people who remember me from six years ago when I turned up late for Nessa's thirtieth dinner party. I didn't remember them probably because I was still getting over the shock of Clayton being there and it had been five weeks since I had last seen him when I left him in New York.

Nessa leaves me alone to go and speak to the caterers and I use the opportunity to nip to the bathroom before dinner is served. I have my foot on the stair when I hear my name.

"Hello Skye" I turn to face the man who addressed me.

Holy fucking shit "Tobias!" I don't hide my shocked surprise. How in the blazing hell did I not see him in the drawing room?

"It's good to see you after all these years" he says softly fiddling nervously with his glass "I don't blame you if wish to see the back of me. I'm as shocked to see you here as well" he offers me a slight smile.

I don't know what to say. My mind is blank and my feet are cemented to the floor. I couldn't walk away even if I wanted to.

"Here, you look as if you could use this" he hands me his glass. I don't even think about it and gulp down the dark amber liquid. It tastes foul whatever it is and it makes me cough as it burns down my throat. At least it kick starts my senses.

"What are you doing here?" I croak out trying not to sound too hostile.

"I could say, what way is that to greet your Uncle after all these years, but I don't deserve anything less" Tobias sighs resigned "I'm a business partner of Chuck's"

I nod, I still don't know what to say to him. We were never close, growing up I wasn't even sure if he knew I existed despite the fact I lived under the same roof as him for fifteen years. I look closely at my Uncle; time hasn't been kind to him. He's got to be late fifties now; I reckon doing a rough calculation. It's uncanny how much he looks like his father, my grandfather. His thinning blonde hair is cut in what I guess to be a number two. His face is heavily lined especially across his forehead and around his pale blue eyes. His rotund physique is covered in a tailor made dark blue suit, his pale blue shirt open at the neck. He cuts the commanding image of a successful businessman.

"Skye, I know we've never been close but…"

"Tobias, there you are" a woman's high pitched baby voice cuts him off. I don't miss his sigh of irritation "I've been looking everywhere for you"

The woman walking towards Tobias is rake thin, as in if she turned sideways she'd disappear and she's over done the fake tan, her skin is tangerine. Her brunette red highlighted hair is cut into an asymmetrical bob, making her heavily made up face look haggard and pinched. The tight red dress she is wearing aside from the fact it clashes with her skin colour does nothing to flatter her figure, actually it makes her thinness even more pronounced. I get the impression that this woman is younger than she looks, probably a couple of years older than me but looks mid to late forties and I don't think it's intentional. For some reason I get the feeling I should know this woman, but I've never met her before of that I am certain.

Tobias turns to face her, in doing so she sees me. Her eyes narrow and her face screws up. I almost laugh out loud when she makes her possessive claim by placing one hand on Tobias's arm, the other draped over his shoulder. Her long red painted false nails look ready to scratch the eyes out of any woman looking to make a move on her man or meal ticket in my uncle's case.

"Now that you've found me Gabrielle what do you want?" Tobias snaps removing himself out of her clutches.

Gabrielle pouts and flutters her fake eye lashes "I missed you" she says in her baby voice fingering his lapel "aren't you going to introduce me to your friend?"

"You're interrupting a private conversation. Go and get me another drink" Tobias says in a commanding tone holding out his empty glass and completely ignoring her request. Now that is more like the cold disdainful behaviour I remember. Gabrielle looks momentarily taken aback at his harshness, quickly recovering herself she takes his glass.

"Don't take too long" she purrs leaning in to kiss Tobias's cheek. She gives me a hateful look that could easily put me six foot under before turning to walk back into the drawing room.

"New mistress or trophy wife in waiting?" I say sardonically, I can't help myself.

Tobias turns back to me with a rueful grin "Wannabe girlfriend" his grin slips as he sighs "Margaret passed away four years ago. Heart attack"

"I didn't know" I mumble. Christ, I feel an utter shit. I had liked my Aunty Margaret, she was a kind woman and one of the few family members who didn't ignore me, at least she'd talk to me if I was in the same room as her.

"It was only a matter of time, all the stress and strain she put herself under over the years because of Alfie and his antics. Then there was his court case for the drugs ring but the final straw was when we found out about…" Tobias pauses, a myriad of emotions crosses his face, guilt, pain, sorrow "I know what Alfie did. I am so, so sorry for what he did to you and I'm sorry for what my father subsequently did" he whispers.

Shocked to my core my legs give out and I sit down heavily on the stairs. I look helplessly up at Tobias, never in a million years did I think I would hear a member of my family apologise for their actions against me, let alone get two, okay one was written in a Will but it still counts in my book. Tobias joins me on the stair, tentatively he reaches out and takes my hand.

"Skye, I can't apologise for what others did to you as that needs to come from them and my apology is never going to undo all the injustice and wrongs that have been done. I can only apologise for my own appalling behaviour towards you. I can put up strong arguments or give excuses but I'm certain you don't care to hear them and I won't insult your intelligence by attempting to put them forward. Can you find it in your heart to forgive me?" Tobias's beseeching eyes search my face.

"Here's your drink honey bun" Gabrielle's baby voice intrudes before I can say anything.

"Will you just fuck off" Tobias roars glaring at Gabrielle making her flinch, she falters to a stop. The muted conversations drifting through from the drawing room all stop.

Nessa appears in the doorway "Is everything okay?" Gabrielle, red faced pushes passed her back into the drawing room. Nessa looks at me and Tobias sat on the stairs "would you two like somewhere more private to talk"

Tobias looks to me "Please, we need to talk" he whispers. I can't argue with him on that score and I'm curious to find out how he knows about what Alfie did.

"Please Nessa" I stand; Tobias follows suit "can we use your office?"

"Of course. Dinner will be served in fifteen minutes" Nessa calls after me as I lead the way.

I sit on the sofa. My legs are still a bit shaky from Tobias's revelations, he remains standing looking uncertain at me.

"Tell me how you found out about Alfie raping me"

Tobias flinches, whether that's from my choice of words or from the expressionless tone of my voice and face, maybe it's a combination of all three. I don't really care; I'm not going to pander to his feelings. He wants to talk well he can have it; I'm taking no prisoners.

"I was… intrigued by the contents of the Will that pertained to you and I started to investigate" Tobias starts to pace "I spoke with the lawyer who tracked you down in New York he told me that you had used ninety-five percent of the words on my father's list, plus a few others that weren't" Tobias snorts "as you know your grandfather never apologised to anyone and that got my curiosity further aroused. What had he done that was so bad that made him break a lifetime's habit of showing no remorse for his actions? Anyway a few months after the funeral I was sorting through his personal effects in his office and came across a file" Tobias stops in front of me and crouches down "it was a file on you"

"Me!" I exclaim, he keeps on delivering these shocks. I don't think my nerves can take anymore.

"The old goat was so proud of you and your achievements and the career you carved out for yourself with no help or interference from him" Tobias smiles wryly "he was prouder of you than any of us put together"

"Huh" it's all I can manage for a response.

"In the file I found various notes that he had written, one told of his biggest regret which was telling you he was disinheriting you and kicking you out as you lay in hospital but there was no mention of why you were in hospital" Tobias takes hold of my hands and squeezes gently "then I came across one that gave an account of you meeting each other at a charity event in London a few months before his death. By the sounds of it you really gave him what for, you did the one thing I never could" I hear the admiration in Tobias's voice "I was too much of a coward"

"He had no hold over me" it's the truth, he couldn't manipulate me "but that still didn't stop the bastard from testing me from beyond the grave"

"I would've loved to witness that" a small smile plays on his lips "being a fly on the wall and all that"

"Saying the air was blue with profanities would be an understatement" I chuckle at the memory "I know I shocked the hell out of Clayton. God knows what damage I did to that poor lawyers' ears"

"My condolences on losing your husband" I suck in a sharp breath. "I've been keeping tabs" Tobias shrugs "you are a phenomenal woman Skye and I can see why father was so proud of you and nothing would make me prouder if people knew I was your uncle. But I won't blame you if you wish to keep your distance"

"The cynic in me wants to know what you're after" I keep my voice flat.

"Reconciliation" Tobias moves to sit beside me "a chance to get to know each other, that's all. I'm not after money, hell I've got enough of my own I don't know what to do with it"

"Gabrielle looks like she'll have a bloody good time spending it for you" I grin, can't help myself, my inner bitch is rearing its head.

Tobias laughs and shakes his head "You can say that again. I've never met anyone so self-centred and money grabbing" something about his description rings a distant bell and I can't place why.

"So how did you find out about what Alfie had done to me?" I ask the question again in a softer tone this time.

"Sorry for digressing" Tobias clears his throat "when all that business with Peter Lancaster confessing to his and Alfie's involvement in the drugs business I had a few phone calls from Detective Sanders" I raise an eyebrow, the detective never told me of his conversations with my uncle "I asked him not to say anything. I didn't think you would react very well to the news" he's got that right; I think my expression says it all because I see the knowing look in his eyes "when he first rang me it was to clarify certain things you had told him around your inheritance. On the second call he was asking if I knew anything about why you had been disinherited. I told the detective all that I knew from your grandfathers' notes and I asked him if he knew why and how you had ended up in hospital, that's when he told me" the genuine sorrow I see in his eyes pulls at my heart "through various contacts I was able to get hold of a copy of the incident report and a record from the hospital the night you were admitted. Skye I can't say how sorry I am" he takes a deep shaky breath "the saddest thing about betrayal is that it never comes from your enemies. It comes from friends and loved ones. I had already disinherited Alfie and cut all ties with him because of the drugs, but this" he sadly shakes his head "I am horrified and ashamed that my own son, my own flesh and blood could commit such a heinous act and to rob you of any..."

"Stop" I say softly holding up my hand "I don't want your pity. I accepted a long time ago I will never have children of my own and I don't dwell on what could have been, it's wasted energy besides" I smile "I have plenty of godchildren to spoil rotten and I get to hand them back when I've had enough"

Tobias throws his head back and laughs, it's heartfelt, warm. I join him. Our laughter breaks the oppressive tension.

"Do you think we could get to know each other, be a proper family?" Tobias asks hopefully.

I look at him for a long time "Let's take it one day at a time" I say eventually.

"I can live with that" he smiles, then he looks at his watch "I think dinner is about to be served, shall we" Tobias stands and holds out his arm.

We walk into the dining room chatting freely arm in arm. Gabrielle's face hardens at the sight of us and I can see she's about to go nuclear.

"I take it you two know each other" Chuck points between us with a nervous laugh.

"Chuck, allow me to introduce you to my niece" Tobias says proudly. My cheeks hurt I'm grinning so much.

The whole room instantly goes quite. Gabrielle's jaw hits the floor.

I try not to watch Nessa and Chuck say goodnight to each other. I feel like an interloper, actually I am. I'm stealing their together quality time. I busy myself with the laptop, opening up Skype in readiness for Shelley and Simon to connect. Nessa had contacted them calling an emergency session whilst I was talking with Tobias in the office. I really hope she hasn't caused them any unnecessary alarm, especially Shelley.

"Well it has been a very eventful night" Nessa says sitting down next to me and pats my leg "you my dear certainly know how to make a dinner party interesting"

I roll my eyes at her "It's not my fault your guests lead dull boring lives" I retort.

"Compared to you they do" she laughs.

Tobias insisted on sitting next to me during dinner and had asked one question after another about my life as a famous artist, business interests and my life in America which prompted everyone else to feel free to ask any question of me they liked, and I chose not to answer a huge bulk of them. In return I threw Tobias his questions back at him. When he left, with a very disgruntled Gabrielle in tow, we made a promise to keep in touch. Tobias whispered in my ear as he hugged me that he wished he had done something sooner about mending bridges and he'd call me tomorrow. Time will tell.

The laptop chimes "What in the hell has been going on?" Simon's shrill voice comes through the tinny speakers.

I look at the screen to see the anxious faces of my two best friends. I smile I'm so happy to see them. I fill them in on my conversation with my uncle and for a while we dissect his motives which range from how genuine the reconciliation he wants is through to trying to get his hands on what remains of the inheritance. I gave a huge chunk away to various charities in the UK and America which I told Tobias about.

"But that's not the reason why I called this session" Nessa finally cuts in "something has happened and it's messing with Skye's head, not that she'll admit it. Although she has admitted something has happened"

Everyone looks at me expectantly; I feel my cheeks burning. I look down at my hands and try to order my thoughts, how to start I ponder.

There is no way in hell I'm going to blurt out I had the most amazing sex of my life with a complete stranger and I didn't even know his name up until I met him again yesterday morning.

"On the train coming down from Fort William I met a guy" I hear myself say. The words tumble out of my mouth as I tell them everything, well not everything they don't need to know about the kink but I do admit to the best sex… ever "the connection was so strong, so intense. I mean stronger and more intense than I had with Clayton. It felt so right" I finish in a low voice.

"First question" Simon says breaking the stunned silence "what did he look like?"

"Same height as Clayton but a bigger in build, more muscular. Jet black shoulder length hair and he had the most amazing green eyes. In the looks department think of Jason Momoa, he even had the same scar thing" I point to my eyebrow.

"Oh my god" Shelley says clutching her chest "seriously?" I nod.

"You lucky bitch!" Simon says in awe. Nessa laughs at my friend's reaction "Second question. You said he was a stranger and you didn't know his name but you called him Caleb. Why did you call him that if you don't know his name?"

"At the time of sleeping with him I didn't know his name. I saw him again yesterday morning when I went for my meeting with Mr Benenati at The Gentlemen's Club. The man who runs the place used his name, but I still don't know his surname"

"What happened at the club" Shelley says softly.

I tell them everything. Falling through the door and landing on my arse to the breath taking passionate kiss, how I felt the air crackling and thrumming around us, the sexual attraction and tension, how it made me feel being back in his arms "If Dario hadn't knocked on the door when he did, heaven knows what would have happened" I finish.

"Oh I think we have a very good idea sweet thing since you were in a sex club of all places" Simon snorts.

"So what's the problem?" says Shelley quickly cutting Simon off.

"I don't know" I throw my hands up in exasperation "I mean I had already reconciled with myself that it was time to move on, to start living again. And believe me I feel really, really alive. It's almost as if I've been reawakened from a long hibernation. I used to feel as if I had a huge gaping hole in my chest" I place my hand over my heart "and now, it's closed with my shattered heart mended" I whisper.

"What do you feel guilty about?" Nessa question surprises me, I frown and shake my head, there's nothing I can think of "I think, and you can shout me down after I've said my piece" she looks at me with a raised eyebrow, daring me to challenge her "I think, unconsciously you are feeling guilty about not being loyal to Clayton's memory and that you have also experienced something so amazing, so life affirming so soon after his death. This is something that you unconsciously thought would never happen or find anything like you had with Clayton ever again only you have found something even better. What's going on up here" she taps the side of my head "is playing out in your behaviour. It makes sense now why you've been so distant and irritable"

I look at her open mouthed, it does make sense. I just put it down to feeling horny. I didn't think I'd have a cat in hells chance of ever bettering my sex life, albeit brief as it was but to have the electrifying kind of connection as well – the mind boggles.

"Skye you have some fantastic memories of your time together with Clayton" Shelley says kindly "but that's all they are. No one will take them away from you but Skye, you can't feel guilty about living your life and enjoying it. No man will replace Clayton, hell if someone does try more fool him because whoever he is will have some big boots to follow"

"Another thing Skye" Simon adds "don't even think about comparing them"

"Too late" I mutter; I've already been doing that.

"Then any relationship you have or hope to have is doomed as you'll be making them compete with your memories of a dead man and no one can live up to those" Simon sighs "I'm sorry if it sounds harsh but you've got to look at it differently. You have needs and this Caleb guy sounds like he's the first man to attract your attention, okay you may never see him again but let yourself have fun and experience fun again. Allow yourself to be happy even if it's just for a small moment in time"

"Simon's right" Shelley says "appreciate the present moment and the special something that happens in that time, it'll never come again. So don't let those special things, happy or sad, pass you by because soon they'll just become a memory too, better to live with having the memory rather than the regret of what could have been"

Nessa reaches for my hand and squeezes. I look at each of my friends in turn, seeing so much unconditional love it makes my eyes fill with tears, tears of gratitude, joy and love. I take a deep breath and puff out loudly.

"I love you all so much. Thanks" I smile and wipe my face "from now on I'm going to allow myself to move on and have fun" because that's the biggest realisation of all for me, even though I had accepted it was time to move on. I hadn't allowed myself to move on. Now I'm going to allow myself to let go and live.

CHAPTER ELEVEN

SKYE

There's something exhilarating about hurtling down the motorway on a motorcycle with the sound of the wind whooshing around you and buffering your body on a bright warmish spring midmorning. The sense of freedom, and recklessness my friends would argue, is indescribable. I feel like I'm flying as I weave in and out of the cars I overtake. I'm thankful it's Sunday, less traffic means I can go faster. I open the throttle and the growling machine beneath me responds.

"Slow down Evel Knievel" Paul's voice crackles in my ear.

"Spoilsport" I mutter under my breath slowing down, just a touch. I glance back over my shoulder and see Paul and Alan catching me up fast on their Harley's "Evel was a daredevil not a racer" I retort "so if you have to call me a name call me Carl Fogarty at least he won the World Superbike championship four times" I hear Alan's laughter and Paul's muttered curse in my earpiece as I speed off again grinning like a maniac.

I know there will be hell to pay from Paul when we finally get to Dove Mill for breaking security protocol but right now, I don't care. I'm allowing myself to have fun and no one is going to piss on my chips today. This morning I woke up feeling light and happy, as if a huge weight that I didn't know I was carrying had been lifted. Of course after last night the hypothetical weight has been lifted.

Sleep didn't come easily to me as my mind kept throwing things up so in the end I spent a couple of hours lying in bed thinking through everything that had been discussed and realised my friends were right in all they said. Especially the 'allowing' thing. By simply saying 'I allow myself to…' then fill in the blank it's unbelievable how powerful that simple act is at liberating my mind and emotions from any self-imposed restrictions and grief.

For the first time in a long time I bounded out of bed, literally, refreshed and raring to go. I slept like a log, plus I got a solid ten hours another thing I hadn't done for a long time. I think Nessa banned the kids from disturbing me, which I am grateful for, because when I arrived down for breakfast they pounced on me. As quickly as they lovingly greeted me they disappeared running out of the kitchen in a high state of excitement and before I could ask Nessa what had got into them, besides all the E numbers, they were back each carrying a present.

"These are your birthday presents" Ella says handing over hers – it's heavy, she steps back to let her brothers hand over theirs "and this is your Christmas present from all of us" she helps her brothers place a large box on the table.

I'm about to say they are way too early when I realise Ella meant these are my presents for my last birthday and Christmas, due to Clayton's death I was in no fit state to celebrate either with anyone.

Like a kid on Christmas morning I tear into the wrapping paper with gusto, making the kids laugh and squeal in delight. All my gifts were for riding my new motorcycle. A pair of leather gloves, a pair of heeled riding boots – being a short arse the extra inches will help when I put my feet down – and fantastic one piece leathers, black with purple and pink panels to match the colours of my motorcycle. The last present being a metallic purple crash helmet. Not bothering with breakfast I head straight back upstairs to put my leathers and boots on.

"Close your eyes Daddy. Aunty Skye looks too sexy in her outfit" Ella calls out as I came downstairs. Chuck laughs as Ella climbs on his knee to cover his eyes when I walk into the kitchen.

"Your Daddy has seen me in tighter fitting dresses than these leathers" I chuckle.

"Yes, but they weren't made of leather" Nessa laughs "all you need now is a whip" she whispers in my ear handing me a drink of tea.

Seeing signs for the junction we need I slow down and move over into the first lane, within a few minutes Paul and Alan are behind me and we're taking the exit. It's not long when we're off the dual carriage way and on the country lane heading towards Henley-on-Thames. I take it slower through the lanes as it's Alan's first visit to the UK and he won't be used to the twisting roads plus he'll get to see more of the countryside but the other reason is mainly because I think Paul has had enough heart attacks on this journey to last him a lifetime.

We draw quite a lot of attention as we ride through the town centre. I guess it's unusual to see two Harley Fat Boy's and a Ducati Monster S4R together or we're the first people to be seen out on motorcycles this lovely spring day then again it could simply be the growling noise of the engines. If we're drawing this kind of attention in a large town god knows what's going to happen when we get to the village, I definitely picked the wrong mode of transport if I wanted stealth. Well at least it will give them something to speculate about, I snigger to myself. Before long we're travelling north out of Henley and back into the countryside, the tree lined lanes give way to the occasional building, low hedges and open fields.

Prior to coming to England, I tracked down the relative to the previous owner of Dove Mill Hall that lives in the village. Lady Joyce Farringdon, I've spoken with her twice the last time being yesterday morning. When I told her I was planning on visiting the Hall she offered to meet me and she would talk me through what the Hall and the grounds had looked like, she also had photographs that she could show me. I jumped at her offer, she recommended that we meet outside the local mini supermarket and we follow her to the Hall as the side road leading to the Hall can be easily missed if you didn't know the way, which we don't.

I slow down further when I recognise the land marks Lady Farringdon had given me on the approach to the village. A large Regency period mansion seen clearly from the road, followed by a small grouping of quaint thatched roofed cottages. I wonder briefly if any of these belong to me. As we pass I see the curtains twitching in a few houses. Let's see how well the jungle drums work around this place. A little further down the road the houses become more frequent. They're a mix of old world thatched chocolate box cottages, to small terraces and larger town houses made from lime and sandstone bricks.

A small grouping of shops sit facing the village green the mini supermarket being the largest, brightest and most modern looking with ample parking at the front. I notice a long low white building directly opposite with people coming out holding drinks, some take a seat at the wooden picnic tables others sit on the low wall that marks the pubs boundary, all are blatantly staring our way. The sound of our bikes obviously drawing them out of what I assume is the local pub.

We pull into the mini supermarket parking spaces and switch off our machines, the following silence is quiet eerie. I flip up my visor and look across at the pub's patrons staring back at me. Now I know what the animals feel like at the zoo, although I'm used to being stared at or the focus of attention I find this level of scrutiny is quiet disconcerting. Above the door is a sign 'The Coach House', on closer inspection the building looks really old. The uneven pitched slate tiled roof and small leaded windows all add old world character. Further along the building there appears to be an archway of some sort splitting it in two with a cobbled pathway leading into a court yard, the building on the other side of the archway looks neglected. By the looks of it, it's possible the building is one of the original stagecoach inns travellers used, putting the buildings age at least seventeenth century.

"I'm getting a drink, do you want anything" Alan says getting off his Harley and taking his helmet off. His short light brown hair is flattened to his head; he runs his hand through it not that it does much for it. He looks rather menacing in his black leathers but then being six foot two, built like a barn with a broken nose kind of adds to the bad boy image.

"I'll have a drink and grab a sandwich if they have any" I say taking off my gloves.

I turn to watch Alan as he walks into the store, the young female shop assistant blushes at being caught ogling and suddenly finds something to do. I pull my phone out and start sending a text to Lady Farringdon to let her know we've arrived. Just as I hit send a Range Rover pulls up in front of us.

"Ms Darcy" a woman calls out.

I get off my bike and walk over smiling although she can't see it because of the helmet, idiot I think to myself "Lady Farringdon?" her smile gets wider and nods. I shake her outstretched hand "I just sent you a text, pleased to finally meet you and please call me Skye"

"Likewise and call me Joyce, this is my husband Bertie" I lean in through the window and shake his offered hand. They seem like a nice couple "you'll be able to follow us as the road is quite clear and free from any debris, as soon as you contacted me I had someone go down and make getting to the Hall as easy as possible"

"That's very thoughtful of you" I'm touched "I'll reimburse you of any expense you've incurred"

"No you won't" Joyce waves a dismissive hand "are you ready?"

I turn back to the shop to see Alan at the counter paying for our things "We will in a minute" I gesture to Alan coming out carrying a bag "I think that's a good idea before the whole village comes out and gawps at us"

Joyce and Bertie laugh "It'll give them all something to talk about in the pub tonight. I think Chris the landlord will be happy, I bet he'll be as busy tonight as he was when news broke the Hall had been sold" says Bertie.

We pull out of the car park following the Range Rover, our movements are tracked by every observer. Some people take out their phones and take pictures of our convoy, others appear to text or make calls. Jungle drums are working just fine, effective and efficient I muse to myself. We reach a fork in the road, nestled in the middle of where the road splits, is a lovely old church surrounded by a grave yard. The church is made from the same grey stone as the wall that surrounds it. With perfect timing the church bells start to ring and the heavy wooden doors open, the vicar steps out followed by his congregation. At the sound of us passing more people rush out. The Farringdon's take the left fork. As I follow on the right set back from the road we pass three very sorry looking neglected cottages with beautifully tended gardens. How strange. I have no doubt whatsoever that those are mine.

About half a mile down the lane the Farringdon's Range Rover indicates to turn left and disappears into the hedgerow. Joyce was bloody right; I would have missed this turning. The road, although cleared of any debris was still a nightmare to negotiate thanks to the years of neglect, dodging the pot holes really tested my skills at handling a motorcycle. It was like taking my CBT test all over again. On either side of the road are trees forming a natural covered avenue, in the summer and autumn the leaf covered canopy must look spectacular. At the end of the avenue the road widens continuing on for another two hundred meters or so and opens into a circular turnaround, a stone fountain covered in moss and weeds sits in the middle. Getting off my bike I look back down the avenue and realise what I thought was a lane is actually the driveway leading to the Hall.

I place my helmet on the handle bars and review the remains of the Hall. The steps leading up to and the portico are intact and so is most of the left side of the building, the right side obviously got the worst of the fire with half the structure gone or collapsed in on itself. There's no roof or glass in the windows and there appears to be half a forest growing inside with ivy covering the external walls.

"Dove Mill Hall was a spectacular building, I loved growing up here" Joyce's voice is wistful tinged with a hint of sadness as she stands beside me. I nod and leave her to her memories.

"Here, you left this in the car" Bertie breaks Joyce out of her reverie by tenderly touching her shoulder and hands her a folder. She gives him such a sweet smile I feel myself go all mushy inside.

"I appreciate everything you've done; I know this must be hard for you" I say with as much sincerity as I can. If it was me in her shoes, I would be gutted seeing something that held so many fond memories about to be ripped apart and rebuilt and I wouldn't be any part of it anymore.

Joyce lets out a huge sigh "I won't insult you by denying it but being here is also giving me closure. In a way I can now finally move on and hopefully the village gossips will have something else to speculate about" she gives me a cheeky grin, making me laugh "I'm sorry but I have to ask. My uncle told me that the place was bought by an American called Mr Blake" she pauses obviously trying to formulate her question. I put her out of her misery.

"It was. Mr Blake was my husband. He bought this for me as an anniversary present. I'm an artist and my work takes me all over the world. I have a number of commissions coming up which means relocating to England for at least twelve months. He bought this as he thought I would enjoy renovating it, turning it into a home for us to use as a base"

"What a lovely gesture, your husband obviously knows you very well" Joyce smiles at me, I feel a twinge of sadness.

"I can't help but notice you used past tense when referring to your husband" says Bertie, he makes an 'humph' sound and rubs his ribs. I smile at the scowl Joyce gives him.

"It's okay, no offense was made nor taken and you're right" I nod at Bertie "my husband passed away not long after our anniversary" Joyce's hand covers her mouth, her eyes stricken. Bertie grimaces at his imagined faux pas "he was in a car accident and died a few days later"

"I am so, so very sorry" Joyce says distraught.

"Don't worry about it. You weren't to know. How could you know, I mean he was a very wealthy well-known businessman in America and the accident and his death did make the news and I would be amazed if that news made it across the pond" I plaster a smile on my face to reassure them "and to clear the matter up about my name. I'm very well known in my field of work and I have a number of business interests that uses my name as the brand so I kept it. Only a handful of people refer to me as Mrs Blake, it also helps if I ever want to travel incognito" I wink making them laugh.

"So would it help if we don't refer to you as Mrs Blake, keep the locals guessing" Bertie says with a wicked glint in his eye.

"Who am I to spoil your fun?" my smile broadens "it would certainly stop people harassing the shit out of me… plus it'll stop people trying to screw as much money out of me as possible for lousy workmanship when I start on this" I gesture to the Hall.

"You've sussed out the locals already and you've only been here ten minutes" Bertie chuckles heartily "I'm curious, who are the two gentlemen with you"

I glance back at Paul and Alan, both are sitting sideways on their bikes taking in their surroundings and pointing things out to each other, no doubt working out the security details "The blonde is Paul Boyd and the other is Alan Parker they are my…" I shrug "I suppose you'd call them bodyguards. Paul is in charge of my security and both of them are American"

Joyce starts giggling "Oh dear" she splutters, her giggling turns in real guffaws, she tries to talk but every time she does sets off another bout. Bertie and I smile watching her hysterics. After a few minutes she's calmed down enough to speak "he went into the shop" she points at Alan and sets of laughing again.

I start laughing as I realise what's tickled her so much "Alan" I call out "did you speak to anyone in the store"

"Yes ma'am, the young lady who served me" he drawls making his accent very evident "is that a problem?" he looks confused.

"Not at all" I snigger "just be prepared to be mistaken as Mr Blake" Bertie starts to chuckle as he's cottoned on "in fact I think we could have some real fun causing confusion with these two" Alan brings over my drink and sandwich, Paul follows. I introduce them "so, are you two up to causing mischief and mayhem with the locals?" I say nonchalantly as I take a bite out of my sandwich.

Paul laughs "That's your middle name. We just follow orders"

"Yeah right" I snort.

"Not to cause you any alarm but we're being watched" says Paul.

"How in the blazes do you know that?" Bertie says startled and somewhat impressed.

"Over my left shoulder, in the distance is a building on the hill that overlooks us. Sunlight is reflecting off the glass on a pair of binoculars" we all look in the direction and sure enough I see the flash and glint of a bright reflective light "do you know who it could be?"

"That's Caleb Raven's place" my stomach somersaults at the name, is this the same Caleb as my Mystery Man "it could be him or any one of his grooms" Bertie says.

My stomach drops to the floor and my heart is in my mouth the odds are getting shorter and shorter "Grooms?" I manage to squeak out.

"Yes, he's a horse trainer" Joyce says. How in the hell I remain on my feet I do not know! I feel light headed my heart is pounding so hard "actually he's been using the top field" Joyce points in the direction of where the field will be "to turn out the horses. Years back Caleb's uncle lost the land in a game of cards to my grandfather. I don't know the full story but needless to say my grandfather felt bad and let his uncle carry on using the land for the horses. My uncle continued with the arrangement when grandfather passed. Caleb's own uncle passed away a few years later and things stayed as they are now. I suppose now he's trespassing on your land"

"What's he like?" I can't resist asking.

"He's a good chap. Works hard although he can have a short fuse" Bertie says "bloody good trainer and he knows his horses. He recently returned from a buying trip for me in America" now what are the chances Caleb is the buyer Mike told me about I wonder "got me and my syndicate some fine horses, although he did say there was one horse he wanted but the owner wouldn't sell and in his words he offered silly money and they still refused" I mentally do a silly dance shouting he is, he is.

"You said he has a short fuse; does that mean he has a nasty temper?" I try to sound inquisitive.

"I put it down to that awful ex-wife of his Gabrielle" says Joyce.

Oh this just gets better and better, then like a bolt of lightning comprehension hits. The skinny Umpa Lumpa I met last night was his wife. Oh my fucking god!

"The poor man works his socks off to build an outstanding reputation as a trainer and the minute he makes a decent living the money grabbing bitch shows up and fleeces him" Joyce spits, she really doesn't like Gabrielle "I'm just glad that this time he filed for divorce. He really seems determined to be rid of her once and for all"

"I'm sure Skye isn't interested in his personal life" Bertie puts a hand on Joyce's arm. I have to refrain from slapping him and saying Oh yes I do. Joyce gathers her composure "will you let him continue to use the upper field for the horses?" asks Bertie.

I shrug "At this stage I don't see why not. It's not as if it's going to be at the top of my priority list" Bertie visibly relaxes, of course he'll have a vested interest he's probably got his horses stabled with Caleb "my main concern is this place, the cottages and the farm. I take it those neglected looking cottages we passed before turning into here are mine" Joyce nods "I think it's safe to say the horses can stay where they are for quite some time because I'll have my work cut out with this lot"

"On that note" Joyce opens the file and pulls out some photographs "I do have some photo's that show the interior back at home, would you like to come back for dinner and I can show you them"

"That will be lovely, although I have to be in London for three as I have a meeting. I can be back by five, six at the latest depending on how long the meeting goes on for"

"Let's say six, you have my number if anything changes and we'll show you where we live on the way back" Joyce smiles warmly. I like this woman, she may talk posh but she's down to earth.

I spend the next half an hour listening to Joyce as she describes the Hall, mentioning and pointing out things the photographs didn't show. We walk around the building, daring to venture inside to get a feel for the interior. I don't spend too long inside as Paul gets twitchy and he's yet to tear a strip off me for speeding away from him and Alan on the motorway.

On the way back through the village there seems to be a suspiciously large amount of people out for a lunchtime stroll and the pub is doing a roaring trade going by the amount of people stood outside. So far, I like what I see of the village. My mind is buzzing with possibilities and ideas, already I have a mental list of people to contact. I can't wait to get started.

DOVE MILL VILLAGE

Lucy hated working Sunday's in the shop with a passion, it was so dull. She only did it to keep the peace between her Mum and Dad. It also meant that she couldn't go out clubbing on Saturday nights in Henley-on-Thames because she had to be up early – and sober – to open up the shop and sort out the Sunday newspapers. God! The family business sucked. At twenty-four years of age she already felt like she was fifty. But this Sunday all that changed… when that sexy beast of an American walked in.

Now, at nine o'clock she is sitting next to her best friend Sally at the bar slowly getting plastered with all the drinks being bought her and enjoying the attention coming her way, especially from Rex who normally didn't look twice at her. All because people were hungry for first hand gossip about the three mysterious leather clad, motorbike riders who came to the village then followed the Farringdon's to Dove Mill Hall and she was the only person to speak to one of them. Sally is just as intoxicated as Lucy all thanks to her friend.

Within seconds of the American leaving the store Lucy was on the phone to Sally telling her about the visitors and the Farringdon's. Sally ended the call and on a hunch ran straight to Caleb's office, thankfully he was out all day so she wouldn't have to explain herself. It took her a few minutes to find what she was looking for because Caleb never bothered to file any paperwork and had a habit of leaving things where he left them so the office looked as if a bomb had gone off. She eventually found the binoculars on the window sill under a week's worth of Racing Post newspapers.

Running as fast as she could, Sally went to the highest point of the hill behind Caleb's house to get the best view point to look down on Dove Mill Hall. Panting and with shaky hands due to the adrenaline rush she carefully took the military grade binoculars out of the case, thanking whoever and whatever that Caleb had brought them back with him from his recent trip abroad. Putting them to her eyes she quickly worked out how to zoom in and out, just in time to see the Farringdon's and the visitors pull up in front of the Hall. Sally, could now give detailed descriptions of the three visitors and what they did for the half hour they spent with the Farringdon's.

"I'm telling you Sal, that American was fucking fit for an older man" Lucy slurs quietly "I mean Rex is gorgeous but this guy had a hard edge to him. I wouldn't say no to a tangle with him between the sheets"

"I know what you mean" giggles Sally "I wouldn't pass up a tangle with the other guy"

"Tangle with who" the deep gruff voice of her boss coming from behind makes Sally yelp and blush furiously as she looks up at him. She relaxes a little when she sees Caleb smiling with a curious glint in his sparkling green eyes, he raises a quizzical eyebrow expecting an answer. Now he is definitely someone she would rugby tackle into bed and sod the age difference. Before she can answer Rex makes an appearance.

"Have the girls told you about the three visitors checking out Dove Mill Hall today?" Rex says draping an arm over Caleb's shoulder.

"So that's why the place is heaving" Caleb says looking around the pub "the gossip vultures coming to get their fix"

"Two men and a woman. One of them was American" Lucy says straightening her back thrusting out her flat chest. The sexy beast American forgotten. Caleb was the older man all her friends, including herself, wanted to get in the sack. All of them envied Sally for having him as her boss. Lucy is thrilled to have Caleb's undivided attention, his intense green eyes on her.

"What did they look like?" demanded Caleb.

"I only got to see one of them, he came into the shop" Lucy quivers at the scowl Caleb gives her "they were riding motorbikes, the other man and woman stayed outside and kept their helmets on" Lucy adds in a rush.

"I saw what they looked like" Sally says in a small voice "I got your binoculars and went up onto the hill" Sally looks down at the floor, chewing her lip. All her happy feelings heading straight out the door as she's certain Caleb is about to tear a strip off her for neglecting her duties, the horses and the yard for the sake of gathering gossip, which she knew he hated. Caleb's roar of laughter snaps her head up "you're not mad at me?"

"No Sally" Caleb gently rubs her arm "I would have done exactly the same thing had I been around. What did you see?"

"Tell him everything, start from the beginning" Rex says handing Caleb a bottle of Corona.

"Well just before lunch they pulled up in front of the shop on their motorbikes. I tell you, you could hear them five minutes before they came into view" says Lucy excited at having a new audience.

"According to Duncan our resident motorcycle enthusiast, the men rode Harley Fat Boys and the woman was on a Ducati Monster S4R" Rex chips in.

"The woman had a gorgeous metallic purple helmet that matched the colour of her bike" Lucy adds enthusiastically. Caleb snorts a laugh at Rex rolling his eyes "one of the men came in the shop and bought drinks and sandwiches. I asked him if they had travelled far and he said London. Then I asked him where they were heading and he said they were meeting someone here. Just then the Farringdon's pulled up in their Range Rover. The woman went over to speak with them"

"What did he look like?"

"Just over six foot, big muscular build. Short light brown hair, a bit shorter than Rex's" Lucy says looking at Rex's hair "pale blue eyes, I think his nose had been broken at some point as it was slightly crooked" Lucy is baffled by Caleb's disappointed expression.

"So then what happened?" Caleb prompts.

"Well he paid for the items and left the shop, a few minutes later they followed the Farringdon's. Going in the direction of the church. I rang Sally"

"On a hunch I went and got your binoculars" Sally picks up the story "As I got to the top of the hill they were all pulling up outside the Hall. The woman spent most of her time speaking with Lady Farringdon and looking at whatever was in the folder Lady Farringdon held, who by the way was pointing a lot at what was in it and at the Hall and surrounding grounds. I think they were pictures. They spent some time walking around the Hall and went inside for a few minutes. They were there for about half an hour"

"Describe the other two"

"The man had really short blonde hair, he's slightly shorter than the brown haired man but still as big in build. The woman looked tiny, even when she stood next to Lady Farringdon" Sally frowns "and her hair appeared to be white blonde"

Caleb chokes on his drink, Rex slaps his back "How long was her hair?" Caleb wheezes between coughs. What are the chances that the mystery woman visitor is his wild kitten? His heart beat erratically at the possibility.

"I don't know. I could tell it was tied back but her hair was hidden underneath her leathers"

Caleb ignores the speculative looks being thrown his way "Has anyone spoken to the Farringdon's?"

"I've been trying off and on for the last couple of hours. Neither are answering their mobiles and I've rung the house only to be told they're not taking calls at present" says Rex miffed.

Caleb nods thoughtfully "So I take it speculation is that one of the men is our mysterious Mr Blake and since Lucy spoke to the brown haired one he is the likely candidate?"

"Got that right" Chris the landlord says laughing heartily as he places dirty empty glasses on the bar "the Goats have already got a book running if anyone's interested. I tell you I don't care who they are, I just hope they come back soon. You won't find me complaining if they keep generating business like this for me"

"Been that good tonight?" laughs Caleb.

"It's been like this all day. Ever since they showed up" Michelle, Chris's wife, says clearing the glasses away "we've had people come in today that haven't been in for years, plus the weekenders have been coming in, most of them delaying their return to the city just to get the latest gossip. Even Simone Fawcett-Fowler has graced us with her presence" Michelle puts on a fake articulated posh voice, the girls snigger into their drinks.

"Now, now my love you mustn't mimic our customers. You'll be giving everyone the wrong impression that we take the piss out of them behind their backs" Chris sternly reprimands his wife.

"Poppycock" retorts Michelle still speaking in the fake posh voice "you as well as these fine people know I would do it to their face. Simone however has her head shoved so far up her own arse she can smell the bullshit she gives out will only darken our door again when hell has frozen over" everyone collapses laughing Michelle's delivery is pitch perfect of impersonating Simone.

"That's bloody brilliant" Rex says wiping his eyes "you should go on Britain's Got Talent. Who else can you do?"

"Don't encourage her Rex" Chris chuckles "I'll have to bar you if you do and I'd hate to lose one of my best customers"

"Come on Chris, you've got to admit it Michelle is uncannily accurate plus Simone does open herself up for ridicule. She's nothing but an ambitious social climber, we potentially have a billionaire moving into the neighbourhood of course Simone is going to want to get her claws into the wife so she can exploit their connections for her dinner parties and social gatherings" says Rex.

"Billionaire's wife is fresh meat to Simone" says Caleb.

"I'd love it if the billionaire's wife was the complete opposite of Simone" Sally says hopefully "now that would be really funny"

"Yeah, someone down to earth, normal like us" adds Lucy.

"I better get some of those spare rooms cleaned, aired and fresh bedding just in case they need somewhere to stay" Michelle says sardonically.

"That's not a bad idea" says Chris, Michelle rolls her eyes "I'm being serious, better to be prepared. Stranger things have happened"

"Me and my big mouth" Michelle mutters as she takes the dirty glasses to the washer.

Five miles away in Henley-on-Thames, Freya Bennett leans forward and rests her aching weary head on the steering wheel of her beloved yet decrepit Ford Fiesta, willing herself to find the energy and courage to drag her twenty stone bulk out of the car and into the house. Her once dream home and safe haven is now a place of terror and torture, a living nightmare. How had her life become so desperate and miserable?

"You allowed it to, you stuck your head in the sand and refused to believe that the man you once loved has turned into a vicious bully" Freya whispers to herself.

For five years she thought she had it all – a beautiful home, a well-paid job she was passionate about and a loving man to share the rest of her life with – before it all changed. Gradually over the following three years the beautiful home has turned into a hazardous shamble. Her job although still well paid is one she now hates due to the unreasonable demands put on her by her bosses, such as working twelve hour days including Sunday, but she couldn't afford to leave not since her once loving man had been made redundant three years ago. In a short space of time their relationship rapidly deteriorated.

At first Freya made excuses for Adam's behaviour towards her. She would tell her friends he was frustrated at not being able to get a new job straight away in his chosen field. He wanted to continue making equal contributions to the running of their home. Or she would say he was under a lot of pressure and working hard because he was starting up his own business, using his redundancy money... but it was all a big fat lie.

Adam quickly squandered his redundancy pay out then he worked his way through the money they had saved up for their wedding and the savings that would be the deposit for buying their own house one day. The small amount of savings Freya managed to squirrel away followed soon after. She hadn't told Adam about this separate bank account, he found the paying in book and cash card as he searched through her belongings looking for cash so he could go out drinking with his new found buddies. That was the first time he hit her. He beat her until she gave him the pin number. No one came to help her, no one answered her screams for help. Her neighbours suddenly seemed to have gone deaf.

Adam controlled her movements, stopped her seeing her friends then stopped her speaking to them. At first she argued back, fought against his controlling ways, but all that got her was a smack in the mouth. She hit him, he hit back harder. She knew her friends were scared of him.

"What friends, you have none" Freya mutters listlessly.

In the beginning a couple of her friends tried to intervene, they even reported the domestic abuse to the police, unfortunately their good intensions had the adverse effect. That was the cause of her first trip to the A&E department. Telling the doctors, she fell down the stairs banging her head on the wall when she landed at the bottom, knocking herself out. Freya wasn't sure how much she had convinced the doctors but Adam playing the concerned, loving boyfriend made the lie more believable. In truth, he was only there to make sure she didn't tell them what actually happened – after repeatedly punching her, he kicked her down the stairs.

Why didn't she just leave? That was a question Freya asked herself a thousand times. At first she believed he wouldn't hit her again, he even said he was sorry and promised to change. He never kept his word. There was a time Freya would have gone to any of her friend's knowing they wouldn't turn her away, but she knew he would come after her and she couldn't bring her problems to her friend's door. Her family lived hundreds of miles away, they didn't like Adam, never had. Only pride kept her from admitting to them they had been right about him all along. Freya even researched shelters for domestic abuse victims during her lunch break at work but she could never bring herself to call.

"He's going to kill me one of these days if I don't get out" Freya thought looking up at the house with dread in her eyes and finally summoning the courage to get out of the car. The reception waiting for her inside will only get worse if she loiters any longer and she was already an hour late as it was. With a heavy heart Freya opens the front door, steps inside and closes it as quietly as possible. The only sound is the TV blaring. Not a good sign, cold dread settles in the pit of her stomach.

"Where the fuck have ya been, ya fat slag?" panic slices through her at the sound of the vicious hateful voice and malicious words.

A heavy hand hits the back of her head, pushing it forward so her forehead slams into the door. She sees stars. Hands roughly grab her shoulders, spinning her around, her back and head hit with the door again with a thud. Shooting pain, from yesterday's bruises, runs across her shoulders and down her spine. The second knock to her head has black dots joining the stars along with a searing headache.

"Answer me ya fuckin' ugly bitch" Adam pulls his arm back but Freya isn't quick enough to dodge the incoming slap, his large palm connects with the side of her face. The whacking sound of flesh hitting flesh reverberates around the narrow hallway; the stinging pain brings tears to her eyes. Freya stifles the scream. It's no good giving it a voice, no one will hear... that's why the TV is on so loud.

"There was more work to sort out than Mr Coleman originally thought" Freya whimpers pitifully, knowing full well Adam wouldn't believe her "I did call and leave a message to say I would be late, did you not get it?"

"Of course I got it" Adam grabs her hair pulling her close, holding her in place next to his red twisted face, the stench of alcohol and stale tobacco assaults her sense of smell. Freya tries desperately not to gag "but ya didn't say when you'd be home ya fuckin' blundering idiot" spittle flies from his mouth and lands on her face. Freya can't stop the involuntary shudder.

Dragging Freya by her hair – she stumbles down the hallway trying to keep up, she can feel her hair ripping out of her scalp – Adam roughly shoves her through the kitchen door.

"Make me somethin' to eat. I'm fuckin' starving because ya were too stupid to leave anything out for me this morning" Adam places a well-aimed kick on her backside. Freya sprawls on the kitchen floor with the force of the blow, the side of her head and shoulder connecting with the cabinet with a sickening thud "get up ya lazy fuckin' cunt" Adam lands another well aimed kick; this time on her ribs before Freya has time to react to the first one. Searing pain shoots across her ribs, Freya screams... silently.

Struggling to her knees, Freya slowly eases herself up using the kitchen cabinets as support. Breathing is difficult, the muscles in her side protesting each time her lungs inflate with air. Taking shallow breaths Freya makes her way to the fridge. It's empty, all the food she bought yesterday for today's dinner is gone.

"Where's all the food gone?" Freya prays that it doesn't sound like an accusation.

"I don't know; you tell me" Adam advances on her. Freya shrinks back against the cabinets "you're the one like the beached whale" he pokes her painfully in the stomach "overweight, blubber belly" he slaps the sides of her flab and viciously wobbles it "I betcha took it all to work with you and stuffed ya fuckin' face all day" he grabs her face, his fingers digging into her cheeks pushing her lips out. Tears roll down Freya's cheeks "yeah, that's whatcha were doing all day. Stuffin' ya fat fuckin' face instead of working like ya said ya were. You disgust me"

"I didn't. Please stop this" Freya begs.

"So I ate it all did I?" Adam let go of her "ya fuckin' bitch" Adam screams in her face.

Freya closes her eyes just before the first punch lands… "He's going to kill me now" is her last thought as she hit the kitchen floor.

Something wet and very cold hits her face, spluttering and gasping for breath Freya lifts her throbbing head. Water trickles into her eyes, at least she thinks its water. Her head is pounding, her body hurts and aches in so many places. Wiping her eyes and hair out of her face, slowly she sits up. She's alone in the kitchen, the blaring sound of the TV is the only thing she can hear.

"You're still alive" Freya murmurs "barely"

Gathering all of her strength Freya gets up, ignoring her protesting knees and pain riddled body, purely concentrating on standing upright. Dizziness has her swaying and grasping onto the kitchen top to steady herself. Blackness threatens to engulf her, claim her again.

"I've got to get out of here, leave now" Freya tells herself "for your own safety and sanity, leave and don't ever come back"

Freya stumbles across the kitchen into the hallway, she creeps past the living room not bothering to look in to see if Adam is in there. She doesn't bother picking up her handbag from where she dropped it by the front door, her survival instinct overrides all thoughts and actions. Cautiously she opens the front door and slips out, freedom.

Freya staggers down the path, walking away from her home leaving everything behind. She has no idea where she is going or how far she has walked – she is aware of people passing by giving her concerned curious glances or blatantly looking the other way, everyone keeps their distance – when reality crashes down on her. Big wracking sobs shake her battered body, trembling she leans against a wall and lowers herself to the cold pavement. Pulling her knees to her chest she wraps her arms around her bruised legs and lets her control slip.

A car pulls up, doors open and close. Someone stands in front of her, she doesn't have the energy to lift her aching head. A waft of floral perfume, not too sweet or over powering reaches her. Gentle soft hands touch her arms and head, she flinches, tries to pull herself into a smaller ball.

"I'm sorry. I'm not going to hurt you" a soft husky voice says kindly "you need help. I want to help you. Will you let me?"

Freya lifts her head to see before her an angel. A stunningly beautiful angel. The angel with sad eyes gently cups her sore battered face.

"You poor woman. My name is Skye. Will you let me help you?"

Freya nods her head; the angel becomes blurred. It doesn't matter, she knows with all her shattered heart and broken body she truly is safe now.

CHAPTER TWELVE

SKYE

I look at the battered and badly bruised sleeping woman lying in the hospital bed. She has taken one hell of a beating. My fists clench as I think about giving the bastard who did this a taste of his own medicine. Paul spotted her staggering down the street last night. I couldn't believe that not one person who passed her stopped to help. Doing a U-turn in the middle of the road he pulled up alongside her as she collapsed to the floor. I wanted to cry at the way she flinched away from my touch, how she trembled and tried to make herself smaller waiting for the next blow to hit home.

Paul and Alan managed to lift her and get her into the car without jostling and hurting her. I rang Joyce who told me where the nearest hospital was. When we arrived the minor injuries department was closed. Fortunately, one of the doctors recognised her. Apparently she's made quite a few visits to them over the last few years, strange how accident prone one person can be. I pulled some strings to get her a bed. The woman stirs. Gently I stroke her lank dark brown hair off her forehead. A huge bruise is forming in the centre, merging with the one at her temple. At first I thought she had fine hair but I soon realise that's because chunks are missing from her scalp. Her eyes flutter open. I sit on the side of the bed so she can see me without having to move.

"Hi, you're in hospital. Do you remember what happened to you?" I ask softly.

Tears leak from her eyes and run down the side of her face into her hair, slowly she nods her head.

"I'm told your name is Freya Bennett" another nod. I give her my warmest smile "my name is Skye Darcy" she gasps "you're in pain let me call the nurse" I get up to press the call button.

"No, no I'm okay" Freya's voice is a hoarse croaky whisper, she lifts her arm feebly to stop me. I take hold of her hand and sit back down.

"There's no need to suffer or put on a brave face" I admonish gently. Freya laughs then winces "you're severely bruised and by the grace of god there are no broken bones, please let me call the nurse" she shakes her head.

"I wasn't gasping in pain" her voice is getting stronger "thank you for stopping to help me Mrs Blake" Freya looks me straight in the eye, her hazel eyes are clear and unwavering. She shocks the shit out of me.

"Well I wasn't expecting you to say that" I laugh, Freya's swollen lips turn up in a slight smile "how do you know who I am?"

"The firm of solicitors I work for handled the sale of Dove Mill Hall"

"Ah! I see" I grin "what do you do there?"

"I'm a PA for two of the partners" Freya winces as she shifts to sit up. My interest is piqued.

"Lie still" I instruct, resting my hand on her shoulder. I press the control on the side of the bed to change the angle "do you like working for them?"

"I used to" Freya sighs heavily, she looks down at her hands and picks at her finger nails, a single tear rolls down her cheek. I pass her a tissue and wait patiently "I always had ambitions of being a lawyer, years ago I started an Open University course studying Law and working in a solicitors gave me added experience and knowledge. I loved it"

"So what happened?" I gently probe.

Another deep sigh and wince "Three years ago my partner, Adam, was made redundant. At first, well for a few months' things were okay then he… he… changed" Freya's voice breaks, she wipes away the fresh tears.

"He did this to you" I say it as a statement not a question but she answers anyway.

"Yes" Freya blows out a long shaky breath "within three months Adam went through all of his redundancy and our savings. We were supposed to get married and buy a house. Ever since we have been living on my salary. For a short while I secretly managed to put a little aside to pay for my course but he found out"

Freya stops speaking and hangs her head. A wave of anger surges through me. My blood is boiling, I really, really want to get my hands on the fucking pig.

"Correct me if I'm wrong but my guess is that he now takes every penny you make and spends it down the pub, at the bookies and on drugs giving you barely enough to buy food"

Freya nods "I don't think he does drugs; I've never seen him take any" she whispers.

"But that doesn't mean he hasn't" I counter, Freya shrugs "what happened to cause this?" I gesture to her face and body.

"I was asked to go into work" Freya snorts "actually I was told. My bosses know how I desperately need my job and they use it against me. Anyway things took longer than they anticipated. I didn't get home until nine, although I had rung Adam earlier and left a message to say I was going to be working later than originally thought it wasn't good enough. He was waiting for me when I got in, I have no idea what set him off but he used the fact that I didn't give a time as an excuse to start on me"

"Bastard" I hiss, Freya looks up at me startled at my outburst "sorry for my language, not for calling him"

Freya gives me a sad smile "I thought he was going to kill me. When I came to on the kitchen floor, I finally found the courage to get out, so I did. I walked out leaving everything behind. When you found me I had no idea where I was going, I didn't know what to do. I just had to get away, as far away as I could" Freya starts to cry, I wrap my arms around her gently rubbing and soothing her back "I have nowhere to go, no money, no clothes. If you hadn't stopped when you did" she can't finish, her whole body shakes with the choking sobs and hisses of pain.

"Let it all go, let it all out" I whisper gently as I hold her.

After a while her sobs subside "I'm sorry" she pulls herself back "you've done so much for me already. You don't need this"

"Nonsense and you don't need to apologise to me" I say straightening the bed sheets around her. I take hold of her hand and sit down "I have a proposition for you" Freya's eyes snap to mine. I see surprise, curiosity and anxious nervousness flit through them "come and work for me as my PA" I let that sink in "I need an assistant and have done for a while. I could do with someone of your experience on my team and your legal background is an added bonus"

Freya looks at me wide eyed and open mouthed after a few minutes she finds her voice "What happened to your last assistant?" she blurts out.

A stabbing twist of pain radiates out of my gut. It's my turn to look down and collect my thoughts "She died" I whisper, Freya gasps. I look up to see her hand over her mouth, her eyes full of sorrow. I take a deep breath, it never gets easier "Macy and my husband along with one of our body guards were in a car accident nearly six months ago. Macy was killed outright, my husband died from his injuries three days later. Bruce survived although he's still recuperating"

"I'm so sorry" Freya whispers. I nod and try to smile.

"Anyway, the job involves working closely with me on my various business interests, plus numerous other things that come along. Sometimes you'll be mad busy and meet yourself coming back other times you'll be sat around twiddling your thumbs bored shitless. You'll get the usual benefits of dental, healthcare, pension plan and I'll pay you a ridiculous amount of money you won't know what to spend it on. You'll live in, although you don't have to" I add hastily "there's a lot of travel involved, do you have a passport?" Freya mutely nods "good. You'll also work closely with my security team" there's a knock on the door and Paul pops his head round, right on cue "talk of the devil" I laugh "come in and bring Alan" I gesture.

Freya's eyes widen further when she sees the two huge men "Guys meet Freya" both smile and nod "this is Paul Boyd, he's head of my security and this is Alan Parker. I'm talking to Freya about working for me as my PA" the boys smile gets wider "she works as one for a firm of solicitors, she'll be a good addition to the team. What do you think?"

"Yes ma'am" they chorus "we need to get going in ten minutes for your meeting" Paul adds as they leave the room.

"Have a think about it and any questions you have I'll answer when I'm back later at visiting time. The doctors are going to keep you in under observation for one more night by the way. Do you have any burning questions for me now?"

Freya looks at a loss. I've given her a lot to process and she has some big decisions to make.

"What day is it?" Freya frowns.

"Monday and its lunchtime" I say looking at my watch "you were out of it for quite a while. You had us all worried, that's why the doctors want to keep you in for another night"

"Oh my god, work!" Freya says in panic sitting up suddenly, her face screws up in agony. I help ease her back down.

"Give me the number and I'll ring telling them you won't be in for the rest of the week due to illness. All you need to worry about now is getting your strength back and healing, understood" I say sternly. Freya nods meekly and recites a number, I put it in my phone "excellent. Right I'll see you later. The nursing staff have my number should you need me for anything" I stand and walk to the door.

"Ms Darcy" I turn to see Freya's battered and bruised face smiling with hope and joy shining through her eyes "I would love to come and work for you"

"Excellent" I grin "shall I tell them you won't be coming back" I wiggle my phone. Freya nods, her grin getting wider. Her joy is obviously overriding any pain she's feeling "I'll see you later, now get some rest. Oh and call me Skye" I wink. I hear her laugh then a hiss and groan of pain as I close the door behind me.

A couple of hours later I'm sitting in The Coach House waiting for Paul and Alan to come back. I left Alan in Henley-on-Thames with instructions to buy at least two weeks-worth of clothes, underwear and shoes for Freya. Plus, make up, toiletries, handbags and anything else he thought of that I'd forgotten and suitcases to put it in since all Freya had in the world was the clothes she stood up in, actually she didn't have those anymore as the doctors cut them off her.

Paul and I headed to Dove Mill to meet with the locksmith at the cottages. I got the locks changed because no one knew where the keys were. Then we went to the Hall to meet with the architect and surveyor, both are contacts of Chuck's and more than accommodating at such short notice plus they're up for the challenge of working to a tight deadline. I informed them I wanted to meet up Friday to see the reports and the architect's first draft. After seeing the interior photograph's Joyce showed me last night I had a good idea of what I wanted.

On that thought I pull out my phone and send a text to Elliot the interior designer asking him to call me at his earliest convenience. I look around the pub; this really would be good to use as a base over the next week. At one end there is a pool table. I could use that area for the meeting on Friday, plenty of space to spread out and get everyone together; project manager, architect, stone masons, builders etc. Hmm I wonder if the landlord will let me.

"What are the odds for that American bloke being Mr Blake?"

Immediately my attention snaps in the opposite direction. The voice asking the question is one of three men huddled around a table by the log fire. The Coach House has a real rustic country feel to it, low beams, stone floor and in between the seating along the walls are short wooden panels jutting out to form booths. I have a clear view of the men yet they can't see me.

"Odds on favourite" a man in a shiny grey suit says.

"Shit" one dressed in dusty work clothes mutters.

"So what are people saying who the other man and the woman are?" a casually dressed good looking blonde haired man says.

Bloody hell, that's me they're talking about. The man in the shiny grey suit flicks through the pages of a note book and turns it around so blondie can read it. I'm willing him to read out loud, much to my chagrin he doesn't. Suddenly blondie is laughing.

"I don't believe it!" he exclaims "you cheeky bastards" he laughs harder "I'll have twenty quid on me" he pulls out his wallet and puts the money on the table "word of advice, don't let Caleb see this or hear about it. He'll rip your fucking head off"

My heart stutters at the mention of Caleb.

"Give me some credit. Do you really think I would walk up to him and say "Hey Caleb fancy having a bet on yourself as the first person to fuck Mrs Blake?" I like my head attached to my shoulders thank you very much" shiny suit says indignantly.

My jaw hits the table.

"I apologise for their bad language Miss" I drag my eyes away and look up to see a friendly faced portly middle aged man with thinning grey hair, he's holding empty glasses in one hand and a cloth in the other. He frowns at the three men.

"It's okay!" I smile brightly at him "are you Chris the landlord?"

He looks at me open mouthed then shakes his head and smiles "Yes I am. I've not seen you around before, I take it you're new to the area?" I nod, putting the cloth under his arm he holds out his hand "Christopher Tunstone at your service and you are?"

"Skye Darcy, pleased to meet you" I shake his hand, leaning forward I whisper "although I'm also known as Mrs Blake but let's keep that between us for now. I quite fancy having a bet" I wink and incline my head in the direction of the three men. I know the grin on my face reflects the thrill of mischief I'm feeling.

Chris's face is a picture. Shock, horror then amusement. He roars laughing, bending over double and slaps his knees. He wipes his eyes using the cloth when he finally gets control of himself.

"Welcome to Dove Mill village" he chuckles.

"Thank you. Lady Farringdon told me you might have rooms to rent. I would like to book four if you have them. Ideally from tomorrow through to Sunday, possibly a couple of days longer" I can see I've shocked him again "if you don't can you recommend a hotel or bed and breakfast somewhere close by"

"No, no. I mean yes" he's flustered "sorry, yes we have rooms available and from tomorrow will be fine. Would you require meals?"

"Yes please. I plan on using this as a base whilst I'm here. If it's okay with you I'd like to use this for various meetings and on Friday, I'll be having quite a few people coming to see me. I know it's being cheeky but I was thinking of taking over that area" I point towards the pool table "would it be possible?"

"Absolutely, do you know how many people will be coming and do you require food?" Chris obviously has a keen eye for spotting a business opportunity, I like him – a man after my own heart.

"No idea to the first and yes to the second" I smile warmly "it's likely I'll be commandeering the area for at least four to five hours with people coming in and out during that time. Is it going to upset your regulars having no pool table on a Friday from lunchtime to late afternoon?"

"Are you kidding me!" chuckles Chris "when word gets out there's a beautiful mystery blonde staying here all they'll be bothered about is finding out who you are and what you're doing"

I laugh with him. Paul and Alan walk in, scanning the pub. I wave them over. The few customers that are in, including the three men, all fall silent and avidly watch every step they take towards me and Chris.

"Guys, meet Chris the landlord. This is Paul Boyd and Alan Parker" they shake hands and murmur please to meet you "we'll be staying here as of tomorrow through to Sunday, maybe a few days longer depending on how things pan out on Friday"

"Yes ma'am" they chorus. Chris is looking at them with open fascination. Paul glances at his watch "I suggest we head off now if you want to get the start of visiting" I nod and finish my drink.

Standing I hold out my hand to Chris "We'll see you tomorrow, what time can we check in?"

"Any time after ten thirty" Chris's smile falters "erm, people are going to ask me who you are. What do you want me to say?"

"Give them our names and I'd appreciate it not mentioning Mrs Blake. As for what we're doing here say you don't know as you didn't ask" I smile wickedly and point at Paul and Alan "tell them they're both American. That'll put the rumour mill into meltdown and bugger up the betting" we all laugh at the devious plan.

"Will we have the pleasure of meeting Mr Blake soon?" Chris murmurs, the familiar stab of grief twists my gut.

"No" I take a deep breath "Mr Blake passed away nearly six months ago, he was killed in a car accident"

Mortified horror flashes across Chris's face "I'm so sorry, please accept my condolences for your loss and be assured of my utmost discretion"

"Thank you" I reach out and squeeze his arm. I plaster a big smile on my face "you have a lovely pub. I'm looking forward to staying with you"

Chris walks outside with us, he nods and waves to curious bystanders. He chuckles when an elderly plump woman stops in the middle of crossing the road and stares open mouthed in our direction "Marjorie Brennan the village busy body" he mutters to me.

"I take it that means you're going to be busy for the rest of the day" I snort.

"I'm hoping all week with you being here" he winks at me.

"Good to know I'm helping the local economy" I deadpan getting into the SUV. Paul couldn't have found a more ominous vehicle if he tried, talk about making a statement. The Mercedes Benz is huge, all black including the windows. Chris looks at it impressed, I roll down the window "see you tomorrow morning" I call and wave as Paul drives off.

Turning to look out the rear window I see the old lady waddle as fast as she can towards Chris. I swear to god I can already hear the beat of the gossip drums.

I poke my head around the door of Freya's private room to see her sat up in bed busily writing. Her shiny round face is a multi-colour hue of purple, red and yellow. The door creaks as I push it further open, Freya is concentrating so hard she doesn't hear it or me as I wheel in two large suitcases with Alan's help.

"Hey, how are you feeling?"

Freya startles at the sound of my voice, then laughs at herself which turns into a wince "A lot better, sore but a lot better" she eyes the suitcases "what they for?"

"The contents of these cases is your new wardrobe. I have no idea what is inside as I sent Alan to do the shopping"

"I take no credit; it was all done by the stores personal shopper" says Alan smiling broadly at Freya "we can take anything back you don't like"

Freya is frozen with shock, her mouth hangs open, only her eyes move as they follow Alan as he leaves the room. I lie the cases down flat and open them. A sharp knock on the door and Alan is back with Paul carrying a number of bags.

"Forgot the shoes" he says sheepishly. I roll my eyes at him.

"Thank you" Freya whispers, I turn to see tears rolling down her cheeks "I... I don't know... I"

"Shh" I go to her and wrap my arms around her, gently rubbing her shoulders "feel up to giving me a fashion show" I say softly after a few minutes. Freya mutely nods.

I help her out of bed, the pale blue hospital gown doesn't quiet fasten properly at the back due to her large size – thankfully Paul and Alan left discretely whilst I comforted Freya – and I can see the extent of the bruising across her shoulders and lower back. I clamp down on the rising anger the sight of her injuries prompt. Fortunately, during the shopping spree Alan saw fit to get nightwear for Freya including a lovely pink fluffy bathrobe.

"Here, I think you'll be more comfortable wearing this whilst we look through" I hold up the bathrobe so Freya can put her arms through the sleeves. It fits perfectly. I pull the tags off.

"I can't believe you've done all of this for me. I can't thank you enough you've done so much" Freya's voice wavers with so much emotion.

"Your part of the family now and I look after my family" I smile at her puzzled face "don't worry you'll get to meet them, now let's see what we've got" I bend down and pick up a handful of clothes.

An hour later we have two piles, keeping and reject. The reject pile is relatively small, only a few items didn't fit and couple that didn't suit her. Thankfully all the underwear fitted so did the shoes, boots and trainers.

"The doctor tells me you'll be free to leave tomorrow around ten in the morning. Alan will be here to collect you, so what I propose is that you go with him to the store to take these back and get yourself a couple of coats plus anything else you want or need" I hold my hand up to stop Freya objecting "that's an order not a request" I say sternly "you need a decent coat, plus get some more jumpers and cardigans as well"

"Yes ma'am" Freya mimics an American accent making me laugh.

"Now the next part of my proposal you're not going to like" Freya's smile slips "you need to go back to your house to get your passport, birth certificate and any other important documents or valuable personal items you'll need" Freya looks frightened, in fact she's trembling. I clear the bed of clothes dumping them in the cases "come on in you get" I say softly "now Alan is going to be with you at all times, he won't let anything happen to you. He's there to protect you, understand?" Freya nods "after tomorrow you'll never go back there again so it's imperative you get those essential things. Everything else leave behind, it can be replaced. The less time spent in the house the better"

"I understand, fortunately I have all those documents hidden in one place" Freya smiles pleased with herself "but I don't have a key to get in"

"Don't worry about that, let's just say Alan has some rather questionable skills" I wink and tap the side of my nose "when you're finished at the house, you'll come and join me in Dove Mill village as from tomorrow we're staying at The Coach House until Sunday at least whilst I get the ball rolling on the renovations for the Hall and cottages. Now, what questions do you have for me?"

Freya leans over and picks up a note book off the side table, tears off five sheets and waves them at me. I can see they're filled. I smile, it pleases me that she really has been giving her new role a lot of thought.

"But first I want to know, if Adam is there tomorrow what will happen if he starts on me?" I hear the apprehension in her voice.

"I could be mean and say what would you like to happen but I won't put you in that position" I smile menacingly "I have given Alan my full permission to break the bastard's neck and give him a kicking he's not going to forget in a hurry. That's what I would do if I was there hence the reason why I'm not going to be with you" Freya looks at me in disbelief "I might be small but I know how to put someone down three, four times the size of me. I spar daily with Paul and Alan, when we get to New York I'll introduce you to Phillipee my other sparring partner but I digress. If Adam starts then Alan will put him down, minus the broken neck"

"Good" Freya says with conviction. She picks up her list of questions but something occurs to me.

"Before you start" I point to the list "I take it your house is rented" Freya nods "if you've not thought about it then I suggest you contact the landlord and notify them you've left, also do the same with your utility providers if any of the bills are in your name. Likewise close all your bank accounts. We'll open another one at my bank"

"Christ I hadn't thought about any of that, thank you" Freya opens the note book and starts to make a list "oh did you manage to speak to my boss, I mean my old employer?"

"Yes, I did. He was sorry to hear you were ill. I don't think he believed me and he was speechless when I told him you wouldn't be coming back. He asked if you could ring him when you were feeling better"

"I'll ring him tomorrow" Freya says thoughtfully "he is a complete and utter twat but he's always been kind to me. Actually, would you mind if I went in to see him?"

"Not at all, just tell Alan where to take you" getting off the bed I gesture to her forgotten list in her hands "fire away with the first question"

"You mentioned you travel a lot with your work, will I need work permits or visas?" Freya reads from her list.

"Good question" I say picking up the clothes I'd dumped in the cases, folding them neatly I answer her questions. The majority are business related and a few personal ones thrown in for good measure. I think I'm honest, open and candid in my replies. Freya's growing confidence, assertiveness and enthusiasm certainly makes me think I made the right decision in offering her a job and it wasn't made out of pity for her dire situation.

"Final question, promise" Freya smiles "tell me the kind of things your last assistant, Macy?" I nod "did for you that wasn't in her job description"

"Bloody hell, now you're asking!" I bark out a laugh and sit beside her on the bed "she did a lot of things. She was like a big sister to me and she looked after me like a sister would"

"You miss her a lot, I can see" says Freya softly, taking hold of my hand.

"I do" I take a deep breath to hold back the tears that threaten to fall "I treated her like a sister and friend, she always kept reminding me she was an employee. I kept reminding her that I paid my best friends for their services I used and she was no different. She protected me from the day to day noise so I could concentrate on my main business. When I work on commissions I lose all track of time, I forget to eat and drink, sleep even. Macy would take it on herself to make sure I ate and when she thought I had been working for too long she would prize the pencil or paint brush out of my hand and frog march me to bed. God, I've lost count of how many times she did that" I smile fondly at the memories that flit through my mind "she was also Paul's wife"

Freya sucks in a sharp breath and slowly lets it out "Were they together long?" she asks tentatively.

"Kind of, I suppose" I frown, what do you class as a long time "Macy was working for me before Paul joined me. They would have been married four years next month and I know they hooked up for a couple of years but they never made their relationship public knowledge. Paul has a son, Jack, from his previous marriage who you'll get to meet, he treated Macy like a Mom. Even called her that too"

"It must have been awful for you, losing two people you love dearly at the same time. I can't even begin to imagine what it must be like" whispers Freya.

"Yeah, I did lose it for a while but I have a small group of supportive friends who love me unconditionally and put up with any crap I throw at them, within reason"

"I hope, if it's not too presumptuous, that in time I will be included in that small group" Freya gives a tentative smile "I really appreciate the opportunity you have given me Skye. You saved my life and I pray that I won't let you down"

"I know you won't and I know you'll be good at it. I already have a really good feeling about you being on board" I squeeze her hand "one other thing that I've just thought of you'll need to add to your list of things to do tomorrow. Call your family and tell them everything that's happened, you'll probably be surprised at how supportive and understanding they are. We'll make arrangements to visit them before we leave the country" Freya's eyes widen in surprise "now that dickhead is out of your life you've no reason not to reach out to them"

A knock on the door and a nurse coming in cuts short our conversation "Visiting time is over I'm afraid" she says apologetically. I nod and stand.

"Get a good night's sleep. Alan will be here around ten and I'll see you later in the day. Goodnight"

"Goodnight" Freya waves as I head out the door.

"How is she?" asks Paul

"A lot better, still quite sore though but she's going to be alright" I smile "she looking forward to starting her new life and job. Oh that reminds me Alan, Freya was talking about going to see her old boss she'll let you know where to take her" Alan nods "I also told her you have my permission to break that dickhead of an ex-boyfriend's neck should he start anything when you go to the house tomorrow since I can't be there to do it personally" Alan's deep rumbling menacing laugh tells me everything I need to know.

Climbing into the SUV my phone rings, by the time I fight to get it out of my pocket it's rung off. The missed call is from Tobias. I smile as he's maintaining our promise of keeping in touch, he rang me yesterday and I feel slightly guilty of not making the first move today. I hit the call button, he picks up on the first ring.

"Skye, thank you for calling me back" I hear the warm pleased tone in the brisk words.

"I couldn't get my phone out of my pocket quick enough" I laugh "how are you?"

"I'm good" he chuckles "how's your day been?"

I fill him in telling him about the Hall and cottages, I briefly mention Freya and how I'll be staying in Dove Mill village for the rest of the week. In turn Tobias tells me about his day.

"Actually, I have a favour to ask" he clears his throat nervously. Here we go, it didn't take him long to get the begging bowl out, my snide side quips "I've been invited to a dinner party on Wednesday and I wondered if you would do me the honour of being my plus one, if you're free that is" wow! I wasn't expecting that "I should also add that the dinner party is in Dove Mill"

"Really!" I can't hide my surprise "If I accept it's not going to cause any problems between you and Gabrielle is it?"

"There is no me and Gabrielle, there never has been" Tobias sounds so adamant I believe him.

"In that case I'd love to go as you're plus one"

"Excellent, I'll call you tomorrow morning with the details. I'll let you go now, enjoy the rest of your evening my dear"

"You too, goodnight Tobias" I hang up.

CALEB

This was a bad idea, although it sounded good at the time, in practise it's not working for me. This tosser is supposed to be showing me how much he wants to be a better Dom and all he's doing is tickling her with the flogger. The gentle sound of thwacking fills the room. Lyndsey, one of the staff Sub's is stood facing the wall, her hands cuffed to each arm of the

St Andrews cross, she's bent forward slightly so her arse juts out giving the men watching a good view. With a sigh I push myself off the wall.

"Okay, stop Austin" I call out; the wannabe Dom immediately obeys by stepping back.

I walk over to Lyndsey. I run my hand down her back and over her arse, the skin isn't even warm. From the length of time Austin has been flogging her, the skin should be warm and a nice rosy pink. I don't need to put my hand between her legs to see how turned on she is, or not in this case. Suddenly in my mind's eye my hands are running over a tiny waist, slim hips and the nice tight round arse of my Wild Kitten. She's arching into my touch, making that sexy as fuck low throaty moan. My dick finally decides to get with the programme and is instantly hard. Concentrate and focus on the lesson you idiot. I take the flogger from Austin and turn to address the group of five men.

"When you use this kind of flogger and for the length of time Austin has used it, you should be able to see a nice rosy pinkness to your subs skin" I don't point out the obvious "when you work with a new sub, like in this case, you need to gage their tolerance or likeness for pain. So here's a tip when you do your first session together, have your sub tell you. Lyndsey" she lifts her head turning her blindfolded eyes in the direction of my voice "I want you to answer my questions honestly, there will be no repercussions, understand?"

"Yes Master Raven" Lyndsey says with confidence.

"Did the flogging hurt you, cause you any discomfort or pain?"

"No, Master Raven"

"Tell me how it felt"

"It... it tickled" I hear the slight uncertainty in her voice.

"Did it give you any pleasure?"

"No Master Raven" she whispers with a cringe.

I lean close to her "It's okay, thank you for your honesty. Are you up to receiving some pain?" I murmur.

Her breath catches "Yes Master Raven" her voice is a breathy whisper; she trembles with anticipation.

I chuckle as I straighten. Lyndsey is the ideal Sub to train new Dom's. I had watched Rex put her through a rigorous session yesterday when we short listed Subs volunteering their services to help with the mentoring programme. She outshone them all and lasted the longest. It also helps she's a true masochist.

"You are all familiar with the meaning of the red, yellow, green safe words" the men all nod "we are going to use these with the following meaning attached. Lyndsey"

"Yes Master Raven"

"Each time Austin strikes you I want you to use green if you want him to strike harder. Yellow if the strike is right for you and you want him to continue with that level of force. Red means he's hitting too hard but you want him to continue. Do you understand?"

"Yes Master Raven" Lyndsey says with a sure voice.

"What is your safe word?"

"Candyfloss, Master Raven"

I smile, I'd love to know how she came up with that one "Use your safe word if you want to stop completely. Repeat back the meaning of each colour"

Lyndsey dutifully repeats back the meanings, I look at Austin "You repeat the meanings and add Lyndsey's safe word" Austin repeats them "excellent, now everyone is clear. The guidelines have been set so we can commence. As you know you can use any words you wish during the session but it is important that each party understands the meanings so your play remains safe and consensual"

I move over and stand next to Austin "Now, I'm going to show you how to strike using the flogger so that it causes pain, without bruising, that turns to pleasure. Lyndsey I want you to be vocal" Lyndsey nods her head "gentlemen I want you to hear as well as see how turned on Lyndsey becomes by the force of the strikes applied. In time you will able to judge these things with your sub being quiet as you'll be reading how her body responds. For the purpose of this session, pay attention to both. Any questions before we begin?" all I see are eager grinning faces as they shake their heads.

I stand and demonstrate the moves, how to flick the wrist, control the movement of the arm and how to put power into the strike without causing yourself or the sub any injury. I hand the flogger back to Austin, then position myself behind him. Lyndsey sensing movement, tenses.

"Start with the light strikes first to warm up the skin" I instruct. Austin does this for a few minutes "Lyndsey on the next strike I want you to start using the colours" she nods her head.

I take hold of Austin's hand gripping the flogger "Relax your arm and hand. I want you to feel the amount of power I use so you can replicate it on your own, understand"

"Yes Sir"

Jesus the guys is already excited and we haven't even started yet. I swing my arm back and flick my wrist with no real power, the resounding thwack already indicates I've struck harder.

"Green" Lyndsey's body responds by arching. Instantly I'm transported back to the train and I've got my riding crop in my hand. Concentrate.

With each strike I increase the force and it's not long before Lyndsey is groaning "Yellow". I release Austin and step back, letting him continue. He does well. Discreetly I check the time, ten minutes to go. After five minutes I call a stop.

"Well done Austin. Now feel how turned on she is"

Austin steps forward and puts his hand between her legs "She's soaking" Lyndsey's head falls back, letting out a low moan of pleasure as Austin continues to massage her sex and clit. He looks at me hopeful.

"Would you like to come Lyndsey?"

"Yes Master Raven, please" she moans.

I look at Austin "She is your sub for this session, reward her as you see fit, then see to her aftercare" Austin has his pants undone and round his knees before I finish speaking "gentlemen on the next session we will discuss your thoughts on the correlation between what you heard and saw. Enjoy the rest of your evening"

I leave the private room with the sound of Lyndsey and Austin's orgasms ringing in my ears. I collect my coat from the cloakroom and I'm out the front door before anyone can collar me asking stupid questions about how the first mentoring lesson went. I need fresh air and a beer.

The cold early evening air clears my head as I quickly get in my dilapidated Land Rover. I wind the window down, being the outdoorsy type I prefer the cold to hot or warm stuffy places. I understand the heating needs to be on in the Club but sometimes I find it too stifling. My thoughts turn to the session, it got better. Reflecting back, I make mental notes of how to run future sessions. What didn't work and how things could be changed to make it work. What worked and how could it be made better. I also make a note to get feedback from the mentees. In a few weeks the mentees will be asked to select a mentor they wish to work with on a one to one basis. Likewise, each mentor will select a mentee from the requests. I've got a feeling I'm going to be inundated considering each of my sessions are fully booked with a waiting list as long as Harry's arm.

My phone going off makes me jump "Fuck" I curse clutching my chest, I pull my phone out of my jacket pocket and hit the speaker button "Hello" I can hear distorted voices and music in the background. Someone has butt dialled me "Hello" I shout.

"Caleb, can you hear me" Rex's voice shouts back.

"Yes, I can hear you" the background noise disappears.

"That's better" I hear a door shut "it's fucking crazy in there. Where are you?" his words slur slightly.

"Heading home back from the club" I look at the passing road sign "I'm about half an hour away. Why?"

"Shit, I forgot you had your first session tonight, how'd it go? No don't answer, just get back here quick as you can. I've got loads to tell you" Rex hung up.

"Jerk" I mutter under my breath but I put my foot down and my clapped out Land Rover grumbles as I ask her to pick up speed.

Twenty minutes later I walk in through the front door of the pub to be met by a wall of bodies. Fucking hell, the place is never this packed on a Monday night, certainly not at nine o' clock. Pushing my way to the bar I pick up snippets of excited babble.

"No it was the GL350 model, I saw it with my own eyes. It was huge"

"Yes, two men and a woman"

"We think they're the same ones that came yesterday on the motorbikes"

"None of them are called Blake, but both men are American"

I spot Chris sat at the end of the bar, he looks six sheets to the wind. So it appears our mystery visitors have been again today and it's Chris's turn to get the free drinks. I smile and wave to him, he gestures for me to come over. Rex appears next to him.

"Buddy" Rex yells when he sees me "mate have we got some juicy news for you" he waves his beer bottle in the air, his face is red and shiny with a huge grin.

"Well I've sussed out our three mystery visitors have been round again" I laugh at Rex's face, I've stolen his thunder "go on fill me in" I nod my thanks to Michelle when a bottle of Corona lands in front of me, she walks off before I can pay for it. Puzzled I look at Chris.

"First drink is on the house" he slurs cheerfully.

"Business that good" I raise an eyebrow.

"And going to get even better, at least until Sunday" Chris sways on his stool "our mystery guests are back tomorrow morning and will be staying here" he flings his arm out, narrowly missing Rex's face "all thanks to Lady Farringdon recommending us" Chris looks so happy I can't help but smile with him.

"How did that come about?" my curiosity is well and truly piqued.

"The woman is called Skye Darcy, she was sat over there" Chris points in the general direction of the seating area not far from the fireplace "she overheard him, Will and Bill talking about the book being run on her and her companions" I burst out laughing.

"And yes it has screwed up the betting" Will's put on pissed off voice comes from behind me, I laugh even harder at that.

"I apologised to her for their bad language. She said she was okay with it and wouldn't mind having a bet herself" Chris is chuckling to himself, I get the sneaky suspicion there's more to that than he's letting on "she knew who I was and mentioned Lady Farringdon had told her we had rooms available. She booked four and she'll be using this place as a base, for meetings and the like" Chris waves his hand in a come closer motion, we all lean in "where the pool table is, she'll be taking over that section all Friday afternoon for some big meeting" Chris taps the side of his nose indicating that it's a big secret, not that it'll stay that way for long now he's let the cat out of the bag.

"The two guys are American" Rex says picking up the thread "big bastards, I'll tell you. From the descriptions one of them is definitely the guy that went into the mini supermarket yesterday"

"That's Alan Parker" Chris says giving a knowing nod "the other one is Paul Boyd, both of them will be staying here"

"So who's the fourth person?" that stumps them, I look at the confused and puzzled faces "you said she's booked four rooms?"

"Come to think of it she didn't mention another name" the wrinkles on Chris's forehead get deeper "guess we'll find out tomorrow"

"Maybe that's Mrs Blake" says Will eagerly. Chris opens his mouth to say something but quickly closes it again. He definitely knows something and for whatever reason he's keeping tight-lipped.

"Good job you thought to freshen those rooms up on Sunday" I wink at Michelle as she places more drinks in front of us.

"That's all it was" Michelle rolls her eyes at her husband "guess what I've been doing all afternoon whilst he's been getting pissed" she holds up her hands. Her usually manicured painted long nails are cut short with chipped nail varnish.

"You know I will make it up to you my love" Chris blows her a sloppy wet kiss. I bite the inside of my cheek to stop laughing. I hear Rex and Will sniggering behind me. We all know not to get on the wrong side of Michelle.

"Don't worry you most definitely will" Michelle retorts but she smiles fondly at her husband before heading off down the opposite end of the bar.

"That's going to hurt your bank balance" Rex openly laughs now Michelle is out of ear shot.

"My darling wife is worth every penny" he blows her a kiss again. He's well and truly drunk. Michelle waves her arm as if to bat away the incoming kiss.

"So what did you think of this… Skye Darcy, it sounds like she has a sense of humour" I put the question out to the three of them.

"Oh she does" Chris chuckles "I took an instant liking to her and she's very beautiful"

"She's fucking stunning you mean" Rex and Will chorus together "she's a natural beauty, not a stitch of make up on her face" adds Will.

"Mascara" says Chris "that's the only make up she wore"

"White blonde curly hair down to her waist, big tits" says Rex. My heart is thumping in my chest he's describing Kitten, my wild kitten has a name Skye Darcy "big full lips, not as big as Angelina Jolie's but not far off and she's petite" Rex's eyes widen as he looks at me "do you remember…"

"Yes I do" I cut him off sharply.

Rex has the good graces to look sorry for his near blunder. I'm not having him blurt out the description of my fantasy ideal woman. Only she isn't a fantasy any more, she's flesh and blood. She has a name and she's mine.

'Get real, you've seen each other twice' my conscious sneers 'First time was a couple of hours spent having incredible sex, the other was a couple of minutes kissing the life out of each other. Yesterday you were hopeful it was her when you heard the descriptions of the mystery visitors. How can you claim her as yours when you've only just found out her name?'

There is definitely an attraction to each other. For Christ's sake I felt it on both occasions. This 'thing' chemistry, connection whatever the fuck you want to call it is triggering all kinds of possessive shit inside me. A thought flitters through my mind but it's gone before I can make sense of it.

"Has anyone managed to speak to the Farringdon's yet?" Will's question snaps me out of my thoughts.

"As far as I know they've not returned anyone's call" says Rex pulling out his phone, he frowns at it as if wondering why it's not ringing "hey Caleb, ring Bertie, he'll pick up if you call"

I shake my head "Oh no! I'm not getting dragged in to the gossip, rumour mill. As much fun it is to hear it. I'm not chasing it, besides it's late and I'm heading home to bed"

I say goodnight as my friend's protest to stay for one more drink but I decline. If I do stay I won't be getting up at the crack of dawn to see to the horses. Being responsible and not drink driving I decide to leave the car and walk home. All the way I conjure up different fantasies of how I can run into my wild kitten, my Skye Darcy. I say her name out loud, my body stirs in response. Christ I'm going to be a walking hard on if I keep this up.

As I fall asleep the image of Lyndsey shackled to the St Andrews cross comes to mind. The image shifts and morphs until it's Skye stood shackled to the cross. Her long blonde hair falling over her arched back, her pert tight arse thrusting out and her pussy wet with need for me. I sigh deeply, letting the fantasy play out.

CHAPTER THIRTEEN

SKYE

Where am I and what day is it? My brain is mush as I open my eyes and look around the unfamiliar room. It's been a long time since I've had to work that out. I yawn and stretch. One thing I do know is this bed is bloody comfortable and I've had a good night's sleep, I roll over. "Shit!" Startled I scramble and just manage to stop myself falling out and face planting the floor. The jolt and shock wakes me up. Laughing at myself I sit up. I'm in a single bed. The Coach House. I suddenly remember.

"Just goes to show I how used I am to being in a humongous bed" I mutter as I untangle myself from the bed sheets and get out.

The room is compact, comfortable and practical. The bedding, wallpaper and curtains match, it's like being in the middle of a meadow in the height of summer with the explosion of wild flowers covering every surface. I go to the sink in the corner of the room to wash and clean my teeth. When we arrived yesterday Chris and Michelle couldn't apologise enough for us having to share the bathroom and toilet that's situated at the end of the hallway.

I volunteered to take the smallest room. Paul and Alan only conceded when I pointed out neither of them would fit in the bed. Freya was too tired to put up any argument. I didn't push her for information about her day, she'll tell me in her own time. All Alan would say is that dickhead ex-boyfriend got a smack and he would let Freya do the honours in regaling the story.

I put my jogging pants and hoodie on deciding to go for a brisk early morning walk. It's been a while since I did any form of exercise and I'm feeling it both mentally and physically, mind you I did have a good workout on the train the other day, my whole body tightens. I smile at the memories of our athletic prowess. I don't feel as guilty now.

I look out the small window to see a clear blue sky, the sun just peaking over the hills in the distance. Signs of life can be seen dotted around the village green as people begin their day. Walking down the hallway I marvel at the amount of character this building has. The floor is uneven and creeks like mad, the walls bow in and out in places, the wooden beams have dents and small holes in them. I absolutely love this place. Chris told me the history of the building last night as we sat in their dining room eating dinner.

The Coach House first started trading for business in sixteen eighty-five, this particular building was erected in place of the original when it burnt down in seventeen twenty-nine. Chris and Michelle have been licensee for nearly twenty years. "At least we're no longer treated as outsiders" joked Michelle.

Chris and Michelle have really made us all feel welcome and opened their home up to us. After dinner we sat in the lounge chilling out and watched TV. If we disappointed the regulars and gossips by not putting in an appearance Chris and Michelle kept it to themselves. I know they had a busy night because we could hear the muted noise filtering through the floor. They also know how to keep their mouths shut, I expected questions about Freya and her injuries but they kept quiet that's not to say that they aren't curious, they are. I could see it in the side long looks or when they thought no one was watching they studied Freya's face.

Making my way down the rickety creaking stairs voices drift up to me through the open door at the bottom. Hearing what's being discussed I slow down and creep the rest of the way. You'll go to hell for eavesdropping, I admonish myself. I feel a twinge of guilt then shove it aside, I'm already on my way there anyway.

"Why didn't you tell me sooner?" I recognise Michelle's voice, it's full of hurt. Please don't say he's having an affair, they seem such a solid couple.

"I'm sorry my love. I did intend to tell you but with all of the excitement of our visitors. I just couldn't bring myself to burst our bubble of happiness" Chris replies. He's full of genuine remorse.

"How long have the brewery given us?" Michelle sighs in resignation.

I inch towards the door and peer round it. Michelle is stood in the pub's kitchen leaning against the fridge. Chris is stood facing her holding a letter in his hands.

"It says they are giving us the option to buy the building and we have four weeks to come up with the money. If we don't take them up on their offer they'll be closing us down and selling the building" Chris paraphrases.

"We'll never find that kind of money in time" Michelle wails, throwing her arms up in the air "no bank is going to give us a business loan. We've barely been making enough to live off for the last eighteen months"

Michelle drops her head into her hands. Chris wraps his arms around her. If it wasn't for their distressing news it would make a touching scene. Michelle lifts her head "the only thing that is saving us this month is that we have guests staying and all this business over Dove Mill Hall has gripped the villager's imagination so they're flocking here every night for the latest snippet of gossip"

"I know my love, I know" Chris murmurs and places a kiss on her forehead.

My heart goes out to them. I'm saddened at their news; this truly is a beautiful building it seems such as shame that what appears to be a place at the heart of the community is going to be ripped away. I have to do something. Before I can put my brain in gear I step into the kitchen, tentatively knocking on the door to get their attention.

"Sorry, I don't mean to intrude" I apologise as Chris and Michelle break apart startled "I couldn't help over hearing what you were saying. May I?" I gesture to the letter in Chris's hands.

He's too shocked to do anything but hand over the letter. I smile and read. Yep, Chris and Michelle are about to lose their home and livelihood. An idea occurs to me.

"If you owned this building and had free reign to do what you wished with the business what would you do?" I put the question to both of them.

"What's the point, we'll never have the money to do what we want?" says Michelle, she can't keep the antagonism and frustration out of her voice.

"Humour me" I smile at them "forget about the money for a moment, just imagine six months from now, you've got the business running as you want. Describe to me what it looks like?"

"Well the pub is a free house with guest ales" Chris starts tentatively "Michelle is running the kitchen and serving the kind of food we've always dreamed of. We have a separate eating area. Outside in the beer garden we have a family come children's play area, along with a barbeque area" Chris is getting into his stride, his eyes glow with enthusiasm and passion.

"We have upgraded and converted all the rooms into decent bedrooms and run a bed and breakfast offering weekend and midweek breaks" Michelle adds, mirroring Chris's enthusiasm "the courtyard and barn are renovated and used for weddings and other functions"

Their vision for the business has me feeling excited at the possibilities "Will you show me around the rest of the building?"

Chris and Michelle look at each other and shrug "Sure" says Chris "this way"

The place is huge. The pub and the area we are staying in is like the tip of an ice burg. The areas that are not in use do need a lot of work. I listen carefully to everything they say as they show me the changes they would make and why. I'm thrilled that they share the same vision and dream. When we get to the courtyard I realise it's the cobbled entrance that I had seen on Sunday. When Michelle describes how she plans to use it and the restoration, I'm sold.

"How would you market the place and what sort of promotions would you do to attract your target customers?" I drag my eyes from the courtyard to see two identical frowns, their faces are filled with uncertainty.

"We've never thought about that" Chris admits sheepishly, Michelle shrugs and shakes her head.

"Don't worry about it" I wave dismissively, I gaze around the courtyard imaging a wedding taking place "I have a proposition for you to consider" I turn back to face them "I'll buy this place and put up the money for all the renovations and alterations. We form a partnership or create a company, either way I will be a silent partner. A very silent partner" I reiterate "you two get free reign on how this place is run. My only caveat is that I put the marketing plan together and I have a say on the interior design of the bedrooms"

Chris and Michelle are motionless, their expressions identical, wide eyes and jaws unhinged "I realise this has come as a big shock to you and I don't expect an answer straight away. Discuss it and let me know your thoughts, my offer isn't set in stone and I'm willing to… negotiate terms. Although that would be done anyway when the paper work is drawn up" I smile at them.

Chris recovers first "Are you serious, I mean this isn't a wind up is it?" he looks around as if expecting to see a film crew to suddenly materialise out of nowhere.

"I'm deadly serious" I confirm.

"And you can afford it?" Michelle's voice comes out like a squeak.

"Yes I can afford it?" I smile at her.

"Of course she can afford it, she's a…" Chris blushes and clears his throat, he shuffles his feet. Michelle slaps her husband's arm at his almost faux pas "I'm sorry I didn't mean to be offensive" he mumbles.

"Hey don't fret. You can say it. I'm a billionaire and a multiple one at that" I laugh "anyway as I said, have a think about it, for as long as you want. I won't be offended if you decide to get funding elsewhere. This is a beautiful building and I would hate to see it disappear, plus I truly believe in your vision for the place"

"Can you give us a minute?" says Michelle.

I nod and walk away towards the archway. Village life has started with a vengeance, the mini supermarket is busy with people calling in picking up newspapers, milk, bread and other small items for breakfast and the morning cuppa. A few doors down I notice a café filled with a mix of clientele, some look to be office workers' others in manual trade. The hardware store, someone is bringing out an assortment of items and arranging a display of every day household items. There appears to be a book store, it has other items in the window I can't make out as it's still in darkness along with the boutiques on either side of it.

The clip clopping sound of multiple horse hooves, has me moving further out into the street trying to locate them. I spot them as they enter from the direction of the church. My heart does a funny flip flop and drops to my stomach. I feel giddy and my lower stomach muscles clench. I suddenly realise my body is reacting at the mere possibility of seeing Caleb again.

"We have made our decision" Chris's voice startles me "sorry. We would like to accept your offer"

"Yay!" I clap my hands in joy and hug them both, they laugh at my enthusiasm.

"So what happens now?" Michelle askes timidly.

"First breakfast" right on cue my stomach growls "can't discuss business on an empty stomach" I say patting my flat tummy.

"I need to go to the shop. I didn't have chance yesterday to buy things in for breakfast" says Michelle apologetically.

"I'll come with you and help" I volunteer as Chris hands a wad of cash over to Michelle. I take my phone out and send a text to Paul on my whereabouts.

"Good idea, you can show me what kind of things you like to eat" Michelle surprises me, I was expecting to rebuff her 'no its okay, not necessary' comment.

We set off to the mini supermarket cutting across the green. The two horse riders are dismounting one heads into the shop whilst the other leads four horses on to the green. Neither of them has long jet black hair nor are they broad and tall enough. The stab of disappointment surprises me. I wasn't aware of how much I was looking forward to seeing him again. I wonder if I'll have the same reaction towards him as last time. *Of course you bloody will. You were creaming your knickers just at the thought of seeing him a few moments ago.*

"What have you done that's made you so rich?" Michelle blurts out "I'm sorry, I didn't mean for it to come out like that. Curiosity makes my mouth disengage from my brain"

"Ha! I like you, I really do" I chuckle, Michelle blushes "I'm an artist and my work is in high demand. I do private commissions and businesses hire me. Due to some shrewd business decisions on my part when I first started out over ten years ago, I receive royalty payments on certain products, mostly video games. These games have turned out to be the biggest selling games of all time and continue to be. And I have a number of other business interests" I shrug "then six years ago I inherited over a billion and a half pounds from my grandfather. I take it Chris told you about my husband?" Michelle nods "he left the bulk of his fortune to me, including his business. In the time we had been together I helped him triple his money" I give a derisive laugh "even without my husband and grandfather's money I would still be a billionaire. Some people say I have the Midas touch when it comes to business" I wiggle my fingers.

"Let's hope that magic rubs off on us" Michelle laughs and winks.

As we near the horses, they lift their heads as we approach. They are magnificent animals. I'm not big on horse breeds but these look to be Thoroughbreds. A chestnut coloured one breaks rank and walks over to us.

"Hey big fella, aren't you gorgeous" I croon. The horse stops and lowers its head allowing me to stroke his nose. I move round and pat his neck and pull his ear. The horse leans into me for more.

"He really likes you" Michelle laughs "you're braver than I am"

I take hold of his reigns "Come on let's get you back with the others" I make a clicking noise and the horse follows "it's down to not letting the horse pick up on your nerves. Just like it would be with any animal really"

"Oh my god, I'm so sorry Michelle" a red faced harassed looking woman rushes towards us, I guess her to be mid-twenties "he's a bugger for wandering off. I hope he didn't scare you. He's a big softie truly he is"

"I'm fine Sally, although he has taken a liking to Skye" Michelle points at me, the girl stops dead in her tracks, her red face turns white.

"He's beautiful, what's his name?" I smile at the woman.

"He's called Wonderwall, after the Oasis song" a slim built man of a similar age with messy sandy hair and a cheeky grin says coming up behind the woman "I'm Marty, this is Sally" he holds out his hand "you must be Skye Darcy"

I laugh "Yes I am" I shake his hand. Sally is still rooted to the spot.

"Wonderwall should be named Wander Off" he laughs as I hand the reigns over to him "you're obviously used to being around horses"

"I am. I have two of my own, really it would be more accurate to say one and a half since one is a miniature" I stroke and pat the other horses as they surround us.

"How often do you ride?" Marty seems genuinely interested.

"I don't" I laugh at the confused look on his face "I own horses but I've never even sat on one. It's one of those things I've never got round to learning, but I would love to do it"

"Sally runs the horse riding lessons we offer at the stables" Marty points a thumb in Sally's direction, she nods mutely "next lessons are on Friday if you'd like try" he grins wickedly, challenging me. I take the bait.

"I can't do Friday, what about Saturday?"

"S-s-Saturday's good. It'll have to be a private lesson" Sally stammers.

"Excellent, actually do you offer stabling?" I direct the question at Sally, for some reason she's terrified of me. I get a mute nod "would it be okay if I call up this afternoon to have a look around, say about three?"

Marty and Sally look at each other. I see the subtle shrug and nod Marty gives "S-s-sure" Sally's voice is a high quiver.

"How do I find the stables?"

"Take the left fork when you get to the church, about half a mile down the lane you'll see a big sign saying Dove Mill Horse Training and Stables on your left, you can't miss it" Marty says cheerfully.

"Great I'll see you then. Nice meeting you both" I smile and give each of the horses a pat.

I follow Michelle around the shop carrying the basket much to the surprise of the other customers. We both smile and say good morning but don't stop to chat. I add extras as we pick up the ingredients to cook a traditional Full English breakfast. Partway round Paul turns up, taking the basket off me he gives me a half-hearted glare.

"At least I texted you" I smile sweetly at him. Paul snorts in response and shakes his head.

"What would you like for dinner tonight?" Michelle asks looking at both of us.

"I don't mind. What do you fancy Paul?"

"You won't be here?"

"I won't" I sound as confused as I must look. Paul raises an eyebrow at me.

"You have a dinner party to attend" he reminds me.

"Crap! Is it Wednesday?" Michelle and Paul both smile and nod slowly "bloody hell, I got up thinking it was Tuesday" god I could kick myself "sorry Michelle, I do have a dinner party but the others will still need feeding"

"No problem" Michelle picks up a pack of steak, holding it up to Paul who gives her a dazzling smile. Michelle blushes "whose dinner party is it? If you don't mind me asking"

I pull out my phone and search for the text Tobias sent me "Someone who lives round here apparently so I don't have far to go, here it is… Mrs Simone Fawcett-Fowler. Do you know her?"

"Oh you poor love" Michelle chuckles.

"Aw crap! That sounds ominous" I groan "tell me, what she like?"

"I'm surprised she's managed to bag you for a dinner party so soon" Michelle's grin is positively evil.

"She doesn't know I'm going. I got invited as someone else's plus one at short notice. Dish the dirt, all of it" I look at her expectantly.

"Simone is best described as a social climber. She doesn't give us common folk the time of day unless she's after something. She and her husband Fred, moved here about ten years ago. He's got something to do with investments. Fred is lovely by the way, down to earth. Simone however plays at being posh, from what I've heard she grew up on a council estate in a rough part of London, Elephant and Castle I think, that's the gossip anyway. She worked as a cleaner in Fred's office, that's how she met him. She is on every committee the village has plus a number of ones that are based in Henley. And she likes to be seen doing things for charity and good causes which wouldn't be so bad if she didn't bully people into giving. Hence the reason she's not very popular, most people run and hide when they see her walking down the street"

Michelle stops talking whilst we queue and pay for the groceries, too many ears, picking up again as we head back to the pub "Chances are the Farringdon's will be there along with Lord Baxter, stay away from him he's known as Lord Broke, behind his back of course. Rumour has it he's on the hunt for a rich wife" Michelle snorts giving me a sideways glance.

"Duly noted and thanks. Who else is likely to be there?" I'm intrigued and fascinated.

"Knowing Simone she'll only have invited the titled, rich and highly influential people. Without a shadow of a doubt there will be some of Fred's business associates and their partners. As for other locals possibly Remington Davies, known as Rex. He's the local playboy and womaniser, if he's not taking a woman as his plus one then my guess is he'll take Caleb Raven, his best friend. Sally and Marty who you met earlier, Caleb's their boss" my heart thumps in my chest and my stomach somersaults, thankfully I keep walking without missing a step "the only other possible guests would be any of the celebrities that live around here and if they can be bothered to make the trip up from London"

"The invite says smart casual, so I'm guessing it'll be anything but casual?"

"You catch on quick"

"Bloody fucking hell" I mutter under my breath. Michelle gives me a sympathetic look as we enter the pub.

During breakfast Chris, Michelle and I thrash out the finer details of our working relationship, the majority of it is me giving them reassurances that I won't interfere with the day to day running of the place. Freya, without being asked, takes notes and offers suggestions on things to be included into the agreement that we will each sign. At the same time, I put calls in to the architect, surveyor and Elliot asking them to come over for this new project. All of them agree to come today, I give Michelle as the point of contact for when they arrive since I'll be out the majority of the day on other business. I even call Simon.

"If you are not a sex god Adonis begging to come over and shag me to death this better be good" his sleep filled voice grumbles down the phone.

"Doh! I forgot about the time difference" I laugh apologetically.

"Skye, is everything okay?" Simon is suddenly wide awake and alert.

"Yes, sorry for waking you but I have need of your services. How soon can you get to England? I would offer to send the plane but it'll be quicker taking a domestic flight" Freya, Chris and Michelle all look at me stunned when I say that.

"At a guess probably early tomorrow morning" I can hear Simon moving around.

"Text or email me when you know your flight number and arrival time. I'll send Alan to meet you" I look at Alan who nods.

"Oh you naughty evil woman, you know how to dangle the carrot to tempt me" Simon mock scolds "hang on a minute" I can hear the tapping on a keyboard "how long do you need me for?"

"We'll be flying back to New York on Tuesday if you want to come back with us, otherwise you can head back on Saturday or Sunday"

I stay quiet as Simon mutters to himself as he rearranges his diary.

"Right, if I can get on it, there's a flight that will get me into Heathrow tomorrow morning at eight and I'll come back with you on Tuesday. I'll text you to confirm in a few hours I've got a couple of meetings I need to move first. What's the job?"

"I'm buying a pub"

Simon roars laughing "You've been in England all of five minutes and already you're building your business empire"

"Bye Simon, I'll see you tomorrow" I grin as I hang up "we'll need another bed making up" I say to Michelle "Simon is one of my best friends and is a marketing and PR guru, he'll come up with the marketing strategy for the business"

"Jesus, you don't hang around do you" Chris chuckles. I wink at him.

Suddenly an idea occurs to me, I mentally kick myself for not thinking of it sooner. "Listen, I have someone you can talk to who will tell you honestly what it's like to work with me in a business partnership, his name is Matthew Butler" I scribble his number down on a piece of paper "he's in America, I'll send him your number and ask him to ring you. I put him in exactly the same situation as you almost six years ago and he's still working with me. How's that sound?"

Chris does the gold fish thing with his mouth.

"That sounds like a great idea" Michelle says frowning at her husband "give him my number, it's my night off tonight"

I send a text to Matthew asking him to contact Michelle, mentally calculating the time difference so he'll know when to call her, last thing I want to do is piss off my business partners by not being considerate about the time zones.

An hour later I've showered and changed clothes, deciding to wear a flowery shirt dress with knee length heeled boots, grabbing a cardigan I head off to find the others. They're in the living room. Paul and Alan are reading newspapers. Freya is on the phone. I sit down next to her on the sofa, she slides her note pad round so I can see it and taps at a word 'brewery'.

"Yes that's right… send all correspondence to me, Freya Bennett. I'll email my contact details to you shortly, what's your email address?" she makes a note using short hand. I'm impressed "thank you for your help, bye" Freya looks at me uncertainly, the bruises on her face are turning from purple to black and yellow in places "hope you don't mind but I thought I'd find out who to speak to at the Brewery about buying the pub, you know get the ball rolling"

"Excellent, good thinking batman" I like people taking the initiative, I look down at the battered note pad, she needs equipment "what have you got planned for today, no let me rephrase. Give me an update on where you're up to with sorting out the things we discussed on Monday"

Freya goes through each item on her list. The woman doesn't hang around, I can see we're going to get along just fine.

"I take it you got your passport yesterday" Freya nods "fantastic, now you'll need to apply for a visa waver. That can be done online. When we get to America we'll sort out getting a more permanent one. Which means we need to get you kitted out equipment wise. Alan" he looks up from his paper "when Freya has finished her other things take her into town to get a laptop, tablet" I look at the ancient mobile phone in her hand "and a new phone plus any stationery she needs. Go to London to get them if you have to. Get everything up and running, call Greg Milton if you can't get access to the servers"

"Yes ma'am"

I turn back to Freya to see tears rolling down her cheeks "Hey, what's the matter" I say softly, I take her hand in mine and rub the back of it. Paul and Alan get up and discretely leave us, cowards.

"I'm sorry" Freya blubbers wiping furiously at her eyes "you've done so much for me. I can't believe the amount of kindness and generosity you have already shown me. I'm not used to it. You'll never know how grateful I am, I can never thank you enough" she lets out a big shaky breath "I keep thinking this is all a dream and I'm going to wake up any second and I'll be back to my pathetic miserable existence"

"Don't go pinching yourself, you've got enough bruises as it is" Freya barks a watery laugh at my poor joke "tell me what happened yesterday maybe talking about that will convince you you're now living your dream. All Alan would say is that he gave dickhead a smack"

"Oh Skye, you should have seen it. Alan was amazing. When you said he was there to protect me and wouldn't let anything happen to me I thought you were speaking figuratively" I grin "I know better now" she snorts a derisive laugh.

"So come on, spill"

"Adam wasn't in when we got there. Alan… used his questionable skills to get us inside" she grins mischievously at me "just like you said I got the important things I needed first, I was in the kitchen making a note of account and telephone numbers for who I need to ring about moving out when Adam came home. He didn't see Alan, anyway Adam starts calling me his usual derogatory names only this time he adds whore and slut into the mix as he comes at me with his fist raised. Alan steps in front of me and says "That's no way to speak to a lady" Adam's face was a picture" Freya pulls a stupefied, gormless face "then he says "Who the fuck are you and what the fuck are you doing in my house?" Alan ever the gentlemen says politely "We'll be leaving shortly when Freya has everything she needs" Adam then decides to play tough guy; god knows why because Alan is twice the size of him. Adam made a grab for me, the next thing I know Alan had Adam by the throat pinned up against the wall, his feet off the floor. Alan says all menacingly "I don't want any trouble, but you ever lay a finger on her again I'll give you a taste of your own medicine. Now are you going to behave" Adam nods so Alan let him go but the stupid idiot decides to take a swing at Alan"

"Ooh!" I make a wincing face.

"Yeah!" Freya agrees "let's just say Adam will have one hell of a headache this morning along with a broken nose and possibly a rib or two as well"

"Was he conscious when you left?"

Freya nods "He was screaming that he was going to call the police. I said go ahead and I'll tell them you walked into the door or better yet you fell down the stairs. That shut him up" Freya says smugly then her smile slips becoming serious once more "you know for years I put up with his bullying, telling me I'm ugly, fat, stupid and useless that I was lucky to have him as no one would ever love me and I believed him. I still do" she finishes on a whisper. My heart goes out to her.

"What do you believe?"

"All of it" I see the pain and self-loathing in her eyes "I mean look at me" she gestures to herself.

"So what are you going to do about it?" my question shocks her "how badly do you want to change?"

"I... I... I" she gives up and looks blankly at me.

"Freya, you're not a victim anymore so stop playing one" I say softly "you are responsible for your own actions, thoughts and what comes out of your mouth. No one can make you do or say anything, sure they can threaten and intimidate you but it's your choice to submit or comply with their demands or not. To submit or comply usually means you fear the consequences. You are out of your negative and toxic environment so now you can change your thoughts and actions. Ask yourself this; from today, this minute, how much of what happens to you now is in your control? Then think about what isn't in your control and ask how much of that can you influence?"

I pause to let what I'm saying sink in "You can choose to be miserable and dwell on the past, think poor me or scream and shout, stamp your feet blame others for your problems and life choices or you can choose to be happy and focus on the future by taking control and responsibility. You can make it whatever you want, you can look however you want, all by simply changing how you think and behave"

Freya looks at me in admiration "You sound as if you're talking from personal experience"

"I am" I say solemnly "one day I'll tell you about it"

"Will you help me?" I smile and nod "I want to lose weight. I wish to be like you; I want to be beautiful like you"

"You know you should never compare yourself to other people, you may wish to be like them and they may appear to have it all but they may be miserable and lonely. This isn't all it's cracked up to be" I run a hand up and down my body "I get called plastic and Barbie by spiteful jealous women and men treat me like a bimbo, who openly leer and make crude remarks normally about finding out if my hair colour is natural"

"Oh my god!" squeals Freya "seriously!" I nod chuckling at her reaction "but I would love to one day walk in to a place and every man's head turn in my direction, following me as I walk past" she sighs wistfully.

"You're on. I will help you achieve that goal. Starting tomorrow morning before breakfast we will go out for a brisk walk and when we get to New York I will introduce you to Phillipee. The fitness training programme he creates for you, Paul and Alan will make sure you follow it when we're on the move. Up for the challenge?"

"Hell yes!" Freya holds her hand up for a high five.

CALEB

What the fuck has got into my staff? All morning and early afternoon they have been cleaning. The yard is so clean you could eat off the floor and they've pulled up all the weeds. The horses have been groomed to within an inch of their lives, their coats are so shiny you can see the reflection of your face. All tack although cleaned every day has been given an extra polish. The dogs haven't escaped the cleaning frenzy either, they've been bathed and brushed. Sally has even attacked my office, the cheeky sod turfed me out whilst she cleaned for a solid hour. I was too dumbstruck to ask her what the hell she's playing at. I can see the surface of my desk, I've not seen that for… I forget how long. Marty rushes past with a bucket and starts cleaning the outside windows. I get up determined to find out the reason for their frantic behaviour. I get to the door when my phone rings on the desk. I go back to answer it.

"Caleb, I need a huge favour" Rex greets me urgently.

"Whatever it is the answer is no"

"Ah mate! Don't be like that" he wines "come with me as my plus one for Simone Fawcett-Fowler's dinner party tonight"

"The answer is definitely no. I'd rather stick pins in my eyes than go to that" I laugh.

"Please. I'll owe you, please, please, say yes" he begs pitifully.

"Why don't you ring her and cancel?"

"I can't. I forgot all about it and I've just bumped into Fred. The crafty bastard tricked me into saying I was looking forward to tonight when he could tell I'd forgotten about the dinner party. I'm on my knees here mate, please come with me. I'll let you have first crack at the decent women there, fuck any of the women" if he was stood in front of me he'll be wiggling his eyebrows right now.

"Alright" I sigh heavily relenting to his pleas.

"I'll pick you up at seven. Its smart casual so no jeans" Rex hangs up before I can tell him I've changed my mind.

Cursing under my breath I head upstairs to dig out my suit and to see if I have a clean shirt. Riffling through my pathetic excuse of a wardrobe

I'm surprised to find that I have not one but three clean shirts and my suit has been dry cleaned. I begrudgingly send a mental thank you to Gabrielle, for all her faults one thing she was good at was making sure I had clean dress clothes. I hear the dogs start barking as a car pulls into the yard but I don't bother to look out of the window to see who it is.

Best try the suit on, see if it still fits. I strip out of my clothes and dump them in the wash basket. I know my body has changed over the last few months. My shoulders and arms are roped with muscles, my back, chest and abdomen are ripped. I'm leaner with more definition than I've ever had in my life. The jacket fits fine, it emphasises the width of my shoulders. The trousers are a little loose resting on my hips. I rummage around and find a belt. I look at the clock, ten past three. Sod it, I'll get a shower now.

Fifteen minutes later my nails are scrubbed clean, I've shaved and showered. I'm drying myself off when I hear my name being called. Wrapping a towel around my waist I open the bedroom door and lean out over the bannister looking down to see a flustered Sally at the foot of the stairs.

"What is it?" I say concerned.

"We have a visitor and you need to speak to her, now" Sally gives me a meaningful look and moves back into the living room come office, not giving me the chance to reply.

Fuck it, whoever they are can take me as they find me. I walk into the living room rubbing a towel over my head to dry my hair "How can I help you?"

"Caleb, this is Mrs Skye Darcy" Sally says in a strained voice.

"Miss or Ms, it's never been Mrs" says a husky voice followed by a throaty laugh.

My skin tingles and my cock twitches to life. The name registers in my brain, I whip the towel off my head and push my hair out of my face. My wild kitten is standing before me. Masses of white blonde curly hair surrounding her, shimmering like an angelic aura. Her amused yellow green eyes greedily travel up and down my body, my skin tightens feeling the caressing burn. A slow smile spreads across her luscious full lips, her pink tongue darts out and runs along her lower lip then her teeth drag and bite it. My whole body reacts as I remember the feel of those soft caressing lips and tongue then the delicate drag of her teeth across my skin. I can't breathe.

Somehow I find my voice "Thanks Sally, I'll take it from here"

Sally's out the door before I finish speaking and my feet are moving, before I know it Kitten is in my arms and I'm kissing her, roughly. Our lips mold perfectly together. My tongue invades her mouth, dipping, weaving, tasting. I can't supress the groan of pleasure, she tastes so fucking good. I pick her up, her legs wrap around me and I'm on the move taking her upstairs. Without breaking the kiss, I lower her onto my bed. I settle myself over the top of her and nestle in between her legs.

Her hands explore my back, the feel of small delicate hands molding to my taut muscles, her nails gently dragging over my skin sends charges of electricity hurtling around my body and the burn of her touch makes my nerve endings feel as if I've been electrocuted. The stinging pleasure makes my muscles twitch involuntary. My cock grows thicker, more painful. I know she will make me come this way if I'm not careful.

Her body is just as soft and pliable as I remember, she smells wonderful. A faint fruity and floral perfume mixed with her heady musky natural feminine scent. I break the kiss and work my way along her jaw.

"I never thought I'd see you again" I murmur.

"Neither did I"

Her throaty laugh has my hips grinding into her. She pushes her head back as I work my way down her throat to her chest. It's then that I realise she's wearing a dress, with buttons down the front. How convenient. Slowly I start to undo them, placing kisses on the exposed skin. Kitten sighs and arches her back thrusting her lace covered ample chest forward, begging to be touched. I slip my hand behind her back and unclasp her bra. Pushing it up so her heavy tits spring free.

Taking my weight onto my elbows, I cup each tit and start to gently knead. I run my tongue over the pale silk fleshy globe working my way inwards to the nipple. I spend time circling the light pink areola before teasing her erect distended nipple into my mouth, sucking and biting gently bringing it to a succulent red colour. Kitten cries out, her hips surge upwards catching my erection in just the right way. We both moan. I switch to the other breast, marvelling at the swelling softness as I continue to caress and squeeze as my tongue dances and flicks across her reddening nipple.

I undo the remaining buttons on her dress. I rear up, pulling her with me. I take off the dress and white lacy bra. Lying her back down I kiss my way from her mouth down between her breasts, pausing to run my tongue over the thudding pulse of her heart in the hollow of her throat and in the arch of her rib cage. Down her stomach, dipping my tongue into her belly button before I continue down her flat taut stomach. I place kisses from hip to hip as I pull the white lace knickers down. I notice a thin white scar and kiss along it. I lean up and lift her legs to remove her knickers. I debate for a few seconds whether to leave her boots on. They're high heeled tan knee length. I undo the zip slowly and kiss down her calf as I pull each one off, her knickers follow quickly.

I gaze down at her magnificent delicate slender body spread out before me. I'm going to devour her. My mouth waters at the very thought and I swallow convulsively. I'm going to enjoy this delectable feast. I remove the towel, my cock pulses and throbs as it springs free. My wild kittens rapturous lust filled gaze runs greedily over my body enflaming my blood and singular lust for her.

Slowly running my hands over her legs, thighs, stomach, waist, chest, shoulders and arms my wild kitten's body responds by lifting into my hands, making the fucking sexiest low groan I've ever heard. Electric tingles dance along my nerve endings collating in my spine and shoot straight down to my cock in response. Her flawless pale skin is warm and silky-smooth. I lower my head and kiss, lick and graze my teeth all over her. Working my way down to her pussy. As I get lower spreading her legs wider with my shoulders, her hands tangle in my hair. The pulling and tugging tells me where she wants me to go.

"Patience my wild kitten" I murmur. I blow lightly over her sex, she whimpers and mewls low in her throat. Fuck I love that sound. I blow again just so I can hear it.

Placing my hands under her pert buttocks I lift her to me. Fuck, every part of her fits perfectly in my hands. I run my nose along the apex of her thighs breathing deeply just as if I was snorting cocaine only I'm taking the hit of her concentrated intoxicating scent and arousal giving me an even bigger natural high than any chemical could. Stiffening my tongue, I run the arrow tip along her cleft from anus to clit. I flatten my tongue and do the same again. Her mellifluous juices coat my tongue, oh fuck, like a starving man I devour her.

"Oh god, Caleb"

Hearing her moan my name is nearly my undoing. My cock swells and my balls draw up tightening. My hips grind into the mattress. I delve my tongue into her folds, her sweet creaminess explodes across my taste buds.

Never have I tasted anything so exquisite. Stiffening my tongue, I push up the hood covering her clitoris and flick the hard knot of nerves endings. Kitten jerks, her legs twitch and clench around my head, her nails scratch my scalp as her fingers fist in my hair, pulling hard. Her cries and moans of pleasure heat my blood, my cock throbs painfully, he wants in on the action.

Her hips circle and gyrate against my mouth, she's close. Lifting her hips higher I thrust and stab my tongue deep inside her hot wet entrance.

"Caleb!" Kitten cries out as her orgasm takes over her body. Her arms fly out to the sides, her hands fist in the sheets. She pushes back her head and shoulders, arching her back, lifting her pelvis higher. I hold her firmly in place as I continue fucking her with my tongue. Her honeyed creamy juices flood my mouth, I greedily swallow and delve my tongue in to collect more of her delicious nectar.

When there is no more to be had I move over her still convulsing body, lifting and hooking one leg over my hip. Her chest expands and falls rapidly gasping for breath. Her body glistens with a sheen of perspiration. Her glorious long hair fans out around her, she looks like a goddess.
My lustful need for her consumes me. Fisting my cock, I guide it to her entrance and push slowly in.

"Oh yes" Kitten moans and arches into my hips taking me deeper.

I close my eyes, absorbing the amazing feel of the constricting velvety smooth grasping walls of her cunt molding around my cock, the tight grip sucks me in deeper. A deep growl rumbles at the back of my throat in appreciation. She's mine. I drop my head against her forehead, I breathe deeply fighting the urge to pound into her. I want to savour this for as long as I can. I want to make to love her. To Skye, my wild kitten, my goddess. Slowly I open my eyes to see sparkling yellow green eyes, flushed rosy cheeks and smiling full luscious lips.

"Are you okay now" she whispers.

"Yes" I whisper back smiling "just reacquainting myself with the feel of your deliciously tight pussy around my dick"

"Good" Skye rotates her hips, clenching her muscles around me, mine automatically circle with her "oh yes" she groans as I pull back and re-enter her moist, hot wetness leisurely.

I lower my head, she meets me partway, our lips and tongues join in a gentle unhurried dance. I circle and thrust my hips at the same leisurely pace, gradually increasing and deliberately stroking deep inside her tight cunt. Her muscles grasp and hold on to me with each withdrawal, I feel the spasms rippling along the length of my shaft as her orgasm builds, her head starts to thrash from side to side as her legs wrap around my hips, the heels of her feet digging into my arse pushing me deeper as she raises her hips to meet my thrusts.

I lift onto my elbows; my hands frame her beautiful face holding her still. I claim her mouth and start to pump faster. Heavy pressure builds in my lower stomach, spikes of pleasure shoot up my dick. Her nails dig into my back and drag upwards, the unexpected pain triggers my orgasm.

"Fuck" I hiss pumping faster and harder all control... gone. I pound into her.

"Yes... oh Caleb! ... yes!"

Her pulsing, twitching soft body beneath me sends me over the edge.

"Skye" her name rips from my throat as I feel my body explode, shattering in pleasure. I collapse on top of her as my body shakes and shudders. I empty everything I have into her.

Soothing hands running up and down my back brings me round. I'm totally spent. I feel sleepy. I kiss the side of her neck then lift my head.

"Hi" Skye smiles at me.

"Hi" I grin back at her; a thought occurs to me "why did you say you've never been married?"

"I didn't say that" her smile gets bigger. I frown.

"Yes you did. When Sally introduced you, you said you've never been a Mrs or was what you told me on the train a lie?" I raise a questioning eyebrow.

Her dazzling beaming smile stays in place "Everything I told you on the train is true. And what I said was Miss or Ms, it's never been Mrs. As in it's never been Mrs Darcy"

I know I'm frowning at her as I think this through. She's been married but she has never been Mrs Darcy, so that means she had a different name. A surge of possessive jealousy takes me by surprise at the thought of her being with another man. Fragments of previous conversations and the recent odd behaviour of certain close friends and acquaintances whisper through my mind. Things slot into place with a resounding click. Of course it all makes sense now. I look at her stunningly beautiful face. I bend and kiss her deeply. Moving my lips to her ear I bite her ear lobe. I grind my hips stroking my still hard cock deep inside her. My wild kitten raises her hips in response and purrs with deep desire at the back of her throat.

"It's a pleasure to make your acquaintance… Mrs Blake"

I check my appearance in the full length mirror, straightening the crisp white shirt – I've decided not to wear a tie – and adjusting the sleeves so they peaked out under the cuffs of my suit jacket. The Armani suit is one of the few extravagant luxury items I have ever bought for myself, the other are the onyx cuff links set in platinum with my initials encrusted in diamonds sat in the cuffs of my shirt.

Picking up the Tom Ford cologne, a Christmas present from the staff, I squirt myself with it. I don't wear shit like this often but I'll be damned if I was going to give Simone fucking Fawcett-Fowler a reason to look down on me during her pathetic excuse of a dinner party. I'll show the stuck up bitch I can look expensive so I might as well smell it too.

Hearing the distant low guttural growl of an approaching car I head out of the bedroom, taking one final look around the room to make sure I've got everything my eyes fall on the still rumpled bed sheets. Images of Skye naked writhing and groaning in pleasure play across my mind. Walking to the bed I lift one of the pillows and inhale deeply, the ghost of her scent fills my nostrils. My body reacts instantly. Fuck, how can a woman, a practical stranger have such an effect on me? I'm tempted to tell Rex to shove the dinner party and go to The Coach House to see her, demand to see her. The two hours we spent making love felt like it happened days ago instead of being just over an hour and half when she left my bed. You're suffering from withdrawal symptoms; I tell myself as I force my feet to move in the direction of the door.

"Looking good my man" Rex grins at me as I lower myself down into the Porsche "I forgot how well you scrub up"

"You're a fucking twat, you know that don't you" I retort, Rex laughs heartily as he drives out of the yard "who's going to this dinner party?"

"Fred said there'll be about twelve people. The Farringdon's and Baxter for definite, some associates of his from London plus their partners and a couple of women from Henley that are on one of the many committees Simone is on, he didn't know which"

"Thanks for roping me in to a night of fucking tedious small talk and boredom" I gripe "you owe me big time"

"Change of subject, I've spoken with Harry earlier this afternoon" Rex says smoothly switching topics "he says you've been getting some incredible feedback from the sessions you've been doing. As a direct result the waiting list for the mentoring programme has tripled and he's had fifty new members sign up all have said they've heard about what you're doing at the club"

I look at Rex in astonishment, I've only delivered two demonstrations and they were to the same five men. I had gotten their feedback at the start of our second session, it was all positive and constructive. I had absolutely no idea they had been that impressed they were spreading the word.

"And" Rex continues as he turns into Simone's driveway "I have it on good authority that all the staff Subs are fighting over who gets to be your next volunteer, so now Barney has created a rota to keep them from tearing each other's eyes out"

"Is this your subtle way of telling me that Harry won't let me quit any time soon" I say getting out the car. Rex winks and makes a clicking sound at me "great, fucking great" I mutter.

I continue muttering and cursing under my breath as we walk towards Pendle Manor, actually it used to be the Old Rectory but Simone renamed it not long after her and Fred moved to the village. She wanted it to be grander than it essentially is. It's common knowledge that Simone was a cleaner working for Fred's investments firm when she caught his eye, after a short torrid affair he left his wife of fifteen years for her. A quick divorce and a few months later Simone became the latest Mrs Fawcett-Fowler. Since then she has clawed her way up the social ladder, reinventing herself by taking elocution and etiquette lessons. Simone behaves how she thinks the rich and gentry behave, sometimes her gaffs produce hilarious outcomes. I should know I've seen plenty of them. What irks her most is someone of common decent having better connections than her and I'm one of those people.

The social circle Simone and Fred circulate in they are paupers in comparison, yes they probably have a fair few hundred thousand or not far off a million in the bank but that's pin money to the tens of millions some of their acquaintances have. Simone collects wealthy contacts just like someone would collect stamps, comic books or antiques. The hired butler for the evening answers the door and shows us into the drawing room.

"Rex, darling so good of you to come" Simone calls out as she walks towards us.

Rex kisses her cheek "Simone looking beautiful as ever"

"Oh you scoundrel" Simone playfully slaps his chest. I know Rex has fucked her in the past, on more than one occasion. Another reason why she doesn't like me, I've rebuffed her advances. I won't give her the time of day "and you've brought Mr Raven as your guest, lovely to see you" her tone says it isn't.

I give her my best smile "Mrs Fawcett-Fowler" I drop my voice into a seductive purr as I kiss the back of her hand. She blushes, her eyes dilate and I see the pulse at the base of her throat jump and beat rapidly. My smile becomes wicked as she's temporarily captivated by me. I hear Rex snigger, that snaps her out of the trance. Simone looks around uncertain, nervously touching and patting her hair whilst the other hand goes to her throat.

"Err... let me introduce you to the other guests. We're just waiting for two more" she says flustered. Simone snaps her fingers and a waitress rushes over with a tray filled with champagne. Rex picks up two flutes and hands one to me "allow me to introduce you to…" I switch off as Simone drones on about each person and their accomplishments.

I look around the cluttered drawing room, it's as if someone has had antique diarrhoea. Spindly chairs that look as if they'll snap in two if someone as big as me sat in it. Ornaments and vases covering every surface. Country scene oil paintings – probably fakes or by some unknown artist done in the style of a famous one – cover the walls. It wouldn't be so bad if the antiques were of the same period or similar in style so the pieces complimented each other. Instead the room looks like it's an antique shop or junk shop depending on your point of view. I spot Bertie and Joyce Farringdon talking to Baxter, I make my way over to them.

"Caleb, my boy" Bertie greets me warmly "didn't know you were invited tonight" he murmurs.

"I wasn't, got conned in to coming by Rex this afternoon" the three of them laugh at my chagrin "I'd sooner be in The Coach House"

"Wouldn't we all" Baxter says quietly "especially if it meant getting a glimpse of a certain visitor staying there, quite the catch, so I hear?"

"When is the expected arrival date of the new horses?" Joyce says, expertly ignoring Baxter's implied invitation to give up any new gossip. I smile knowingly at Joyce – she doesn't want to talk about Skye any more than I do – she winks back.

"I'll have confirmed dates tomorrow but my guess, it'll probably be end of next week"

The sound of the doorbell chiming stops all conversation.

"Ah good, our last guests have arrived" announces Simone.

The door opens, the butler steps aside revealing Tobias Belling. My hackles rise as the short fat bald fucker walks in, no doubt Gabrielle will be close behind. I turn away so I don't have to see the smug bitch's face. At the sound of the whole room drawing in a sharp breath, I turn around to see my wild kitten stepping into room.

Her curly white blonde hair is swept up and piled on top of her head, exposing her long slender neck. Her ears glitter with multiple ruby earrings. Her scrumptious body is covered in a simple form fitting pale pink off the shoulder dress, it finishes about two inches above her knees. At the end of her silken legs are dark pink high heels. My wild kitten is the epitome of the sex siren goddess I know her to be. My mind has shut down but my body hasn't.

Belling turns to my kitten and holds out his arm, smiling she links him. What in the fucking hell is she doing with that bastard? My mind screams. A hand landing on my chest draws my attention. I look down at it, confused. I follow the arm and look into Joyce's concerned face.

"Now is not the time, nor the place Caleb" she whispers, I realise someone else is holding my arm, it's Bertie. They're attempting to hold me back. I hadn't realised I started to move towards Skye "I know it must be difficult seeing him, can you let your anger towards him go?"

I nod. Joyce and Bertie let go of me but keep close, not that either of them could do anything to stop me should I decide to thump the fucker. Luckily no one else saw what happened, their attention being consumed by the stunning beauty of Skye.

"Mr Belling, so lovely of you and your companion to join us" says Simone, her etiquette lessons kicking in.

"Mrs Fawcett-Fowler, thank you for inviting me, may I introduce you to Skye Darcy"

Belling looks like the cat that caught the canary, his face is so fucking smug. It takes all of my will power not to walk over and smash my fist in to it.

"Hubba, hubba, hubba" Baxter murmurs under his breath "I have just seen the new Lady Baxter"

"Get in line, she's Mrs Davies first" counters Rex.

"Down boys and behave" chuckles Joyce.

I want to scream "Back off you fuckers, she's mine!" and smash their heads together but instead I watch Simone simper and fawn all over Skye. Tobias hands her a glass of champagne, she takes a sip and fleetingly she pulls a face like you do when you bite into a lemon. She doesn't like champagne it occurs to me. Her eyes scan the room; I realise she's taking in the décor rather than the people. Her eyes snap back to Simone and takes a few steps to follow her when she spots my group. A huge dazzling smile spreads across her face as her eyes briefly lock on my mine. My heart stops and my dick pulses.

"Joyce, Bertie" Skye's husky voice calls out "so good to see you again" she walks over to our group with a startled Simone hot on her heels. Belling stays talking with Fred but his eyes follow Skye.

"Skye what a lovely surprise. Simone didn't say you were coming tonight" Joyce greets her with a hug of genuine affection. Bertie kisses both Skye's cheeks. I want to kiss and bite those luscious lips.

"I'm a last minute plus one" laughs Skye.

"I believe you managed to get rooms at The Coach House" a throat being cleared stops Joyce mid-sentence "how rude of me" she laughs taking the hint "allow me to introduce you"

"To Lord Baxter" Simone jumps in. If Joyce Farringdon had been anyone else, Simone would be throwing the filthiest look possible her way right now.

"A pleasure to meet you" says Baxter taking hold of Skye's hand and kisses the back of it.

He holds her gaze and speaks Russian to her. It's his pickup line and party trick to seducing women. The phrase says something about how beautiful they are, how they've stolen his heart and he'll follow them to the end of the world or some other soppy shit like that.

Skye stares at him with an amused puzzled look, then she astounds us all by speaking fluent Russian back. Baxter looks at her open mouthed. She says something else her eyes glint mischievously as she continues speaking Russian, then she starts laughing. My whole body hums at the sexy throaty sound.

"You have no idea what I have just said" she removes her hand from Baxter's "and I'm guessing that what you actually said to me is completely different to what you think you said"

I can't help it, I collapse laughing. Rex joins me. Joyce and Bertie do their best to smother their mirth. Simone is torn between joining in the laughter or to remain aloof. Her etiquette training wins out, it's telling her not to laugh at her guest's cock up.

"All these years Baxter you think you've been telling the ladies that their beauty rivals Aphrodite herself, they've stolen your heart and the air from your lungs, you are their slave and you'll follow them to the ends of the earth" splutters Rex "Remington Davies, you can call me Rex" he says to Skye, kissing the back of her hand "please tells us what he actually said"

Skye shakes her head "That would be unfair of me. However, I will say Lord Baxter expect a smack in the mouth should you ever say that to a Russian woman"

"So why didn't you smack him in the mouth?" the question is out of my mouth before I can stop it. Skye's grin gets even wider.

"Because I asked him who had taught him Russian, when he didn't respond I asked him to translate what I had just said, if he had done any of that then I would have" Skye's eyes darken "it's a pleasure to make your acquaintance Mr Raven" a slow seductive smile spreads across her lips.

"It's a pleasure to make your acquaintance… Ms Darcy" keeping eye contact I raise her hand to my lips, the tip of my tongue snakes a lazy pattern on the back. A shiver runs through her, I feel the pulse in her wrist pick up speed and see a faint blush bloom across her cheeks.

"How do you know who he is?" Rex's question breaks the moment.

"Powers of deduction and I have my sources" Skye grins wickedly "it's amazing what you find out from local gossip and rumours especially when people don't know who you are" her eyes briefly flick to mine, then Joyce and Bertie. I get the subtle message, keep her true identity secret "or know that you're listening" she winks at Rex.

I laugh and slap Rex on the back, he looks sheepish as the others look bemused. The butler comes in and announces dinner is ready to be served. Tobias Belling comes over to Skye, he gives me a curt nod as he holds out his arm to her. Skye doesn't miss the hostility in my expression as she smiles warmly at the fucker. How in god's name does she know that little shit?

In the dining room everyone finds their seat. I can see Simone is dying to rearrange the seating plan so she can have Skye near or next to her but most guests have already taken their seat. To my utter joy Skye is sat directly opposite me. Joyce is to my right; I have no idea who the woman is on my left. Bertie is to Skye's left, Tobias to her right. I have a sneaking suspicion that Simone placed me where I am thinking or hoping I would be sat opposite Gabrielle. Small talk picks up around the table as the first course is served.

"How are you finding The Coach House and the village?" Joyce asks Skye.

"Great, it's the ideal base and Chris and Michelle are lovely. Thank you for putting me on to them" Skye smiles "everyone I've met so far are really nice"

I stretch my legs out and accidentally kick someone's feet. Skye jumps, her eye's flick to me, I mouth sorry. A devilish thought comes to me, under the table I artfully move my legs and to either side of hers, using my feet I hook her legs and start to lift them. Skye continues to listen to Bertie whilst she eats, with the odd flick of her eyes to me. I can see a slight frown on her face, she's obviously wondering what the hell I'm doing. Suddenly her legs disappear and her feet are on my crotch. I nearly choke on my salad.

"Are you okay?" Skye's husky voice is all innocence yet her look is positively salacious.

I take a drink of water and clear my throat "Yes, thank you" I put my hands under the table. I move the table cloth so it covers more of my lap. Gripping her slender ankles, I slide off her shoes, I shift in my seat and place her feet against me. Her toes flex as she feels my erection, with one hand holding her feet in place I flex my hips. I continue to eat one handed.

During the main course the conversation turns to horses. Bertie is telling Skye about his polo buddies and the new horses I recently acquired on his behalf, plus the ones I bought for the syndicate. She seems to have a genuine interest in the topic and asks where I got them from. Bertie gives her a rundown of the countries he sent me to.

"Do you have horses?" asks Bertie.

"Yes, I have two" she snorts a laugh "actually I should say it's more like one and a half, since one is a miniature. They're currently stabled with friends, however I do need to find somewhere else for them and get them into training"

"Well, why not have our very own trainer take them for you?" Bertie points his knife in my direction.

"Bertie, stop coercing Skye" Joyce admonishes him.

Skye laughs "It's okay, I was thinking the same thing. I met Sally and Marty this morning along with the delightful Wonderwall"

So that's why she was at the stables this afternoon. We never got chance to talk considering we were too busy fucking the life out of each other.

"By all means come up to the stables and have a look around" I grin at her and grind my hips into her feet. Her toes flex and grip me, I swear my straining cock gets thicker and pushes uncomfortably against the fly of my trousers "what breeds are your horses and whereabouts are they currently stabled?"

"The miniature is a Falabella and the other is a Friesian Sport horse, all of them are on a ranch in Tennessee" my eyes snap to hers, my fork halts halfway to my mouth, Skye's lips tilt in a slight smile.

Bertie chuckles "Caleb, visited a place in Tennessee, said he saw a belter of a horse but the owner wouldn't sell apparently they said…"

"Money isn't an incentive to sell" Skye finishes for him, her sparkling knowing eyes never leave mine.

I drop my knife and fork in shock, the clatter draws the other guest's attention "Fuck me! You own Dark Moon" I exclaim in the ensuing silence, of course Mike's comment makes sense now.

"I do" Skye nods her head and raises her wine glass to me. I throw my head back and laugh heartily.

"What's so funny? Please share with the rest of us" Simone calls down the table.

"We've just discovered that we have a mutual friend" Skye says "Caleb tried to buy a horse from him recently, the horse he tried to buy is mine" polite laughter follows Skye's statement.

"It's amazing how small the world is, isn't it my dear" Tobias fucking Belling says, his hand covers Skye's and gives it an affectionate squeeze. I want to rip his fucking hands off her.

"How did you two meet?" says Simone quick as a flash, she's obviously been waiting for the opportunity to ask.

Tobias looks at Skye before answering. I don't miss the imperceptible nod of her head, she's giving him permission… how strange!

"This lovely young lady is my niece" he declares proudly.

"Bloody hell, you're Lord Matthew Belling's granddaughter!" Bertie says in astonishment.

Skye winces, I feel her feet start to withdraw from between my legs. I grasp her ankles to stop her and put her feet back firmly where they belong. Her eyes widen in surprise. I apply pressure a silent command to keep them where they are.

"Bertie, you're embarrassing the poor girl" reprimands Joyce.

I smile at Skye because I know the blush has nothing to do with what Bertie has just said.

"I'm sorry" Bertie says contritely "I knew your grandfather and he often spoke about you, he was very proud of your accomplishments"

Skye jolts and looks completely stunned at Bertie. Why is that? I wonder, surely she would know what her own family thinks about her?

"What is it exactly you do?" asks Fred, he's sensing fresh blood and the potential to fleece money from an unsuspecting new investor, a very wealthy investor.

"I'm an artist and designer" says Skye.

"Oh so that's why you're here. You're overseeing the restoration and interior design of Dove Mill Hall for the new owner Mrs Blake" Simone smiles gloating to her other guests that she's been clever working out Skye's reasons for being in the village.

"Partly, plus I have other business to attend to whilst I'm here" I admire how Skye cleverly answers Simone.

"What's your other business" says Rex getting in on the act.

The all too familiar mischievous glint flashes in her eyes at the same time she moves her feet rubbing my dick applying just the right amount of pressure. I fight to supress the moan at the back of my throat.

"I have a client who recently bought an exclusive club on the outskirts of Windsor, he owns a number of others clubs just like it around the world. He commissions me to do all the paintings for them" Rex's jaw hits the table, so do a number of others "at the moment I'm gathering preliminary information in readiness for when I start working on the commission towards the end of the year"

"What's the name of this club? I think we should become members Fred don't you?" Simone smiles sweetly at her husband.

"No, I don't. We have enough memberships to exclusive clubs already" snaps Fred shifting in his seat uncomfortably, he knows what the club is. I bet he's a bloody member himself! I smother the snort of laughter. I catch Bertie and Joyce's eyes; they look away quickly biting their lips. I daren't look at Rex. Skye is grinning from ear to ear, she's sussed out who the other members are sat around the table.

"Have you decided yet when you'll be leaving?" says Tobias to Skye.

"If everything goes according to plan on Friday then we'll be leaving Sunday afternoon for Cumbria then fly out to New York on Tuesday"

Shit, this news unsettles me. Tobias looks as unhappy as I feel "So soon, when will you be back?" he asks quietly.

Skye shrugs "Six months maybe" Tobias looks distraught "we'll keep in touch I promise" Skye pats his arm.

"It seems so unfair that after all these years we are only just getting to know each other" he whispers.

What the fuck does he mean by that? I glance around the table no-one else has heard him as various conversations have sprung up around them whilst the waitresses clear the table and serve desert. Baxter and Rex start competing for Skye's attention by asking mundane questions.

Ignoring my desert, I put my hands under the table and massage her feet. Pressing my thumbs into the soles of her feet, gently tugging and pulling on her toes, sliding my fingers back and forth in between them. The suggestive action has her squirming in her seat, the lovely rose blush colours her cheeks, spreading down her neck onto her chest. Her breathing becomes shallow.

"Ladies shall we" Simone calls out and stands.

I reluctantly let go of Skye's feet. She's the last to stand and leave. As she sashays out of the room I admire the sway of her hips, so does every other fucking male. The men follow Fred into his study where the butler serves brandy and cigars. Rex and Baxter come and stand by me, we're the only none smokers.

"I can't believe Harry didn't tell me about her" Rex grumbles into his brandy.

"I bet she's worth a pretty penny" murmurs Baxter keeping his eyes on Tobias "I heard a rumour that when his old man died he only got a fraction of the fortune and the identity of the major beneficiary was sworn to secrecy. Speculation was rife that the old man left it to some love child. Maybe she's not his niece but his half-sister"

I look at Baxter in disbelief. I'd met Lord Belling once about ten years ago, if Skye was his daughter which I doubt he would have fathered her in his mid to late fifties at least. His reputation in business was legendary, a ruthless cold hearted controlling bastard. His son Tobias is a chip off the old block according to my sources, namely Bertie. What puzzles me is his relationship with Skye, from what I've seen tonight she is the one very much in control. Tobias was careful about how he worded things when people asked anything personal about them, how he would look to her for cues, the subtle nods or shakes of her head giving permission to divulge or deflect.

I don't join Rex and Baxter in their speculations about how genuine Tobias's information is or her perceived wealth. I'm not going to betray her true identity, one thing I have realised tonight is that Bertie and Joyce Farringdon also know who she is and I know Chris and Michelle do too.

"Excuse me I'm going to the bathroom" I murmur.

SKYE

I grip the sink, taking a deep calming breath to steady my nerves. I still can't believe what I did with my feet during dinner. The soles of my feet and toes tingle with the memory of Caleb's thick hard cock against them. All through dinner I played with his cock… with my feet!

I look at myself in the mirror. My eyes are bright, my cheeks flushed, my tits feel heavy and my nipples are aching. I touch them trying to lessen the ache. It doesn't work. All it does is make my core clench and the heaviness between my legs increases. How can a man playing with my feet make me feel so wanton and horny?

Someone trying the door handle snaps me out of my mental debate. I straighten my dress, grab my clutch and open the door.

"Hello Kitten"

Holy fucking shit!

Six foot four inches of pure virile male has me in his arms and kissing the life out of me in a nanosecond. My brain switches off and my body enjoys the pleasure ride. On some level I'm aware of being moved and I hear the door shutting with the lock clicking into place all the while my lips and tongue are hungrily devouring the man who triggers so much lust in me I don't recognise myself.

Caleb breaks the kiss, both of us are breathing heavily. My back is against the door; his hands are either side of my head. He lowers his forearms against the door effectively bringing his head down to my level, eye level.

"Tell me what your relationship with Tobias Belling is?" Caleb's deep gruff voice brokers no argument, he's expecting an answer, and his emerald green eyes tell me as much.

Defiance raises its head and growls. I owe him nothing "Why?" I challenge.

"I want to know what you are doing here with that fucking piece of shit" the vehemence of his words surprises me at first, then I remember his wife being with Tobias at Nessa's dinner party and the hostility I felt oozing out of Caleb every time he looked at Tobias this evening.

"Are you angry with me being here with him or with the fact that your wife left you for him? Sorry you threw her out. I stand corrected"

Caleb closes his eyes, takes a deep breath then slowly opens them "Don't push me kitten. Right now it's taking all my control not to bend you over and spank the fucking shit out of you for the information. Answer me"

Bursts of heat flash all over my whole body and I feel my juices flow between my thighs at his threat. I lean forward and kiss him, attack him more like. I push my tongue into his mouth, claiming him as mine. I goad him to take me. Christ I want him to spank me, to fuck me… hard. My body is screaming out for it. Caleb pulls away. I whimper at the loss.

"Turn round and put your hands on the door" he commands.

I do as I'm told; his hands are on my hips roughly pulling up my dress to my waist. I push my arse out and widen my stance in readiness. Caleb hisses in a breath.

"Jesus fucking Christ, I hope you're ready for me Skye because you look too fuckable for your own good like this"

I feel his rough callused hand running gently over my waist and bum. His fingers following the suspender straps down to the tops of my stockings. I push my bum up trying to get more of his scorching touch against my skin. He pulls my knickers down to my thighs. His fingers separate my outer lips, circling, probing.

"You're soaking" Caleb groans "keep quiet, this is going to be hard and fast"

I bite back the protest when he removes his fingers, my sex is throbbing for attention. Hearing the sound of his buckle and zipper being undone has anticipation shooting through me. I feel the bulbous head of his cock poking and probing at my entrance, he pushes in slightly then his hands grip my hips.

"Remember to keep quiet"

He thrusts forward, I clench my teeth and lips together. The sudden penetration shocks my body; my internal muscles clamp down hard on the thick length in ecstasy. I can't stop the muffled strangled shout of joy at the back of my throat. The throaty animalistic growl Caleb makes has the hair on my arms and neck standing on end and the sound goes straight between my legs. Caleb's head rests between my shoulder blades, he's composing his control. Every time he's entered me he has to do this. I flex my muscles, working his cock and me at the same time.

"Kitten you're making me come" he growls, I keep clenching and releasing his cock, he hasn't told me to stop but then again I don't think I can "shit, I coming"

He starts to move, hard and fast he pummels in to me over and over again. His thighs and balls smack my backside and clit simultaneously. I lock my arms as he pulls me back onto him as he thrusts forward, harder and faster, in and out. My eyes roll to the back of my head, my whole body is on fire, the heaviness in my lower stomach is building painfully fast, rising ready to burst, electric currents feel as if they're snapping and frying my nerve endings. I surrender to the sensations and the waves of pleasure that start my climax.

"Come with me, now Kitten"

Caleb's guttural command, the hard deep thrust and all the sensations in my body collide and detonate. I shatter. I feel Caleb's arms wrap around me, his hard body shuddering and jerking along with mine as we ride out our orgasms. Our gasping ragged breaths are taken in unison as we try to get much needed air into our lungs. After a few minutes Caleb pulls out of me. I wince at the loss of him inside me and the heat of his body. I feel the flow of semen trickle down my thighs.

"Shit, stay as you are Kitten" he murmurs. Within seconds he's back, wiping me with tissue, when he's finished he turns me around "I'm sorry, every time I lose control with you. I should use a condom but I get so carried away" he pulls my knickers up and pulls my dress down.

"I'm to blame just as much as you. You have the same effect on me" I sigh; I'm not going to explain I can't get pregnant. We look at each other; I can see he's holding something back just as he can probably see I am too "we better get back before people notice we're missing"

Caleb runs his hands through his long jet black hair "Yeah you're right" he leans over and unlocks the door.

"Caleb" I put my hand on his arm, he looks at me expectantly "I just want you to know that the way I am with you, I've never... I'm not..." I'm struggling to find the right words to say I'm not normally this free and easy or whatever the current phrase is for giving it up so willingly.

His eyes soften "Me neither" he bends and kisses me so tenderly my toes curl.

We walk back towards the drawing room where we hear the other guests, Caleb has me tucked into his side all the way and I revel in the warmth of his hard body.

"Will you answer my questions?" he says softly "please"

I stop, Caleb's hands rest on my waist pulling me closer to him. I look up at his handsome face, I see a sadness and longing in his eyes. I reach up and touch the side of his face, he turns and kisses my palm. I smile as the memory of Clayton doing the same thing echoes through my mind.

"Tobias is my uncle. We recently met at a dinner party. It was at one of my closest friends in London. I've been estranged from my family since I was eighteen and it was quite a shock for both of us to see each other after all these years. Tobias was there with Gabrielle" Caleb starts at that bit of news "the anorexic Umpa Lumpa description was quite apt I must say" I smile at Caleb's chuckle "that along with the things Tobias said about her matched with some of the other things you said about her on the train. At the time he said Gabrielle was a wannabe girlfriend, when he asked me to come here tonight I told him I didn't want to cause problems with him and her. Tobias said there has never been anything between them, that's not to say he hasn't fucked her, he probably has. Tobias is keen to make up for lost time, but the cynic in me..." I pause and sigh. Caleb remains quiet, looking at me steadily "you know who I am and no doubt how much I am worth"

"I do and I have no idea but from the gossip tonight I imagine it's a fair bit"

I can't help the smile. I appreciate his honesty.

"Tobias is cut from the same cloth as my grandfather and he was a ruthless, manipulative bastard"

"So the cynic in you thinks he's after something" Caleb finishes for me. I nod.

The door to the drawing room opens, Caleb and I step further apart before whoever is coming out can see how intimate we look stood so close together.

"Oh there you are. I was coming to look for you" says Simone "is everything okay?" she's burning with curiosity as she looks to each of us.

"Absolutely" I give her a dazzling smile "you have a beautiful home"

The distraction works, Simone starts giving me the history of the place. Caleb gives me a salacious smile and winks as we enter the drawing room he bends and whispers in my ear "I still haven't forgotten about the spanking kitten"

Oh sweet lord.

CHAPTER FOURTEEN

SKYE

It's just before lunch time and muted sounds of conversation surround Freya and me as we sit at the bar in The Coach House. I'm tucking in to a tuna fish melt toastie – I've developed quite a taste for them – with a healthy side order of fat chunky chips, as I go through my contact list giving Freya a rundown of who my friends and most important business contacts are so she'll know who's call I'll take without question should she need to interrupt me when I'm working. Freya is inputting the information in to her new tablet.

"Clive Platt" I say dipping a chip into the pot of mayonnaise "is the captain and he'll organise the flight crew. You just need to call him with dates, times and destinations he'll sort everything else out"

"What kind of plane is it?"

"737 Boeing Business Jet" I smile at Freya's awed expression as she looks at me "yeah it's a big bugger, you'll be arriving in style to see your family" I wink at her "now as for cars this is where you'll liaise with Paul, actually you'll liaise with Paul on all travel arrangements" I correct myself "but he'll source the vehicles we need. Any questions?"

Smiling Freya shakes her head "It's as clear as mud"

I laugh, I like her sense of humour "Joking aside, I know it's only been a few days but tell me how you feel about the job so far"

"I absolutely love it" I can see Freya practically hugging herself "Paul and Alan have been so supportive and kind. You are the best boss I have ever had the privilege of working for"

"Let's revisit that in six months, you'll probably change your mind" I snort "right, tomorrow is going to be manic and I'll apologise now if I seem to be firing instructions at you or pointing people in your direction for whatever reason. If at any time it gets too much please say something, you're still recovering" I look over her face, the bruises are fading nicely and she's done well on our morning walks but I've seen her wincing on occasion "promise me" she nods "no playing the martyr" I raise a stern eyebrow.

"I promise" Freya chuckles "scout's honour" she crosses her heart and holds up the three finger salute.

A blast of cold air hits me square in the back and blows my hair as the door opens.

"Please tell me this place has ghosts"

"Simon!" I squeal in delight jumping off the bar stool and throw myself at my best friend "god I've missed you" I squeeze him hard.

"I've missed you too baby girl" he hugs me back just as fiercely.

The pub has gone so quiet you could hear a pin drop. I pull away and turn back to the bar "Simon meet Freya, my new PA"

Simon startles Freya by giving her a hug, gently. He's mindful of her injuries "It's a pleasure to finally put a face to a name. Skye has told me a lot about you, all good I may add and it takes a lot to impress the socks off our Skye so keep up the good work" she blushes at his compliment.

"Thank you and it's good to finally meet you too" she stumbles through her words.

"How was the flight?" I ask sitting back on my stool.

"Flight was fine it was the bloody delay taking off that was the pain in the arse" Alan comes in carrying Simon's case "but at least I had a gorgeous hunk of a man to feast my travel weary eyes on at the end of my journey" Simon gives a dramatic sigh as Alan walks past rolling his eyes. Simon smiles at Freya and winks "Alan is my man crush, has been for the last five years"

"Yeah and I'm waiting for the day that Alan finally has enough of your advances and slaps me with a sexual harassment complaint" Freya looks from me to Simon bemused "don't worry, you'll get used to him" I jerk my thumb at Simon "just be warned he fights dirty if there's a good looking man around"

My phone buzzes at the same time Freya's tablet pings, both are my appointment reminders and Paul comes out of the door that leads to the upstairs living quarters. He has my oversized bag in his hand.

"Well I have to love and leave you" I say to Simon "Freya will introduce you to Chris and Michelle when they get back from the wholesalers and I'll catch up with you later" I give him a hug.

"See you later"

"Would you like me to show you to your room?" I hear Freya tentatively ask Simon as I walk out the door into the bright sun light.

It's that bright I shield my watering eyes. Paul hands me a pair of sunglasses, gratefully I put them on and take my bag off him.

"I want to nip into the shop over there, do I have time?" I point to the book store across the green. I discovered yesterday that it also sold art materials.

"Yes you do. I'll get the car and meet you outside" he hands me a wad of money. I take it off him feeling like a kid getting their monthly allowance off their father. We've done this for years, me not carrying money or cards simply as a precaution "don't take too long though" he grins at me knowing full well that I will and he'll have to turf me out of the shop.

I jog across the green and bound into the shop "Good afternoon" I say cheerfully and smile at the startled shop assistant. I soon lose myself in selecting the art materials I need and browsing through the book shelves. I'm pleased to see they have a good selection of photographic books, two in particular catch my eye. One is full of erotic shots, the other is scenic landscapes – just what I need to give me inspiration. I make my way to the counter with my haul of goods as Paul comes in to hurry me up no doubt.

On the drive to The Gentleman's Club I take my time looking through the erotic poses, the timing of finding this book is perfect considering I'm about to spend the afternoon in a sex club trying to get new ideas for something I've painted a hundred times before. I was starting to worry that I would have to rehash drawings I'd done before, that's not something I like doing. I like to be original with each picture I produce. I'm only fifteen minutes late when Paul pulls into the drive way of the club. He parks next to a bright orange Porsche.

"I'll be back at five, call me if you need picking up sooner" Paul says as I climb out the SUV. He's heading in to London to see a company specialising in security electronics in preparation for tomorrow's meeting when we finalise plans on the Hall.

"Will do" I call as I shut the door and wave bye.

I make my way to Harry Davies office, remembering the way from my last visit. His door is slightly a jar.

"I can't believe you didn't tell me; she's fucking gorgeous" a familiar man's voice sounding slightly pissed off halts my raised hand as I'm about to knock on the door.

"Just because you're my cousin doesn't mean I have to discuss everything to do with my business" I recognise Harry's voice who sounds just as pissed off. I knock on the door "come in" Harry calls out sharply.

Harry jumps to his feet as soon as he sees me, the scowl disappearing to be replaced by a warm smile. I smile back at him.

"So sorry I'm late Mr Davies" I shake his hand, the man sat at his desk rises to his feet. I realise now why his voice sounded familiar "good to see you again as well Mr Davies"

"Please call me Rex" he puts his hand over his heart and bows slightly, he takes my hand and kisses the back of it "after last night I thought we had got past all the formalities" he flashes a wide smile, one that no doubt has women swooning in their thousands, only I'm immune to it. I remove my hand and refrain from wiping the back of if down the leg of my jeans.

"You've met?" Harry sounds slightly incredulous, his scowl is back in place as he looks at his cousin. As different as they are in physique and stature I detect the family resemblance.

"I'm currently staying in Dove Mill village and last night I had the pleasure of attending a dinner party which Rex along with Caleb Raven were there"

Harry's scowl vanishes in an instant at the mention of Caleb, he gives his cousin a knowing look and a wide smile, almost gloating. Whatever it is that I've said has obviously given him an insight into his conversation with his cousin before I arrived.

"Ms Darcy, I am instructed by Mr Benenati to assist and give you whatever it is you need, whenever and for as long as required" Harry says keeping things formal and professional.

"Fantastic, all I need is access to one of the rooms for a few hours" I smile at Harry, in my peripheral vision I can see the lecherous look on Rex's face "preferably one where I won't be disturbed" I add, I can see Harry gets my drift.

"I have just the room and it locks from the inside once you're in it" he says reaching into his desk and pulls out a plastic key card roughly the size of a credit card "please follow me. I won't be long Rex" Harry throws over his shoulder stopping his cousin in his tracks.

I follow Harry up the stairs and down the plush corridor. The thick red carpet has flecks of gold in it to match the brushed gold wall paper. The soft lighting comes from the hidden spot lights behind the cornices along the length of both walls. Halfway down Harry stops outside a door, swipes the card and pushes the door open. He steps in first, switching on the light. He hands me the card.

"If you need anything there is a phone on the bedside cabinet" he points into the room, I follow his direction and spot it straightaway "dial one and that will give you the bar, this is room six. Dial zero and you'll get me. I'll ensure you are not disturbed"

Translation, I'll make sure Rex stays away from you.

"Thank you"

Harry nods and without another word, leaves. I close the door and flick over the lock. I look around the room. The layout is identical to the one I first saw Caleb in almost a week ago. I settle down in the middle of the floor, open my bag and pull out my art book and pencils, the erotic photographic book and my iPod. I sit facing the St Andrews cross, switch on my music putting one of the buds in my ear. I close my eyes take a deep breath in through my nose letting it out slowly through my mouth, in and out slowly.

My mind quietens, all I hear is the heavy rifts of Fiver Finger Death Punch, one of my favourite rock bands, telling me they're Bad Company. After a few minutes I gradually open my eyes and focus on the cross. Caleb's whispered words from last night about spanking me drift through my mind and I see myself facing the cross with my arms stretched out to the sides with my hands cuffed to the cross. Caleb is stood to the side of me, naked from the waist up. He's wearing tight jodhpurs with riding boots in his hand is a whip, one of his large hands cups my bum. A blast of heat runs over my skin as I remember his touch. I pick up my pencil and start to draw.

CALEB

I look at my watch, shit, I'm running late. If I don't get a move on, I'll be having Harry on my case. I pat each of my pockets trying to locate my phone. Kitchen table, I spin round and sprint back into the house, grab my phone and head back out to the car. I don't even have time to shower or change clothes. I'm still in my riding gear.

"Well he can't have it both ways" I mutter to myself, if Harry has a problem with me turning up like this he can find someone else to run the daytime demonstrations or all of them for that matter.

I know full well Harry doesn't give a toss what I wear and my building irritation is more to do with Baxter and Rex trying to muscle in on Skye last night. I learnt a hell of a lot about her during the dinner party just by simply watching and listening. She shocked the shit out of everyone when her phone rang and she answered it speaking fluent Chinese.

When she finished the call Baxter the condescending prick said "Russian and Chinese, I'm impressed. I can see there's more to you than just a pretty face"

"I also speak French, Italian and Spanish fluently, does that mean I'm also intelligent" retorted Skye.

Not only does she have a sharp tongue but she has a wicked sense of humour and quick wit, coming out with some brilliant one liners to rival Mae West. I chuckle as I recall Rex making a comment about how great and unusual he thought her name is, she responded "If you like that, you should hear my phone number"

I cried laughing when Rex moaned later that she'd given him a duff number and then Skye admitted she used that response all the time to that particular chat up line, plus she didn't take any credit for its originality "I nicked it from a Friends episode" she gleefully informed me.

My phone rings, taking my eyes off the road I take a quick glance at the screen and see Rex calling plus I notice there's ten missed calls from him. I hit the speaker button, keeping an eye out for lurking police.

"Where the fuck have you been?" Rex's tinny voice explodes around me "I've been trying to get hold of you for the last two hours"

"Sorry. I left my phone on the kitchen table this morning and I've been out all day training the horses. What's so urgent?"

"She's here! Skye is here" he says jubilantly.

I don't need to ask where 'here' is. I know instantly he's referring to the club. Two things happen, my dick hardens in anticipation and my stomach rises to my throat in dread. Rex better not have laid a finger on my wild kitten. I'll rip his fucking arms off if he has.

"What's she doing?" I keep my voice neutral.

"I don't know. She's been locked away in room six for the last two hours and Harry won't let me anywhere near her or the room. Specific instructions have been issued to not disturb her" he grumbles sullenly.

Good on Harry, a grin as wide as the Dartford Tunnel spreads across my face "I'm on my way. I have a demo class in half an hour. Tell Harry I might be a few minutes late"

I end the call and put my foot down.

SKYE

I stand up and stretch. I've been sat down for too long. I bend forward and touch my toes then lay my palms down flat on the floor. I feel the pull of the muscles at the back of my legs and down my spine. Oh that feels good. I straighten and shake my arms and legs and roll my neck from side to side. Bending down I pick up my art book and flick through the drawings. I've done a lot more than I thought. I look at my watch, I've been here two and a half hours with another hour and a half before Paul collects me. I check my phone for messages, there isn't any. Freya and Simon obviously have everything in hand.

After using the bathroom, I gather my belongings together deciding to go downstairs to find Harry. I'm sure Dario mentioned to me this place had a dungeon if it has I want to see it, maybe it'll give me more inspiration. Cautiously I open the door a crack and peak out, for some reason I'm half expecting to see Rex waiting for me, I wouldn't put it past him. I'm relieved to find the passageway empty. Rex doesn't weird me out nor do I find him creepy, far from it, he's very easy on the eye but knowing he's put it about… a lot by all accounts I don't want him anywhere near me, nor do I want to be another notch on the bedpost.

Feeling safe I step out into the hallway, the heavy wooden door swings closed of its own accord. I push down on the handle just to make sure it's locked. I hear voices as I walk towards the stairs. Male and female, the woman sounds as if she's flirting and she's being all giggly. They appear at the top of the stairs and stop at the first door, the man is very tall with long jet black wavy hair. My heart thumps painfully against my breast bone. Caleb holds the door open for a tall woman who has bright red short dyed hair, she's wearing a bathrobe. He smiles at her as he says something, I don't hear what he says but whatever it is the woman places her hand on his chest and laughs as she passes into the room the hand on his chest drags slowly down his stomach.

I feel sick, my legs become wobbly as I get closer. You have no claim on him, my mind admonishes. I do, he's mine I snarl back. I want to run in to that room and drag the bitch out by her hair. I grip my art book tighter to my chest to give my hands something less destructive to do. The magnitude at the sudden surge of complete irrational jealousy I feel scares me. He's a member of a sex club, this is the very place you saw him for the second time what did you expect? He's not seen you, he'll go into that room without looking this way. Keep walking.

Caleb's head snaps in my direction. I can't even fake a smile as I get near him. His expression is impassive. I feel something inside my chest crack, I can't look at him anymore. I put my head down as I pass.

"Skye" his deep gravelly voice calls softly.

He hasn't called me Kitten. That really hurts for some reason. I keep walking. My feet disappear off the floor as two huge arms wrap around me, lifting me. I'm trapped. I could kick and scream but I don't have the energy. I hang limp in his arms.

"It's not what you think" his hot breath tickles my ear. His nose pushes my hair out of the way as he places a kiss at the side of my jaw.

"You're a member here Caleb, there's nothing to think" my voice is flat, monotone.

"Let me explain" his voice is more of a growl, my skin prickles.

"You don't owe me an explanation, you don't owe me anything" I whisper softly, fighting to get the words past the huge lump in my throat. I feel like crying, why did I have to go and fall for a guy like him?

The world moves at lightning speed, when it stops my back is against the wall one of Caleb's huge hands is at my throat, his thumb and fingers framing my face gently but firmly holding my head in place. My skin burns at his touch and close proximity, it's a wonderful scorching burn. His other hand is flat against the wall close to my head he's positioned himself so he can look me in the eye, only my eyes are closed. I draw in a shaky breath, I smell horses, leather, hay, fresh outdoors and underneath his heavenly intoxicating musky slightly spicy male scent. My insides liquefy as his essence surrounds me.

"Look at me" he commands; his fingers tighten slightly on my jaw "Look. At. Me" I force my eyes open and look into hard emerald eyes "what do you mean?"

I sigh and close my eyes again, he wants me to spell it out.

"Eyes. Open. Now" he grits out. He's fighting to hold his temper back, am I going to see this famous temper Bertie told me about? I don't want to antagonise him so I comply.

"Caleb, we are two people who barely know each other, we've had… no I have had some of the best sex of my life with you. You are a Dom and a member of a sex club. I… I'm going to be leaving in a few days and you… life goes on"

"Oh Skye, kitten baby" Caleb sighs, he rests his forehead against mine "I'm in charge of running the mentor programme. I'm the lead mentor for Dom's. In that room right now are five men all waiting for me to give them a demonstration. Yes, I'm a member here but you are the only woman I have been with since we met on the train" I gasp in surprise "no one has ever affected me like you do. I don't even get turned on in these sessions but the minute you enter my mind and I imagine doing those things to you, I'm hard as iron. We have a connection and I know you feel it too. I can't resist the magnetic pull you have on me. I don't want to resist it. Now, you are going to come in that room and watch me in action then after the session is over I'm going to take you to my room and fuck you into to next week" my mouth pops open at his candid directness "that's after I've spanked the shit out of you for saying there is nothing between us" my muscles clench with desire and anticipation.

Caleb kisses me tenderly, then steers me into the room with his hand resting at the nape of my neck. A strange calm settles over me. I feel reassured by his words, his sincerity. I believe him! And he can't resist me just like I can't resist him. We're drawn to each other. That explains our reaction to each other a hell of a lot. The magnetic pull is so strong it won't be denied even if we did try to fight it, it would be fruitless, wasted energy. The inevitable is going to happen whether we like it or not. We're meant to be together, destiny demands it. Ah! Crap... he is my true soul mate. Well at least I'm not playing catch up this time, I reconcile with myself.

In the room there are indeed five men all stood chatting in a loose semi-circle and they're all dressed the same. Black t-shirt and trousers, bare feet and they all wear a black wrist band. In front of them the red haired woman is knelt on the floor in the submissive pose, she's still wearing the bathrobe and peeking out from under the cuff I notice a blue and white wrist band.

"Gentlemen, I apologise for my lateness. An unexpected urgent matter cropped up" at the sound of Caleb's voice the room falls silent, the men suddenly alert and attentive. They all eye me curiously a few give me lecherous looks. Caleb doesn't introduce me nor does he say why I'm present. He points me in the direction to a place against the wall. Without a word I go to it and sit down.

I have a very good advantage point. This room is different to all the others, there is no bed. In fact, it doesn't have any furniture in it at all. I look at Caleb and realise that he's wearing black and tan knee length riding boots, cream jodhpurs that show off his muscled thighs. He pulls off the thick woollen jumper to reveal a well-worn Iron Maiden t-shirt that clings to his chest and stomach. Oh! I've died and gone to heaven. Caleb brings the jumper over to me. I can't help but run my eyes appreciatively over his fine physique, my eyes rest on his crotch. I can see the swell of his cock getting bigger, I lick my lips and swallow convulsively as my mouth pools with saliva. The magnetic pull and connection he mentioned earlier… I'm feeling it now, boy am I!

"Keep that up kitten and we'll be giving a different kind of demonstration than the one I intend for these gentlemen" Caleb's voice is deep and guttural as he bends placing his jumper next to me on the floor.

Caleb's hand stretches towards me as if to stroke the side of my face. I can feel electricity jumping from his fingers to my cheek, the faint tingles skittering across the surface of my skin. He clenches his hand, the roped muscles and veins of his forearm standout at the straining tension his fist is creating. Caleb takes a huge step back away from me, slowly releasing a deep breath. He's distancing himself but his lustful burning eyes never leave mine. Holy hell this guy has got control and then some over himself, I'm going to have fun testing that later. I smile at the thought.

"Behave" Caleb mouths.

My smile gets wider, hell no.

CALEB

The licentious look Skye is giving me is testing my control to breaking point. The connection between us, the magnetic pull and her siren call is as tangible as ever. I close my eyes take a deep breath and with every last shred of willpower I have left, which is not a lot, I turn my back on her and face the patiently waiting mentees. I stride purposefully to the centre of the room.

"Gentlemen, let me introduce you to Claire who has kindly volunteered to be your Sub for today's session" I look at the five men in turn "Mark, I believe it is your turn today to be lead Dom"

"Yes Master Raven" Mark steps forward, his excitement palpable. He's tall but of slight build although from his arms I can see he works out.

Out of the corner of my eye I see Skye shifting her position. She opens the large book on her lap. I angle myself so I can observe her better. She rummages quietly in her bag and pulls out a pen or pencil. Her hand starts to move quickly over the page, is she's drawing? Her eyes flicker up and down between my group and the page. Huh! She is.

"Today's session is about whips"

Skye's head snaps up, her whole body stills. I allow myself to glance in her direction. Her eyes look huge in her face; those luscious lips open in an O shape. Fuck, her open mouth is just the right size for my cock. On cue my dick pulses and throbs against the fly of my jodhpurs.

"Who here has used a bull whip before?" I say dragging my eyes away from Skye and back to the group. No one responds to my question "okay who here would like to learn to use one" two men put their hand up "who would like to have a go" everyone put their hand up.

"As you all know by now I am a big advocate of the Dom experiencing the pain before they inflict it on a Sub, so who wants to have a go now?" no one puts their hands up "thought as much" I chuckle.

"Claire, bring me the bag" as the Sub moves to do my bidding I look at each of the men in turn "the bull whip requires lots of practise if you intend to use it in your play. It is not my intention to teach any of you how to use it but more to highlight the damage it can do in the wrong hands. The bull whip's primary function was to herd cattle, sometimes to train horses. Although the whip is never used on the animal, it is the sound of the crack that gets them moving. The bull whip, like any whip can bruise and break the skin. It also takes skill and practise to make sure you hit your target and nowadays the main use of the bull whip is for showmanship, check out You Tube and you'll see what I mean, plus there are lots of training videos on there as well"

Claire places the bag at my feet and resumes the waiting position. I open the bag, it's full of the whips I'd asked Harry to get me. I pull out a flogger, a knout, a cat o nine tails, horse whip and a bull whip laying them out on the floor next to each other.

"Following in the same vein as the other two sessions I will be demonstrating how to inflict pain without bruising the skin or causing any prolonged injury. However, all Sub's will suffer discomfort after a session with any of these" I point to the whips on the floor "so it is important that you follow through on their aftercare. Mark, secure Claire to the whipping post and explain the use of the colours and safe words"

I get into my stride, although I'm constantly aware of Skye's presence and watchful eyes. For some reason it becomes very important, vital almost, to me that she understands I'm the teacher not a participant. That my sole purpose is to pass on my expert knowledge and experience.

Claire is another Sub who is proving to be good for using to train the Dom's, she has a high tolerance to pain and she reaches sub space quickly. She readily agreed to be taken in and out of sub space so the Dom's could judge for themselves when they moved from a soft flogger to using something harsher like the cat o nine tails or horse whip. I correct stances, arm movements and the applied power to the strike with each man as they take a turn. I even have the men practise on each other so they experience what it is like to be whipped. Some of them are going to walk away with bruises, at least it drove my message home about damage and wrong hands. I check my watch, two minutes left. Time to wrap up. I call a halt to all activity.

"Mark please see to Claire and her after care. Thank you gentlemen that concludes today's session, as always I welcome your feedback which I'll get from you at the beginning of the next session. Alternatively feel free to speak with Harry" I say collecting the various whips and put them back in the bag.

I signal to Skye, she stands gracefully holding her bag and my jumper. I snatch up the bag off the floor and head for the door, thankfully Skye follows. I want her out of the room before any of the men think she's up for grabs. I hold the door open for her to exit. Taking her hand, I lead her to my room.

Dropping the bag on the inside of the door I turn to see Skye checking her watch as she walks in behind me.

"Wherever it is you've got to be or whoever it is you're meeting send them a text saying you're going to be late" it doesn't occur to me to ask her to stay or how long she can spend with me, this is happening, end of.

Skye walks over to the bed and searches through her bag. I wander over to her, she finds what's she's looking for, her phone. Absently I pick up the hard backed book she was drawing in and open it. Fuck me! I nearly drop the book. The roughly drawn pencil image is erotic as hell. I turn the page; the next image is just as sensual.

"Hi, it's me" I look up at the sound of Skye's husky voice, she's watching me. I go back to looking through her art work "no I'm not ready to leave just yet…. Take your time, don't rush back…. That's good news and they don't mind coming to us tomorrow…. Okay, see you in a couple of hours" she hangs up.

The last couple of pages are of me, the majority are quick study drawings with a couple of detailed ones. Skye has captured my likeness with uncanny accuracy. I can see she is seriously talented by these rough sketches; Christ knows what the finished piece will look like.

"These are good. Who did you ring?" I say closing the book.

"Paul" I raise an eyebrow for her to elaborate, Skye smiles coquettishly "and wouldn't you just like to know who he is"

In a split second I grab hold of her, sit down on the edge of the bed and flip her onto her stomach across my knee. The resounding smack of my palm landing on her jean clad arse echoes around the room. Skye yelps, her hands automatically move to her arse trying to protect it. I grasp both wrists in one hand, move them out of the way and spank her again. Skye wriggles and struggles to sit up. I spank her hard three times in quick succession.

"Let's try again, shall we kitten?" her wriggling body is stroking my erection. I thrust my hips upwards. Skye stills. I rub my hand in circles over her buttocks.

"Paul Boyd" the name rings a bell, of course he's one of the two Americans with her "he's one of my bodyguards"

"Where is he now?"

"London, he's at a meeting and will be picking me up on his way back"

I lift her upright, Skye moves her hair out of her face as I cradle her between my legs. Her face is flushed and she's breathing heavily, her eyes are bright.

"So how come you're here without any protection?" I say slowly lifting up her top. Skye dutifully lifts her arms. I place a kiss on her ridiculously flat stomach.

"No one here knows my true identity, when I first turned up" Skye prods my chest "you were still in the village and had no idea I was coming here today. So Paul assessed the security risks and deemed it low" she makes quick work of pulling my t-shirt off me.

Skye's fingers play with my hair at the back of my head. I tighten my arms around her pulling her closer to me, enjoying the skin on skin contact. I bury my face in between her magnificent breasts, inhaling deeply her light floral scent invades my lungs.

"I'll protect you" I murmur against her soft skin as I kiss along the lace trim of her bra and work my way up the centre column of her throat. Skye's head drops back on a blissful sigh; her long hair brushes my forearms.

"I know you will. I feel safe with you" she brings her head forward. Her hands on the side of my head still my movements forcing me to look at her face, her dazzling breath taking smile greets me "I trust you Caleb" her whispered words inflame me in the physical and emotional sense.

There is nothing I wouldn't do for this woman. I will lay down my life for hers if that's what it takes to keep her safe. This elegant and dainty creature before me invokes such strong feelings of passion in me, stronger than I have ever known before and feelings that I didn't even know I was capable of. Her beautiful yellow green eyes see right through me. I'm laid bare before her, there is nothing I can hide from her and she knows it.

"What are you doing to me Skye?" I whisper.

"The same thing that you're doing to me Caleb"

Skye's soft satin smooth full lips kiss lightly at the side of my mouth, then the opposite side before they meld fully to my lips. Slowly moving, gliding caresses I submerse myself into her kiss. Neither of us deepens the kiss but enjoy the gentle sensuous dance our lips and tongues perform. Dipping, twirling and entwining.

I feel Skye starting to pull away. I tighten my arms around her. I'm not finished, a low growl rumbles from deep in my chest and I deepen the kiss. My hand cups the back of her head, my fingers tangling in her hair. I fall backwards on the bed, taking Skye with me. My hands roam over her back and arse, moving from soft silky skin to hard brush cotton. Her body responds with undulating sinuous friction building movements against me, in tandem we groan with pleasure.

Skye shifts, kissing down my throat. My head pushes back to give her better access. Her hands roam over my chest and stomach. My skin sizzles at her touch, leaving a simmering burn as she moves downwards. My cock thickens and throbs painfully against the fly of my trousers, my hips surge upwards impatient for her touch. Skye's hand snakes down my stomach and cups me.

"Oh fuck" I groan at the sudden spurt of pleasure that shoots from my dick to the rest of my body. I can't wait any longer "on your knees kitten" my lust filled voice rasps.

Skye's throaty laugh vibrates against my stomach as she places a final lingering kiss there "Yes Master Raven" she whispers sliding her semi naked body down me.

I sit up to see Skye in the submissive waiting position "Kitten, look at me" obediently she lifts her head. Her large yellow green eyes sparkle, her cheeks flushed rosy pink, her luscious full lips slightly parted, her glorious tits encased in black lace lift and fall with her shallow breaths. I reach out and cup her face, her eyes close briefly at my touch. A contented smile spreads across her lips as she opens her eyes. I shift forward bringing our faces closer together.

"I am yours and yours alone. Till the end of my days I belong to you" Skye pulls in a sharp breath at my affirmation, I have no fucking idea where this is coming from but it feels right saying it "just as you belong to me" my voice is a husky whisper. I seal my words with a kiss.

Releasing her face, I stand, looking down at her upturned face seeing it full of wonder and joy I know soul deep that meeting on the train wasn't a chance encounter it was something else at work; destiny, fate, the universe. I haven't got a fucking clue but I do know I've finally found my other half.

Skye rises to her knees, her hands smooth over the bulge of my erection. I watch her face as she plays with me through the material of my jodhpurs. Her delicate small hands and nimble fingers press rhythmically against my dick.

"Stop teasing me kitten" Skye's eyes full of mischief snap to mine "I want my cock in your tight little mouth just as much as you do"

Skye's husky laugh sends shivers down my spine. With sure deft fingers she opens my pants and pulls them down around my thighs. My cock springs free from its restricting prison of my boxer briefs. Skye's hands are on me in an instant. The fluttering touch of her fingers tracing up and down my shaft makes my eyes roll to the back of my head. My head drops back at the churning sensations stirring through my body.

The light swirling of wetness and the probe of her tongue in the tip of my cock has my head snapping back down. Her large luminous eyes silently laugh. I watch as her lips close around the bulbous head of my dick. My balls tighten at the feel of her hot moist mouth and tongue swirling and pressing against it. My hips thrust forward, my dick wants to be deeper. I want to be deeper.

"No more playing kitten. Suck me hard as I fuck your mouth. I want to come so then I can play with you till my heart's content"

I almost come just by looking at her smile with her mouth stuffed full of my cock. Skye shifts her position, with one hand grasping the base of my cock the other grips my hip. She starts a rhythm of stroking my shaft, taking me deep and sucking as she pulls back. The pressure starting gentle, getting more forceful with each withdrawal. Fucking sweet heaven.

"That's it kitten, take it all. Fuck yeah!" she skilfully works me into a frenzy. I start to pump faster, deeper. My hands delve into her hair and cradle her head, holding her still. I take over fucking her mouth. I feel her lips kiss the base of my cock and the tip hits the back of her throat. Christ, she's deep throating me. I open my eyes to see her concentrating on breathing. A tear leaks out the corner of her closed eyes. I'm too far gone to stop now.

The suction her tight mouth and tongue creates sends my nerve endings crazy with ecstasy. My heart is hammering in my chest and I feel beads of sweat trickle down my chest and in between my shoulder blades. Tension builds in my balls at the surging pleasure Skye is giving me. I feel one of her hands slide between my legs and cup my heavy sack. She hums at the back of her throat. The vibration shoots along my shaft at the same time she squeezes my balls.

"Fuck" I roar as my climax slams into me.

My whole body locks and I release into her mouth. I feel Skye's mouth working me, my hips rock with her rhythm as she sucks me dry, my orgasm keeps on rolling through me. I drag in a lungful of air as the last shudders and tremors shake through my body. I pull Skye to her feet and kiss her deeply, running my tongue around her mouth tasting myself and her.

"You have one clever mouth kitten and give the best blow job ever" I say against her lips, giving her one final kiss before releasing her.

"Why thank you Master Raven" Skye says in a mock southern American accent "how about you show me how clever your mouth can be"

"And you have one dirty mind" I pick her up and throw her onto the bed, Skye squeals then giggles as she fights with her hair. I pull her shoes off then undo her jeans "I accept your challenge, my love" I say as I drag her jeans down her legs.

SKYE

I raise up onto my elbows and watch Caleb peel off my knickers. It's hot, his emerald green eyes burn with lust for me and it increases as he lifts my knees and spreads them apart. My sex spasms and floods with juices. Christ he's just looking at me and I'm a melting mess of need already.

"Lie back and enjoy being pleasured" Caleb's gravelly voice makes my spine tingle.

Closing my eyes, I lie back, taking a deep breath I slowly open them and look at the ceiling, only there's someone looking down at me.

"Holy fucking shit!" I yell pulling myself up onto my knees, almost kicking Caleb in the face in the process.

"What's the matter?" Caleb shouts in alarm, he's next to me on the bed in seconds.

Clutching my pounding heart, I glance up at the ceiling only to see… me and Caleb. It's a mirror, you moron. I start to laugh.

"There's a mirror on the ceiling" I point with a shaky hand.

Caleb frowns "There is?" He looks up; I see his reflected surprise turn to a salacious smile "so there is"

"Sorry, it scared the crap out of me. I wasn't expecting to see someone staring down at me"

"Oh my poor baby you're shaking" Caleb laughs pulling me into his arms "I've got you"

I feel foolish but his large caressing hands soothe me in an instant, I relax in to him and his warmth. I place a kiss in the centre of his chest, unable to resist I nuzzle into him. His fingers press fleetingly in the centre of my back. My bra comes loose. His fingers and nails drag lightly down my arms as he pulls the straps down. His eyes are fixed on my breasts as he discards the bra. My nipples tighten and pucker at the cool air and his heated gaze.

"Lie down kitten" I start to lower myself down "wait" Caleb leans over and grabs some pillows. Placing them behind me. He scoops up my hair in his hands "lie down"

Caleb positions the pillow directly beneath my head then releases my hair, fanning it out around me. He twists and looks up into the mirror. He makes a satisfied grunt, I follow his gaze and look up. My breath gets stuck in my throat as I look at my naked form. My heavy breasts spread outwards, at least they don't fall under my armpits, the soft pink areolas surrounding the darker pink buds of my nipples. My flat stomach and narrow waist flowing out to my hips. I don't quiet have the classic hour glass figure, my hips are slightly narrower to pull it off but I still fall into that category, according to Shelley. My smooth pubic mound leading to the apex of my thighs. The pale creamy whiteness of my skin is flushed pink and stands out against the darker tan colouring of Caleb's skin. The contrast between our colourings stands out even more when he lies down next to me, placing his head next to mine and his long jet black hair mingles with my white blonde hair. Black and white. The disparity in our height shows, my feet make it just past Caleb's knee caps. Caleb stops the fit of giggles threatening to bubble up out of me by placing a hand on my lower stomach.

"Watch and keep your eyes open at all times" he whispers the instruction as he starts to move his hand and fingers in a soft slow caress. Fire ignites in my belly. The heat and burn spreads, following his touch.

He circles my breasts, underneath, in between, across the top but never touching my nipples. They tingle and ache for some form of stimulation. My hands move before my brain realises what they're about to do.

"Oh no you don't kitten" Caleb stops my hands before they get to their destination "hmm, I don't think you're going to keep still"

Caleb is up and off the bed and across the room at the chest of draws before I can blink. I lift on to my elbows and watch him, actually I admire the flex of his taut bum and thighs as he pulls items out of various draws. He turns round catching me ogling him, unabashed and audaciously I drag my eyes up and down his body. Clayton had a good body but Caleb is on another level. His broad shoulders and heavily muscular chest and arms are testament to the active outdoor lifestyle he leads. His stomach is ripped to an inch of its life and yes he has the V thing, but his is the kind that renders intelligent women stupid not only that but he has the thin line of hair starting just underneath his belly button leading down to his public hair, which he keeps trimmed. The V and hair all point directly to his huge thick cock... yep all my brain cells are right there with me drooling, my eyes follow the bobbing swing of his lovely cock as he strides back to the bed, to me.

"You're very naughty kitten" Caleb drops the items on the end of the bed and moves over me, straddling and settling his weight on my hips and lower stomach forcing me to lie back down. I look at him as innocently as I can. He chuckles "that's not going to work. Give me your wrists"

I lift both arms out in front of me. He fastens a leather cuff to each wrist, on the side of the cuff there's a clip. I bring my wrists closer to get a better look, it's a snap hook carabiner. This is new. I've only ever been put in leather cuffs once and they were attached to a chain hanging from the ceiling. There was a time when the very thought of being restrained would send me into a panic attack due to what happened to me at eighteen but Clayton helped me get over that fear, however he never pushed my limits.

I know Caleb is about to do that. My heart starts to thump, but I'm not afraid.

Caleb moves my arms above my head. He lifts up on his knees and stretches to reach something at the head of the bed. His cock is right in my face. I've never been one to resist temptation so I do the only thing a girl can. I open my mouth and take a long delicious lick. Caleb jerks, his hips move back and he looks down at me trying to look stern. I give him my best 'what I didn't do anything' innocent look. His chuckle is dark and sexy as hell. I hear a clinking sound of metal against metal and a click, the sound is repeated then I feel a tug on both wrists as Caleb tests the restraints. I pull for good measure. Caleb's smile is positively wicked.

He moves off me and goes to the foot of the bed, grasps my ankles and pulls me down the bed. My arms stretch but it's not uncomfortable, he spreads my legs. The pressure on my ankles a silent instruction to keep this position. I lift my head and watch Caleb fasten another leather cuff to my ankle and attach it to the restraint. I've never been restrained spread eagled before. I'm completely at Caleb's mercy. Faint panic starts to stir. I lower my head and concentrate on my breathing, closing my eyes desperately trying to keep the fear at bay as I feel Caleb attach the remaining cuff. 'I can't move; I can't move' the faint echoes scream in my mind.

"Open your eyes" Caleb says softly; his fingers trail lightly over my face. I force my eyes open. His tender lust filled expression changes instantly. He must see the panic and fear in my eyes. His eyes move to my throat and chest; he places his hand there "this is your first time being restrained like this" I lie by nodding, there is no way in hell I'm telling him "I'm not going to hurt you"

"I know. I trust you, just… I need a minute" I close my eyes and breathe deeply. I feel Caleb starting to undo the restraints "No" I call out, he stops "I want to do this" I do, I really do want this. I open my eyes to look at him "please, just give me a minute"

Caleb's concern filled eyes soften, he strokes my hair and lowers himself down next to me "Something else is causing the panic" I nod, I should have known he'd see right through me. His eyes roam my face searching for answers "give me your safe word"

I don't have one. I know the standard red, yellow and green as Clayton put those in place when we first started to play but now, I want something different. Something that has significance and meaning. I thought I was free from all of my past, I want to be well and truly free of it. I want freedom to explore my sexuality, I want freedom to experiment without any hindrance. That's it…

"Freedom" I say with clarity and certainty.

"Freedom" Caleb repeats softly "so my wild kitten wants to be set free from whatever haunts her beautiful eyes" his fingers trail and caress my face and throat.

"Yes" I barely whisper.

"Then I am honoured to be the one to lay those ghosts to rest and set you free" his lips seal mine. He kisses me so lovingly, tears unexpectedly spring to my eyes. His lips move over my face, he kisses away my tears "shhh, I've got you my love"

Caleb continues to murmur encouragement and endearments to me as he works his way all over my body with soft kisses, swirls of his tongue, gentle nips of teeth and the tender touch of his rough callused hands. There isn't an inch of my skin that he doesn't touch. It doesn't take long before my body takes over and has shown my bad memories the door. Soon I'm undulating in response to Caleb's expert ministrations.

"Ready to play now kitten" Caleb's gravelly voice and warm breath tickle my ear.

"Yes"

"Open your eyes and watch in the mirror" my heavy eyes slowly peel open. Caleb's loving gorgeous emerald green eyes are the first thing I see "there she is, my beautiful girl" he lowers and kisses me until my toes curl. I whimper when he pulls away.

I lift my head to watch him as he twists to pick something small up off the end of the bed. He raises an eyebrow at me, oh I'm supposed to keep still. I roll my eyes and let my head flop back.

"My wild kitten refuses to be tamed" he chuckles.

"Told you I'm a crap submissive" I retort "I may be sexually submissive but all the other stuff doesn't rock my boat" I lift my head to prove my point making him laugh. It's a lovely sound.

"Oh I could make you behave" the steely tone of his voice leaves me in no doubt how he would achieve that "but, I wouldn't have you any other way. Now lie still and be a good girl for me" he leans in for a kiss. The pressure he applies has my head hitting the pillow in no time.

Caleb trails kisses down my throat to my chest. His tongue swirls and laps at my nipple. I open my eyes remembering I'm supposed to be watching him. Holy cow, this is hot! Caleb covering my spread eagled body.

Seeing the back of his head move in time with what I'm feeling he's doing with his mouth and seeing the muscles of his back and arms flex and move as his hands fondle my breasts is erotic as hell. He sucks hard on my nipple then I feel a pinch.

"Ouch" I yelp at the shock of the sharp pain radiating from my nipple, it quickly turns to a dull ache but its pleasure I feel surging between my legs. I lift my head to see something attached to my nipple "what the hell's that?"

"Nipple clamp" Caleb replies smugly as he sets to work on my other nipple. This time I remain quiet, I know what to expect as soon as he sucks hard on my nipple "good girl, you learn quick" he tugs on the chain that connects the clamps. The sharp sting blooms to pleasure, my hips rotate "I won't leave them on for long since it's your first time"

I lift my head again trying to get a better look, the clamps look like mini gator grips but not as vicious looking, they appear to have a soft leather coating. The chain connecting them is fine gold. Caleb straddles me, shifting forward so his knees are either side of my ribs. Gently he pushes my boobs together and massages them. The pressure of the clamps and the kneading of his hands sends a multitude of sensations straight to my sex. My hips thrust upwards but my movements are hampered because I can't move my legs and feet to get the leverage I want to lift higher.

"Open your eyes"

Shit! I can't help closing my eyes, it's a natural reaction to absorb and handle the churning pleasure in my body. I look into the mirror. Caleb shifts and manoeuvres his cock in between my tits. He rotates his hips and pushes forward and back, stroking himself at the same time stimulating my breasts. I moan not just at the pain and pleasure sensations but at the erotic image reflecting back from the ceiling. Caleb tilts his head back, his emerald green eyes holding mine.

"It looks as good as it feels, doesn't it kitten?"

"Yes" I groan, other areas of my body want attention now.

A few more thrusts and Caleb is moving down my body. His hands and mouth drive me insane, every now and then he tugs on the chain making me cry out. He moves between my legs, thank god. I feel my juices flow as my sex clenches in anticipation for his magical hands and mouth, not forgetting his wicked tongue. Caleb doesn't disappoint. Placing his hands underneath my bum he lifts my hips up a fraction. The pull of the restraints on my wrists and ankles reminds me of how much I am at his mercy. Caleb runs his tongue once along my cleft and places a kiss on my pubic mound before placing my hips back on the bed. No! I want more.

"How long has it been since you were fucked here?" Caleb's question and probing figure at my anus cuts off all protests I'm about to make "answer me kitten, how long?"

My lust addled brain fights through the fog of memories trying to work out when the last time Clayton had taken me that way. Caleb pushes his lubricated finger inside me, the sudden discomfort and pain at the intrusion has me gasping. The memory suddenly becomes crystal clear. We had been on the plane coming back from a business trip in Los Angeles.

"Just over eighteen months ago" I pant out.

"I can tell it's been awhile, you are as tight here as your beautiful pussy is" Caleb moves his finger in and out slowly, reaching up he tugs the chain.

"Ah" my back arches off the bed, the spiking pleasure is intense. My clit throbs and pulses. My heaving chest is causing my nipples to throb in the clamps.

Caleb removes his finger. I sense him moving I open my eyes in time to see him sitting up right "Do you know what this is?" he holds up something torpedo shaped.

"It's either a vibrator or a butt plug" I answer warily.

Caleb gives me a dazzling smile "Well done kitten, it's both. A vibrating butt plug" he squirts lubricant gel over it and his fingers "lift your hips as far as you can for me"

Without questioning him I do it. His fingers are cool with the gel. They slide easily into me. I get lost in the pleasure as he gently thrusts in and out of me. I groan when he penetrates me with the plug easing it in just as gently as he did with his fingers.

"Holy crap" I yelp at the sudden vibrating.

"Sorry kitten, I should have warned you" I lift my head to see Caleb trying to keep a straight face. Sorry, my arse he is. The vibrating turns into short sharp pulses. It is the strangest sensation I've ever experienced "how's that?"

I laugh at the absurdity of the question, Caleb's face is suddenly in front of mine with a confused and bemused look on it.

"What's so funny?"

"Sorry" I try for contrite but I don't think I succeed "it's the first time I've ever been asked how I like my arse vibrating" that sets me off laughing.

"I'm glad you find it amusing" Caleb says. I feel his cock at my entrance just before he thrusts forward.

My giggles catch and die at the back of my throat, turning into long drawn out groans. It's the first time I've been penetrated like this. The fullness, the stretching, the feeling of his cock and the butt plug deep inside me… its mind blowing. Caleb pulls back and thrusts going deeper. I move my arms and legs to wrap them around him, to cradle him taking him deeper still but I can't. The clinking of metal against wood reminds me of the restraints. I pull against them trying to see if I can get any slack, no such luck. Caleb grins at me as he thrusts, with one hand he tugs at the chain connecting the nipple clamps.

"Oh god, Caleb!" I cry out. The unexpected pain in my nipples rapidly blends with the intense heavy pleasure that's building in my lower stomach, the friction of Caleb and the pulsing vibrations have me careering head long for the precipice. My heart is hammering in my chest. I feel sweat breaking out over my skin, I'm burning.

"Your tight pussy feels fucking amazing" Caleb rasps out "you're not to come until I tell you" Caleb's words cut through the crescendo of noise in my appetence for climax.

Hell no! I've no chance of stopping now. I'm too close to the edge. Caleb thrusts deeply, I let go screaming his name as fireworks explode inside of me.

"You really are very naughty kitten" Caleb's gravelly voice rasps in my ear "I told you not to come until I gave you permission to do so"

I open my heavy eye lids as I drag myself back to awareness. The butt plug is still vibrating in my arse, Caleb is slowly thrusting and rotating his hips. My body snaps back to full alert as pleasure reignites.

"Oops!" I'm not sorry so I'm not going to apologise, instead I clench my muscles hard around his cock. I groan along with Caleb.

Caleb clenches his eyes tight, he's fighting to keep control. I squeeze him again. A deep sexy growl vibrates out of his chest. I do it again.

"Fuck" Caleb hisses, he rears up. Twists slightly reaching for my ankle. I hear a click and my leg is free. Moving quickly, he shifts my leg so it's resting on his shoulder then leans forward planting his fists and braces his arms on either side of my stretched out arms.

He starts to move fast, in and out, in and out. Driving harder with each thrust. His balls slap against the butt plug, enhancing the pulsing vibration. The burning embers of my previous climax burst into an inferno. My frazzled nerve endings spark back to life with a vengeance as pleasure sensations crash around my body with each plunge Caleb makes. I feel a sharp tug on my nipples as the clamps are removed. The rush of blood and the surrounding hot warmth of Caleb's mouth has me mindless with desire to orgasm again. My head is thrashing side to side as I fight to stave off the looming climax.

"Caleb" I call out

"Now, Skye"

Caleb slams in to me. We both shout as our orgasms claim us, taking us on a blissful roller coaster ride of agonised pleasure. Caleb moves his hips in sensuous slow movements prolonging the ride. Our bodies shake and shudder in unison, our laboured breathing and hammering hearts beat in sync.

It takes me a few minutes for me to find my voice to speak. I only do it because I'm beginning to feel uncomfortable with the position I'm in.

"Caleb, release me please" I whisper the words into his ear.

His head is buried in the crook of my neck. His warm gusting breath and heavy heaving body a welcome weight pushing me further into the mattress. He places a soft kiss on my shoulder and lifts his head. His eyes are unfocused for a few seconds as he looks down at me, then seems to remember I have one leg over his shoulder whilst the other along with my arms are tied down.

He gently eases out of me and removes the butt plug, then makes quick work of unhooking the cuffs. He lies down on his back and pulls me on top of him seeming content to hold me close. One hand plays with my hair whilst the other strokes lightly up and down my back. I rest my head on his chest, he has very little hair considering how dark he is, a fine light smattering, just enough for me to play with.

"I'm not normally one to ask how it was for you" Caleb whispers into my hair, he kisses the top of my head. I still, I sense a but coming "but seeing your fear and panic at the beginning, I have to ask"

I lift my head and look into his concern filled emerald eyes. I inch up and kiss him slowly. His arms tighten around me pulling me closer. He breaks the kiss "As much as I love kissing you that doesn't answer my question" he chuckles.

"It was... fabulous, fantastic, great, earth shattering" I grin at him "has that stroked your ego enough, or do I need to find some more adjectives?"

Caleb's deep rumbling laugh vibrates through me, my nipples harden and tingle. He runs his fingers down the side of my cheek "It was the same for me too" he kisses me tenderly "as it is each and every time with you" he murmurs against my lips.

"Ditto"

I snuggle back down onto his chest. We stay in companionable silence, neither of us feeling the need to talk, for quite a while. Our fingers drawing lazy patterns on each other's skin. I find the feel of Caleb's rough callused hands strangely therapeutic, lulling me into a light slumber.

"Skye?"

"Hmmm" it's too much bother to form words.

"Will you answer a really personal question for me?" I hear the cautious hesitancy in Caleb's gravelly voice.

"Ask your question and then I'll decide and let you know"

"Fair enough" Caleb chuckles, I love the sound as it rumbles down my ear "actually I suppose I'm after clarification really" he tugs on my hair so I lift my head to look at him "how much of the lifestyle did you and your husband lead?"

"We didn't" I smile at his confusion.

"But you know the submissive pose. You've let me do some… you know kinky stuff without protest. In fact, I would go as far to say you loved it and correct me if I'm wrong but I think you'd let me do a whole lot more. What I don't understand is your reaction to the cuffs"

A shiver of lust and desire runs through me. He's right. I'd let him tie me in knots, literally, given the chance. I run my fingers lightly over his chest, the tip of my fingers circle his nipple as I contemplate my answer. I watch it pucker and distend as I decide honesty is always best. I select my words carefully so as not to arouse too much suspicion to instigate an interrogation from him about my past.

"Clayton was a dominant but he wasn't into the lifestyle. When he was in college he and a friend went through the training, he always said it was because he was a curious horny teenager" I snort a laugh at the memory "but his focus was mainly building his business empire. However, there were certain things he liked to do and I liked him doing them to me but first I had to get over some issues and he helped me." I look at Caleb gaging his reaction, his expression remains attentive.

"He always said that it was my choice if I wanted to be more active in the Dom-Sub lifestyle. I looked into it even spoke with a submissive, I spent a day with her and she showed me the pose and talked me through how to act and told me about her experiences. I knew I wouldn't go the whole way purely because I worked too hard for my independence and control over my life. I will never completely surrender control in or out of the bedroom. Especially out of the bedroom, the thought of being at someone's beck and call and doing things in a way of their choosing just does nothing for me even if it does mean giving the Dom pleasure and there is no way in hell I will let anyone beat me into behaving a certain way. And before you say the sub has all the power, I get that but it still won't change my mind"

I let out a heavy sigh, I've said more than I intended. I start to move to sit up but Caleb's arms tighten, keeping me in place.

"You don't have to give me the details but I'm guessing these issues you mentioned were of a previous bad sexual experience and as far as the independence and control stems from the way you were brought up" Caleb's voice is soft.

"Yes" I whisper.

Caleb's fingers lightly trace the side of my face, his eyes burning with curiosity and I see flashes of anger. I feel his protectiveness in the strength of his hold on me. I'm thankful that he keeps his inquisitiveness to himself. He tenderly kisses me.

"Tell me about the kind of things you did that you liked" Caleb's request surprises me, he chuckles at the expression on my face "don't get me wrong the thought of you being with someone else drives me bat shit crazy but you are mine now and I want to do lots of naughty kinky things with you and to you, so what do you like?"

I'm stunned, that's the second time in less than an hour he has said I belong to him. A warmth blooms through me. I like the sound of it. If it came from anyone else, I'd more than likely laugh in their face after I'd slapped it. But this feels right.

"I know you like it rough and you like to be spanked, especially with the riding crop" it's as if Caleb's deep gravelly voice is talking directly to my pussy. I squeeze my thighs at the sudden surge of desire pooling there "I will shackle you to this bed and spank it out of you"

Oh, sweet lord "Yes please" I whisper.

I can't believe I've just said that. My inner slut goddess is running around my head ripping her robes off in lust driven ecstasy shouting 'It's about bloody time, bring it on!'

"As you wish kitten" Caleb growls.

Flaming hell and heavens above, what have I unleashed?

CALEB

I sit up cradling Skye to me, my wild kitten has just thrown down the gauntlet. She is a paradox, on the one hand she won't conform to behaving as a traditional Sub and being punished is a big no-no yet she willing lets herself be spanked because she is reluctant to give information.

"Lie face down with your arms out stretched"

I move off the bed and watch Skye obediently follow my instructions. Her long wild curly hair flows around her, covering her luscious body except her peachy taut arse. My semi hard cock is at full attention in a split second.

"Do you have a hair tie?"

Skye lifts her head, her puzzled look suddenly changes to a big grin as realisation dawns why I asked the question, she blows at the hair covering her face "In my bag, inside pocket there should be a black scrunchie"

I find it straight away. Skye rises to her knees and takes it from me and makes quick work of tying her hair up, she lies back down in position when she's done. In the meantime, I get the leather throng flogger and riding crop out of the bag.

"Lift up your beautiful arse for me kitten"

I collect the four pillows and place them under her. I run my hand over her back, arse and thighs, circling and stroking. Skye's response is instant; she pushes into my hand. My dick gets harder. I've never known a woman to be so responsive to my touch, my hands aren't the softest in fact I'm acutely aware of how rough they are. I may have a reputation as a brilliant Dom but I've known Sub's to cringe at my touch, it's one of the reasons why I touch them as little as possible. But my wild kitten practically purrs when I do this. She's addictive.

Remembering how she brought her hands to cover herself when I spanked her earlier I decide to shackle them to the bed, she's still wearing the cuffs. I move to the end of the bed taking hold of her wrist I click it into place, securing the other wrist I look down into Skye's excited yellow green eyes. She wants this badly. My cock jerks at the sight of her prone position. I climb up on to the bed behind her. I adjust the spread of her knees. Her pussy glistens further confirming how badly she wants to be spanked.

"You really are looking forward to this aren't you my lovely kitten?" I run my fingers around her lips, spreading the mix of my semen and her juices over to her anus and back down to her clit. Skye groans as I let my fingers dance, teasing out more of her creamy juice "when I'm done spanking you I'm going to fuck you here" I press my finger against the tight puckered entrance of her back passage, the lift and push back of her hips tells me she wants it now "patience kitten, first you have yet to tell me what I want to know" Skye whimpers as I move off her.

Getting off the bed I pick up the leather throng flogger, I then spy the vibrator at the foot of the bed. My sadistic side kicks in.

"You're not allowed to come until I tell you" I say parting her lips and insert the vibrator. Skye gasps as I switch it on to the lowest setting "comfortable enough?"

Skye doesn't answer, she's concentrating on breathing. I slap her bottom just at the juncture of her buttock and thigh,

"Yes Master" Skye yelps and jerks.

"Remember to safe word if it gets too much and you want to stop" an idea comes to me "if you want me to hit harder say green. If it's just right and you want more of the same say yellow. If it's too hard say red. To stop completely use your safe word, understand?"

"Yes Master" Skye says clearly and without hesitation.

"I'm going to warm up your skin using the leather flogger, I will be starting lightly building up to heavier strikes start to use the colours from that point on, understand?"

"Yes Master"

"Now start telling me about the things you've done that you like"

I flick my wrist in a figure of eight, the soft swish of the leather throngs cutting through the air then the equally soft thwack of landing against the skin on her back has my body tingling all over. Skye lets out a sound that is a mix of a moan and sigh saturated with pleasure.

"We role played. I would dress up and we would act out certain scenarios"

I like the sound of that "Describe them to me"

Swish, thwack, swish, thwack.

"Clayton would ring me mid-morning saying I had to attend a disciplinary hearing for unsatisfactory work and poor performance meeting targets. I knew I had to dress up in my naughty secretary outfit and be at his office for lunch. I would wear a tightly fitted low cut cleavage revealing top or blouse with a tight fitting pencil skirt that finished at my knee but the split at the back finished about an inch from my bum. Black seamed stockings and killer heels. When I arrived and he was on the phone the majority of the time I would suck him off, he would always tell me not to make him come… but of course I always did. He would bend me over his desk and spank me then fuck me hard. Sometimes he would sit me on his desk with my skirt around my waist and go down on me whilst he conducted a telephone conference call, if it was a particularly long meeting he would fuck me as well"

Christ my imagination is running riot. My cock and balls ache. I increase the force of the swing. The swish and thwack becoming louder. Skye's groaning resonates deep within me.

"Tell me more"

"Other times Clayton would phone saying he wanted a girl. Blonde, big tits, petite. I knew then I had to turn up in my stripper come hooker outfit" Skye sighs deeply "green"

It takes me a second to realise she wants it harder. I oblige.

"I have a tartan micro mini skirt" a throaty chuckle "Clayton called it a belt because it is so short. It just about covers my bum but when I walk it flashes my cheeks" Skye's hips undulate against the pillows "green. Hmmm, yes" she moans "I would wear a tight fitting jersey top with buttons down the front, revealing as much bra and cleavage as possible. Sometimes I would wear hold up stockings and I have a pair of clear hooker shoes, the ones where the soles light up when you walk"

She's going to have me coming soon. I increase the strikes of the flogger.

"Sometimes Clayton would have me dance and strip. He would be sat in a chair and I would give him a lap dance. He wasn't allowed to touch me" Skye arches her back and mewls as she undulates her hips "other times he would bind my wrists using his tie and fuck me hard in various different positions around his office"

I put the flogger down and pick up the riding crop. I trail the tip over her back and down to her arse. Skye tenses when she realises what it is. I flick my wrist, the resounding smack of leather hitting flesh and Skye's throaty groan makes my skin prickle with desire.

"Green" she purrs lifting her arse in the air. How can I refuse her when she responds like this? I raise my arm and hit harder "yes! Yellow" Skye calls out. I repeat the move.

"Tell me more kitten, I know there is more" my heart is hammering in my chest, a heated mist of perspiration coats my skin.

"I would dress up in my naughty nurse outfit whenever he was ill, or faked illness" I hope to fuck it isn't one of those tacky rubber or PVC outfits "it's a figure hugging original nurses uniform only it's very short and has poppers running up the front" Skye's breathing is getting laboured, she pants heavily between words "I wear white stockings and suspenders with white platform high heeled shoes"

"When was the last time you played?" I pull the vibrator out and with three sharp taps with the crop I hit her pussy.

"Oh god!" Skye gasps, her breathing is laboured. I reinsert the vibrator.

I swing my arm back and hit hard "Answer me kitten, when?"

"Argh" Skye's chest lifts off the bed "we sort of played at Halloween" she pants out "other than that it had been months"

I hit hard again "How long?" I demand.

"Fuck, yes" Skye yells arching again, the red welts across her arse stand out against her pale skin "I don't… six… no, nine months maybe"

"Tell me about Halloween" again I hit hard, the strike landing directly below the other two.

"Jesus! You, son of a bitch!" Skye screams, she pulls hard on the restraints lifting her torso like before, her hips grind down into the pillows. My cock is painfully hard, demanding attention "please Caleb… Master"

"You're close to coming aren't you kitten?" I flick the crop, landing the strike at the juncture of her arse and thighs.

"Argh! Yes" Skye cries out pulling on the wrist restraints "please Caleb… please" she begs.

"Not yet. Tell me now"

Skye is really struggling; her hips undulate trying to get friction. Her slick body is a glorious quivering mass of need to climax. I softly tap over her back, buttocks and thighs working every inch, including the red welts. Her body responds by lifting and writhing. It's fucking magnificent.

"Part of my costume… sharp teeth made" Skye labours to say "Clayton… bite him all over… blow job, argh!"

It's enough for me to fill in the blanks. I feel a pang of jealousy; he was a lucky bastard having someone so willing to play like that, whenever he wanted.

I turn off the vibrator and step back. I want to know more, only this time it's her fantasies I want, not her husbands. I watch Skye slowly come back from the brink of orgasm, when her laboured breathing returns to normal, she lifts her head and looks at me. I see the confusion in her beautiful yellow green eyes. I lower myself so we're eye level.

"Thank you kitten, you've told me what he wanted and you no doubt enjoyed playing along. Now, I want to know your deepest, darkest fantasies. What are the games you've always wanted to play but have never told a soul? Those are the things I want to hear"

"Oh fuck!" Skye whispers dropping her head down.

Standing, I chuckle, because she knows I know she will tell me, even if it is under duress, kind of. I run my hand over her back and arse, down in between her legs, I switch the vibrator back on. A low resigned moan comes from Skye. I trail the riding crop over her skin and start a light tapping over every inch of her skin, arms, legs, buttocks, back, shoulders.

"I'll make this easy for you kitten. I already know you have a fantasy of being fucked by two men. Your body told me that on the train" Skye nods her head "have you ever fantasied about being with a woman?"

"No" Skye says clearly, her hips grind in to the pillows "girl on girl does nothing for me"

"So tell me what does" I bring the crop down hard on her buttocks.

"Argh!" Skye cries out, pulling on the restraints. I admire the muscle definition of her arms and back, she really does take care of her body. I start the tapping over her body, slightly harder this time.

"I'm waiting kitten" I add a touch of impatience to my voice. Skye visibly tenses waiting the next hard blow. I don't deliver, it'll come when she least expects it.

Skye's head drops to the mattress "Three men" it's barely a whisper and it stops me dead in my tracks.

"Go on"

A heavy sigh, but nothing follows. I raise my arm ready to deliver the hardest blow.

"Two are playing with my tits, the other on my pussy" Skye's words are muffled but I hear them as clear as day. My mind is a riot of possibilities "and being watched" she adds more clearly.

My control snaps. Moving quickly, I grab the gel and climb on the bed positioning myself behind her. I coat my dick with the gel and her puckered opening. The tension in her body is palpable, sliding my fingers down reaching between her legs I increase the speed of the vibrator then moving down I locate her clitoris. My fingertips gently tease the sides of tight knot until she relaxes and moans giving herself over to the pleasure. The shaft of my cock massages the crack of her arse, gliding smoothly the gel mixes with her juices, after a few minutes I guide my dick to her rear entrance. Gently pushing through the resistance, I still when Skye cries out.

"Breathe deeply kitten" I continue to massage her clit as I run my other hand over her back, soothing her. She relaxes, I push further in.

Fuck she is so tight. I can feel the pulsating thrum of the vibrator through the thin membrane wall pushing against my cock. That and the clenching muscles of her arse has my dick thickening and my balls drawing up as carnal pleasure erupts from the sensations. I pull back and ease back in. My eyes roll to the back of my head, I fight to keep control as I repeat the motion over and over again, going deeper with each penetration.

"Oh, god. I can't hold on much longer" Skye half whimpers and groans. Her muscle spasms tell me as much.

"Yes, you can" I bark out as I start to move faster, thrusting harder when Skye pushes back onto me taking me to the root.

I grasp her hips and pull her back on to me as I thrust forward, she feels fucking amazing. My control snaps when her muscles grip me hard and squeeze. A red haze descends caused by my debauchery and the animalistic carnal need I have to possess my wild kitten, my Skye. Pummelling in to her harder and faster, the slap of flesh hitting flesh drives me on. My blood feels as if it's on fire. My pulse pounds in my ears muffling Skye's cries of pleasure. The pressure in my groin builds and builds, sweat is pouring off me as the desperate need for release increases.

"Caleb" Skye screaming my name and her tightening around me as her climax takes over her body triggers my orgasm.

"Argh. Skye!" I bellow throwing my head back as my whole body locks and my release explodes from me. The aftershocks have me collapsing forward, I crouch over Skye pulling her close to me feeling the shudders and convulses of her body matching mine.

When I can breathe properly, I ease out of her and remove the vibrator. Releasing her from the cuffs I massage her shoulders and trail kisses along her skin. Gently I move her off the pillows and wrap her in my arms, Skye snuggles in to me. Her soft smooth body fits perfectly against mine.

"You know I can't help thinking that you are genetically engineered specifically for me" I murmur into her hair.

"I bet you say that to all the girls" Skye says sleepily.

A flash of annoyance has me lifting her chin forcing her eyes to meet mine "I have never said that to anyone in my life" I can't hide she's just pissed me off nor can I stop scowling at her.

Skye lifts her hand and strokes my face "I apologise, that was insensitive of me" Skye kisses me, gently and sensuously "forgive me" she murmurs looking at me with wide luminous yellow green eyes.

I roll her on to her back "Kiss me again and I might" I grumble. Skye's throaty chuckle has my cock stirring to life. I silence her by claiming her mouth.

"I need to answer my phone" Skye mumbles against my lips.

I pull back and look at her puzzled I didn't hear a phone ring, then the faint sound of music reaches my ears. Reluctantly, I lift myself and Skye slides out from under me. She hangs over the bed and grabs her bag. 'Born in the USA' gets louder as she pulls her phone out.

"Where are you?" she says as a way of greeting "I'll be ten minutes" she hangs up.

I crawl over to Skye and kiss her long and slow. I burn the feel of her lips and her taste into my memory. I don't know when I'll next be able to do this, then inspiration hits.

"I want to see you tonight, come down into the bar. I'll be there about seven thirty"

"Okay" whispers Skye.

We both dress quickly. Skye straightens the bed sheets whilst I clean the toys and put them away along with the whips. At the door I lean down to give Skye a final kiss. I don't want to make what we have going on common knowledge and I have a sneaky suspicion that it's the same for her as well. I step out into the hallway first to make sure the coast is clear; I signal to Skye. She joins me with a broad smile on her face.

"What?" I ask curious, I know from that smile something amuses her.

"I feel like a naughty kid whose about to get caught with their hand in the cookie jar"

"So long as your hand is in my cookie jar I'll make sure we don't get caught" I wink at her.

"Caleb!" Skye squeals and bursts in to laughter as we walk hand in hand down the corridor. I let go when we get to the stairs. I fight the urge to tuck her into my side and never let her go.

"I need to see Harry before I leave" Skye turns to me at the foot of the stairs.

"I do too"

I don't but I'll grab whatever remaining seconds I can before I start counting down the minutes till seven thirty. I glance at the grandfather clock, that's one hundred and fifty and counting. We're half way across the foyer when Harry comes out of the restaurant with Rex.

"Ms Darcy, I trust you got everything you need" Harry smiles at her, I don't miss his curious eyes flicking to me.

"I did thank you and Mr Raven was very kind letting me sit in on his session" Skye's smile is dazzling "it was very helpful and he's given me lots of inspiration" she gives me a saucy wink. I feel myself blush, for fucks sake what's that all about?

Harry laughs, he's delighted. Rex looks like he's sucking on a lemon.

"Glad to be of service" I mock a bow, Skye responds by dipping into a curtsey.

"Will you be visiting here again?" says Rex hopefully.

"No, I have everything I need for now" I notice Skye moving back slightly her smile slips a little, she doesn't much care for Rex "I'm assuming Mr Benenati has given you the time frame I'm working to for the paintings" Skye says to Harry.

"He has indeed and I look forward to seeing the finished master pieces. I must admit, after he showed me the ones you've produced for his other clubs I can't wait" Harry beams at her.

The front door opens and we all turn to see who's coming in. I recognise the guy as Skye's bodyguard, she nods to him and turns back to Harry.

"It was a pleasure meeting you again Mr Davies" she holds out her hand "and I'll see you sometime in the autumn. Mr Benenati will let you know of the exact date"

"I look forward to it" says Harry warmly.

Skye nods to Rex, turning to me a with a wicked smile and mischief dancing in her eyes she says "And I'll see you later for that drink"

We all watch as she walks out, her bodyguard reaches out and takes her bag off her shoulder. At the door Skye turns back and waves, then she's gone.

"You're meeting her for a drink!" Rex splutters incredulously.

I shrug "Sure, she wants to thank me for this afternoon" I hope I sound and look nonchalant.

"Some of your mentees were disappointed she wasn't the sub for the session" Harry chuckles, that doesn't surprise me "they're hoping she'll be there for the next session so expect questions when she's not. Good feedback again by the way. Two of the guys wanted to know if they paid for private lessons would you teach them how to use the bull whip" now that does surprise me "have a think and let me know" Harry looks at his watch "excuse me gentlemen I have a meeting to attend"

I hand the bag of whips over to Harry and shake his hand. Rex follows me as I head for the front door. I glance at the clock, one hundred and forty-two minutes to go.

"Harry, hang on a minute" calls out Rex and walks back towards his cousin "what did you mean by finished master pieces?"

Harry smiles broadly "Don't you know? Ms Darcy is a world renowned highly sort after artist. Mr Benenati commissions her to produce paintings for all of his clubs. He's commissioning twenty for this place and believe me her paintings don't come cheap"

"So she'll be back in the autumn with all the paintings?" Rex clarifies.

"No, she's only here on a short business trip and returning here at some point in the autumn to go through the preliminary ideas she has. My understanding is she won't be starting the commission until the end of the year. Mr Benenati tells me she has a two year waiting list but she's brought him forward a year to coincide with other work commitments she has whilst being in England" Harry turns to walk away then stops "you know Ms Darcy is a very astute businesswoman, don't make the mistake of underestimating her" Harry looks directly at me when he says that. He dips his head and leaves.

Rex turns to face me, a thoughtful frown on his face. I can see the cogs turning formulating some sort of scheme no doubt to hook and reel Skye in. Harry's words bounce around my head as I get in my Land Rover 'astute businesswoman' it sounds like he's been doing his homework on her and it's about time I did my own.

CHAPTER FIFTEEN

SKYE

The pub is quiet when I arrive back, with less than a handful of customers calling in for a quick drink on their way home from work. I nod and smile as they stare open mouthed at me. I spot Simon and Freya sitting in a far corner with Chris and Michelle close to the log fire. As I approach them I can see Simon is holding court, Freya is frantically taking notes as Chris and Michelle look at Simon in awe.

"So as I mentioned at the start these are the four campaigns I think we should kick off with" Simon points to something I can't see "This place has so much character it would be criminal not to exploit it and I'm going to recommend to Skye that we focus on these four target markets first" again he points to something "Give me your thoughts"

"I hope you haven't bamboozled these lovely people" I speak over Simon as I walk around the table and see a note pad filled with Simon's looping handwriting and diagrams.

"Hey, baby girl just in time" Simon grins at me as I sit down gingerly and very carefully next to him, my bum is so tender "I'll bring you up to speed in a minute first I want Chris and Michelle's thoughts on my proposal"

"I'm amazed you've thought of all of this in such a short space of time" says Chris, his admiration written all over his face.

"I'm not sure about the haunted angle. I love the other three" says Michelle, she winces apologetically.

"This place has ghosts!" I exclaim. Chris and Michelle nod sheepishly and look slightly worried "how cool is that. Wow!" I'm impressed and my painful arse is temporarily forgotten.

"See I told you she'd love it" Simon crows.

"Seriously it doesn't bother you?" Michelle says slightly stunned.

I shake my head "I love all that supernatural stuff. Hey do you think we can get one of those paranormal TV shows interested to film here?" I say excited, the others laugh at me "I'm being serious" I grin.

"Let's not get too far ahead of ourselves" Simon says patting my knee "what are you not sure about Michelle?"

"Well won't it put people off staying here if they learn it's haunted?"

"Not if we do the campaigns the way I suggest. You see the haunted angle will only be blatantly publicised to those people who are interested in that kind of thing. With the other three target markets there will be no mention whatsoever and they'll only learn about it once they're here. Some people won't believe it, such as the out and out sceptics. The majority of people staying in such an old place like this will expect some sort of unexplained phenomena to occur and it's their stories we need to collect to attract more of the believers"

I can see Simon has won Michelle round. Chris is already sold.

"No decisions need to be made just yet" I say "mull it all over, have a chat and put down your own ideas and we'll get together before we leave on Sunday" Chris and Michelle nod. My stomach growls loudly.

"What would you like to eat" Michelle laughs getting up "I have some of those burgers you like"

"Yes please, with bacon and cheese" I say eagerly "and those curly fries if there's any left"

"What would you like to drink" Chris says standing also.

"Budweiser please"

Simon and Freya bring me up to speed on what's happened today. Simon is gushing about how quaint the village is, it seems Freya has acted as tour guide and took him over to Henley for a few hours as well. He runs through all of his PR and marketing ideas for the pub. I love each one and tell him to go with whatever Chris and Michelle feel most comfortable with, we can always revisit his more outlandish ideas at a later date.

Paul and Alan joins us when the food arrives. Freya gives an update on her personal business and tells me someone from the brewery is coming over tomorrow with the relevant paperwork to sign for the sale of the premises.

Freya flicks a nervous glance in Paul and Alan's direction "I told them you're a cash buyer, I hope that's okay"

"Of course" I smile reassuringly at her.

"Also I spoke to Joshua Blake" my face drops in shock. Freya looks scared to death now "I told him to expect a call from the legal department of the brewery in the next day or so. I wasn't sure who to call about the money side, Joshua said he will sort it out" Freya is frantically wringing her hands.

I lean over and put mine over hers "You did the right thing, stop worrying. I like it that you're taking the initiative. And thank you Alan and Simon for pointing her in the right direction"

The guys laugh and Freya sags in relief. As much as I loathe using Joshua because he'll blab to the rest of his family, I have no choice at present and I don't want Freya thinking she's done something wrong if I say anything different. Paul talks through his meeting with the security electronics company – I was too wrapped up reliving my afternoon with Caleb on the journey home plus my burning arse from the spanking put paid to any coherent conversation – and his ideas for wiring up the Hall and the cottages. The company's managing director is coming himself along with the sales rep Paul spoke with to view the plans so he can give an estimation on cost.

I'm looking through the emails on Freya's tablet and giving her instructions when in my peripheral vision I notice Paul and Alan shifting position. I look up to see them watching an extremely nervous middle-aged man approaching our tables. I mentally put him mid to late fifties with his well-worn craggy face and short dark grey hair swept back off his brow. He's wearing a cheap dark suit and looks very uncomfortable in it. He tugs on the collar of his shirt. In his hands he's holding a cap, when's he's not tugging at his shirt his hands are twisting the cap. He looks wearily at Paul and Alan. He opens and closes his mouth a few times, words fail him.

"How can I help you?" I ask softly and smile, hoping to put him at ease.

"My name is Frank Appleton, Ms Darcy" he stutters "I'm a... I'm..." he laughs nervously.

"Come and take a seat along with a deep breath" Paul and Alan stand and move so Frank can sit down, his eyes flick anxiously at them "don't worry they won't bite unless I tell them to" I wink at Frank and he lets out a genuine startled laugh "come on" I pat the seat next to me encouraging him, it works "what can I get you to drink Frank?"

His eyes widen in surprise "Pint of bitter please"

Alan goes to the bar to get the round in, Paul clears the empty plates off the table.

"So tell me Frank what service do you offer?"

"How did you..." he stops himself "sorry, I'm a gardener" he takes a deep breath.

Something clicks into place. When I was looking around the cottages earlier in the week I noticed the gardens seemed to be well tended considering they have been empty for the best part of five years since the last of the tenants left.

"So you're the gentleman who's been tending to the gardens at the cottages" I exclaim and I can see I've shocked the shit out of Frank "I wondered who had been looking after them and I've been meaning to ask Joyce"

Frank blushes "Guilty as charged" he laughs "I started working for Lady Farringdon's grandfather as a lad. I used to look after the cottages as well, then the fire happened. When the cottages became vacant I couldn't bear to see the gardens become eyesores" he shrugs.

This is a man passionate about what he does. Alan places the drinks on the table. Frank takes a large mouthful, draining half of his drink in one gulp. He's building up courage to ask me for a job. I decide to help him along.

"So what have you been doing since then?"

"I had my own gardening business for a while but had to take alternative employment when the work began to dry up. Now I do Lord and Lady Farringdon's gardens once a month, Mrs Fawcett-Fowler hires me when she wants to hold a garden party, some of the outsiders" Frank looks at me sheepishly "sorry I meant no offense"

"None taken" I smile at him.

"Some of the people who have weekend homes here occasionally hire me, usually at the beginning of spring and end of autumn. Anyway" Frank clears his throat and tugs at the collar of his shirt "I was wondering if you could put a word in for me, you know with the new owners of the Hall. I understand you're here on their behalf" Frank starts picking nervously at his cap "I can get references if you need them"

He looks at me with such earnest open honesty and hope, my heart melts.

"If the new owner offered you a full time position, what would you do with your other customers?"

Frank blinks several times, shifts in his seat and clears his throat "I hadn't thought about that happening… well I'd give them notice and put them in touch with some contacts I have over in Henley. Do you think the new owner will do that, offer me a full time position?" again the hopefulness in his voice tugs at my heart.

I shrug "Maybe. Tell you what be here tomorrow around twelve thirty, forgive me I should ask can you be here for that time?"

"Y-y-yes" Frank stutters in shock.

"Excellent we'll talk more about it then"

Frank returns my smile and gets up "Thank you Ms Darcy, thanks so much. I'll see you tomorrow"

I watch him walk away with an expression that looks not too dissimilar to someone who's won the lottery. I feel really good about it.

"Nobody here knows who you are, do they?" Simon mutters under his breath to me.

"Only seven people know I'm Mrs Blake the owner of Dove Mill Hall, the rest think I'm the designer overseeing the work being done and I haven't felt the burning need to correct them"

Simon roars laughing, he throws his arm around my shoulders pulling me to him. He plants a big soppy wet kiss on my cheek "I've missed your cunning evil streak baby girl. So besides Chris and Michelle who are the others?"

"Lord and Lady Farringdon, the last owner was Lady Farringdon's uncle. Farmers Joe senior and junior who I met yesterday and the lovely Freya here, she knew who I was before I offered her a job"

Freya blushes like mad "I worked for the Law firm that dealt with the sale of the Hall. I knew her name from all the paperwork I had to check"

"How did Chris and Michelle find out?"

Simon is on one of his gossip gathering missions so I fill him in on the overheard betting conversation and Chris being stood by me at the time, how he had apologised for the men's bad language and I had revealed my identity.

"And neither of them have said a word to anyone" Simon says in wonder. I shake my head "so I take it no one knows you're buying the pub"

"Nope, although the cat might be let out of the bag tomorrow with the brewery coming here and if that doesn't give the game away Chris and Michelle will be involved in meetings with the architect, interior designer and any of the contractors that turn up"

"Tomorrow is going to be fun!" Simon says gleefully clapping his hands.

"And manic" Freya adds "on that note, if you don't need me I think I'll go and sort this lot out and turn in for an early night"

I can see Freya is looking tired so I don't push for her to stay for another drink "That's fine and thanks for all the good work you've done today. See you in the morning"

Freya flushes as she gathers her things together "Good night"

I watch her move through the pub, I'm surprised to see so many people in now. I glance at my watch fifteen minutes past seven, blimey the time has flown by. A bout of giddiness and butterflies hit my stomach, fifteen more minutes and I'll see Caleb again.

"She's a good find" Simon murmurs, I look at him watching her thoughtfully.

"Yeah, I think so too"

"Freya told me her story today, you know about her ex-boyfriend" I raise an eyebrow at him "okay I dragged it out of her" he holds his hands up "I told her that I'd get the story from you if she didn't spill"

"Simon" I sigh heavily exasperated "I hope you haven't scared the poor woman off; I would like to keep her longer than a week"

Simon puts his arm around me again "Skye please, give me some credit" I snort a laugh as I put my head on his shoulder "besides she's in for the long haul" Simon links the fingers of his free hand in mine "she sees you as her guardian angel and says you saved her life"

"I wouldn't go that far"

"I don't know Skye. Listening to her talk about the frequency that shit of an ex used to beat her I think it was only a matter of weeks before he put her down for good"

"Well at least Alan gave him a taste of his own medicine when she went to collect her things" I feel a surge of gratification that justice had been dealt on her behalf.

Mentioning Alan, it makes me realise he and Paul are absent. I look around and see both of them stood at the end of the bar with Freya. I also spot Caleb stood next to them. I smile when he raises his bottle to me in a salute.

"You know, tall dark and handsome" Simon pauses "add dangerous into that mix, has been staring at you for the last half of an hour" startled I look at Simon "at first I thought it was me he wanted but when I put my arm around you and kissed your cheek he looked as if he was about to rip me to shreds"

"He probably would" I laugh, now its Simon's turn to look surprised "that's mystery man from the train and yes I've been tapping him all week.

Oh and he also knows who I am, so that's eight not seven people who know my real identity"

"You lucky bitch! That's the Jason Momoa look-a-like" Simon says wide eyed. Nodding I collapse into a fit of giggles, Simon joins me "you lucky, lucky bitch. I have got to get a picture of him to show Shelley. She will not believe me"

"Come on I'll introduce you to him" I stand, picking up my bottle of Bud.

I make my way towards Caleb not taking my eyes off him for a second. A sexy as sin smile slowly spreads across his face the closer I get. Christ I want to ravish him and he is so rocking the bad boy image. Faded black jeans that deliciously hug his crotch and thighs, a black fitted t-shirt and black leather jacket. His shoulder length jet black wavy hair frames his beautiful chiselled face. His emerald green eyes sparkle with amusement. It takes every ounce of restraint I possess not to crawl up his sculpted body to get to those decadently sinful lips. There is no way in hell that I'm going to last the night without feeling those lips on me, anywhere on me. I take my jacket off, not because it's warm in the pub but from the simple fact I feel like I'm going to combust any minute from the fire burning deep inside me.

CALEB

I got back home in record time, within fifteen minutes I shaved, showered, changed clothes and was back in my car heading for the pub deciding to do my research on Skye first thing tomorrow morning. I'm going to be way too early but I can't hang around at home waiting for the time to pass so instead like some love struck puppy I'm going to sit at the bar and wait.

The pub is surprisingly busy for early evening on a Thursday, it doesn't get busier until around nine when people come in just before the quiz starts. Marie and Chris are rushed off their feet. I go to my usual spot at the end of the bar and wait to be served.

"Excuse me sir"

A deep American drawl comes from behind me. I turn and move to the side coming face to face with the blonde haired bodyguard. He has a stack of dirty plates in his hands, as he goes to put them on the bar Michelle materialises in front of us.

"Oh thank you Paul, I was just coming to clear the tables. Was everything alright"

"Yes ma'am. Delicious as always" smiles Paul. Michelle blushes. I've never seen her so coy. I can't help smiling at her, she avoids looking at me.

"Would you like anything else?" Michelle's cheeks are turning beetroot now.

"No thank you ma'am and Ms Darcy will let you know if she does"

The guy might be polite but he's still a mean looking bastard. She fancies him, it dawns on me. Michelle finally looks at me and grinning I wink at her. Michelle huffs and rolls her eyes taking the plates and disappears out the back. The other American bodyguard appears and hands Paul a drink, belatedly I realise Skye must be somewhere in the pub and that's why it's so busy. I scan the room until I spot her sat in the far corner by the fire. Frank Appleton is sat on one side, my eyes nearly pop out of my head the guy is in a fucking suit. In all the years I've known him I have only ever seen him wear a suit for a wedding and a funeral, bet it's the same one. He looks really nervous; his flat cap is going to be pulled to shreds if he keeps twisting it in his hands.

"Scotch or bottle Caleb" Marie's breathy voice intrudes on my observations.

"Bottle please" I turn back to see a rather harassed looking Marie "been busy long?"

"Only the last half an hour. Within ten minutes of our guest making a show" she nods in Skye's direction "everyone started coming in saying they wanted a good seat for the quiz" Marie snorts a derisive laugh as she places my drink on the bar and I pay "it's amazing how much excitement they're causing" suddenly realising two of the pubs guests are stood next to me all colour drains from Marie's face "I'm so sorry. I didn't mean to be rude" poor girl looks as if she's about to burst into tears.

Both men chuckle "No offense has been taken ma'am" says Paul.

"Besides Ms Darcy causes this kind of reaction wherever she goes" the other one says. I can't remember his name for the life of me "and if she's causing this much trouble now tomorrow is going to be bedlam" again both men laugh, leaving me wondering what the hell they're talking about.

"I'll make sure to be wearing my running shoes" says Marie putting the money in the till and laughs with them. Now I'm really intrigued.

I turn round and lean against the bar to watch Skye and her companions. The large woman has some serious bruises on her face, she looks familiar but I can't place her. The slim man sitting next to her looks high maintenance with his coiffured hair and designer clothes. Frank sitting on her opposite side looks like the poor relation in comparison. Skye however is giving Frank her full attention. The other man's eyes roam the bar as he talks to the large woman, they meet mine. I hold his hard gaze for a few seconds before breaking contact and look at Skye.

Frank stands and makes his way back to the bar, he's practically floating on cloud nine. He looks completely dazed and like the cat that got the cream at the same time. Over his shoulder I see high maintenance guy laughing, puts his arm around Skye and kisses her cheek.

"She's mine" the thought snarls through my mind. My hand tightens around the bottle; it takes everything I have not to launch the fucking thing at his head. Skye doesn't pull away from him; she looks at him fondly. Whoever he is, they're close I realise. Frank passes me and I hear him muttering "lovely woman, what a lovely woman" to himself. A few minutes later the large woman stands, she comes away looking flushed but pleased with herself, not in a smug way but happy at being recognised for something well done. As she gets closer I can see the extent of the bruising, she must have been in one hell of an accident to get bruises like that. She stops beside the bodyguards.

"Paul, Alan, I'm going up see you in the morning"

"Goodnight Freya"

I hear them say in unison as I watch high maintenance guy still with his arm around Skye link hands with her, she rests her head on his shoulder. No doubt about it they are exceptionally close. I feel insanely jealous of the intimate pose and show of affection. I want to do that with her. I want everyone to know she's mine. Skye's eyes suddenly snap to mine, my whole body tightens and an incredible warmth spreads through me at her dazzling smile. I raise the bottle in my hand, tipping it in her direction in acknowledgement.

High maintenance says something to her, whatever it is she's surprised then she's laughing. The throaty sexy sound drifts over the chattering sounds that surround me. I lip read 'You lucky bitch' from the guy's lips as his eyes rove up and down my body. Skye stands, picks up her drink and walks towards me. She's not changed and her hair is still tied in the messy ponytail.

I admire her jean clad legs, the sway of her hips and the flash of her mid riff as her t-shirt moves when she pulls off her jacket. Her eyes shimmer with lust for me, as always my body responds to her siren call. My dick presses uncomfortably against the fly buttons on my jeans. A discomfort I welcome if it means I get to spend the next couple of hours in my wild kitten's company.

"Hi, glad you could make it" Skye's husky voice washes over me, goose bumps break out along my arms "Caleb, I'd like you to meet one of my oldest and best friends Simon Hanson. Simon this is Caleb Raven"

"Pleased to meet you" I smile at the guy and shake his hand. His grip is surprisingly strong.

"Oh the pleasure is all mine sweet thing" Simon fans himself with his hand "Alan, I'm afraid you've been bumped down to second place in the man crush stakes"

Skye, Alan and Paul laugh. Rex suddenly appears at my side.

"Oh, no wait a minute Alan, make that third place" Simon says eying Rex.

"Now I'm crushed" Alan retorts good naturedly.

"And I'll pass on the second or first place, you're too high maintenance for me" I say joining everyone else laughing. Rex stands there looking confused at us all.

"Simon behave yourself" Skye admonishes with a giggle and slaps his arm "this is Rex Davies a friend of Caleb's"

"Please to meet you" Rex says uncertainly shaking Simon's hand.

"Well I've died and gone to seventh gay heaven" Simon winks at Rex "if all the locals look like these two I am definitely moving in with you when your house is ready baby girl. There's enough eye candy around here to send me into a diabetic shock"

"I thought that was a given anyway" Skye rolls her eyes at him "right I'm nipping upstairs to dump my things and freshen up. I won't be long"

Skye moves to Paul and Alan, speaking to them quietly for a few minutes. Paul follows her as she makes her way round the bar and disappears through the staff only door.

I down my drink and signal to Marie, she comes over with a bottle of Corona and I indicate to the others each saying what they want "Take for Skye and Paul's drink and one for yourself" I say handing over the cash.

"How do you know Skye?" says Rex to Simon as I hand the drinks out, this should be good.

"I could answer that by saying I know her very well but I'm guessing you want to know how I met her and how long have I known her" chuckles Simon.

Judging from his response it's obvious he gets asked that question a lot. I catch Alan's eye and his knowing smile tells me I'm right.

"We met fourteen years ago in her first week attending the Royal College of Art, within a few weeks along with another friend, Shelley, we were living together" Simon smirks at Rex's shocked face "then a year later Skye got the opportunity to study at the New York Academy of Art. When she moved to America she took me and Shelley with her. Now Goldilocks it's your turn to get down and personal" Simon grins mischievously.

I throw my head back and laugh. I like this guy. He's unashamedly hitting on Rex at the same time turning the tables on him, clearly Simon is not going to answer any more questions about Skye until he gets something in return. Rex is dumbfounded for a few minutes.

"Come on handsome, tell me about yourself" Simon raises an expectant eyebrow.

"Rex is our local Lothario and he's a wealthy one at that" I supply.

"Oh Rex, I'm going to have fun converting you" teases Simon "Alan will tell you, I don't give up easily and I've been working on him for nearly six years"

"He doesn't and he has" Alan drawls straight-faced but his eyes crinkle with humour.

Rex finally finds his voice and sense of humour "Sorry to disappoint but I'm only into women"

"That won't stop him" Alan snorts.

Simon smiles and nods his head in agreement.

"What about him?" Rex points at me.

"I already know all about Mr Tall, Dark, Handsome and Dangerous here" Simon pats my arm, his comment wipes the smile off my face. He already knows about me! How can he? He's only just met me. My smile returns full force when it dawns on me that Skye must have told him about me. Simon gives a subtle nod of his head answering my unspoken question "besides right this moment I'm into blondes, so spill the details Goldilocks"

Giving a dramatic sigh and shaking his head Rex gives in "I have lived in Dove Mill off and on all my life. Moving here permanently when I inherited Millington Lodge and the family estate just over nine years ago before that I lived and worked in the city. Caleb is my oldest and best friend" Rex raises his bottle and clinks mine.

"What about number of marriages, wife, kids, love children?"

"None, no, never and don't know" Rex laughs.

Simon keeps throwing questions at Rex for the next ten minutes and he answers occasionally dragging me into their good natured sparring. Rex throws questions about Skye back but I notice how Simon craftily side steps the really personal ones or completely ignores them, for some reason Rex mentions how unusual Skye's name is and asks which of her parents named her.

"Oh please tell me you actually said that to her" Simon says gleefully.

"At a dinner party last night" I say to confirm "she replied if you like that you should hear my phone number"

"And she gave you a dud number" Simon squeals unable to contain his mirth.

"What's the best put down you've heard Skye come out with?" I ask.

"God there are so many" Simon takes a couple of deep breathes as he thinks, when his eyes light up I know it's going to be good "we were attending this big posh charity gala. Lots of political big hitters, business moguls and famous celebrities. The President's wife was there as well. Any way there was this guy who kept following Skye around all night, full of bullshit and spouting it as well. He was one of those types that no matter what you have done or achieved he had gone one better, you know the type I mean?"

"I've climbed Snowdon; he's climbed Everest" I say.

"Exactly" Simon nods "so Skye is stood talking to the President's wife and a couple of A list Hollywood stars when this guy butts in on the conversation, that's the final straw for her and she snaps "I've met some pricks in my time but you sir, are a cactus" the guy starts huffing and puffing how rude she is when she says "Oh! Have I offended you with my opinion? You should hear the ones I keep to myself" I tell you me and Michelle had to hold each other up we were laughing so hard. I nearly wet myself"

Rex and I are holding on to each other laughing hard. I wipe my eyes and gasp trying to get air into my lungs. I've got a stitch, grasping my side I straighten to my full height to find the majority of the pub looking in our direction with puzzled bemusement. The 'staff only' door opens and the white blonde head of Skye appears. I watch her progress back. Halfway she stops and talks to Sally and Marty, I can see them introducing her to Davy who hadn't been around yesterday afternoon when she called up at the yard. After a few minutes of chatting with my staff Skye looks up in my direction and smiles, my staff all turn around and smile at me. My feet are moving towards her before my brain registers what's happening.

"What?" I look expectantly at them all.

"Nothing" Skye says innocently "I was talking about you not to you" my staff do a piss poor job of stifling their sniggers "good seeing you again Sally and Marty and nice meeting you Davy, enjoy your evening. Shall we?" Skye grins and moves around me to get back to the others.

My eyes roam up and down Skye's body as she weaves in and out of people smiling and saying hello as she passes. She's wearing a red flowery skirt that flares out at her hips and finishes a couple of inches above her knees revealing those fine shapely smooth legs. Oh fuck me! She's wearing red high heels – images of those fine legs and red heels wrapped around my head flit through my mind – making the sway of her hips more pronounced as she walks. Her top is pale pink cap sleeved button down jersey, revealing just the right amount of cleavage and hugs her curves, emphasising her tiny waist. Jesus, I'm not going to last the night without touching her. My fingers are twitching already.

Marie places a bottle of Budweiser in front of Skye when she reaches the bar "Wow! Now that's what I call service" says Skye smiling at Marie.

"Is Paul not with you?" Marie says looking around trying to spot him.

"No, he'll be down in a while"

"Speaking to Jack?" asks Simon.

Skye nods then downs half her drink and lets out a huge belch "Excuse me. I needed that" she laughs at the stunned faces around her.

"Such a classy bird" Simon's caustic remark is softened by their laughter as they high five.

"Have you been behaving yourself?" Skye raises an eyebrow at Simon.

"Of course I have" Simon says indignantly then he grins impishly "well I could have behaved but I didn't want to. I mean where's the fun in that? So in my defence I have been as well behaved as I can be being surrounded by these fine specimens" he clutches his heart and sighs dramatically, fluttering his eye lashes at Rex. Skye rolls her eyes at her friend.

"Actually Simon has been entertaining us with stories of your one liners" says Rex. Skye frowns and looks puzzled.

"Like the one you delivered last night when Rex commented on your name" I say smiling. A mischievous grin spreads across her face.

"I only told them about the guy that annoyed the shit out of you at the charity gala in Washington" I see worry flicker through Simon's eyes.

"When I was stood with Michelle, Sandra and Cameron?" Simon nods "now that was funny" Skye chuckles at the memory "although as I told you last night, I can't claim credit for originality they're all nicked"

"I'm impressed by the fact you rub shoulders with the First Lady and Hollywood stars" says Rex.

Shit, I'm impressed as well but I keep it to myself when I see a flash of irritation cross Skye's face. I search my mind for something to say to change the subject but I'm distracted when Skye suddenly jerks and pulls her phone out of her pocket. Her eyes flick to Simon before she answers.

"Shelley, is everything okay?" Simon moves closer to her side in an instant. Skye holds the phone so he can hear the person on the other end "he's here listening"

"Hey honey, you okay?" Simon's voice is as marred with concern as Skye's.

Both listen intently, a mix of emotions cross their faces "Plans are to fly back Tuesday morning. We should be landing at JFK around lunchtime but we can be there Sunday… are you sure, okay… let me know immediately if things change… promise… I'll put the plane on standby and we can be in the air within the hour or thereabouts… take care, give our love to Phil and the kids" Skye hangs up.

"Is everything okay?" Alan murmurs.

"Yeah so far. Shelley's doctors are concerned and are talking of doing a C section possibly Thursday next week at the latest. They're admitting her today so they can keep a closer eye on her over the next forty-eight hours. From Saturday we need to be in the air at a moment's notice"

Alan nods "I'll see to it" he starts to move away.

"Alan" he comes back "tell Freya that if we have to leave she can still visit her family and follow us to the States as originally planned"

"Will do ma'am. If it's okay with you under the circumstances, I'll stay with her"

"Yes, good idea"

Alan strides through the pub with purpose, people are quick to move out of his way.

"Such a shame he's straight" Simon sighs "he could be my knight in shining armour. I'm getting jealous of Freya"

"You've got nowhere in all the years Alan has worked for me, considering you've been hitting on him since day one don't you think it's time to concede defeat?"

"Never!" Simon mocks horror putting both hands on his cheeks.

"What makes him Freya's knight in shining armour?" I've got about twenty questions running through my head based on their short conversation and that's the one that pops out.

Simon looks at Skye, she shrugs and nods "The bruises on Freya's face and the ones you can't see come courtesy of her ex-boyfriend" Simon leans in to me whispering "cutting a long story short Skye found her at the beginning of the week badly beaten in the street. She's now working for Skye as her PA, when she went to get her personal effects the other day Alan went with her. Ex turned up and decided to play macho man. Alan gave him a taste of his own medicine"

I know my eyes must be wide, they feel as if they're out on stalks. Then a memory jumps out and I realise why Freya looked familiar. Last summer I had to rush Davy to the hospital after he'd been kicked by one of the horses, whilst we were there Freya had been brought in. I remember her boyfriend as being overly concerned and attentive. One of the nurses I know told me that Freya was a regular only they couldn't do anything because she kept to the pathetic story the boyfriend gave out.

"Good, he's a nasty piece of work from what I've heard" I murmur.

"You know him" Skye says startled.

"No not personally" I tell her about Davy last summer and what the nurse told me.

Our conversation gets interrupted by the appearance of Paul "All sorted?" Skye asks, he nods "how's Jack?"

"Good, usual complaint about his mom's new boyfriend and he wants to know when you're going back to Mike and Penny's and can he come"

"Ah bless him" Skye chuckles "hey! Maybe Caleb can find him a job at the stables when he comes to stay later in the year" I raise an eyebrow at her "Jack is Paul's son and he wants a career working with horses. He's worked for Mike on the ranch and knows his way around horses. Mike says Jack is a natural, ring him I'm sure he'll give Jack a glowing reference, you won't have to pay him anything he'll work for free just to get experience"

"I like the sound of that" I laugh "how old is he Paul?"

"Twelve, he'll be thirteen in September. Do you know Mr Holstead?"

"I do. He's an old friend and I was at his ranch the other week buying horses. I believe I left a day or two before you arrived" Paul can't hide his surprise "I tried to talk Mike in to selling me Dark Moon and I found out last night that Skye owns him"

"Jack was with Ms Darcy watching Dark Moon being born, they ended up being drafted in to help when difficulties arose and time was of the essence" it's my turn to be surprised "the lad kept his cool the whole time" Paul says proudly.

"It's one of the most amazing experiences of my life" says Skye. I understand now more than ever why Skye will never sell the horse, money isn't the incentive to sell not because she's absolutely loaded but because she has an emotional connection to Dark Moon "I'm just thankful that I had been Shelley's birthing partner otherwise I'd have been passing out but Jack showed just how much he's a chip off the old block, as stoic as his old man" Skye winks at Paul.

"Less of the old if you don't mind" he mutters under his breath "Talking of Mrs Cotterill, the plane is on standby from six tomorrow evening. Freya is arranging it so we can take a helicopter from High Wycombe airport to Heathrow should it be rush hour when we need to leave"

"Excellent" says Skye.

"If you don't need me I'm going to go up and go through some things with Freya"

"I'm good and thanks Paul"

Paul nods and disappears into the crowded pub.

"How long has Paul and Alan worked for you?" even though they are her employees I can see she doesn't treat them as such and the question is out of my mouth before I can stop it.

"Almost ten years for Paul and five and a half years for Alan"

Suddenly Skye's eyes widen in alarm and she stumbles forward. I catch her before she can fall, the feel of her voluptuous body against mine makes me groan. The person who backed into her turns round to apologise as I reluctantly set Skye on her feet and let go. Skye stays in close proximity. My skin is tingling as my body hums with electricity and desire. My hands find their way back onto her waist and gently I pull her back into me. She moves willingly.

"Watch what you're doing dickhead" Rex shouts aggressively from his end of the bar and glares at the young lad, I realise its Jay one of the part time bar staff.

"I'm so sorry" he says again, I can see the poor lad is mortified "I tripped, I didn't mean"

"It's okay, no harm done" says Skye patting his arm smiling warmly at him.

I catch the slight frown crinkling between her eyebrows when she looks at Rex as she moves aside — her body is now flush with mine. I inhale deeply drawing her heady scent deep into my lungs — so Jay can put the empty glasses on the bar. Fireworks are going off around my body and my dick throbs. I really, really want to drag her upstairs.

"Oh before I forget" Skye suddenly brightens "there's two things I need to discuss with you"

"Seriously, you want to talk business now" I say.

Skye leans in to me, if I didn't have my jacket on I would feel the heat of her body against mine "Hang on a minute" frigging idiot, why didn't you think of that sooner. I take my leather jacket off and hang it on the end of the brass bar that runs around the bar. I lean on the bar and dip my head "what were you going to say"

I savour the feel of Skye's breasts rubbing against my arm as she leans in to me again, her heat and faint fruity floral scent enveloping me. My hand automatically snakes around her waist to hold her in place.

"If I don't do it now we'll never get round to discussing business because every time we're alone all we want to do is fuck each other senseless"

I can't help but laugh, Skye grins at me wickedly "You're right kitten and it's taking all of my will power not to drag you upstairs or back to my place" I growl softly in her ear. I feel the tremor of desire my words send through her body.

"Down boy" Skye mouths as she pulls away. In my peripheral vision I can see people giving us speculative looks. Rex isn't looking too happy about something, whether that's from Simon keeping him away from Skye or me I don't know, I suspect it's the latter.

"I understand from Joyce that you had an arrangement with her uncle about using the top field" Skye's words jolt me off my lust cloud like a kick up the backside. I tense as all euphoric feelings evaporate in an instant. Skye senses my unease "don't worry all I want to say is that you can continue to use the field for as long as you want" relief has me sagging against the bar "on the proviso that someday you tell me the story behind your uncle losing the land in a game of cards to her grandfather. Joyce was sketchy on the details"

"Deal" I smile at her "and the other thing?"

"I want you to train Dark Moon"

"Fuck me! Seriously, for real" I bark out. The conversations going on around us all stop.

"Yes for real and I'm serious" Skye says very solemnly "and I would love to do the other soon" she murmurs under her breath so only I can hear.

All I can do is gawp at her. I have no idea what to say, never in a million years did I think she would say those words. I had envisaged trying to persuade her to sell him to me but the thought offering to train her horse had never crossed my mind.

"What have you said to Caleb to put him into a state of shock?" says Rex, he's finally managed to sidle next to us. Skye doesn't answer him instead she puts something into my hand.

"Here drink this" Skye lifts the tumbler to my lips, the volatile vapours I smell tells me its scotch. I knock it back the burn brings back my senses and awareness of my surroundings.

"Skye wants me to train Dark Moon" I say in wonder, my voice made hoarse from the scotch, excitement at the thought starts to stir my blood "thank you, I would love to train him"

"Excellent" Skye smiles "I look forward to seeing him win the Grand National in years to come" she raises her bottle in salute to me before taking a drink.

The image of her raising that bottle to her lips and watching her throat work as she swallows has me instantly back on my lust cloud of happiness, in fact I'm soaring high above it I feel so giddy.

"This calls for a celebration, Chris brings us a bottle of champagne" calls out Rex.

"None for me thanks" says Skye.

"Of course you must have some. I insist on it" Rex says a tad forcefully.

"She doesn't like champagne" I say along with another voice, Simon.

"How do you know that?" Skye and Rex say together looking at me.

"I noticed last night, when you took a sip you pulled a face sort of like you do when sucking on a lemon" Skye laughs nodding "and you didn't touch any for the rest of the night preferring to drink something else"

"She says champagne is like drinking lemonade with vinegar in it" Simon snorts "our Skye here has very simple if not singular tastes, by all accounts she's rather a cheap date"

"Hey! I take exception to being called cheap" Skye scowls at Simon.

"Baby girl nobody could ever call you cheap, you're more high maintenance than I am. I simply meant that you don't have expensive tastes where alcohol is concerned"

"But I'm high maintenance, since when?" Skye is still scowling at Simon; he opens his mouth to respond but I jump in.

"Dangerous territory. Quit while you're ahead, otherwise you'll be digging your own grave"

"Spoken by a man with experience" says Rex.

"Been there and done that several times… I never learn" I say it like wearing a badge of honour, I wink at Skye. She throws her head back and laughs. The deep sexy throaty laugh makes my blood sing.

"I'm sorry baby girl I didn't mean to offend you, I was only referring to…" Simon stops when he sees me raising my hand and I slash the cutting movement across my throat "give me a shovel and point me in the direction of the grave yard" he chuckles.

Chris places and ice bucket on the bar with the champagne bottle poking out of it, he places four flutes on the bar. While Rex makes quick work of opening and pouring the champagne Skye picks up one of the glasses and pours lager in to it.

"Will you be taking part in the quiz?" Chris looks at us all "five pounds per team to enter, no more than six in a team. Winners gets the pot"

"Sounds like fun" Simon says to Skye who nods "all we need now is a karaoke night"

"That's tomorrow" Chris and I say together.

"Oh we are so going to be doing that baby girl and no arguments" Simon says grinning at Skye, she sighs and shakes her head in resignation.

"Put us in for the quiz" I say to Chris handing over the entry fee. Chris gives me a sheet of paper and a pen "we need a team name any ideas?"

"I have" Simon says snatching the paper and pen off me.

He scribbles something down and gleefully hands it to Skye, her eyes widen and her mouth pops open, then she chuckles. Before she can say anything I take the paper out of her hands to see what he has written '(I've always wanted to be a) Pheasant Plucker'

"Try saying that fast when you've had a skin full" Simon says cheekily. Unable to help myself I burst out laughing. Rex takes the paper off me, reads it and rolls his eyes.

Skye signals to Marie for another bottle of Bud "Does anyone else want another drink?" she asks our group in general. Simon and Rex shake their heads; I lift my bottle to check what's left. Skye points to the bottle and Marie nods "can I buy you a drink Mrs Brennan?"

Fuck, I hadn't realised the old busy body had worked her way to our side of the bar. How long has she been stood there? And how much has she heard? I hope to god she's only just arrived, the thought of her eavesdropping on our conversation makes me feel really uneasy, speculation will be rife as it is without her adding fuel to the fire. Marjorie Brennan looks completely stunned at Skye, her mouth opening and closing with no sound coming out. Marie places two bottles of lager in front of Skye.

"Thank you Marie, and a drink for Mrs Brennan" Skye indicates to the woman still doing a good impersonation of a fish. Marie smirks at Marjorie before moving to the optics.

"Well that's a first" Rex snorts "Marjorie Brennan rendered speechless"

Marie places a glass with a shot of clear liquid in front of her along with a bottle of Coke "Th… th… thank you Ms Darcy" Marjorie manages to stutter through her shock "you know who I am" the words are almost whispered. Skye nods, winks and raises her bottle in salute to Marjorie.

"So you'll be leaving us on Sunday" Rex says "where are you off to?" although he directs the question at Skye its Simon that answers.

"Up North so Freya can see her family before we fly to New York on Tuesday, our friend Shelley is about to have twins so we might be heading back sooner if the babies decide to come early"

"Or the doctors decide to give her an emergency C section" Skye adds.

"Is that likely to happen?" I say seeing the worry in Skye's beautiful yellow green eyes.

"There's a strong possibility, she nearly died with her last pregnancy and the doctors have kept a very close eye on her throughout this one especially since she's carrying twins"

"Well I can tell with a figure like yours you've never had kids" Rex leers. Skye's relaxed demeanour changes instantly; she stands straight, her back and shoulders stiffen, her expression becomes impassive. It's as if metal shutters are coming down fast. I notice Simon flick a nervous look at Skye. This is obviously a taboo subject for some reason. Rex hasn't picked up on the changes in Skye, the idiot steps into her personal space, slipping his arm around her waist pulling her closer in to him "but whenever you decide to have them, give me a shout as I'm more than happy to oblige" he gives her his trade mark dazzling smile. It's the smile that I've seen a thousand times and every time the woman he bestows it on succumbs. Skye doesn't respond, well she does but not in the way Rex or I expect which is usually a simpering quivering mess.

In a deft move Skye steps easily out of his hold, the move brings her back into close proximity to me. My fingers twitch and flex longing to reach out to her. Skye completely blanks Rex and I can see he's beginning to realise that he's made a huge blunder. The once relaxed happy atmosphere is now strained. Rex looks at me bewildered, he has that 'what did I say' look of innocence on his face. Fucking twat, I want to slap him.

"Simon before I forget. I plan on getting a haircut when we get back, do you fancy coming" Skye says very matter of fact.

"Yay! A trip to Vegas" Simon gleefully shouts clapping his hands "I am so there, baby girl"

Simon's very over the top response makes me laugh subsequently breaking the tension. Skye grins at me, then I realise what has just been said "You're going to Vegas to get a haircut" I can't hide my disbelief.

Skye nods "David is the only stylist who can work wonders with this lot" Skye points to her head "and he just happens to live in Vegas"

Out of the corner of my eye I can see Marjorie Brennan's astounded face looking at Skye, let's see how quickly that snippet of information works its way around the village.

"Good evening ladies and gentlemen, the quiz will begin in a few minutes so get yourselves sorted and ready to start" Chris's voice coming through the sound system halts all conversation.

Simon hands Skye the pen and she turns to the bar with the sheet of paper taking a side step so she's right next to me. I lean on the bar and stealthily inch closer. My fingers slide under her top finding the warm flesh of her taut stomach. Skye steps closer as Simon and Rex gather around her, my fingers slide further over her stomach, it's impossible to keep my fingers still and they draw lazy circles over her silk smooth skin. I take a deep breath and a hit of her sexy as hell feminine scent. My dick pulses threatening to explode.

SKYE

A sudden thrill rushes through me as Caleb's fingers glide and circle my tummy, I don't quite supress the shiver of desire that ends up pooling between my legs. If my clit had a voice, it would be screaming bloody blue murder for those magical fingers to head south, pronto. I use the opportunity to move closer into Caleb when Simon and Rex crowd round me in readiness for the quiz to start. The heat from his body enhances his mouth watering masculine scent, a musky earthy outdoors smell with hint of citrus. Christ, at this rate I'm going to end up in a puddle on the floor.

Caleb shifts position, lifting his leg to place his foot on the brass foot rest bar that runs around the bottom of the bar. It means his thigh is now resting against my hips, during the last flurry of activity of people getting drinks in before the quiz starts unnoticed I drop my hand onto his leg running my fingers and dragging my nails the length of his thigh, Caleb hisses in a sharp breath as I get dangerously close to his crotch.

"Careful kitten" the low rumble full of warning is said for my ears only. Unable to help myself I look at him and grin, wickedness surges through me. Caleb's eyes sparkle with equal wickedness. Bring it on!

The high pitched squeal of the microphone makes everyone wince and look towards the source, all plans of naughtiness temporarily forgotten.

"Sorry folks" Chris half laughs apologising.

"Sorry my arse" Rex grumbles sticking a finger in his ear and wiggling it about.

"First question" Chris carries on, a sudden flurry of paper, low murmurs and an air of expectation fills the pub "there's a point for each correct answer with this question. There are five boroughs that make up New York City, name each of them"

"Oh this is just too easy" Simon mutters, I'm already writing them down before the words are out of his mouth.

"Next question" Chris calls out, a few people shout back "Hang on a minute" and frantic whispered discussions can be heard around us "moving on, question two for one point name the American rock band whose name is also the term used by Allied pilots in World War Two to describe UFO's"

"Where in the fuck did he get these questions from?" Rex mutters under his breath.

"Don't worry mate, Skye's already written the answer down" Caleb chuckles. I twist and lean in to Caleb lifting the paper so Rex can see.

"Foo Fighters" Rex frowns at me "are you sure?"

"Believe me, Skye is what you would call a metal head or rock chick so you can bet your sweet tight arse she's right" Simon says smugly before I can answer. Not that I could have given an answer as eloquently because Caleb's large warm hand kneads and caresses my bum, it takes everything I have to keep the groan locked in my throat, so I nod my head instead.

"Question three for one point. Lisa Gherardini, according to several sources is believed to be the model for what?" Chris reads out.

I've written the answer down before Chris finishes speaking, Rex leans in to me reading over my shoulder. I resist the urge to push back or stamp on his foot for invading my personal space and his crass suggestion about fathering my children earlier. However, he uses the opportunity to put his hands on my waist. I want to rip his hands away, my skin is crawling, shrivelling in on itself at the contact. Strange how Rex has the complete opposite effect on me compared to Caleb.

"Mona Lisa, hmm I guess it would be farcical if you didn't know that, what with you being an artist"

I'm sure Rex meant it as a compliment but to me it sounds condescending, telling him to fuck right off is on the tip of my tongue when I see Simon's infinitesimal shake of his head so instead I smile sweetly.

"Put like that I guess it would be wouldn't it?" I load as much sarcasm as I can get away with into my voice. It does the trick, Rex takes his hands off me and steps back. Out of the corner of my eye I see Caleb shrug and shake his head no doubt in response to whatever Rex was mouthing behind my back.

"Question four, in Japan what is a gaijin?" the question distracts me from turning round and asking Rex what the hell his problem is? Instead I write the answer down.

"Christ, is there anything you don't know? I daren't ask if you're sure" Rex splutters.

I turn and step back in to Caleb so my back is flush with his front, discretely I lower my arm and put it behind my back angling myself so my hand settles on his crotch. I cup and flex my fingers and hand, feeling how deliciously hard he is. A low growl vibrates against my back. Slowly moving my fingers, I explore his erection through his jeans.

"I take it you've never seen Fast and Furious: Tokyo Drift" Simon playfully punches Rex on the shoulder.

"No I haven't" Rex says puzzled.

"It's one of my favourite films, the lead character gets called it, that's how I know what it means" I feel a heavy gust of hot breath on the back of my neck, Caleb is struggling but he doesn't stop my fingers nor move my hand.

"Question five, one point for each correct answer. Since the introduction of the Premier League in England which ten players have scored the most goals? And before anyone asks its Premier League goals only" Chris clarifies.

"Now it's your chance to shine, I don't know this" I push the pen and paper towards Rex. I start to move out of the way so he and Caleb can confer but a large hand grasps my hip a silent command to stay put, I don't need telling twice.

The quiz progresses, as a team we find that each of us has areas of specialist knowledge and useless information meaning that we all give our fair share of answers. I'm fascinated that the whole pub takes the quiz very seriously and any group found cheating, and by that I mean using their mobile phones to get the answers off the internet, are disqualified and they have to buy everyone in the pub a drink. A great forfeit and deterrent. Throughout the whole time Caleb's fingers caress my stomach and on a few occasions when I lean down to write his hand cups my breast, his thumb circling my aching erect nipple. It takes all my will power not rip my clothes off, lie down on the bar with my legs spread and beg him to fuck me.

After three quarters of an hour Chris announces a fifteen-minute break before part two begins. I take the opportunity to visit the ladies and I try desperately to gather some form of decorum. Running my wrists under cold water in a vain attempt to cool my boiling blood and a cold damp cloth at the back of my neck has little effect. Looking in the mirror at my overly bright eyes and flushed cheeks I straighten my top and skirt. It's no good my raging hormones are still that… raging. I step out into the empty corridor, my heels clicking on the stone flags. Passing the gents toilets, I hear muffled raucous laughter and banter from within. Suddenly I'm grabbed from behind, a large hand covers my mouth and nose. An arm that feels like banded steel wraps around my middle and lifts me easily off my feet and then I'm in blackness.

"Keep quiet" a gravelly rumble and warm breath gusts in my ear. I breathe in just before the hand moves from my mouth. I get a hit of familiar masculine outdoorsy with a hint of citrus smell. My fight induced muscles turn to liquid in an instant and my whole body goes lax. A light flicks on and I turn to see Caleb. His intense green eyes dark with need, need for me.

Without thinking I drop to my knees and open his jeans. The buttons pop open easily enough to reveal my lover is commando. His huge cock is angry looking. The shaft red and the glans almost purple, semen seeps out of the eye, he's that close to coming.

My tongue darts out and laps up the tangy slightly salty cum. Caleb hisses as I take him deep into my mouth. His fingers dig into my hair and gently massage my scalp as I fist him with one hand and start to stroke whilst my mouth sucks greedily and my tongue swirls around the head of his cock. It's not long before Caleb takes over, his hips pump faster, his cock pushing deeper into my mouth touching the back of my throat. With both hands resting on the side of his thighs I feel the straining muscles as he fucks my mouth, I breathe deeply through my nose praying my gage reflex doesn't kick in.

Caleb's fingers tighten in my hair, the pulling and slight sting of pain on my scalp along with the feel of his cock thickening in my mouth tells me he's about to come. I hollow my cheeks and suck hard as he withdraws. Caleb's whole body stiffens as his climax hits and he spills into my mouth. My eyes water and lungs burn for air as he seems to take forever coming. I swallow and suck every last drop from him as his shuddering body rides out the last of his orgasm.

"Skye" Caleb's voice is a hoarse whisper as he untangles his fingers from my hair and reaches for me. He kisses me hard, his tongue taking over from his cock in fucking my mouth. I'm lost to him. I rub myself against his rock hard body.

Suddenly his lips are gone and he's turning me around, he pushes my hair out of the way and nibbles at my neck, one hand cups my breast whilst the other is heading south.

"Open your eyes kitten and look in the mirror" Caleb whispers.

Lifting my head, I do as he says and it's the first time I take in where we are. The disabled toilet. A huge mirror takes up half the wall. The hand cupping my breast snakes underneath my top, his rough callused hand gently moves over my stomach back to my breast to find the lace covered nipple. His other hand grasps my skirt and drags it upwards. I take hold of my skirt and lift it so his other hand quickly finds its way inside my knickers.

"Put your arms up around my neck" Caleb instructs. I do as he says "now watch"

I feel Caleb's fingers part my sex and move lightly, flickering and tantalising over my clit. But I can't see any of that all I see is the movement of his hand underneath the material of my skirt, likewise his other hand is gently cupping, squeezing my breast with his thumb and fingers pinching, pulling and rolling my nipple but again all I see is the movement of his hand under the material of my top.

The scene playing out in the mirror is hot as hell. My hips start moving, circling and lifting. Caleb cups my sex and his talented fingers enter me, the base of his hand pushing against my pelvic bone and clit giving me the stimulation I need, my internal muscles greedily grip his fingers as they move in and out of me in a languid manner. My breathing is laboured and I fight to keep my eyes open to watch this erotic scene. I look so wanton as my body moves sinuously to Caleb's touch. I can see for myself how much I love everything about this lewd act.

"You said one of your fantasies is to be watched being fucked, but I also know you like to watch, don't you kitten?" Caleb's voice purrs down my ear like the devil himself.

I nod, no point in lying. Christ, this man has a direct link to my deepest darkest fantasies, how does he do that?

"Have you done that often, answer me truthfully kitten"

"No, once sort of, by accident" I pant out.

"Explain" Caleb commands, I watch his hands moving under the material of my clothes, his touch and the feelings of pleasure are causing havoc with my mind and body.

"I saw a man masturbating, he was watching a couple have sex but I couldn't see them, only hear them. Oh god!" I cry out as Caleb thrusts his fingers deep inside me.

"So now it's a fantasy to watch properly. Don't deny it, your body and greedy cunt is telling me, yes" I nod, helpless to the thought and pleasure surges through me "but more importantly you want to be watched being fucked" Caleb thrusts his fingers deep again and strokes my g-spot, pleasure spikes, my eyes roll to the back of my head. A low moan leaves me as image after image of Caleb fucking me in various positions and being surrounded by watching men, flash through my mind "Look at you, my beautiful wild kitten is such a slut" Caleb's gravelly voice stirs me even more "you can't get enough of me or my touch. You love me touching you like this" his fingers squeeze my nipple "and your tight greedy cunt" he starts to thrust faster "is begging to be fucked"

"Oh god" I pant as my fingers tighten in Caleb's hair "Caleb" I call out desperately as my climax suddenly gets to the brink as the pleasure sensations coalesce between my legs.

"Shh, not a sound my wonderful slutty kitten"

Caleb bites down and sucks on the juncture of my neck and shoulder, the sharp sting and feel of his mouth, it's enough to tip me over the edge. Wave after wave of pleasure rolls through me. I lose all sense of where I am. All I know… I'm floating, yet my body was shuddering and jerking. It seems to take forever to come back down from the incredible high. Caleb gently removes his hands, he straightens my top and skirt whilst I try to untangle my fingers from his hair.

I help Caleb straighten out his clothes, he's hard again. I smile as the thought of taking him in my mouth for a second time crosses my mind.

"We'll be missed if you do" Caleb says reading my thoughts, he pulls me into his arms and kisses me tenderly "god you're an amazing woman. I'm sorry if my foul mouth upset you. I didn't mean it"

"I quite liked being called a slutty kitten" I pout.

Caleb's hand connects with my bum as I step out into the corridor, thankfully no one is around "You're my slutty kitten, get it right" Caleb growls playfully in my ear but I detect the hint of possessiveness again… and I like it, a lot.

CHAPTER SIXTEEN

CALEB

"Shit!" I curse as everything in the cabinet decides to jump out and land all over the fucking bathroom floor. I bend down to pick them up, the room tilts, bad idea. I straighten gingerly, my head is pounding. Through blurry bloodshot eyes I see the box of paracetamol in the sink. I take two out and wash them down with water praying the pain killers will kick in pronto. It's been a long time since I've had a hangover I muse, as I wash my face and clean my teeth I try and work out when that was but come up with zilch.

Dressed and ready for the working day I step out into the yard, the early spring morning freshness does little to clear my muggy head. The dogs pad over with tails wagging to greet me. I stroke and pet them. They're not mine they belong to the grooms; I forget which dog belongs to who but they all seem to follow Sally around.

I enter the stables as Marty and Davy are turning out Wonderwall and All on the Nose, they take one look at me and burst out laughing, Sally's head pops out of the tack room.

"Good lord you look rough" she says joining the laughter "I think you best go back to bed for another eight hours"

"I haven't seen you looking this hungover since Rex took you out to celebrate" Davy suddenly stops talking, realising that he's about to say when I kicked Gabrielle out for the final time.

"It's okay you can say it; I was trying to work out when the last time was any way. Thanks for the reminder" I pat Davy on the shoulder.

"Seriously though boss, go back to bed. You look like shit" says Marty.

I look at each of their grinning faces "That bad, huh?" they all nod "why is it that when you have such a good night you pay for it in the morning?"

"It's called balance or sod's law" Sally says giggling "anyway you need your beauty sleep because you'll be doing it all again tonight at the karaoke"

I groan as I remember Simon threatening to take over the night unless each person in our group promised to sing at least one song. Skye told us Simon loved to sing which was a shame because he's tone deaf. Rex volunteered me for a couple of songs, I stupidly agreed to take his slot as well as my own.

"We can manage" Sally says softly "go back to bed"

I nod and wave bye in surrender. I gladly crawl back into bed, falling asleep with a smile on my face as my mind replays Skye jumping into my arms when Chris announced our team as winners of the quiz, the scene changes to her being on her knees taking my aching cock in her mouth.

I gradually come awake to silence. It's too quiet and dark. Fuck! Don't say I've slept the whole day. I jump out of bed and wrench the curtains open. I'm blinded by sunlight. You muppet, it's quiet because the window is shut and it's dark because of the curtains, I always sleep with the window slightly open so I can hear the horses, I must've shut it earlier without realising. My heart slows down from trying to jack knife out of my chest. I stumble back to the bed, my eyes adjusting to the light, picking up my phone off the cabinet I check the time. It's eleven. I rub my face trying to wake up some more, at least the hangover headache has gone. My phone vibrating makes me jump. I look down to see Rex calling me.

"Morning" my voice sounds as if I've drunk a gallon of scotch.

"Whoa! Mate you sound rough" Rex sounds too cheerful.

"You should have heard and seen me a six o' clock this morning. I was that bad the staff ordered me back to bed. I just woke up"

"Man it was a good night" Rex laughs heartily "I'm heading to the pub now, want me to pick you up?"

"No I'm good. I've a few things to do here. I'll see you in about an hour"

"Will do. I'll save you a seat" Rex hung up.

Last night Skye, inadvertently, mentioned her first meeting was due to start at eleven thirty and of course that golden nugget of information was overheard by the flapping ears of Marjorie Brennan, it was around the pub within seconds. Chris joked that he was going to need more chairs which progressed to charging people for a seat. Skye joked about roping off the area around the pool table and anyone desperate enough wanting to know what was going on could pay a VIP entrance fee.

Downstairs in the living room come office I switch on the old computer and wait for it to kick in to life. Sitting down I check the messages Sally has left, none are urgent and can wait. I bring up Google and contemplate what to put in the search, in the end I type 'Skye Darcy' the first listing is a link to her website. I click on it.

Skye's stunningly beautiful smiling face appears, the picture is in black and white. Skye is relaxed, her smile is one I've seen many times and it reaches her sparkling eyes. Underneath are words of welcome, at the side is a 'Gallery' button which brings up samples of Skye's work. Each piece is stunning and so realistic they look like photographs. There is another button saying 'Jewellery' this takes me to another website. This time there is a picture of Skye linking arms with a man who looks late-twenties called Matthew, both are casually dressed. The jewellery is a collaboration, Skye designs the pieces and Matthew and his team makes them. The website also states most of the designs come from paintings Skye has done and thanks are given to those clients who have granted permission for the artwork to be shown next to the item of jewellery. I click through the links to view rings, bracelets, necklaces and earrings. There are also arm bands, head pieces and what appears to be full body jewellery. I quickly work out there are three price ranges. I'm impressed no matter what budget you've got there's something you could afford, all the pieces are truly exquisite and original. On the jewellery website there's a link that takes me back to Skye's page, the other link on her website takes me to an auction house.

West End Fine Art Auctions have two offices one in London the other New York. There's a brief history about the London auction house and it appears Skye bought the struggling business nine years ago, she opened the New York branch just over five years ago. Both businesses are a huge success mainly down to Skye's approach to helping other artists sell their work offering an alternative to selling through a Gallery. The interesting thing I find about this website is it plays down Skye's connection as the owner, the information is there in the 'About Us' page but the rest of the site promotes the artists whose work is up for the next auction.

I go back to Google and click on the Wikipedia link. There's nothing about Skye's life before she went to America. It does mention she is the sole owner of Darcy Enterprise Holdings under which she has an extensive property portfolio mainly due to buying derelict buildings and renovating them. It also mentions how she became successful as an artist. Early on in her career she was commissioned by a video game company to do a series of designs and paintings based on their best-selling game, rather than take a flat fee Skye negotiated a percentage in royalties for every marketing item that used her designs. At the time the game company were losing business to their competitor hand over fist so they gladly accepted Skye's terms, today the same game company held the number one slot and has done since the re-launch of their ailing game using Skye's artwork. The CEO of the game company is quoted as crediting Skye as the person to turn around their business's fortune. Since then other game companies and corporate businesses hired Skye. The page went on to mention various film projects she has been involved in, the collaborations with other artists and her other business interest being involved in her husband's private equity and property business.

 Back on Google I scroll down the page randomly clicking on the links some show pictures of Skye at conventions posing with fans and signing the games merchandise. I watch a video titled Las Vegas, the footage is from a convention six years ago, Skye is on stage with three other artists. Other links show her dressed to the nines attending various functions. I spot Simon in a few of those photographs, in others she's stood with a tall woman with short dark hair. My heart jumps into my throat when I find one of Skye stood with a tall dark haired man. Skye is smiling at the camera the man is looking at her mesmerised and smiling tenderly, there's no caption but I have a sneaky feeling it must be Clayton. He's a good looking fucker, was, I mentally correct myself. The guy screamed money, everything about him. His suit, watch, shoes even his bloody hair is well groomed.

 Feeling deflated I click off and go back to Google, on the second page I find an article in a business magazine. The article mainly focused on Clayton Blake — the head and shoulder photograph confirms for me the last picture of Skye and the dark haired man, he was her husband — and how he built his business empire starting out on his own whilst at college then going to work for his father starting at the bottom, eventually taking over when his father passed away. The article quoted Clayton from a recent interview he had given to another business journal where he gave full credit to his beautiful wife helping to triple the business's turnover since they met "She sees things I nor my staff don't. For years I've been trying to get her to work with me full time but she turns me down flat. I love inviting her in to meetings to discuss the new proposals and ventures we are considering investing in. Skye has this incredible sixth sense when it comes to business, she has saved not just my business but other investors a fortune time and time again at the same time she's made us a fortune" Mr Blake laughs "if you ask her what she bases her decision on she'll tell you her bullshit meter is going off the scale or it feels right. I don't care what people say but I've learnt to listen to my wife"

'It is always a tragedy when a forward thinking, dynamic and charismatic business leader's life is cruelly cut short especially in one so young as in Clayton Blake's case a few days after his thirty sixth birthday. It is rumoured that Mr Blake has left the bulk of his fortune to his wife, Skye Darcy, a multi billionaire in her own right is now estimated to be worth in the region of ten billion dollars'.

The last paragraph turns my blood cold, I quickly open a new tab to change dollars in to pounds. "Holy fucking shit" I mutter as I see it converts to just over six point five billion and the article said estimated so it could be more. I go back to the article scrolling to the beginning to see when it had been published, it went out in December a month after his death.

Skye is way out of my league. Her whole life couldn't be any more different to mine. It's no surprise now why she has two body guards permanently with her and a PA. I bet she has a whole fleet of staff and servants at her beck and call in all her mansions and penthouses. She even has her own plane for fucks sake, not a jet a plane. She has the kind of wealth that can put a plane on standby to fly her and her entourage wherever she wants at a moment's notice. Shit! I'm barely keeping this business afloat and Skye juggles multiple successful businesses all at once.

What does she see in me? Apart from the fact we've had some pretty amazing sex and fucked at every opportunity, we've had a good time. Is that it? I'm her bit of rough, a pleasant distraction whilst she's here. I bet she's been laughing about me with her rich friends, Simon implied as much last night that Skye had been talking about me. Fucking rich bitch.

I slap that thought away. She's not like that, it doesn't appear to be her nature. What do you know? Apart from when you talked on the train you've not had an in depth conversation with her since, when you've seen each other all you've done is fuck each other's brains out. Yes, we're attracted to each other, there's definitely chemistry between us but that's it. Take away the sex what do we have? There is nothing I can give her, she has it all already or she can buy a more expensive version herself. I'd never be able to keep a woman like her and I'm kidding myself otherwise.

Well, she'll be gone in a few days might as well enjoy the ride whilst it lasts, I decide as I switch off the computer and head for the shower. So why does my heart feel so heavy and I feel sick to my stomach at that very thought?

On the walk down to the pub I meet Frank Appleton, he's in his suit again, freshly shaven and his dark grey hair slicked back, there's no cap insight.

"Hey Frank where's the interview?" I joke in a way of greeting as I pat his shoulder.

Frank turns green and tugs at the collar of his shirt and takes a deep breath "Not an interview" he frowns his ruddy face wrinkling "I don't think it is anyway, just want to create the right impression, that's all" he nods and points in the direction of the pub.

We arrive about fifteen minutes after midday. The place is rammed, it's as if every person in the village including the weekenders has taken Friday afternoon off work.

"Where the fuck did all these people come from?" I mutter under my breath, Frank chuckles as we fight our way to the bar.

"Mr Appleton" a deep American drawl comes from behind us, we both turn to see Paul "if you'll follow me please sir"

All the colour drains from Frank's face, I don't blame him. Paul is one scary looking son of a bitch; you wouldn't want to mess with him. Without a word Frank steps forward as Paul turns to lead him round the bar and through the staff entrance.

"What was that about?" Rex's eager voice hisses in my ear.

"Dunno" I shrug "Paul asked Frank to follow him. What's been happening?"

I look over towards the pool table area to see a group of strangers with various folders and long tubes setting up.

"Nothing much, those guys turned up about five minutes before you and there's been no sign of Skye" Rex says rather disappointed "come to think of it Chris and Michelle haven't been around either and I would've thought with the place being this busy it'll be all hands on deck"

Behind the bar with Marie are two other women, Becks and Sara, who work part time usually in the evening, all three were serving two or more customers at one time. A few minutes later the staff door opens, Chris and Michelle appear with three gentlemen all dressed in a very sharp business suits. All had ridiculous grins on their faces as they shake hands. One of the suits makes a comment and gestures to the crowded pub "Too late now" I lip read Chris, the suits laugh. All eyes follow them as they made their way out. Chris comes behind the bar and starts serving as Michelle heads to the group of strangers by the pool table.

314

"Caleb my boy what can I get you?" Chris booms grinning manically.

"Two bottles of Corona. You look as if Christmas has come early" I raise an inquisitive eyebrow at him.

"It has, it most certainly has" Chris winks as he hands over the drinks.

"What do you think he means by that?" Rex mutters speculatively in my ear.

"No idea" I say turning to lean on the bar and settle in to watch the Skye Darcy show like every other muppet in the pub.

SKYE

I shuffle in to the kitchen squinting against the brightness, even raising my hand to shield my eyes doesn't help. My tongue feels furry and too big for my mouth, my head and eyes feel as if little men wearing big hob nail boots are having a stomping party and forgot to invite me.

"Oh dear, you look rough" Freya says trying to sound sympathetic and failing miserably. The others all laugh.

"Sit down" Michelle guides me to a chair "a nice greasy breakfast will have you right as rain in no time"

"I didn't think I had that much to drink last night" I groan as my head hits the table, making the cutlery rattle.

"It was the Southern Comfort that did it" Chris chuckles, I hear the clink of a glass and the fizz of its contents being put in front of me "here drink this, it'll help"

Slowly I lift my head, picking up the glass I down the drink in one go "Yuk!" I screw my face up and shiver at the taste "hair of the dog will probably do just as well" I hand the glass back to Chris just as Simon shuffles in.

"Oh baby girl you look as rough as I feel" he croaks sitting down next to Freya "why didn't you stop me last night, you're supposed to be the responsible one"

"It was my night off" I retort and laugh as he hangs his head in his hands.

Chris materialises with another fizzing glass of what he'd given me and silently hands it to Simon who drinks it without question.

"Eww" Simon pulls a disgusted face and shudders as he hands back the glass.

"Here you go, eat up" Michelle places a plate of bacon and fried eggs in front of us.

My stomach grumbles instead of revolting at the smell. I reach for the bread and make myself an egg and bacon butty. Half way through I start to feel human again.

As I eat Freya gives me an update on the things we went through yesterday and the changes to the meetings taking place today, it's nothing major mainly other people being brought along for me to meet who will play a key role in the restoration work. The phone ringing makes everyone jump, I realise my headache has gone. As Michelle picks it up a thought occurs to me.

"Chris, I have a favour to ask"

"Sure whatever you need" Chris says without hearing my favour, it makes me smile.

"Do you mind if I bring Frank Appleton up here for a meeting, he approached me last night about putting in a word with the owner of the Hall to do the gardening, I've decided to offer him the job but I need to tell him who I am and I'd rather do that in private"

"Of course, bring him up. I believe he's bloody good at what he does and a lot of people round here take advantage of his good nature. It couldn't happen to a nicer man" Chris beams.

"Excuse me everyone. I have Mr Singleton on from the brewery. He's reached Henley and wants to know can he come to us now, apparently he set off early allowing for traffic and there wasn't any" Michelle grins, Chris and I nod "that's fine Mr Singleton. We'll see you shortly" Michelle hangs up.

"Right, I'm getting a shower now that I feel fully human again. Thanks for breakfast and whatever that concoction was. It's certainly done the trick"

"You're welcome" Michelle and Chris call out as I head out the door.

Mr Singleton, it turns out, is the brewery's Managing Director, he brought with him the company solicitor and Finance Director. It soon becomes apparent that I, or my team, were not what they were expecting. To me, they came thinking they would be dealing with some two-bit yokel who liked the idea of owning their own pub. Luckily they came prepared and brought all the contracts. Freya copies the documents and emails them to Joshua. Within half an hour Joshua calls me via Skype. After the solicitor and the Finance Director answer his questions Joshua says he's satisfied and happy for me to go ahead and sign. I know I shock the shit out of the Finance Director when I ask him for the bank details the money is to be deposited in to and Freya completes the transaction as soon as he finishes giving the last number.

"The money is in your account" says Freya "have someone in your accounts department to verify that now and send me an acknowledging email" we both look at the FD expectantly

"Oh, yes, right away" he says somewhat flummoxed as he fumbles for his phone.

While he made his call I address at the solicitor "Have the deeds couriered here for Chris and Michelle's attention immediately"

"Of course" he says picking up his phone a lot more calmly.

"I wish all business transactions would go as quickly and smoothly as this one" Mr Singleton says smiling at me "what are your plans for this place, if you don't mind sharing that is?"

"I'm just the silent business partner, that's down to Chris and Michelle they sold me their dream for this place so by rights they'll tell you"

Mr Singleton couldn't hide his surprise, and his surprise increases further when Chris and Michelle tell him their plans and of Simon's marketing strategy to promote the different areas of the business.

"Why didn't you approach me with this business plan?" says Mr Singleton.

"Would you have listened?" I threw at him before Chris and Michelle can answer "or would you have made a decision based on numbers?"

Mr Singleton gives me a wry smile "I take your point Ms Darcy, making a decision based on numbers is why I have just sold this place to you and it is you who is backing this venture because you listened" he laughs and shakes his head "I have learnt a valuable lesson today"

"My grandfather used to say "Listen first and do the numbers second. If the numbers don't add up but you see belief, passion and determination that is what will make it work to balance the books" he was a mean old bastard but by god he was right about that"

"Sounds like he was also a wise man"

"He had his moments when he wasn't scaring the shit out of people"

"May I ask who your grandfather was?" curiosity is rolling of Mr Singleton. There's a strong possibility he knew of or had actually met my grandfather.

"Lord Matthew Belling" I watch closely for his reaction. Mr Singleton's eyes widen and his jaw pops open, yep he knew him.

"You're Skye Darcy the artist" I nod "I'm so sorry I've just made the connection. Tobias is an old friend of mine. I knew your grandfather he would often talk about you, Tobias too. It's a pleasure to finally meet you" Mr Singleton says in awe.

"Wow, it's true what they say about it being a small world" Michelle says taking the words right out of my mouth.

My phone buzzes, looking down I see a message from Paul saying Frank has arrived and he's on his way up. I stand and hold out my hand to Mr Singleton "It was a pleasure doing business with you, unfortunately I have another meeting" the men all stand and I shake their hands and say goodbye.

I meet Frank in the living room, it's more comfortable and less formal. Frank is in his rough woollen suit again; he desperately wants to make a good impression. I find myself smiling fondly at him as he walks in to the room, he's nervous as hell and he keeps tugging at the neck of his shirt collar.

"Hi Frank, good to see you again" I do my best to make him feel relaxed "this is Freya, she's my PA" Frank nods and does a slight bow towards Freya "now before we start how about removing that tie and unbuttoning your shirt before it strangles you. I appreciate you want to give a good impression but I'd sooner have you comfortable"

Frank barks out a nervous laugh as he gratefully undoes the tie and opens the top button "The misses will kill me if she finds out"

"I won't tell her if you don't" I pat his arm and Frank visibly relaxes as he settles into the seat "I thought it best to do this part of the meeting away from prying eyes and flapping ears" I point to the floor indicating to the low muffled noise from the bar below "it sounds too busy to have this kind of conversation plus it wouldn't be fair on you" uncertainty flashes across Frank's face "it took a lot of courage to approach me last night and I admire your integrity so I would like to offer you the position of Head Gardener or Grounds Keeper, tell you what you can make up your own title, how's that"

"I don't... you spoke to..." Frank pauses takes a deep breath and runs his hand through his hair messing up the slick look "you spoke to Mrs Blake and she's already said yes?"

His shock and disbelief are enduring. I lean forward and take hold of his work worn hand "Frank, I am Mrs Blake" Frank's eyes almost pop out of his head "and I had quite a long conversation with myself and we agreed to offer you the job"

"I... yes, yes I accept" Frank says getting over his shock and enthusiasm breaks through.

"The job will entail looking after all of the grounds, not just the garden but the woodland areas, the orchard and the cottages, sometimes there might be other jobs that you'll be asked to oversee or sort out. You'll have a budget and you can hire whoever you need to help. The hiring and firing will be your decision; you won't have to run that by me. The only stipulation I have is that the people you hire are discreet. Are you okay with that?"

"Yes, yes Mrs Blake" says Frank eagerly.

"Okay, first off drop the Mrs Blake" worry flashes across his face, I squeeze his hand "very few people call me that and I only use it if I want to go incognito but being here Darcy works better" Frank laughs and nods his understanding "do you have any questions before I continue?"

"Will I get to meet Mr Blake?" Frank's question takes me off guard "I'm sorry if I've said anything to upset you" Frank says quietly.

"I wasn't expecting that" I try to smile "my husband passed away in November, he was in a car accident and died a few days later from his injuries"

"I'm sorry to hear that" Frank pats my hand in a fatherly manner. I feel a rush of warmth and gratitude towards him, he genuinely does feel sorry for my loss. I've heard so many people say it but not actually mean it. I take a few deep breaths "when can I start?"

That makes me laugh and his question breaks the chains of sorrow that are starting to engulf me "You don't know what the salary and benefits are yet"

Frank shrugs "It's my dream job, you can pay me a pittance and it wouldn't make me change my mind"

I roll my eyes at him "I was thinking forty grand a year, you'll have private health care and dental plus a pension and thirty days' holiday plus bank holidays on top and you can start now. How's that sound?"

Frank's eyes fill up "Where do I sign?" his voice cracks with emotion.

"Freya will draw up a contract of employment for you to sign later. Give her your address and bank details plus whatever else she asks for" I stand "I'll be back in a minute then we'll go downstairs I understand that Martin the architect has brought a landscape architect with him, I want you to work closely together on the restoration of the garden, you're the one in charge of that project"

"Thank you so much Ms Darcy for this opportunity" Frank stands and holds out his hand.

"Welcome to the team" I say shaking it.

I head to the bathroom to freshen up, then my bedroom and check my reflection in the mirror. At least my eyes are no longer puffy but I do look at little pasty. I put mascara on then lip balm for my dry lips, putting the little pot in one of the many pockets of my combats. I've had these trousers for years and they are so comfy. I squirt some hair product on my hands then tip my head down and run the product through my damp hair. With the exception of when it is wet I never brush and comb my hair instead I put loads of product in it to stop it frizzing, the result gives me large ringlet type curls. Flicking my head back my hair falls all around in a wild curly mess, my cheeks are flushed bringing some much needed colour and my eyes look large and bright. I smile at myself, a couple of hours ago I was a hungover mess, now I'm ready to take on the world.

Back in the living room Frank is on his phone relaying information to Freya, after hearing a series of numbers I realise it's his bank details. I sit down and wait for him to finish. Freya double checks the information and says she'll drop the paperwork off at his house in the morning.

"Before we head down stairs do you have any other questions?" I say to Frank.

"Will I be working to a budget for the renovation of the garden and the rest of the grounds?"

"Good question, the short answer is no" I grin at him "the longer answer is you'll have a credit card you can use, Freya will organise that for you. Use the card if we can't be invoiced. I trust your judgement and expertise in all matters to do with the grounds. As far as taking on staff let me know how many you need, for how long and salary and I'll make sure the funds are available. Freya will give you an email address and mobile number as a means to contact me, actually I should say contact Freya who will make sure I get your messages. Anything you're unsure of and want clarification on get in touch. When we get downstairs and have the meeting with the landscape architect I'll tell you what I like, what I want and don't want. Anything else?"

"Not at the moment" Frank says rubbing his work worn hands together, he's eager to get started.

We all stand and make our way downstairs, the volume of the pub getting louder and louder. Frank pushes the door open and a wall of noise hits us.

"Bloody hell" I mutter "I knew it would be busy but this is frigging ridiculous"

"Welcome to the freak show" Freya mutters back with a nervous laugh.

"You okay?" I run a critical eye over Freya, most of her bruises are covered with subtle make up. Her dark brown hair is shiny but in desperate need of a good cut. David will sort that out, I mentally make a note.

"Yeah, I'm good. Just not used to being in the thick of the action and centre of attention" Freya takes a deep breath "but I'm excited and raring to go" she gives me a huge dazzling smile that reaches her eyes, she's not faking it.

"Good. Now remember if things get too much, shout" I give her a stern look, Freya salutes me making me laugh "in case I forget to say it later, thanks for all your hard work today"

Freya beams as she takes a seat at the bar, it doesn't escape my attention that Alan has been keeping it for her. He really is developing a soft spot for Freya, a very protective one at that.

"Come on Frank let's get this show on the road" I look up at him, he's grinning from ear to ear. He looks like someone who has hit the jackpot. As we make our way over to the pool table area I spot Caleb leaning against the bar, Rex is next to him. I smile and wave to them, both raise their bottles in salute to me. My attention is pulled away immediately by Martin.

"Ms Darcy so good to see you again" he shakes my hand, his grip strong and sure "we have everything ready" he gestures to the pool table. The whole surface is covered in plans.

"Excellent, I understand you've brought a landscape architect with you"

"Yes, I hope you don't mind" Martin makes a come here gesture to someone "this is Charlie Tanner" he says as a tall gangly blonde haired man joins us.

"Pleased to meet you" we say together and shake hands "this is Frank Appleton. He's in charge of the garden restoration and all the grounds I want you two to work very closely together. Frank was a gardener for the original owners of the Hall, now he's my head honcho"

Charlie's eyes widen then he grins "Excellent that makes my job a hell of a lot easier"

"Frank, why don't you take Charlie over to the Hall and show him the layout of the land and you can show him how the gardens were" a thought occurs to me "do you need a car?"

"It's okay we can take mine" Charlie offers before Frank can say anything.

"Right I'll see you both back here later, take as long as you need" I watch the pub patron's reaction to Frank and Charlie leaving together, it makes me smile. People will be gossiping about this day for months to come. I turn my attention back to Martin "Show me what you've got"

CALEB

The woman is a machine. For five hours I've watched her along with everyone else as she's moved from one group of people to the next and back again. With a simple hand movement, she has commanded people to her side in an instant. She's consulted, listened, given instructions, put people together and sent them on their way to wherever; only for them to come back hours later to make a report. It's been very interesting to watch this powerful, dominant, extremely wealthy businesswoman in action, yet she has willingly submitted to me. My cock twitches, as I remember her dropping to her knees last night. I feel a secretive smile pull at my lips.

My favourite moments have been when certain villagers have been unexpectedly summonsed, the funniest being the first when Bill Makin got singled out. Skye stood by the pool table looking at the plans with two men, who appeared to be responsible for the rebuild of the Hall. One of the men was making notes on whatever Skye was saying, she then called Michelle over after a brief conversation all four turned to face the watching crowd. Michelle pointed giving a description of someone. Skye spotted the person and made a 'come here' gesture to Bill. Comically he looked around then pointed to himself, Skye smiled and nodded making the gesture again.

It was strange to see Bill, who is so confident and cocky, to look unsure and nervous. Michelle did the introductions then left the group to discuss business. Whatever it was appeared to be good news because

Bill got the same look on his face that Frank Appleton had when he came back from his meeting with Skye. In turn Bill looked out to the crowd and pointed to certain people indicating for them to come over. Stan Williams who is a joiner, Mal Barton a plasterer, Steve Jamieson a plumber, Ken Fritz an electrician all made their way to him and Skye. Within minutes the other four had the biggest fucking grin on their faces matching Bill's. Each of the guys dug in their pockets and handed business cards to the man who was making notes. After a few more minutes the five of them left and headed for the bar. Bill came and stood next to me and Rex.

"We've all been hired" Bill freely volunteers in an 'I can't believe that's just happened' daze.

"Who are those two blokes" Rex tips his bottle in the direction of the pool table.

"The red haired one taking notes is Keith Hart, Project Manager. The other is Martin Atkinson he's the architect" Bill leans in "according to Ms Darcy there's a directive to use as many local businesses and tradesmen as possible for the restoration of the Hall and other properties in the estate"

I feel my heart swelling with pride as I look at Skye. Almost single handed she is boosting the villages economy and winning the hearts of those that live here without even knowing it, if she is aware of it she's being low key and down to earth about it. Skye maybe ridiculously wealthy but looking at her now you wouldn't have a fucking clue, dressed in khaki combats that showed off her fit tight arse to perfection and a purple and pink tie dyed t-shirt she looked like any other young woman.

At some point Chris switched on the air conditioning; with so many people crammed into the pub it was getting uncomfortably hot. Skye must have been stood directly under the cold air as she spoke with Michelle, Simon and another bloke who was dressed so flamboyantly I pegged him as gay. In my book only a gay man would and could get away with wearing tight fitting purple trousers, a yellow paisley shirt with a red scarf tied around his neck. Skye was shivering, Paul who had been keeping an eye on the crowded pub got off his stool removed his fleece jacket and put it around Skye. She carried on talking as she put her arms through the sleeves. Paul turned to leave, Skye's hand shot out and squeezed his arm, a silent thanks. The gray fleece drowned her. It finished at her knees, Skye had to roll the sleeves back then she zipped it up.

After her conversation finished Skye slowly turned to face me, a sly smile on her lips. She looked down at the jacket and back at me giving a saucy wink. I looked at the jacket, across the front was big red scrawling letters. I took a mouthful of my beer then my brain registered what the lettering said… 'Wild Cat'. I choked on my drink and sprayed it all over Rex with Skye's throaty laugh ringing in my ears.

Two hours in to the meetings Bill, Stan, Mal, Steve and Ken were summoned again this time they sat with Michelle. I could see Steve's face and whatever Michelle said surprised the hell out of him, I could see from the backs of the others they had the same reaction. A genuine smile and words of congratulations from Steve was followed by claps and laughter from the others. Michelle introduced them to flamboyant guy, once again business cards were handed over. After that meeting word soon spread around the pub that Chris and Michelle now owned it. The three men in suits and Chris's manic smiling made sense, also Michelle had been spending all her time with Simon and the flamboyantly dressed guy whose name I now know is Elliot, he is an interior designer and project manager for the refurbishment of the pub and the rest of the work that will be carried out.

"We're going to refurbish all the rooms upstairs and convert the old barn and coaching stables so we'll have a function room to hire out and we'll be running a bed and breakfast as well" Chris beams when he tells me and Rex his plans "we'll also operate as a free house with guest beers and the outside garden will be overhauled to make a proper family and children's play area and there'll be a purpose built barbeque area"

"That's fantastic news Chris, what made you decide to buy the pub?" says Rex.

"We got a letter from the brewery saying they were going to sell it and gave us first option to buy. If we didn't then they were going to shut the place down by the end of the month"

"Jesus, that's a bit harsh" I bark out.

"They're number's men" Chris shrugs "although when they saw how packed the pub was they joked about changing their mind. I told them too late" he laughs.

The whole atmosphere in the pub became jovial and rowdy as good news after goods news quickly spread. Quite a few people attempted to approach Skye directly, they didn't get far when Paul and Alan closed ranks. Word soon got round that if you didn't have anything to offer in connection to the restoration of the Hall or any of the other properties for that matter, you were politely turned away. A couple of people hand over business cards which are passed to Freya.

Shortly after Chris and Michelle's news broke the next biggest surprise of the day was seeing Farmers Joe senior and junior come in to the pub. Joe senior is a mean old bastard and he's got worse with age especially now he relies so heavily on his son to get around. The poor sod is riddled with arthritis and can barely walk so it's very rare for him to come in to the village. Joe junior pushes his old man in what looks like a brand new wheelchair through the pub towards me and Rex.

"Hi guys" Joe smiles and shakes our hands "what do you want to drink Dad?"

"Guinness" the old man snaps as he looks around, his harsh wrinkled face softens when he sees Skye. Joe senior raises a gnarled arthritic hand to wave to her. Skye gives him a heart stopping dazzling smile and makes her way over to us with Elliot behind her.

"Mr Porter, so good to see you and thank you for coming" Skye bends and kisses his cheek, the old man blushes and looks chuffed to bits.

"Not that I had any choice in the matter" he tries for grumpy but fails miserably much to the amusement of me and everyone around us.

"This is Elliot, who I told you about" Skye steps aside so the old man can see him, Joe senior's face is a picture when he gets a load of Elliot.

"Pleased to meet you Mr Porter" Elliot says politely and gently shakes Joe's hand.

"You mean I've got to spend the afternoon with this ponce?" and the old man is back to his normal snappy self. Joe junior looks mortified at Skye, she smiles and winks at him.

"Oh come on, you little ray of sunshine, you know you're going to love every minute of it" Skye says getting behind his wheelchair and pushes him towards the pool table.

"And besides you're just how I like my men, mean and nasty" Elliot says patting the old man's shoulder. Joe senior shocks the shit out of me by laughing.

"I think that's the first time I've ever heard your old man laugh"

"You should have heard him the other day" Joe junior nods in Skye's direction "Ms Darcy came to the farm and you know what dad's like he was downright rude to her the second she set foot in the house. Without turning a hair, she said to him "You remind me of my grandfather. He was a mean old cantankerous git just like you" well that shocked the hell out of him" Joe junior laughs shaking his head "then the old bugger roars laughing. After that he was like putty in her hands"

"What was Skye doing out at the farm" Rex says frowning.

"Well she does…" I kick Joe's ankle to stop him, he was about to let the cat out of the bag. Joe looks at me puzzled, I subtly shake my head, thank fuck Joe cottoned on "she's overseeing all the properties in the estate and she came to have a look around to see what needed doing. That's why we're here to get all the work arranged"

A few minutes later Rex disappears to the gents giving me chance to have a quiet word with Joe "Sorry about kicking you but only a handful of people know her true identity" I mutter in Joe's ear.

Wonder then amusement crosses his face "You know but Rex doesn't" Joe correctly guesses, I nod "who else knows?" he whispers, looking around furtively. Thankfully no-one is paying us any attention.

"Me, the Farringdon's, Chris and Michelle"

"That's it" Joe says stunned "oh dad is going to have a field day when I tell him" Joe looks at his father fondly. Joe senior is surrounded by people, Michelle brings him his pint of Guinness and a plate of food. The old goat is already loving the attention.

"What work is being done?" I change to a safer subject before Rex comes back.

"Everything, the place is being gutted. New roof, re-wire, central heating, double glazed windows, new kitchen, bathroom and furniture. You name it, it's being done. Including all the outhouses, the barns and we're getting all new machinery as well"

"Bloody hell, but it's about fucking time. Your place was being held together by the cobwebs"

"Aye that it is" Joe laughs and takes a sip of his juice "I'll tell you something else" Joe lowers his voice looking around furtively again "Ms Darcy will be paying for a full time house keeper come carer for dad. She was horrified to learn that dad suffered so badly and we couldn't afford the care he needed. Then she made a few phone calls, anyway cutting a long story short because we only manage the farm technically we're her employees so now we have pensions, private healthcare and dental. Not only that but she's changed the profit share and made it so we get ninety percent of the proceeds from the sale of produce. Late yesterday afternoon, a bloke turns up with that wheelchair and a brand new Range Rover for me that has this lift contraption to help get dad in and out of it. Then we get a phone call from a Harley Street specialist saying dad has an appointment next week for a full medical and to discuss his arthritis"

"Fucking hell" I whisper in awe.

"I know and that's not all" Joe steps closer "Dad asked her what she intended to do about the Mill, she had no idea there was one. We took her out to see it and dad told her how it used to be operational making flour only since old man Cookson lost the family fortune he couldn't afford to get it repaired so he shut it down. Ms Darcy fell in love with the place she asked if we knew of anyone who could work it if she got restored. Dad told her about Nick and his lads, she told him to talk to them" Joe grins widely.

"And?" I raise an eyebrow.

"And what?" Rex says appearing at Joe's shoulder "what have I missed?"

"My cousin Nick and his lads are coming back to the village to work the Mill"

"Mate that's bloody fantastic news" I slap Joe's back in delight.

"What! Wait is the Mill being restored as well?" Rex says astounded, Joe nods gleefully.

"Excuse me Mr Porter" a timid female voice has us all turning round to face Freya, she smiles warily at me and Rex before shifting her gaze to Joe "Ms Darcy asks if you would take the architect and surveyor up to the Mill and show them around"

"Yes, certainly, now?" Joe says putting his drink down on the bar, Freya nods and walks back to the pool table area "catch up with you later guys" Joe pats both mine and Rex's shoulder and follows her.

It was fascinating to watch Skye's team attend to her every need without her saying anything, they seemed to pre-empt Skye. On one occasion Skye kept shifting her hair out of the way as she looked down at plans, then she started patting pockets. Alan went over to her and took hold of her hair and tied it back whilst she remained bent, a thumbs up sign was all the acknowledgment she gave. Freya and Simon would regularly hand her a bottle of water or juice, even Michelle got in on the act by putting a plate of sandwiches in her hands as she talked to Elliot and a couple of other people who had loads of sample folders.

But my all-time favourite moment is when Miles Cunningham got his Z list celebrity nose pushed out of joint, not by Skye but an eleven-year-old boy. It was late afternoon when Miles showed his face in the pub, he did his usual thing where he stood pretending to look round for someone but we all knew he was really waiting to be recognised and to be pointed at. Very few of the villager's pander to his ego and everyone in the pub was more taken with Skye so we ignored him.

"Look at that fucking ponce" Rex growls in my ear as Miles made his way to the bar.

"No thanks, there's a much better view that way" I tip my bottle in Skye's direction.

Rex for some reason despises Miles and I've never been able to fathom why or get to the bottom of it. Rex says it's because Miles is an utter prick, end of. I've never bothered to find out if the feeling is mutual since Miles always looks down his nose at me. Unfortunately, Miles chose to park his unwelcome presence right next to us. Thankfully Marjorie Brennan, who is a fan, stroked his ego by talking about how fantastic he had been all this week on the telly blah, blah, fucking blah, hurl. When the fan fest finishes she starts telling him what's been happening in the pub, most of the things she tells him are only partially right but that's Marjorie for you, she often got the wrong end of the stick.

Skye's meetings finish, the architect and his team pack up along with Elliot and his people, all of them shout a cheerful goodbye to everyone in the pub. Skye makes her way over to me, well not me per say since Paul, Alan and Freya are close by. Skye chats with them briefly, Paul hands something to her and she goes behind the bar. Skye speaks to each of the bar staff then disappears through the door that leads to the kitchen. One by one each of the staff follow her only to return a few minutes later grinning from ear to ear.

"What was that all about?" Rex asks Marie, only she refuses to say anything, just shakes her head and her smile gets wider "never mind I'll get it out of her later" Rex mutters to me.

Since the 'Skye Darcy Show' was over the pub started to empty, most people going home for dinner and to get ready for the karaoke tonight. Michelle and Skye came out ten minutes later talking about food, my stomach growls reminding me that I hadn't eaten anything all day, being sensible I switched to soft drinks after the one Corona. Skye heard my stomach and smiles.

"I'm not the only one that needs feeding" Skye says to Michelle nodding her head in my direction.

"Stop shifting the focus to someone else, you only ate half a sandwich earlier, now what do you want to eat" Michelle says sternly.

"The same as last night please. What!" Skye exclaims as Michelle and the others roll their eyes at her.

"You'll be looking like a burger soon" laughs Freya.

"They're delicious, I might as well make the most of it whilst I'm here" Skye says haughtily as she comes back round to my side of the bar "what are you guys having?"

Paul, Alan and Freya put their order in, then Skye surprises me, Rex, Miles and Marjorie by asking what we want. Marjorie and Miles say they're okay and about to go home before I can answer Michelle looks at me and Rex saying "The usual" we both nod.

"Ohmigod, ohmigod, Dad, Dad, ohmigod" a highly excited child's voice has everyone turning round "it is, it is ohmigod I can't believe it" the young boy stood staring and pointing in our direction whilst he tugs on his father's arm.

"Sorry, he's a bit star struck" the lad's father says smiling.

"It's okay I'm used to it" Miles says stepping forward, preening "it happens all the time"

"Who are you?" the young lad says in disgust, frowning at Miles and looking him up and down.

Rex and I burst out laughing. Rex is hanging on to me, this is the best put down I've witnessed to deflate an over blown pretentious ego, my sides are aching. Poor Miles looks totally thrown, he has that 'if I'm not the star then who is' kind of expression on his face.

"Miles Cunningham, I present the regional news on the TV" Miles says loudly to drown out our laughter.

"Dad can I have the car keys" the lad says bouncing on the balls of his feet completely ignoring Miles which makes us laugh harder. His father duly hands over the keys "I'll be back in a minute, don't go anywhere" he shouts to no-one in particular and runs out of the pub.

"I apologise, he's quite excited. The other day he overheard one of his school friends mention you were staying here and he's begged me all week to bring him" dad says looking at Skye "I'm just thankful you are still here otherwise he'd never forgive me if we arrived only to find out you had been and gone"

"You're lucky, I'm leaving on Sunday" Skye says smiling.

Rex is sniggering down my ear "Get a load of Miles's face" he says gleefully.

Miles is in a state of utter shock and confusion now; he has no idea who Skye is. The door bursts open and the young lad is back with an armful of packaged toys and posters. Without a word Paul hands Skye, a marker pen.

"So young man what's your name" Skye says taking a seat at the nearest table.

"Edward" he says breathlessly as he drops everything onto the table, some of the toys fall to the floor. I bend to pick up the one that lands at my feet. Rex does the same thing. The figure is of a muscled bound warrior, the one Rex has is a hooded figure in a swirling cloak, long blade swords in both hands "thanks mister" Edward says taking the toys back.

"Your dad tells me you heard from school friends I was here" Skye says as she starts signing the backs of the toy packages.

"One of the boys in the year above me has an older cousin that lives in this village. He was boasting that his cousin had seen you but no one would believe him. God, I can't believe it you're really here" Edward reaches out and touches Skye's hair, she doesn't flinch or move away like she did with the guy on the train, instead she gives him a dazzling smile.

"And how far have you made your poor dad drive just to see if the rumour was true"

"Not far only from Reading, but dad doesn't mind he's a big fan, just don't tell my mum" Edward stage whispers.

"I won't" Skye stage whispers back and winks at dad. Dad blushes.

Everyone gathers round to look at the three posters when they're unrolled, two are of scantily clad female warriors, looking beautiful but fierce. The third is of a warrior King sat on his throne with two voluptuous practically naked women sat at his feet. Skye signs all three putting a personal message to Edward on each.

"There you go" Skye says capping the pen.

Edward flings his arms around Skye's neck "Thank you so much, can I have a picture with you?" he says releasing her.

"Sure, you got your phone or camera?"

Edward pulls his smart phone out of his pocket, Paul takes it from him. Skye poses with Edward and his dad, then with Edward on his own, in the last one Skye kisses his cheek.

"He won't have a wash now" his dad jokes as his son held his face in wonder "thank you so much for your time"

"My pleasure, safe journey home" Skye calls out as they left the pub.

"Does this mean I'm going to be inundated with fans now" Chris says with a wink as he clears the bar of empty glasses.

"Maybe" Skye shrugs "but chances are by the time word gets round I won't be here"

"You'll have to take pictures Chris and put them up around the bar as proof she was here" suggests Simon. Chris's eyes light up and grins at Skye.

Skye rolls her eyes and stands "Right, I'll be back in a five minutes" she says walking towards the staff door. Freya follows her.

"But you said she was just a designer" Miles's nasty accusing voice drew everyone's attention.

"I… I was told… I…" poor Marjorie stammers.

Simon slid off his stool and went to Marjorie putting his arm around the old dear "Don't you fret sweetie" he says kindly to her "Marjorie is correct Skye is a designer, you've just seen a mere smidgeon of some of the things she designs. You're the numpty for assuming the kind of designer she is" Simon glares at Miles.

Miles narrows his eyes at Simon, its obvious Miles is dying to say something cutting but can't risk looking more of a twat than he already does. Fortunately for Miles his phone rings, using that as an excuse he leaves the pub.

"Who is that…" Simon abruptly stops talking and covers Marjorie's ears up "wanker?" he finishes.

"That wanker reads the local news on the TV" Marjorie says before anyone else can answer "he's so full of himself I wouldn't be surprised if he shat mini me's"

Those of us that know Marjorie well gawp open mouthed at her, she never insults anyone and it's extremely rare to hear her swear.

"I like you Marjorie. Chris get this lady a pint of whatever she wants" Simon says laughing.

"I'm paying" Rex calls out "Marjorie, you my dear lady are my favourite person today and I'm pinching your description of Miles. He's so full of himself he's shitting mini me's, that's fucking brilliant"

"I'm confused" Marjorie says cupping her face in her wrinkled hands "does Ms Darcy design toys?" she frowns bewildered at Simon.

"Skye is a very famous artist in the Fantasy and Science Fiction genre. Sometimes video game companies' pay a fortune for her services to redesign an existing product or come up with new characters but that is only a small fraction of what she does" explains Simon.

"Oh" Marjorie says but the confusion is still in her face "so what she doing at the Hall for Mr and Mrs Blake?"

Simon doesn't hesitate "Well one of the other things Skye loves to do is restore old buildings, it's kind of like a hobby, so when the opportunity arose she jumped at it"

Clever, very clever Simon. He told the truth but didn't correct Marjorie on her presumption. Simon looks directly at me and winks. Trying to keep my face straight I make my way to the toilets otherwise I'll give the game away.

I ponder on everything I've seen today. Skye may be the richest person I or anyone else will ever meet but she is so down to earth, generous, considerate and caring and she has a wicked sense of humour. Yet she is candid, commanding and focused, not forgetting hugely talented. Christ, what a fucking dickhead I was this morning thinking Skye would only see me as a distraction, her bit of rough on the side. Those kind of thoughts would never enter her head. Skye treats everyone as her equal; that was very evident today.

Sighing at myself for being such a knob I wash my hands and rinse my face, make the most of the time you have left together, she'll be gone on Sunday for god knows how long. The thought leaves a very bitter taste in my mouth. I don't like it; I don't like it one fucking bit.

SKYE

Opening the staff only door I see Freya following me, behind her I can see Caleb scowling at the self-proclaimed TV celebrity Miles somebody, huh he certainly did think he was someone, pretentious git. Then I notice everyone else has the same expression, Simon gets off his stool and goes to Marjorie. I'll find out what it's all about later.

"You okay Freya?" she's looking tired, I put my arm around her waist as we head upstairs.

"Yeah" it's said wearily "I've really enjoyed today, learnt a lot too"

"I'm glad, you've been a real trooper" I hug her gently, mindful of her bruised ribs "what are you planning to do once we've eaten?"

"Well I'm going to go through all the action points from today, list them in order of priority and have an early night"

"No you're not" I smile at her puzzlement "tonight you're letting your hair down with me. That's an order" I add before she can object "you deserve down time, we all do. So I'm going to freshen up, change my top and I'll see you back downstairs ready to party in five minutes"

"Yes ma'am" Freya says smiling and mock salutes me as I shut the bathroom door.

Today has gone better than I imagined, everyone came fully prepared and in some cases pre-empted me which has saved a lot of time. I got a real kick out of telling the local tradesmen there was a directive to use as many local businesses as possible. I mentally pat myself on the back for my quick thinking at least they won't feel put out when others are brought in from outside the area because work on the Hall will be going on twenty-four seven, plus there's all the work that will be going on at the farm and Mill, not forgetting the cottages and pub.

After freshening up I head for my bedroom, I smile as the floral décor assaults my eyes. I've grown quite fond of the feeling of sleeping in a summer meadow but it's a bit much and at least Michelle agreed it was overkill. I'm glad we agreed on the décor that Elliot presented he really captured the subtly of modern with a hint of country.

I go through my clothes deciding what to wear, my mind wonders to Frank Appleton. The guy is just bursting with ideas and enthusiasm, I'm so pleased that he and Charlie Tanner are two like-minded souls. It was three hours later when both of them returned from the Hall. Frank took the initiative and called on Lady Farringdon to see if she had any photographs of the gardens, which she did. Turns out she went with them to the Hall as well and between the two of them they were able to reconstruct the gardens for Charlie, who had drawn some rough plans to show me.

I, in turn gave them a list of my favourite flowers and instructions to build a herb garden as close to the kitchen as possible. I also told them that if they planned for statues and fountains that I was going to source or design them myself, ideas of faeries, elves and pixies were already popping into my head. Charlie grinned at me saying "I would've been disappointed if you went with the standard Greek or Roman figures, especially an artist of your reputation and calibre" he scored brownie points for doing his homework.

I decide to wear a white spaghetti strap t-shirt with a white long sleeved lace crop top that finishes at my rib cage, the front can be fastened or left open, I chose to leave it open. After a few minutes debating with myself I decide to keep my comfy combats on changing my shoes to ballet pumps. Touching up my mascara a knock on the door makes me jump.

"Yeah" I shout.

"Dinner's ready" Freya's voice filters through.

"I'll be two minutes"

I put eyeliner on and smudge it, giving my eyes a smoky look. A squirt of perfume then grabbing my lip gloss I stick it into a side leg pocket then head out.

Downstairs everyone is seated and tucking in to their food. Someone has rearranged the tables pulling three together forming a nice cosy group.

"Come on baby girl" Simon waves me over to a seat in between him and Caleb. Simon smirks at me as I sit down "I got you a Budweiser" he points at the bottle with his fork.

"Cheers" I say lifting the bottle and taking a much welcomed swig.

The bacon cheese burger on my plate looks huge and smells delicious, Michelle has also done me a big side order of fat chunky chips served with an equally big pot of mayonnaise. My mouth fills with saliva and my stomach rumbles in anticipation for the feast before me.

"I think you're going to lose your bet Rex" Caleb chuckles "the sounds coming from Skye's stomach tells me this lot will be gone in five minutes"

"Nah, not five minutes. Fifteen maybe" I wink at Caleb as I pick my burger up and bite into it "hmm" I groan as the tang of tomato, saltiness of the bacon, the creaminess of the melted cheese and the flavour of the beef hit my taste buds.

For the next ten minutes the table is silent as we all tuck in, the squeak of knives and forks against porcelain, the clink of glasses being picked up and placed down. The occasional burp or hum of appreciation are the only sounds. All the men are working their way through steaks, Freya is having grilled chicken, baked potato and salad. My heart swells as I watch her sat between Alan and Paul, they've really taken her under their wing. I noticed throughout the day how they kept checking she was okay and I could see they were giving her a running commentary on how to read me when I was in business mode. It was good training for her especially if I ever do a convention. It's been three years since I last did one, maybe it's time to put myself out there again. I vaguely remember getting an email a few months ago from Giles Miller the organiser of the Fantasy and Science Fiction conventions I did in Las Vegas, mentally I make a note to get Freya to find it.

"Skye" Simon's hand on my arm brings me out of my reverie.

"Hmm" I look at his amused face; I've obviously missed something.

"Michelle was asking you if everything was okay"

I look up to see Michelle stood between me and Caleb, everyone is grinning at me "Sorry Michelle I was miles away"

"I can see that" she laughs genially "I was going to ask if everything was okay with the food but I can see my question is redundant" she nods at my empty plate and I've polished off all the chips, blimey I must have been hungry.

"I could eat it all again it was that delicious" I smile widely at her.

"Well I have chocolate fudge cake if you want some of that instead?"

My eyes light up "Yes please with ice cream"

"Anyone else for dessert. I also have apple pie and cheesecake" Michelle says as we hand over the empty plates. Paul, Alan and Simon put in their requests.

"Who've you lost the bet to Rex?" I grin wickedly at the look of disbelief on his face.

"Me" Simon pipes up at the same time Rex nods in his direction "I told him you were the equivalent to a human dustbin albeit a very skinny one"

"It's nice to see a woman with such a healthy appetite" says Caleb winking at me. I feel myself blush as I pick up on his insinuation.

A loud commotion and clattering noise draws everyone's attention to the entrance of the pub and away from me, thank god. Chris rushes from behind the bar and holds the doors open, the person coming through says a relieved thanks. The man recognises Chris and the two men laugh and joke, a large set of disco lights appear before the man does. He's quite portly with a thick thatch of red hair. Chris points him in the direction of the pool table which I realise has been pushed back against the wall. Giving quite a bit of space for the karaoke with room to dance. Conversation around the table turns to the upcoming song fest, I'm grateful Michelle brings out our desserts at least that will stop Simon bullying people into getting up to sing for a while.

I eat all the chocolate cake and ice-cream. I feel pleasantly stuffed "I thoroughly enjoyed that" I say patting my distended belly as I lean back in my chair, thank god my combats are hipsters and my top is stretchy.

"How many miles jogging tomorrow is that going to take to work off?" says Rex leering at me.

"None. I'm going horse riding. How many hours will I need to do to work it all off Caleb?" I pat his arm and grin wickedly at him.

He returns my grin with a roguish one of his own "Let me see, at least four for the burger and six for the chocolate cake" he takes a mouthful of his Corona.

"Damn, I'll be bow legged by the time you finish with me"

Caleb chokes and sprays his drink all over Rex "For fucks sake that's the second time today you've done that" Rex says disgusted as he wipes down his jeans. The rest of us laugh and I pat Caleb's back as he has a coughing fit.

"Excuse me, I'm just going to the little girl's room" Freya says standing.

"I'll come with you" I stand and rub Caleb's back "you okay now" he nods and waves me away.

We pass the karaoke man on the way to the ladies, he smiles broadly at us as he finishes setting up. Entering the corridor to the toilets a blast of music makes me jump.

"Bloody hell, I nearly wet myself then" Freya laughs crossing her legs "you going to get up?" she says pushing the door open to the ladies.

"Probably. Simon no doubt will be putting me in for a few songs" I say entering a cubicle "what about you?"

"Depends on how much I have to drink" Freya snorts a laugh "to my ears I sound like Whitney Houston or Christina Aguilera but in reality I'm out of tune, well that's what I'm told"

"Don't worry Simon is tone deaf and he loves to sing" I flush the toilet and step out, I start at seeing Marie waiting quietly "sorry I wasn't expecting to see anyone stood there" I laugh at myself as I clutch my heart. Marie grins at me "are you going to be singing tonight Marie?"

"I have the perfect get out clause. I'm working" she says going into the cubicle I've just vacated.

"Blimey, it's going to be a long day for you" I wash my hands, Freya joins me at the sinks "I hope you've had a break before you start the night shift"

"I have, thanks" Maria sounds touched by my concern "I'm not due to start until eight but it's already filling up out there and Chris is by himself" I put on my lip gloss as Freya touches up her make up "so I'll start early. I don't mind, every bit extra helps" Maria says coming out of the cubicle.

"Have you worked for Chris and Michelle long?"

"Off and on for the last five years" Marie sighs "they've been really good to me especially since I had my little boy and I split up with his dad"

Marie says fondly "I moved back to my mum's, it's just the three of us and I'm determined to pay my way" she lifts her chin defiantly.

"Well good for you. Let me know if I can do anything to help, not that I've ever worked behind a bar before but I can collect and wash glasses"

"I'll bear that in mind" Michelle laughs "and thank you again for the tip. It's much appreciated" she says shyly.

"You deserve every penny of it" I squeeze her arm as we head out back to the pub. I'd given the bar staff two hundred pounds each as a thank you tip for looking after me and my visitors "blimey where did all these people spring up from" I mutter getting a feeling of déjà vu, we haven't been gone five minutes and the place is just as full as it was at lunchtime.

"You're good for business" Marie says cheekily and winks as she steps behind the bar and starts serving. She makes me laugh, that girl deserves a pay rise and I admire her determination to make her own way in life and not rely on handouts.

We make our way back to our table only to find two new additions, a blonde haired man and brunette haired woman. I can't see their faces but the woman is sat in my seat. Cheeky bitch, would she jump in my grave as quick. As if she'd heard my snide thought the woman turns to face me.

"Nessa" I yell; she just about stands as I throw my arms around her. We hug tightly. Releasing her I look at the man "Chuck" I move to hug him as well "what are you two doing here?" I'm grinning so widely my cheeks hurt, I can't help it, even though it's only been four days since I last saw them it feels like forever.

Nessa and Chuck look at each other as we sit down only there's no seat for me. Caleb goes to stand to give me his place, I put my hand on his shoulder to keep him seated and move round and sit on his lap. The whole table instantly goes quiet and stares at me and Caleb. Shit!

"Sorry, you don't mind do you" I say turning to look at Caleb, I'm certain he can see the 'Oops! I've just fucked up' message in my eyes.

"No, not at all" Caleb's low gravelly voice sends a shiver down my spine. I feel his large warm hand slowly caress the side of my leg. I'm so wishing I wore a skirt right now, bugger!

"As if any man is going to say any different to having you sat on their knee baby girl" Simon scoffs and rolls his eyes at me for being stupid to think it would bother Caleb.

Caleb's low rumbling laugh makes my toes curl and breaks the stunned silence as the others join him.

"So what brings you to this neck of the woods" I say to Nessa.

"I'm after a favour, a big one" I raise an eyebrow, it's unusual for Nessa to ask me for anything "I know it's short notice but I have a big charity gala to go to tomorrow night will you come with me?"

"Sure, but why isn't Chuck going with you?" I ask puzzled and look at Chuck. They go everywhere together.

Nessa scowls at Chuck, he shrugs and looks sheepish. He's in the dog house no doubt about it. "I fucked up" he holds his hands up "I'm going to be away on business, flying out tomorrow afternoon to Germany"

"Oooh! That's going to cost you" Simon says gleefully. Nessa winks at him.

"It already has" Chuck says glumly "I've learnt my lesson to triple check all of my diaries before I make any business commitments"

Nessa fills me in on the charity gala, where and time. We arrange for me to pick her up, Paul and Alan will be coming with me and Simon invites himself. I don't push Freya when she says she'll stay here. Something suddenly dawns on me I lean over and whisper to Nessa "Have you been introduced to everyone?" she shakes her head.

"Freya" I call across the table "I'd like you to meet two of my very good friends, this is Nessa and Chuck Johnson. Nessa and Chuck meet Freya Bennett, she's my new PA" they shake hands and say pleased to meet you "she's only just joined the team so no horror stories" I twist in Caleb's lap "this is Rex Davies and Caleb Raven" I point to each man.

Nessa's eyes widen and snap to mine when Caleb's name registers. I subtly nod my head to her silent question to confirm its mystery man from the train.

"Ladies and gentlemen" karaoke man says over the speakers "since the pub is so full we thought we'd empty it by starting early. If any of you lovely people would like to get up and sing, or try to, please fill in the slips that Michelle is giving out. I have plenty more here" he holds up a handful of paper "and bring them back to me"

Simon is up out of his seat in an instant, taking a song book from Michelle and half of the slips she has. Simon sits back down and starts flicking through the book, scribbling down songs every few minutes.

"Surely he's not going to do all those himself" Rex says sceptically; he shouts to be heard over karaoke man singing Tom Jones' 'It's not unusual'

"He's writing out everyone's song choices from last night" I grin evilly at Rex reminding him of his promise.

"I thought he was joking. He said he can't sing" Rex says pointing at Simon.

"I can't sing, but I didn't say I won't sing" Simon retorts. We all crack up; it's going to be a fun night I can feel it in my water.

CHAPTER SEVENTEEN

CALEB

I'm hypnotised by the sway of Skye's tight arse as she follows Freya to the ladies. I sigh internally and pinch myself to make sure that the last hour in fact the whole week has been real and not some unbelievable fantastic dream, a wet one at that!

I felt the luckiest bastard alive sitting next to her during dinner considering Rex made such a big thing about arranging the tables and seating. Luckily for me Rex miscalculated the numbers. He forgot about Freya, not surprising since she is so quiet but the real reason he forgot is because she's overweight. Rex is shallow and will shag anything in a skirt, she could be ugly as sin so long as she was slim he'd fuck her. Rex didn't do fat women. The woman could be absolutely stunning but if she carried a bit of timber on her it meant he ignored her, actually that's harsh of me. Rex would speak to the woman and be pleasant but he wouldn't pay attention, just like he did with Freya which is unfair because underneath all the makeup currently hiding her bruises Freya is a pretty woman. So when Freya came back before Skye and sat down next to Alan, Simon quickly got another chair and put it in between us giving me a knowing smile and wink. I'm liking this guy more and more by the minute.

Michelle and Chris brought out the food, when Rex saw what was on Skye's plate then the huge bowl of chunky chips he made the stupid comment "Skye will never eat all of that" Simon's retort of "Oh she will" was immediate. I'm sure Rex is suffering from short term memory loss because the other night at the dinner party Skye was the only woman to clear her plate for each course. I was about to say that when Rex suggested the bet, Simon willing accepted it then added "Skye may be tiny but she's like a human dustbin, you'll be surprised what she can put away"

As we ate it took all my will power to keep my hands above the table and not caress her leg that rubbed against mine. Aside from using the knife to cut her burger in half, Skye didn't use cutlery. She used her fingers to eat. The woman is worth six and a half billion pounds, she's sat in a country pub wearing combats eating burger and chips with her fingers, drinking straight from the bottle. How much more down to earth can you get? Even Simone Fawcett-Fowler who came from a rough council estate and worked as a cleaner before marrying into money wouldn't be seen dead doing what Skye is doing right now.

And by god she could put food away, after the burger and chips she ate a huge slice of chocolate cake and ice cream. She devoured her food with as much enthusiasm as she devoured me. I got a kick seeing the faint blush to her cheeks when she picked up on my double entendre about her healthy appetite although the minx got her own back twenty minutes later. My dick is still twitching at the thought of making her bow legged.

"Nessa, Chuck over here" Simon calling out brings me out of my reverie.

I hear muffled American accents as they hug. The way Simon welcomes the new arrivals, the woman in particular seems to indicate she is someone special to him. Simon grabs a spare stool which the man took.

"Does she know we were coming?" the woman says sitting in Skye's place.

Childishly, I want to turf her out of it. I've enjoyed the closeness of my kitten since I'd been denied that all day, being so near yet so far and all that crap.

Before Simon can answer the woman suddenly looks round, she's older than I first thought and a huge fond smile spreads across her face.

"Nessa" Skye's delighted shout comes from behind, suddenly she's enveloping the woman in a huge hug. The man stands as Skye releases the woman "Chuck" just as enthusiastically she hugs the man.

Well that's me and Rex muscled out of the picture and forgotten about. Being the gentleman I start to stand, I'll let Skye have my seat but the slight pressure of a tiny hand on my shoulder tells me to stay. Skye shocks the shit out of me by sitting in my lap, in front of everyone, holy fuck she doesn't realise what she's just done. The whole table stares at us in surprise.

I feel Skye stiffen, her head whips round. I can see the 'I've just fucked up' look in her beautiful yellow green eyes but as calm as you like, cool as a cucumber she asks do I mind. I want to shout at the top of my lungs 'Hell do I mind? Fuck no!' I just about manage a polite no I don't response but I can't stop my hands from wandering up and down her legs. My dick throbs wanting friction but I do resist the temptation to grind in to her.

Simon makes a 'you're so dumb if you think any man would mind' response to Skye breaking the tension and any forming suspicion. I laugh mainly out of relief. I partly listen to Skye's conversation as Rex bitches in my ear.

"You fucking jammy bastard" Rex says enviously "if I hadn't screwed up the seating, she would be sat on my knee now" I bite my tongue somehow I seriously doubt that "who are these people anyway?"

"No idea" I murmur back. The woman, Nessa, is asking Skye to go to a function tomorrow night "they're friends from the sounds of it"

I look around the pub, as per this afternoon Skye is drawing everyone's attention. I spot Miles Cunningham, he's stood frozen in position, white as a ghost looking directly at our table. I nudge Rex and nod my head in Miles' direction "Wonder what's got him all spooked?"

"Jesus, he does look weird" Rex looks back at our table "don't think it's got anything to do with Skye sat on your knee" he looks back at Miles trying to discern who is the focus of his attention "maybe it's the American's"

Both our attention is brought back to Skye as she calls out to Freya and she introduces them. Skye leans back in to me, I fight the urge to wrap my arms around her, to introduce Rex then me. I see recognition flash through Nessa's eyes at my name, then she looks at Skye I catch the subtle nod of her head answering an unspoken question. A thrilling surge of delight floods my body, I have absolutely no doubt Skye has been talking about me to her friends.

John the DJ snags everyone's attention by announcing the karaoke will start early. Simon is out of his seat and practically rugby tackles Michelle for the song book and slips. John sees me, he lifts the microphone and points to it. I nod, he smiles and gives me the thumbs up. My guilty pleasure is singing on the karaoke, I have a reasonably good voice and without being big headed I'm one of the few good singers the pub has. John and I do a mean rendition of 'Don't Let The Sun Go Down On Me' we take it in turns to be Elton and George.

Skye getting off my knee snaps my attention back to her "I'm getting drinks, who wants what?" she says. Paul and Alan say they'll get them but she waves them away. The order is easy, beer and wine.

"I'll give you a hand" I say standing, Skye smiles and nods.

At the bar Skye patiently waits her turn to be served, I stand behind her unable to resist and going unnoticed I caress her bum. Skye wiggles against me. I've got to her.

"Yes Skye love, what can I get you?" Chris gives her a fond fatherly smile.

"Can you put fifteen bottles of Corona and two bottles of Rose wine into ice buckets please, saves coming back for a while"

"Certainly" Chris laughs, he disappears out to the kitchen.

"How do you know Nessa and Chuck?" I murmur in her ear as she leans back in to me.

"Nessa was a neighbour in the apartment block we moved in to when we first moved to New York, she took us under her wing and became like a big sister to us. Not long after she met Chuck, they moved to London for Nessa's career just over eight years ago. Chuck was an old college friend and business associate of Clayton's but I didn't know that until six years ago"

"So when you say 'us' you mean Simon and Shelley as well" Skye nods "what does Nessa do?"

"Last year she was promoted to Managing Director of the TV station she's worked at since coming here, she's done really well for herself" Skye says proudly "and Chuck has that many fingers in so many pies it's hard to say what he actually does" Skye laughs.

"She knows about us" I say low so only Skye can hear me, thank god for someone killing the song on the karaoke. Skye nods, she doesn't attempt to deny it "who else?"

"I can count my true friends and confidants on one hand" Skye holds up three fingers "they know me so well I don't have to tell them something is wrong they know just by looking at me. Nessa knew something was up the minute I arrived at her house. After the dinner party she called an emergency meeting with Simon and Shelley on Skype" Skye sighs looking around the pub her eyes resting fondly on her best friends "the way I've been behaving with you is so out of character for me. I've never had sex with a complete stranger before. I had a lot to work through and they helped me"

"I get it" I say softly, I really did. She is still grieving for her dead husband and along comes me. Who she herself admitted only last night we can't keep our hands off each other, the attraction is so strong it's off the scale.

The clank of metal has us both turning to the bar. Chris puts the fifteen bottles in one bucket and two bottles of Rose in the other, pouring ice over them. Skye asks for three wine glasses. I grab both buckets and we make our way back to the table. Skye smiles and acknowledges the people who shout hello to her, some even ask if they can buy her a drink, she laughs says thanks then points to me saying she's okay at the moment. I pass Miles who's still stood staring at our table, then it clicks.

As I place the buckets in the centre of the table I bend to mutter in Rex's ear "Skye's friend Nessa is Managing Director of a TV station, what's the betting she's Miles's boss?"

Rex's head swivels round to look at Miles then at Nessa, he has the biggest fucking grin on his face just like he did this afternoon with Marjorie "Today just can't get any fucking better" he croons "how do you know that?" he says as I hand him his drink and sit down.

"I asked" I say taking a swig of the cold beer.

"And Skye just told you" Rex says in disbelief.

"Why wouldn't she?" I know I sound indignant.

"Sorry mate, it's just every time I ask a personal question I get stone walled"

"Ah but I didn't ask a personal question about her, I asked how she knew Nessa and Chuck" Rex looks at me confused "my question was about them not her"

"What's the difference? It still sounds like a personal question to me" Rex is really frowning now.

"It's not personal as in revealing information about herself which is what you were trying to do last night. Instead she's telling me about someone else. In this instance Nessa was a neighbour who took Skye and her friends under her wing when they first moved to New York" I can still see Rex struggling with what I'm trying to get across "think about the young lad this afternoon, do you think he's her only fan, she must have thousands" I nod in Skye's direction as she's talking with Freya, remembering all the photographs I'd seen on the internet of her posing with fans "she's a public figure and people must constantly ask her about personal things, things that she wishes to keep to herself, private. It's second nature to her to avoid answering those kind of questions"

"Ah! I get it now, if it's not too personal she feels safe answering without revealing too much" Rex shakes his head "shit I wish you'd told me that last night. I'm going to have to work twice as hard now to try and win her round"

My gut clenches along with my fist and teeth "Don't try too hard" I manage to loosen my jaw "you may come across as desperate"

"Good point" Rex pats my shoulder getting up, his eyes fixed on Skye.

Shit! He's going to make a move on her. I frantically search my mind to say something that will stall him but I'm saved from the effort by John the DJ.

"Skye Darcy is up next" John announces, cheers and whistles go up around the pub. Skye looks surprised at the DJ then turns and narrows her eyes at Simon. He laughs and turns her giving a gentle push in the direction of the karaoke. Rex curses under his breath. I grin like an idiot and cheer with everyone else. I stand to get a better view of Skye.

She talks to John and goes through the paper slips probably finding out what Simon has put her down for, some of the slips she screws up and throws over her shoulder until she finds the one she likes. John taps on the keyboard, seconds later on the screen 'Black Velvet, Alannah Myles' appears and the slow raunchy beat of the song starts. The pub goes quiet, I'm holding my breath and it seems like everyone else is. I really hope she doesn't suck.

"Mississippi in the middle of a dry spell" Skye's husky voice rings loud and clear. She can sing, fuck me can she sing. Cheers and applause erupts. Skye isn't even looking at the screen; she knows the words off by heart. She sings to the pub, a slow seductive swing of her hips moving to the beat. Skye looks directly at me.

"The boy could sing, knew how to move, everything

Always wanting more, he'd leave you longing for"

Singing the chorus, she focus's back on the rest of the crowd, the pub is going mental as she belts out the song. My skin is tingling all over from the sound of her voice. The next time she sings directly to me I almost barrel my way through the crowd to get to her.

"The way he moved, it was a sin, so sweet and true"

During the instrumental Skye dances provocatively around John, he plays along fanning himself and wiping his face with his handkerchief and wringing it out. When Skye sings 'a new religion that will bring ya to your knees' John and some of the men close by all drop to their knees. Skye barks out a laugh but manages to continue singing. At the end of the song Skye gets a standing ovation, the whistles and cheers shake the rafters. Skye laughing does a mock curtsey and bow.

"God I feel sorry for the poor bugger following her" John says as Skye makes her way back to us "Caleb, you're up" he waves me over.

Skye's eyes are glittering with happiness. As we pass each other I feel Skye's fingers gently trail down the inside of my arm, electric sparks jump and frizz along my skin leaving a pleasant burning path. I take the microphone off John. I've no idea what I'm singing until I hear the music. I don't need to look at the screen I know the words. I look directly at Skye as I launch into 'Sweet Child o' Mine' my heart swells as Skye sings right along with me. During the instrumental Skye stuns the whole pub by head banging. Swirling her hair and body to the music, she's lost in the music and she doesn't fucking care what people think. I don't think my heart can take any more its fit to bursting with pride and happiness.

When I get back to the table Simon is flicking through the book again, he looks at me with a determined glint in his eye "You two are definitely doing some duets together" he says pointing the pen at me then Skye who's stood talking with Nessa and Freya "no arguments"

I hold my hands up in surrender "So long it's not something soppy"

"Ha! That's exactly what she said" Simon says as he writes out the song choice. I try to see what he's writing but the crafty sod covers his hand over the paper.

Taking a fresh bottle out of the bucket I scan the pub, not that I can see much with all the bodies. I notice that Paul and Alan have positioned themselves so that no one can get to Skye. They look relaxed as they chat with Chuck but their eyes tell a different story, alert and ready for action.

"You're right" Rex shouts to be heard over the din of another song being murdered.

"About what?"

"Nessa is Miles's boss, well she's 'the' boss" he shouts gleefully "the fucking twat had the gall to ask me to introduce him"

"Let me guess, you told him to fuck off" I grin at Rex.

"Very politely of course" Rex grins wickedly "I pointed out I couldn't possibly introduce him to someone who I had only just met and hadn't spoken to"

We spend a couple of minutes speculating what moves Miles will pull in order to get introduced to Nessa, the most obvious is getting to Skye but I point out Paul and Alan are on guard duty.

"Next up we have Skye and Caleb" John's announcement brings our discussion to an end. I look over to Skye and hold out my hand.

"What's Simon put us down for?" she says grinning at me as she places her warm tiny hand in mine.

"Not got a clue" I shrug.

"It better not be something bloody soppy" she mutters under her breath as we make our way over to John.

SKYE

I'm having an absolute ball; the night is turning out better than I imagined. The duet I did with Caleb was hysterical, both of us knew the words to 'Dead Ringer for Love' neither of us looked at the screen once. I got a real kick out of pretending to be Cher to his Meat Loaf as we acted out the song. Although, I must admit the chemistry between us is doing funny things to my equilibrium. I feel drunk but I know I'm not. My whole body tingles and I swear to god sparks fly off me whenever I'm in close proximity to him, which is often. The brief touches and caresses are driving me nuts. I just want to crawl up his delicious rock hard body.

"He really is a dish; I can fully understand the attraction" Nessa murmured to me after I introduced her "his friends not bad either"

"Difference is he knows it and uses it, whereas Caleb doesn't" I muttered back. Nessa gave me a knowing nod, she got it.

It warms my heart to see Nessa and Chuck making a point of talking to Freya, and Caleb and Rex for that matter. But it's the time with Freya that touches me the most, of course they'll be speaking to her first whenever they needed to get in touch with me, it's the fact they're taking a genuine interest in her as a person that means more to me.

As the night wears on I sing a few more songs. Someone kept requesting I sing Whitney Houston but I made John the DJ switch the tracks so instead I did 'Teenage Kicks', 'Highway to Hell' and 'Set Fire to the Rain' just to mix it up. On the fourth occasion I'm called up to sing Whitney I take matters into my own hands.

"Freya" I say into the microphone, I wave for her to come over "ladies and gentlemen, someone out there desperately wants to hear Whitney. You may have guessed by now I don't do Whitney" that gets a lot of raucous laughter "however my friend here does, put your hands together for Freya" polite cheers and whistles go up on cue as I hand the microphone to a petrified looking Freya "sing your heart out as if no-one is watching and listening"

I step away but stay close just in case. Simon comes up behind me, his arm resting on my shoulder "Can she sing?" he murmurs. I shrug in answer. I have my fingers and toes crossed hoping I've done the right thing and not pushed her too far. The music starts, Freya takes a deep calming breath and I see a physical change in her. She opens her mouth... and the voice of an angel comes out. My arms are covered in goose bumps and the hair on the back of my neck stands on end.

"Bloody hell she's got a set of lungs on her" Simon yells in my ear clapping furiously at the end of the song.

The pub is in uproar cheering and clapping, some people are calling for more. My smiling face is aching and my hands are sore from clapping so much. I wrap my arms around Freya, she's shaking, the after effects of the adrenaline rush.

"You're a dark horse that was fucking brilliant, we are so doing a duet" I shout to be heard over the noise.

Freya laughs and wipes her eyes with trembling hands "Was it? You're not just saying that are you?" her insecurity hits me in the gut and her words from earlier about being out of tune come back to me, that fucking twat of an ex-boyfriend putting her down.

"Are you kidding me? I bet you'll give Christina a run for her money"

"Just listen to the ovation you're getting" Simon says putting his arm around her "do you really think they'd cheer like that if you were as crap as me"

Simon takes Freya back to our table, I go to see John. The next person is getting ready to sing, the young man looks six sheets to the wind and he's being egged on by his friends. John rolls his eyes as the guy starts to rap, missing half the words.

"I could do with you and your friend being here every week but I know you're not" he gives me a rogue smile "whatcha singin' next"

"Put me and Freya down for It's Raining Men, then me and Nessa for Dancing Queen" John writes them down "that'll do me for the rest of the night"

"One more duet please" John holds up his hands together as in prayer but pleading "with Caleb"

"What you got in mind?" I narrow my eyes at him suspiciously.

"Paradise by the Dashboard Light. It'll be the last song of the night, please say yes, please, please. I'll get down on my knees" John starts to kneel.

"No need to go that far" I laugh "go on then. But if anyone else puts me down for singing I'm not getting up"

"Yes ma'am message received loud and clear" John salutes me "I'll get Freya up instead"

Heading back to our table Miles what's his face steps in front of me. My nose is centimetres from his chest. I step back to go round him; he moves with me. I look up at him, I should have put my heels on instead of flats.

"Ms Darcy, I'm afraid we appear to have gotten off on the wrong foot earlier today" the pompous git states looking down his nose at me. In my peripheral vision I can see Paul, Alan and Caleb descending on me. I hold up my hand to stop them, well Paul and Alan. Caleb keeps coming, he looks as if he's about to rip Miles apart "I'm Miles Cunningham and I wasn't aware we had such an esteemed and famous artist in our mist" interpretation he went home and did his homework "I hope you're enjoying your stay in Dove Mill"

"I am, thank you" I go to side step him again, he moves with me "what is it you want Miles?"

My question throws him, he looks flummoxed. Before he can say anything Caleb is at my side, a look of censure flashes across Miles's face. My back stiffens and my hackles rise.

"Is everything okay Skye" Nessa says from behind me, Miles's eyes widen and his face drains of colour. The TV celebrity looks as if he's seen a ghost, of course he must work at the TV station Nessa runs.

"Nessa" I turn and smile brightly at her and link arms "just getting to know the locals, but I think you already know this…" prat, dickhead, wanker. I wave my hand in front of me "gentleman"

"I hope you are not hounding my friends Miles, otherwise we'll be having words in my office Monday morning" Nessa says linking her other arm with Caleb "enjoy your evening"

We only take a few steps when Caleb starts laughing "I like you" he says kissing Nessa's cheek "please take the pretentious dickhead into your office Monday morning and scare the living shit out of him"

"You're incorrigible" Nessa laughs, turning to me she whispers "I like him, you can keep him"

Back at the table Simon and Rex want to know what happened with Miles, I tell them my bit then let Caleb and Nessa finish off as I go to Freya stood with Alan and Paul.

"Wasn't she fantastic?" I beam linking arms with Freya.

"I was just saying she sang it better than Whitney" Alan smiles at Freya who promptly blushes beetroot "made the hairs on the back of my neck stand on end"

"What hairs!" says Freya touching the back of Alan's neck, he has an all over number one at the back and sides of his head, suddenly realising what she's doing Freya snatches her hand away looking embarrassed. Taking pity, I hand her a glass of wine. Alan being ever the gentleman pretends he hasn't noticed.

Paul nods his head in Miles's direction "He's not going to bother us again" I say answering him "Nessa is his boss and scared the shit out of him" Paul snorts a laugh.

It seems someone from our group gets up to sing every other song. Caleb has a fantastic voice; he really has missed his calling as the lead singer for a rock band. He knocks the socks off Bon Jovi's 'Living on a Prayer' and I almost die of embarrassment when he sings the entire song of 'Blonde, Bad and Beautiful' by Airbourne, much to the drunken delight of the whole pub, to me. Simon got up and sings badly out of tune 'I am what I am' but the whole pub forgives him as he puts his heart and soul in to it.

"Next up we have Freya and Skye" John the DJ calls out over the still cheering crowd.

I make my way over to Freya as she's stood talking to Nessa and Michelle, her eyes are wide with surprise. I grin mischievously "Come on" I shout and hold out my hand to her. In a daze she reaches for my hand.

"What are we singing?" Freya says slightly panicked as we fight our way through the crowd.

"It's Raining Men" I laugh as her eyes light up.

"I love that song" Freya squeals "can I start the song off" she says bouncing on the balls of her feet in excitement.

"Of course, do you mean you want to do the talking bit before the singing starts?" I ask for clarification as I take my microphone off John. Freya nods eagerly taking her microphone.

The rising music starts, the women in the pub recognising the song, so does Simon, all rush and push their way to the dance floor. I start the soft background singing as Freya beings the talking, she puts on the sass to the delight of the crowd. Launching into the song the crowd goes ballistic, I swear to god I see dust particles coming down from the rafters. My and Freya's voices complement each other perfectly. I leave the really high notes to Freya, likewise the lower notes she leaves to me, we harmonise beautifully, even if I do say so myself. Freya really lets herself go, she's having the time of her life. Alan and Paul cheer, clap and whistle loudly with the rest of the pub at the end of the song, Freya is positively glowing. Gone is the shy, nervous, timid woman I found earlier in the week, I can see the confident, self-assured woman she's turning into. I beam proudly at her; she's come such a long way in so short a time.

"That was amazing!" Simon shrieks at us "you did the Weather Girls proud, fucking amazing!" he throws his arms around Freya and me as we make our way back.

"Babe, you killed it" says Rex leering, he works his way in between me and Simon, his arm snakes around my waist pulling me in to his side. He's been doing this all night and my patience is wearing thin. There's only one person who I want to be man handled by and he's currently nowhere to be seen.

"It was a joint effort, I couldn't have killed it without Freya" I slide deftly out of his grip "don't forget to let her know" I smile sweetly at Rex, I'll be damned if he tries to make it all about me "Freya deserves recognition as well"

I look pointedly at the others surrounding Freya, all giving her hugs and praise even the locals are coming over and telling her how fantastic she was. I turn back to face Rex. I'm shocked by the look on his face and I don't like it, not one bit. Revulsion is written all over his face as he looks at her, what the hell is that all about?

"Skye" Nessa says putting her hand on my shoulder to get my attention and unbeknownst to her stops me ripping into Rex and giving him what for "I'm sorry but we have to leave"

"It's all my fault" Chuck laughs raising his hands in surrender "got to be up at the crack of dawn"

"You can't go yet" I wail "we've got a duet to do"

"Dancing Queen?" Nessa grins at me as I nod enthusiastically "as much as I would love to stay and sing it with you, I can't. We've already stayed two hours more than we intended"

"Oh, okay since Chuck has to be up at stupid o'clock" I say sulkily.

"Ha! Don't ever change" Chuck sniggers giving me a hug.

"You'll need to come out to the car with us" Nessa tugs on my hand to follow her "I've got your dress for tomorrow night" she adds seeing my confusion "actually I brought the three you left behind so you've got a choice"

I roll my eyes at her, which she ignores. As we pass Paul and Alan I tell them where I'm going and indicate for them to stay where they are, Simon comes with us to say goodbye. Stepping outside I welcome the blast of the late evening fresh air as it hits me square in the face. Taking a deep breath, the coolness and freshness chase away the stuffiness and heat I've been feeling, the short walk to the car park also perks me up. Chuck opens the boot and lifts out three long dress bags.

"Here you go my love, all freshly laundered" Chuck says handing me the dresses, he kisses my cheek "have a safe journey and I'll see you when you're back later in the year"

"You too, safe travels" I give him a one armed hug.

Chuck gets in the car as Simon takes the dress bags off me "I'll take these inside, see you tomorrow night Nessa" Simon calls out as he walks away.

"See you tomorrow" Nessa says to both of us, then we embrace "I've really enjoyed tonight, it's a fantastic pub and the locals are lovely, especially a certain Mr Raven. I thought Clayton was hot but he's scorching" she murmurs in my ear.

"Down girl and behave" I laugh pulling away "you're married, remember?"

"Spoilsport" Nessa pouts opening the car door "I can window shop" she smirks.

Chuck manoeuvres the Bentley out of the tight parking spot with ease, I wave bye and remain watching until the tail lights disappear from view. Walking slowly along the path back to the pub my thoughts turn to Rex and the look he had given Freya. She didn't deserve whatever contemptuous thoughts or views he had of her. Freya is a gentle soul with a kind heart. I feel anger surge through me, Rex has pissed me off more than I realise. A tall dark figure appears on the path in front of me, all thoughts of tackling Rex and his prejudice against Freya take a back seat as I prepare to take down the big man, should I need to defend myself.

The tall dark figure stops, he's waiting for me, adrenaline spikes and my heart pumps hard in my chest. The broad shoulders, large arms and slim hips suddenly register, a rush of heat flows through my body and my skin is tingling all over. Caleb, I run at him. Caleb's stance changes, his arms open and I launch myself at him. He catches me, lifting my feet off the ground. My arms and legs wrap around him, his lips meet mine before I take my next breath.

We hungrily devour each other, I'm vaguely aware that Caleb is moving. He doesn't break the kiss as he walks god knows where. I'm lost to the feel of his soft lips against mine, his tongue darting in and out of my mouth. I want more of him; my teeth snag his bottom lip. Biting gently and pulling. A low sexy growl rumbles in Caleb's chest, it resonates directly between my legs and my nipples harden thanks to the vibration. Christ, I really want him to fuck me. I don't care that we're outside and we could be caught any minute. My fingers clench in his hair as I pull myself closer to his hard body.

Something rough and hard hits my back. Caleb presses against me, whatever he's got me pinned against is solid, it's a wall the thought manages to filter through my lust filled brain. Caleb shifts, his large hands grip the tops of my thighs and buttocks. His hips grind against mine. Oh sweet Jesus! His erection catches me in just the right spot, my eyes roll to the back of my head when he does it again, and again, and again.

My body is on fire, I'm burning up. Lust filled pleasure is hurtling through my veins, swirling and building in my lower abdomen. Electricity is dancing over the surface of my skin. I feel so alive. My muscles start to gather themselves and the now familiar sensation between my legs tells me I'm not going to last and I don't want to. I tear my lips away from Caleb's.

"I'm coming" I gasp, Caleb thrusts against me again, his jean clad dick perfectly stroking my clit "Caleb" my cry is cut off as he reclaims my mouth, I freefall into the rolling waves of my orgasm as it crashes through me. A low groan reaches my ears and I feel Caleb shuddering against me. I hold on to him tightly as he comes.

"I'm sorry, I didn't mean for this to happen" Caleb whispers as he softly kisses my neck "I only came out to steal a quick kiss"

"Instead we got to make out like a couple of randy teenagers behind the bike shed" I giggle as I unwrap my legs, I keep hold of Caleb as my legs are still wobbly.

"You can say that again" Caleb snorts "last time I did anything like this I was fifteen"

A pang of jealousy hits me, it's unexpected and surprises me. I don't know how to react to it, I've known this man a week and already I feel he's mine, in the possessive sense. Is that possible in so short a time? I didn't have this feeling with Clayton so early on. I know I'm attracted to Caleb just as I was with Clayton but I would argue the attraction is stronger with Caleb and I never felt this possessive over Clayton. By rights I should have been more possessive over Clayton, not only had he been gorgeous but ridiculously wealthy and women threw themselves at him, even when I was with him they would unashamedly hit on him, but it didn't bother me. I laughed and joked with Clayton and my friends about scratching the women's eyes out and ripping off their arms but deep down, I know I didn't care.

So why am I having such a strong reaction to Caleb? Aside from the fact that he's drop dead movie star gorgeous he's by no means rich, from the information I have on him I know he's only just keeping his head above water. Caleb might not have women throwing themselves at him but I've seen them flirt outrageously with him when he interacts with them, I'm not blind. Caleb definitely emits a 'hands off' vibe, he's a dominant through and through. All week I've been getting these unexplained surges of jealousy, it's not like me to suffer from the green eyed monster. Maybe all it needed was meeting the right person to trigger my possessive jealous streak. Huh, go figure!

Caleb's fingers gently trailing down my cheek brings me out of my thoughts "Hey, I was a randy teenager with raging hormones, just looking at a girl, any girl or woman at that age had me..." Caleb shrugs sheepishly "let's just say I was a walking hard on ninety-nine percent of the time"

I laugh at the image in my head and Caleb's rakish grin "Well I was a good girl and never got to make out behind the bike shed" I kiss Caleb's cheek. Caleb gives me a devastating smile, making my heart flip and my knees weak "come on, let's get back before a search party comes looking"

Walking back towards the pub it suddenly occurs to me that Caleb knew I was jealous of his teenage escapades, blimey was I that transparent to him he could read me so well? Pushing the door open I shove the thought away to examine later. Luckily no one seems to notice me and Caleb sneaking in, we split up. Caleb heads for the bar as I make my way back to our table. Simon reaches the table at the same time.

"I've hung the dresses up. I think you should wear the red one" Simon grins mischievously, he leans in "it'll give this lot something to talk about for months when they see you in it" he murmurs in my ear.

I know exactly what he means, the dress is what fashion critics call old Hollywood glamour, and it makes a statement. Shelley designed it to match my ruby choker and earrings. It screams the wearer has money and status plus it flaunts my figure, as do all the dresses Shelley makes for me but in this one I look and feel like some kind of Siren. Jessica Rabbit also springs to mind!

I laugh knowingly at Simon's impish grin "You just love to stir up trouble" I playfully slap his arm "but it will be fun to see their reaction and considering we'll be leaving early Sunday morning I won't be around to answer any intrusive questions"

"What are you two whispering and plotting about?" Rex says putting more bottles into the ice bucket.

"Nothing for you to worry about sweet cheeks" Simon says friskily whilst leaning across the table and walking his fingers up Rex's arm, then squeezes his cheek between his thumb and forefinger.

Before Rex can respond Caleb appears with a bottle of Rose "Chris says this is from about twenty different people who've bought you a drink, the other four bottles he'll keep on ice for you"

"You've certainly made an impression on the locals' baby girl" Simon crows gleefully, pouring the last of the wine out of the one remaining bottle, Caleb places the new bottle he's holding in to the ice bucket.

"That's an understatement" Rex says moving quickly around the table towards me, I've nowhere to go as Paul and Alan are blocking my escape route. Rex's arm snakes around my waist and like a snake it constricts pulling me tight in to his side "from what I've been hearing tonight this little lady is a hero in many people's eyes, even though she is spending someone else's money" Rex presses his lips to the side of my head.

My skin is crawling and there's nothing I can do to stop the shudder of revulsion. The cheeky fucker! Shouts my mind when I register his comment. I had grown up with these types of comments from my grandfather, he was full of them. I called them a warm pricklies. My grandfather would start off saying something nice or complimentary so you'd feel warm and fuzzy inside, then he'd follow up quickly with a stinging put down making you wince and feeling the 'ouch', the only other person I had come across who could do the same thing was Caroline Tanner — the deceased psycho bunny boiler bitch ex-girlfriend of a so called friend.

I look at Caleb. Holy fucking shit! If looks could kill, Rex would be twenty foot under. Then a warm giddy glow spreads through me, I'm not the only one suffering from a healthy dose of the green eyed monster. Caleb has it by the bucket full. Rex seems oblivious to the tension in me and Caleb for that matter, instead he has a smug satisfied look on his face like the cat that got the cream.

"What's the fact that she's spending someone else's money got to do with anyone thinking she's a hero?" Simon says acidly taking hold of my arm and moving me out of Rex's hold. Simon steps forward in to Rex's face and personal space, it's intimidating. Rex is too stunned to react quickly enough to hold on to me "it shouldn't matter who's money is paying for the work that's being done, at least Skye has the initiative and forward thinking to utilise the local talent and workforce meaning the wealth gets spread around where it deserves to be" Simon is on a roll, everyone stood around us stops their conversation to listen "if it wasn't for her everyone in this place would be watching outsiders coming in taking what will no doubt be classed as their jobs, so in my eyes and I agree with all the good folk of Dove Mill, she is a hero and money has fuck all to do with it"

Everyone stood around our table along with a handful of locals standing close enough to hear are gawping at Simon. One of them, Bill, starts to clap a few others follow suit.

"Well said mate" Bill nods his approval at Simon "I, and I'm sure my fellow tradesmen will share my sentiments, we will forever be in your debt for giving us the opportunity to work on the Hall and the other projects going on around the village" my cheeks flame with embarrassment "you ever try and put this beautiful lady down again Rex I won't be held accountable for my actions" Bill's voice is calm and even which makes his threat all the more real.

From Rex's expression I can see he can't quite work out what it is he's said that has everyone so worked up but he does realise that he's screwed up.

"I apologise for causing offense, it wasn't my intention" Rex says looking solemn at Bill and Simon "please forgive me" he says to me. I nod acknowledging him.

Thankfully the strained atmosphere is short lived when Freya and I are called up to the karaoke.

"What was that all about?" Freya whispers to me as we make our way to DJ John. I tell her what Rex had said to set Simon off "the cheeky bastard" Freya hisses indignantly "I'm surprised Simon didn't bitch slap him. I tell you, I would've done had I heard him"

I laugh, hearing Freya readily jump to my defence and she's got Simon sussed in such a short space of time it lightens and lifts my spirit. Taking the microphone off John I look over to our table. Rex is stood next to Caleb; whose large hand grips the nape of Rex's neck. Caleb's head is bent so he can hear whatever Rex is saying, Caleb's face is deadly serious and I watch his sensuous mouth move as he speaks. In the dim lights of the pub I can see the colour drain from Rex's face, Caleb's words and message have hit home. The sound of piano keys snags my attention, a brief flare of panic hits my gut, I have no idea what we're about to sing. Luckily the tune resonates, 'Alone' by Heart. I look at Freya.

"You start off" she says quickly grinning manically at me.

It's a song I know but not all the words by heart, I look at the screen and start to sing. Freya joins in at the chorus our powerful voices harmonising beautifully, the hairs on the back of my neck rise. I indicate to Freya to sing the next verse. I sneak a look over at Caleb, his expression is still serious and he's still listening to Rex but he's watching me. He winks, it's not salacious or suggestive but there's something about it that flicks the incinerator inside me on. I feel the heat spread out from my stomach down to my toes and up to my scalp making all the hairs on my head prickle. I have to force my focus back to the song, Freya and I sing the rest of the verses and chorus together.

"God I love that song" Freya gushes as we hand the mic's back to John "I always wanted to sing it like that but never had the nerve, thank you" Freya surprises me by enveloping me in her arms.

"You're most welcome" I link arms with her as we make our way back to the table "any time you want to sing like that just let me know, in fact I'll get a karaoke machine installed in the games room and you can sing to your hearts content"

Freya laughs, it's a real heart felt joyful laugh. I smile delighted to see her so happy and it's the first time I've heard her really laugh "You might live to regret that" she snorts.

CALEB

Sometimes Rex can be such a fucking twat I want to slap him in to next week, and right now is one of those moments. He's bloody clueless about what he's just said. Hats off to Simon, he jumped to Skye's defence faster than anyone, for a gay guy he's bloody scary, he even scared the shit out of me. I have a sneaking suspicion this isn't the first time he's defended Skye. How in the blazing hell Bill didn't lamp Rex one is beyond me! Bill is one of those guys that hits first and asks questions later, kind of like me. The atmosphere is so tense you can cut it with a knife. Paul and Alan appear to be casually watching the situation, I have no doubt in my mind that one nod from Skye and these two will go nuclear on Rex.

The timing of John calling Skye and Freya up to sing couldn't be more perfect, no sooner have the girls left our group Rex is at my side in an instant. I steel myself for the whinging fest that's about to start. All too often I have to explain to Rex why he's upset someone with the things he's said, only this time he knows he's fucked up, it's written all over his face.

"Tell me what I should have said" Rex says resigned.

"Like hell I will" a hollow humourless laugh escapes me. I slap his back and my hand grips the back of his neck "what the fuck made you say that in the first place"

I dip my head to hear Rex's explanation, my skin prickles and tingles, I'm being watched. I can feel Skye's eyes on me, the urge to turn round and look at her is so strong. I fight with my body to resist her Siren's call. Piano music starts shortly followed by Skye's husky voice and my resistance snaps, my eyes find her only she's not looking at me but at the screen. I have to concentrate to listen to Rex.

"I have no fucking clue. In hindsight it was childish of me. I don't know, I guess hearing everyone gushing about how she's brought so much work to the village and managed to achieve that in only a few hours" Rex shrugs his shoulders "it got to me"

"So you thought to remind everyone that she's spending someone else's money to do it" only I know differently – it's her money. Rex lets out a heavy sigh and nods his head "and that my dear friend was your fuck up"

"I get that now, she's the hero because she has the authority to assign the work force. It's blatantly obvious the villagers don't give a flying fuck who's signing the pay cheques. Christ! I wish I could turn back the clock, I've crashed and burned all the progress I've made tonight with Skye. Do you think she'll be more receptive if I apologise again?"

My fingers flex and grip the back of Rex's neck harder in response to his question. I really, really want to snap it. Skye's eyes meet mine; my heart goes out to her. I wink, hopefully conveying everything is okay, and she has me and practically all of the village looking out for her. A slight smile plays on her full lips and I can see the blush of her cheeks, even from where I'm stood.

"I wouldn't, best leave things well alone" I advise him.

Skye and Freya sing the rest of the song together, their voices blending perfectly. The hairs on my arms and neck stand on end, the only downer is Skye doesn't sing the words to me, had Rex kept his bloody mouth shut she would be singing 'How do I get you alone' directly to me right now. I love my best mate but right now I fucking hate him.

As before the crowd cheer loudly when they finish. I watch the two women Freya is positively glowing, she's on such a high. I briefly see a startled look on Skye's face as Freya envelopes her in an embrace. Freya's larger frame hides Skye from view, when they break apart Skye is looking at Freya with genuine fondness.

"I want to make amends" wines Rex "she's the best looking and fittest piece of arse this place has ever seen. I don't want to let the opportunity to have a piece of her pass by"

I let go of Rex's neck before I actually rip his fucking head off. She's mine! I want to snarl at him but I can't officially claim that, my blood is boiling with frustration.

"If that's the only reason why you want to apologise to her is so you can fuck her, you're shit out of luck" a male acerbic voice comes from behind us. We both turn to see a furious Simon "Skye spots twats like you a mile off, do you really think you're the only dickhead to try it on? Believe me she'll crucify you and I personally can't wait to see it happen. On second thoughts, you know what, go ahead I could do with a good laugh"

Rex is mortified, he stares at Simon with his mouth opening and closing, no sound coming out. I, on the other hand want to roar with laughter, this is fucking brilliant. There is no doubt in my mind that Simon will tell Skye verbatim what Rex has said. After a minute of silence and intense glaring from Simon, Rex concedes defeat and skulks off in the direction of the bar.

I pick up two fresh bottles of beer out of the ice bucket, handing one to Simon "You're one vicious queen, remind me never to get on the wrong side of you" I chuckle.

"Hurt my baby girl and I'll give you the hardest bitch slap I can muster" retorts Simon.

"I'll remember that" I clink bottles with him.

"What's up with Rex and who are you bitch slapping?" Skye's husky voice has me turning to see her beautiful radiant smiling face.

"Rex wants to apologise so he can get to fuck you but unfortunately for him I overheard" says Simon.

"So you bitch slapped him" Skye raises an eyebrow.

"Only verbally baby girl" Simon grins "and I was warning Mr McHottie here what would happen if he ever hurt you"

I throw my head back laughing at Simon's nickname for me, Mr McHottie, that's a new one. Skye's eyes twinkle, she's amused by my reaction "His tongue is sharper and hurts more than his slap" Skye winks "he's more likely to set Paul or Alan on you" that sobers me up pretty quickly.

I look over at the two bodyguards, their relaxed demeanour as they chat with Freya and a couple of the locals' brave enough, or drunk enough to be brave to talk to them doesn't fool me. These guys are on high alert. Paul's eyes, although very subtle, constantly scan the room. Focusing on Alan I notice he's doing the same thing. I've had my suspicions for a while about these two and I'm almost certain they're ex-military, who the fuck am I kidding, of course they're ex-military.

The rest of the night goes without a hitch, after half an hour Rex rejoins the group. He doesn't make any attempt to get in Skye's good books. Skye ignores him, she doesn't give him the cold shoulder per se but she doesn't go out of her way to make conversation with him. I can see Skye is thoroughly enjoying herself mixing with the locals. She flirts back with the men and slaps down anyone who gets too risqué much to the delight of the rest of us. Freya gets called up to sing Christina Aguilera's 'Beautiful'. During the song Skye has tears rolling down her face and she does nothing to hide them, I notice there are a few others wiping their eyes. When Freya comes back, I hear Skye murmur "You are beautiful and don't let anyone tell you any different" as she gently hugs the battered and bruised woman. Freya's chin wobbles as she fights to hold back her tears. It's a really touching moment.

Everyone in the pub is in high spirits, it's a fantastic atmosphere, the best it's ever been. People who rarely set foot in the place have ventured in tonight, even those that look down their noses and shudder at the thought of having to enter the place, have come in, namely Simone la de da Fawcett-Fowler. The look on her face is priceless when Skye and Freya drag Joyce Farringdon up to sing 'Dancing Queen' with them. The woman really doesn't know how to let herself go, although according to Rex she's a goer in the sack. I'll take his word for it. But the best thing about the evening, Skye rarely leaves my side and she always, always positions herself so our bodies could make contact – discreetly of course. The subtle touches and caresses are a huge turn on; it drives me bat shit crazy knowing we won't be sharing a bed tonight but I can't complain when the night ends on a perfect note.

"Ladies and gentlemen" John calls out to get everyone's attention "tonight we have a change to our usual finale" a few groans go up "instead of singing along with me and Caleb, you get the pleasure of singing with Caleb and Skye, guys up you come"

I take hold of Skye's hand and lead the way to cheers and whistles. I don't let go of her hand even when she tries to wriggle free as we take the microphones off John. I do let go when I realise what we're singing. As before, we act out the song 'Paradise by the Dashboard Light'. The chemistry between us is electrifying, it couldn't have been a more apt song to sum up what is happening between us. I time it perfectly to plant a kiss on Skye's cheek just as she launches into 'stop right there, before we go any further…'

When we finish the whole pub goes ballistic. People shout for more. I take the opportunity to grab Skye, wrapping my arms around her, enjoying the feel of her pressed against my body longer than necessary and no one calls me out for doing it. I even manage to sneak a goodnight kiss.

I walk home with Sally and Marty; each relay a surprising amount of gossip they picked up during the night. I correct them on quite a few things, especially the bits that have been blown wildly out of proportion. I'm amazed that Skye's true identify hasn't been discovered. If I could work it out and find it on the internet surely someone else has as well.

"I think it's brilliant that Frank Appleton and all the other tradesmen in the village have been hired. Skye is so down to earth for someone who is incredibly wealthy" Sally gushes.

"How do you know that?" Marty slurs. A sense of foreboding slams into the pit of my stomach as I grab Marty's arm and guide him away from the hidden ditch he's about to fall into "thanks boss"

"I overheard Miles Cunningham and Lord Baxter discussing her. Apparently Baxter was speculating she'd been left a fortune by some relative but Miles said there was no mention of that when he looked her up on the internet apparently she's worth a fortune in her own right. He didn't say how much, just said it was a lot" Sally's face suddenly splits into a wide grin "hey, wouldn't it be awesome if Skye bought the Hall from the new owners? I really like her, at first I was scared of her but she's so likeable.

God I nearly wet myself laughing when she got Lady Farringdon up to sing"

I switch off from Sally's babbling. The girl doesn't know how close to the truth she is but I can't shift the sense of unease I have about Baxter and Cunningham's conversation. Miles is a newsreader, however he was a journalist before moving in to TV, I hope the fucker doesn't do anything stupid if he has unearthed Skye's true identity.

CHAPTER EIGHTEEN

SKYE

I look at the time on my phone and huff, it's still too early to go to Caleb's for my horse riding lesson. Although, they would be up now mucking out and doing whatever else it is they do… no, no, no, I can't go now. I'll look like some desperate brazen hussy. You are! Look at yourself, you're dressed for Christ's sake and have been for the last hour, it's only seven, you've got another two and a half hours to wait.

I flop down on the bed but within seconds I'm back up pacing the room. I'm too agitated to draw; every attempt I've made has me fantasizing Caleb doing those things to me. As I pace the room I think back over our time together and what we've done, more importantly where we have done it. Holy shit! I'm even more into kink than I thought. Clayton had awakened me sexually but Caleb calls to the submissive in me, really calls, like a demon lover calling to the darkest depths of my soul. The very thought excites me, is that wrong? I'm putty in his hands and I've given him complete control, something that I said I would never do for any man, I didn't surrender completely to Clayton. Bloody hell! I don't know how I feel about that.

Caleb has certainly pushed my boundaries and I let him, hell I did it willingly. He has done things to me that Clayton would never have. Lord! My arse is still tender from how hard he whipped me the other day.

That's because Caleb doesn't know about my past, Clayton did. Clayton respected my limits and didn't push. Yes, but Caleb instinctively picked up on those things and still went ahead. I could have used my safe word and I didn't. That's right, I didn't, I agree with myself. I've had the most intense orgasms of my life this past week, a tremor goes through me as my body remembers them. I squeeze my thighs together, it does nothing to alleviate the heaviness and dull throb between my legs. Fuck it! I'm going now. I yank open the bedroom door.

"Morning, I didn't think anyone else would be up this early. Would you like some breakfast?" Michelle smiles from the doorway in to the kitchen, she's in her pyjamas and dressing gown with remnants of last night's makeup around her eyes.

"I'll make it" I say following her in to the kitchen "sit down and I'll put the kettle on"

"Thank you" Michelle says round a yawn; she runs her hand through her bed head hair "goodness me. I could do with another couple of hours' sleep"

"Why don't you go back to bed" I say filling the kettle.

"Too much to do and I need to take yesterday's takings to the bank. I don't fancy having all that money sat in the safe until Monday"

"Can't argue with that" I concede "what time does the bank open?"

"Nine thirty, oh thank you" Michelle says as I place her cup of tea in front of her.

"Paul and Alan will take you" I hold my hand up to halt her protest "I insist. Judging by how busy you were all day and night I can only guess at how much you took. I've got my horse riding lesson, so Paul can drop me off first then take you to the bank. Which reminds me, you need to give me the bill for what I owe"

"It seems criminal to take money from you considering the amount of money we've made off you being here this week" Michelle says getting up and going to one of the overhead cupboards, she pulls out a folder "but from one business woman to another" she hands me a sheaf of paper and lets her sentence go unfinished.

I look at the amount, it's nowhere near enough "This is just for the rooms, what about all the food and drinks we've had?"

Michelle shrugs "Like I said it seems criminal to take money from you, but I'm comfortable with that" she nods at the invoice.

"Fair enough" I laugh. I'll make sure Freya pays extra to cover food and drinks.

Halfway through making breakfast Paul and Alan put in an appearance and as I'm dishing up Simon, Freya and Chris show up. Turns out Chris has been up for hours doing a stock inventory. The verdict doesn't bode well; the pub is almost dry.

"I'm just thankful you're all leaving on Sunday" Chris chuckles good-naturedly "I could do with going to the wholesalers to stock up on the bottled stuff, we've not got enough to see us through the weekend, ale wise we should be okay"

Plans are made and as luck would have it I get dropped off at the stables forty-five minutes early. Sally is nowhere near ready for me. She shows me in to Caleb's office when I finally convince her I'm more than happy to wait until my arranged time. Caleb is nowhere to be seen and I have to bite my tongue to stop myself from asking where he is.

I look around the room and realise it's actually the living room that's been commandeered as the office. The furniture has a worn shabby look, the carpet is thread bare and the curtains look as if they'd stand up by themselves. The place is clean but it's aged. Curiosity has me idly looking through the paperwork on the large wooden desk, most of them are overdue bills. Caleb's words about his ex-wife being a money grabber flit through my mind and I look around the room again with fresh eyes. This place could be beautiful if it had an injection of cash.

I know if I offered the money outright Caleb wouldn't take it. I'd have to be subtle otherwise I'd run the risk of offending him. I need to give this some thought and fast, a possible idea starts to form.

"Leave it with me and I'll get back to you"

Caleb's deep raspy voice along with his footsteps coming down the stairs has me moving away from the desk and sitting down on the sofa. Seconds later Caleb appears in the doorway. My eyes hungrily take in his fit as fuck body. Oh heavens above! He's wearing jodhpurs again, my heart thuds against my rib cage. He looks divine in them, his black t-shirt clings to his torso. The cap sleeves strain under his bulging biceps and I can see the clear definition of his pecs and abs under the cotton material. Desire spikes and floods through me when my eyes reach his lower legs and see riding boots, the only thing that's missing is the riding crop. Oh my sweet lord!

"Kitten"

The low growl of my pet name has me up out my seat, he catches me as I launch myself at him. My arms and legs automatically wrap around him, my hands fist in his hair pulling his head towards me so I can get at his luscious lips. A whimper escapes me as we connect. Caleb's hands cup and need my arse, I rotate and grind my hips against him, feeling his erection getting harder, thicker and longer.

"I need to fuck you right now" Caleb rumbles against my lips, lying me down on the sofa. He kneels up, grasps my leg and pulls my boot off as I'm undoing my jeans. His hands knock mine out of the way, roughly yanking my jeans and knickers down he releases the leg that's minus the boot. Caleb has his jodhpurs around his thighs seconds later. He lowers himself, covering my body. I feel his glans probing my entrance. I lift my hips and he slips inside.

"Oh yes" we moan together, Caleb flexes his hips and sinks a few more inches inside me, another rotation and he's in deep, seated to the root and... the telephone rings.

"Shit, of all the fucking lousy timing" Caleb curses as he starts to pull out of me.

I stop him from moving "Take the call while I fuck you"

Caleb's eyes widen in surprise then a salacious smile spreads across his face. Caleb quickly snatches up the phone "Hello, hang on a minute" he says to the caller.

I point to the sofa "Sit down" Caleb raises and eyebrow "if it pleases you, Master" I say it in my best seductive submissive voice.

Before sitting down Caleb toes off his boots and takes his jodhpurs off, I leave my clothes as they are, there's something decadently debauched about fucking whilst half dressed. I straddle Caleb and lower myself down on to him. Caleb controls my decent by gripping my hips. The slow intrusion and feeling of fullness is everything my body has been craving. Caleb kisses me deeply, his tongue possessing my mouth just as much as his cock is possessing me, before he resumes his call.

"Sorry about keeping you waiting" he rasps in to the phone, his sparkling emerald green eyes hold mine. I undulate and rotate my hips as he listens to the caller "yes, I rang yesterday to make an appointment... sure, I can do any time that suits you... this afternoon is fine" Caleb's tongue darts out and runs along his full bottom lip. I bear down and grind against his hips, the feel of his cock stroking deep inside and the friction against my clit has me repeating the move faster and faster. I lean forward and snag that luscious bottom lip between my teeth, biting and tugging.

Caleb's deep rumbling half growl and groan resonates deep, deep inside me, soul deep. My blood is pounding in my ears. He fists my hair, holding my head firmly in place then claims my mouth. His hips thrust upwards and I ride him, hard.

"Mr Raven... I can do three o' clock. Mr Raven... are you there? Can you hear me? Mr Raven" I hear the tinny shout of a male voice.

"I'll be there" Caleb rasps and drops the phone. Caleb's free hand grasps my hip, stilling my movements "you are so fucking naughty kitten" the next thing I know I'm flat on my back, Caleb lifts my leg over his hip. He positions his hands, one on the back of the sofa the other on the arm rest, and lifts his weight off me. I pull his t-shirt up as it's blocking my view of his fantastic, mouth-watering body. I run my hands over his abs, his muscles twitch and flex as he thrusts slow and deep stroking every inch of me. His golden tanned skin glistens with perspiration. God I can't get enough of him.

I trail licks, kisses and nips on the areas of skin I can get to. My hands slide round his back and down to his tight arse. I knead the taut flexing muscles, digging my nails in and pull him deeper. Caleb rotates his hips and hits the spot that shoots my building orgasm into the stratosphere.

"Oh god, yes!" the strained words rip from the back of my throat "please, again"

"You like that kitten" Caleb hits the spot again making me whimper, I'm becoming frantic with the need to come "I can feel your greedy grasping pussy demanding more, you want more, don't you?" I make an incoherent sound, it's the only reply I can make "I want to hear you, do you want more?"

A strangled wail comes out of me as I grind against him. Caleb stops moving. What the… I force open my heavy eye lids to see hard emerald greens staring back, my chest is rising and falling rapidly, I'm on the brink, at that point of no return. Caleb raises an expectant eyebrow at me. Ooh! He's in Dom mode.

"Yes, I want more. Please Master" I whisper. I flex my fingers kneading his arse and pull him as I raise and grind my hips against him. Not that it moves him but it does give me the friction I need.

"Naughty, naughty kitten" he lowers his head closer to mine "stop trying to top me from the bottom" his whisper holds a threat of punishment if I don't behave. What the hell… in for a penny, in for a pound. I repeat the move "not only are you very naughty, you are extremely greedy. Very well then, I will give you what you want" Caleb lowers further, his lips against my ear "I am going to really enjoy punishing you after your riding lesson"

Caleb rises and shifts his position, placing one foot on the floor. He moves my leg so it's higher up his hip "Don't come until I tell you. I want to hear you but no screaming" he says moving his hands back to their original position. Dipping his head, he gives me a toe curling sensuous kiss, as he does he slowly withdraws. I can feel every ridge. I tense my muscles making the most of it. Caleb lets out a low plaintive groan.

The tip of his cock breaches my entrance, he breaks the kiss by lifting himself. All his muscles tense, his eyes sparkling. I'm mesmerised by his beauty and carnal lust for me. Without warning he thrust forward, plunging hard and deep.

"Argh, yes" I cry out in ecstasy. Caleb delivers each measured stroke with precision, hitting my g-spot time after time and it's not long before I'm fighting to stave off the impending orgasm "please… Master, please" I'm whimpering and begging, for what I have no idea.

"Not yet" Caleb bites out.

His movements pick up, faster and faster he plunges in to me. I'm mindless as this pleasure trip takes me higher and higher, the pressure building inside me is fit to burst like a pressure cooker. I screw my eyes shut and bite down on my lip.

"Fuck! Don't you dare come" Caleb's words are my undoing.

The scream tears from me as my orgasm detonates, Caleb covers my mouth with his hand stemming the sound. My body convulses, it feels like fireworks are going off and shredding my nerve endings, in my head I see stars. Caleb pounds faster chasing his own release and prolonging my orgasm.

"Skye" he calls out as he empties himself. I wrap my arms around him and hold his shuddering body close to me as he rides out his climax. His warm gasping breath tickles my neck and shoulder.

After a few minutes he shifts our positions, so I'm lying on top of him. Amazingly, I can still feel how hard he is as his cock rests against my hip. Caleb strokes my hair, whilst the other hand runs patterns across the exposed skin of my lower back and arse. I feel myself drifting off to sleep.

The sound of horse hooves clattering directly outside the window jerks me awake. Caleb sit's up and stands me on my feet in one swift move.

"Shit" he curses under his breath, grabbing my boot he thrusts it into my hand "quick upstairs. I'll tell Sally you're using the bathroom"

Stifling a fit of giggles, I sprint for the stairs, leaving Caleb to pull on his pants. I hear the front door open as I make it to the top, at the same time the telephone rings. An image of Caleb hopping around the room trying to get his jodhpurs and boots on whilst answering the phone sets me off laughing.

I spend five minutes in the bathroom sorting myself out. I braid my hair and splash cold water over my face in a vain attempt to reduce the flushed just fucked look on my face. Give up, it's not working, I tell myself. Taking a deep breath, I head downstairs. Entering the living room come office, I see Sally stood by the door, Caleb is on the phone, and he's dressed, thankfully he's concentrating on some paperwork on the desk otherwise I don't think I could pull off acting like nothing has just happened.

"Sorry Sally, are you waiting for me?" I ask as nonchalantly and breezily as I can.

Smiling she nods and indicates for me to follow her. As I pass Caleb I can't resist pinching his bum, he jerks and bashes his knee against the desk.

"Shit, ouch. Sorry I just walked into my desk" he says to his caller as he scowls at me rubbing his knee. I can't help smiling at him, I blow a kiss and wave bye at the door. His face softens as he returns my smile and shakes his head.

An hour later I'm back in the yard with Sally. My first lesson over with and I really enjoyed it. I fell off once — giving poor Sally the fright of her life — it was my own stupid fault. Precariously leaning to one side to adjust my stirrup the law of gravity took over. Thankfully the ground was soft. During the lesson I got to know Sally, she's a naturally chatty girl. I was amazed when she told me she had been working for Caleb for almost twelve years, although she admitted she hadn't officially been a member of his staff for the first six years. At school, Sally had been the girl who was mad on horses, I vaguely remember having someone like her in my class. No interest in boys, music, makeup, fashion or shopping, their life revolved around horses.

She told me her parents had bought her a pony for her twelfth birthday, reluctantly giving in after four years of pestering. Unfortunately, tragedy struck and her mother passed away six months later, not long after her father told her he couldn't afford to keep the pony. Caleb had come across her in floods of tears in the stable, when he managed to get what was wrong out of her, he took her home and made an offer to her father.

Caleb would keep the horse and in return Sally would work a few hours a week in the yard for free and that would be payment for the pony's food and stabling. Sally's father relented when he saw how happy the arrangement made his daughter. As it was Sally spent every available spare hour she had at the stables. After leaving school she spent more and more time there, even when she was supposed to be looking for a job. One day, Caleb came to her asking if she would like to work full time for him since one of the grooms had resigned. That was the second happiest day of her life, the first being getting her pony, of course. As we enter the yard Davy comes out to meet us.

"Okay, tell me how to get off this beautiful beast. I can get on and fall off no problem" I laugh "whoa!" I yelp as I'm suddenly air borne.

"There you go" Caleb's raspy voice rumbles in my ear as my feet land on the cobblestones, his hands remain on my waist "did you say you fell off?" he looks me over, assessing for any damage. He frowns at Sally, the poor girl blushes and looks mortified.

I swat his arm "It was a combination of my own stupidity and physics. Poor Sally nearly had a heart attack when I went arse over tit and face planted the floor. Thankfully the ground was soft"

Caleb rolls his eyes at me and takes off my riding hat, handing it to Davy. We both pat the horse's flank as Davy leads him back to the stables.

"Come on" Caleb tugs on my braid, he leans down and whispers in my ear "you've still got that chocolate cake to work off"

Desire instantly pools in my lower abdomen as my heart rate kicks up. Dutifully I follow Caleb in to the house. I have to restrain myself from sprinting up to his bedroom and throwing myself on the bed. My inner slut goddess is already there; stark bollock naked with her legs spread wide, impatiently waiting.

CALEB

I lead Skye to my bedroom. In the hour she had her riding lesson I've done nothing but prepare how I'm going to punish her. I know what I'm about to do will really push her limits. We've never discussed hard limits or dislikes but I know from our short time together being completely restrained is a trigger for her, my instinct is telling me that being gagged and blindfolded at the same time is more than likely to push her over the edge. Being the sadistic selfish bastard that I am, I'm going to do it anyway.

Laid out on the bed is everything I'm going to use on her. Skye's eyes widen in surprise when she sees all of my kinky paraphernalia. Her teeth gnaw her bottom lip, an outward sign of nerves and anxiety. I watch her closely. She remains perfectly still, only her eyes move cataloguing each item in front of her. Skye takes a deep breath and slowly releases it, her eyes drop to the floor and she gracefully lowers to her knees.

Holy fucking shit! I wasn't expecting that. I really thought I was going to have to coerce her, not that I would force her to do something against her will but I was prepared to do some persuading. I walk over to her and inspect her waiting position. For the sheer hell of it, I tap between her parted knees. Without hesitation she moves them further apart. I straighten her shoulders back and gently push her head lower down so her chin almost rests on her chest.

"Perfect" I murmur walking around her "in a minute you're going to stand and remove all your clothes then I want you to resume this position. Do you understand?"

"Yes Master" Skye's husky voice whispers without hesitation.

I go into the bathroom for no other reason than to calm and gain control of myself. I pull off my sweater and t- shirt. I undo the button on my jodhpurs and start to toe my boots off when the image of Skye and the lust filled carnal look she gave me earlier causes me to pause. Skye looked at me like that one other time, in the club when she had watched me give the demonstration. My naughty kitten has a thing for me in jodhpurs and riding boots, hmm, this is going to be interesting. I smile at my reflection. I wash and scrub my hands and nails, not that they need it but I want to build Skye's anticipation by making her wait as long as possible.

Back in the bedroom, Skye hasn't moved a muscle I spend a few minutes admiring her. Time to play, I reach over and pick up the riding crop. Standing with my feet hip width apart I rest my hands on my hips, the crop lies flat against my thigh.

"Well done kitten. Take your clothes off, now" I command.

Keeping her gaze lowered, Skye lifts gracefully to her feet in one smooth movement. Her hand rises going straight to the zip on her jacket. Taking it off she looks around obviously deciding where to put it, her eyes lift to me. The sharp intake of breath, the blush of her cheeks and the way her lustful eyes hungrily travel up and down my body confirms my suspicion. Her eyes lower to my crotch, the tip of her tongue darts out licking her lips. I feel a smile tug at the corners of my mouth, I know she likes what she sees and exactly what she wants.

"Only good girls get what they want kitten" I purposely grab my crotch and hardening dick "you have to earn this by getting back in to my good books" my voice is rougher than normal. Skye's eyes snap to mine, her cheeks blaze red. Using the riding crop, I point to the chair by the door. Skye's breath hitches when she sees the crop "don't make me wait kitten. Your punishment is already going to test you"

That gets Skye moving, in no time at all she's back in the waiting position gloriously naked. My cock is aching; I need to take the edge off otherwise I'm not going to last. Standing in front of her I unzip my pants

"Hands behind your back" Skye complies "lift up on to your knees" she rises "open your mouth" she does. I bite back the moan, she's being an absolute star "I'm going to fuck your mouth, you will take everything I give you and you will swallow"

I take my cock in hand and stroke the shaft, the heaviness in my balls increases "Kiss it" I command placing the tip to her open mouth. Her lips close enveloping the head, her tongue swirls and drawing back she sucks just like you would on a lolly pop. My eyes roll to the back of my head as pleasure shots straight up my spine. My brain registers the naughty minx didn't kiss it as I intended.

Gently cupping her head in my hands I ready myself "Open wider" I slide in slowly, watching my cock disappear into the wet hot velvety depths of her mouth, I ease back out Skye hollows her cheeks creating suction, her tongue presses up against my shaft and swirls around the head "mmm, that's feels good kitten" I spend a few minutes enjoying her mouth and the delights of her talented tongue, letting the pleasure sensations build around my body. Each time I push deeper until I feel the back of her throat "oh, yeah!"

I start to rock back and forth faster, and faster. My breathing comes in short pants as I chase my release. Her mouth is so fucking snug like her pussy. My fingers shift in her hair, gripping and holding tighter. My balls draw up as the pleasure sensations all gather and merge. Looking down at Skye with her arms locked behind her back, her lips and jaw relaxed allowing me to plunge unhindered into her mouth, heightens my pleasure. Slowly her eyes open and lock with mine, the lust and trust I see sends me over the edge.

"Argh" the noise rips from my throat as I release into her mouth. I hold still as my orgasm crashes through me. Feeling Skye's mouth and tongue working me I shudder as she draws out the last remnants of pleasure. I let her lick me clean "Stand" I hoarsely command. I kiss her gently, tasting myself, as I release my fingers from her hair "thank you, I needed that" a smug smile plays at her lips "that doesn't get you out of your punishment" her smile falters and she drops her eyes to the floor.

Stepping away from her I fasten my pants, Skye still has her arms behind her back, thrusting out her beautiful tits. Unable to resist I lower my head taking one of the succulent nubs in my mouth. I suck and swirl my tongue around it then pull back letting the tit pop from my mouth. I capture it again, suck hard and bite. Skye gasps, then releases as a low groan. I straighten, place my hands on her shoulders and turn her to face the bed.

"Tell me why you are being punished"

"I came when you didn't give me permission" Skye says in a clear confident voice.

"Why else?"

Skye looks at me confused "I… I… don't recall, I'm sorry Master" her head drops, her eyes downcast. My dick stirs to life.

"Look at me" her gaze lifts to me "you tried topping me and I still owe you a spanking for Wednesday" Skye looks really puzzled, her eyes drift off to the distance and chews her bottom lip as she searches for the memory. I let her think.

"The bathroom, at the dinner party" Skye whispers, her eyes widen when I nod then they instantly darken a smile plays across her lips "I'd forgotten about that"

"I know" I mouth, tearing my gaze away from her I reach down and pick up the first item "now I'm going to be using everything you see. I want you to answer me honestly and no hesitating. If you know what the item is I want you to tell me and if you have used it before, understand?" Skye nods "Do you know what this is?"

"Yes, Master" Skye says softly "it's a love egg and yes I have had one used on me before, multiple times"

My stomach twists at the thought of her having played using these multiple times. I do my best to squash my reaction and concentrate on the here and now. I reach for the lubricant.

"Bend over and touch your toes, good girl, widen your stance a little more, excellent" I run my hand over her arse, letting my finger brush over her rear opening and over her vulva parting her to tease her clit "Oh kitten, you are so wet" I insert a finger inside, her greedy cunt grips my finger "you are such a naughty wanton girl, I don't need to use any lube" I thrust my finger in and out, hearing the squelching of her juices. Removing my finger, I spread her wetness around the love egg then part her labia, easing the egg inside her. I help her stand "okay?" Skye nods, then she lets out a yelp "this one vibrates" I grin holding up the remote "you are not allowed to come" Skye's eyes narrow which makes me grin all the more. I know she's cursing me to hell and back.

I pick up the next item, it's a belt with a long narrow piece of silk material dangling from the middle. Skye shrugs and shakes her head "This fastens around your waist" I buckle the belt, the material hanging at the front "open your legs" I reach through her parted legs for the material and pull it back and upwards, wrapping it through the belt and pulling it tight. Skye's breath hitches "feel that kitten" she nods. I adjust the material at the front making sure it lies snugly against her clit and the crack of her arse, the excess material is securely wrapped around the belt, don't want it getting tangled up with the whip.

I increase the vibration of the egg and run my nail over the silk covered sensitive bud of her clit. Skye's head falls back, a low guttural moan emits from her, it goes straight to my cock. I reduce the vibration, can't have her coming just yet. I pick up the next items and hold them in my palm.

"Nipple clamps" a wicked glint and smile light up her face "the one and only time was when you put them on me the other day"

I feel a surge of pleasure at her words. Lifting one of her heavy breasts I knead the flesh, steadily increasing the pressure, studying her face until I see the first wince of pain. I keep building the pressure and lower my head, taking the already erect hard nipple in my mouth. I worry it with my tongue, flicking and circling before closing my mouth drawing as much in as I can. I bite down on the nipple.

"Oh god" Skye shudders.

"You like your tits being played with, don't you kitten?" I attach the nipple clamp.

"Yes" Skye yelps, her eyes fly open, pain flashes through them quickly followed by desire.

I repeat the process, only this time I spend longer playing. Skye starts to squirm. I run my finger lightly over the silk material between her legs. Her breathing becomes ragged then I attach the nipple clamp.

"Ooohh! God" a plaintive cry full of desperate need to climax, music to my ears.

"So decadent and responsive but we have a long way to go yet, so you need to control yourself kitten" my voice is low and full of warning. I lightly trail my fingers over her swelling breasts then tug on the chain that connects the clamps. I'm rewarded with a muffled whimper.

"Now I know you know what these are" I say reaching for the leather cuffs, Skye holds her wrists out "tell me how many times have you been in cuffs like these?" I attach the first one.

"This will be the third time"

My hands still attaching the second one. So few, I stop myself from saying. Again I derive an obscure sense of pleasure from her admission. Skye gives me a shy smile that I can't help responding to it with one of my own. I pick up the last item and hold it up.

"I know what it is but never had one used on me" Skye's voice is wary.

"I need you to tell me what you think it is" I keep my voice as soft as I can.

"Spreader bar" she whispers.

I notice the pulse in the base of her throat has increased and she starts to chew her lip. Mindful that I'm about to push her limits I gently guide her to sit on the edge of the bed. I make quick work of attaching the cuffs to her ankles. Stepping back, I look at her. Christ she looks so fucking beautiful. I put my hand down my pants and adjust my dick. He wants to party now.

"In a few minutes I'm going to secure you to the bed. You will be face down with your arms spread, wrists attached to the chain that wraps around the posts and head board" Skye eyes follow the direction I point "tell me have you ever been bound, blindfolded and gagged all at the same time before?"

Skye's whole body jerks and starts to tremble, the pulse in her neck jumps crazily. I know if I put my hand on her chest I'll feel how hard her heart will be beating, more like a jack hammer just as it did the other day, only this time it'll be worse. Skye's head drops down, her eyes close tight. She knows what's coming and from her physical response I'm preparing myself to hear her safe word.

Skye raises her head "Yes" she barely whispers looking at me with haunted eyes.

Jesus, what the hell happened to her? The imploring look not to pry kills the question being given a voice. I raise my hand and gently run the back of my fingers down the side of her face then tenderly cup it with both hands, Skye's nuzzles in to the touch.

"I am only ever going to give you pleasure, everything I do to you will be about discovering and experiencing the true depths of your sexuality. I will never hurt you. I do want to blindfold and gag you, will you let me?" Skye closes her eyes; I feel the tremors rolling through her body. This is too much for her, call it quits. Skye draws in a deep breath and lets it out. Opening them I see determination and trust in her gorgeous yellow green eyes, she nods her assent taking my breath away "you beautiful girl, thank you Skye" I kiss her reverently because I know she's granted me something she vowed never to give up, to anyone – complete control.

I lift her in my arms and carry her round to the side of the bed. I help her get onto her front. I raise her torso by stacking pillows and cushions underneath her stomach. Silently she watches me attach the cuffs to the chain, she tugs to see how much give there is – there's none.

From the bedside cabinet I pick up a little brass bell. I place it in her hand, without waiting for any instruction she lets go of it. For a small bell it makes a surprisingly loud noise. I pick it up and place it back in her hand.

"Happy?" she nods "release that and everything will stop immediately" again Skye nods.

Under Skye's watchful eyes I strip off my remaining clothes and climb on to the bed, straddling her. Her arse is in just the right position for rubbing my cock against her. I have to fight the urge not to claim her arse.

"Open your mouth kitten" my voice is rough with lust and desire. I place the ball in her mouth and fasten the gag at the back of her head "now for the mask"

SKYE

Ohmygod, ohmygod, ohmygod. I bite down on the ball to stop the scream that's trying to work its way free as my world plunges in to darkness. Bile rises up and burns the back of my throat. Uncontrollable tremors make my muscles spasm as adrenalin pumps through my veins. My whole body breaks out in a cold sweat. Palpitations make me light headed and my breathing erratic.

What the fuck are you playing at girl? My common sense screeches at me.

Freedom… I want freedom.

Then let go of the bell you silly cow. My fingers flex.

No! I want this.

You crazy bitch, look at the state of you! How in the hell can you want something like this after what happened to you? You're out of your fucking mind if you want to please him this way.

"Christ you look so fucking beautiful" Caleb's voice rasping darkly in my ear and grinding his erection in the crack of my arse along with the low vibration of the love egg and the friction of the silk material tormenting my pussy slams the door shut on my common sense. A strange calm suddenly comes over me… I can do this. I know I can.

Besides, this isn't for him… it's for me.

Caleb's hands cup my aching swollen breasts, his fingers digging in causes a dull throbbing pain in my clamped nipples but feeling his rigid manhood and wishing it was inside me, has me moaning. Only the sound vibrates at the back of my throat. I try pushing back against Caleb but I can't move or get any leverage. The spreader bar and the position Caleb has me in put paid to that.

"Hmm, I am so going to fuck your arse now. Usually I would administer punishment first but I can't wait, you are just so fuckable"

Caleb's weight lifts off me. I feel him tug at the material wrapped around the belt at my waist. The movement causes friction and pressure against my clit as he loosens it. I feel him move across me as if he's reaching for something. I draw in a sharp breath as cold liquid touches my rear passage, lube.

Pressure, then a sharp pain as Caleb pushes in to me. My whole body tenses, I pull on my restraints riding out the pain, breathing heavily through my nose. The vibration from the love egg intensifies, the pain turns in to a dark decadent swirling pleasure in the lower depths of my belly. My body relaxes enjoying the sensations building within me. Caleb's gentle callused hands stroking along my skin stirs my blood and passions even more, I feel the bloom of perspiration mist across every surface of my body. His hands cup my breasts, a tug on the nipple clamps sends spears of sharp pain straight to my pussy. He pushes all the way in. A delirious scream gets blocked by the ball, my teeth clamp down on it. My entire being is awash with the dark swirling pleasure, rising higher and higher. I'm floating and flying at the same time with each deep thrust Caleb makes, it takes me further to a place I have never been, I never knew existed. I want to get there so much. I'm helpless to stop it. I won't stop it. Caleb stops moving, halting my climb to nirvana.

"Remember kitten, you are not allowed to orgasm until I give permission"

Fuck! Fuck! Fuckerty fuck. I want to scream at the top of my lungs. I know I'm not going to succeed, no matter how hard I try. My internal muscles are already cramping and going into delicious spasms. This isn't right, I should be fighting to be set free. How can something so wrong, so twisted, so depraved, be so… fucking… wonderful?

Caleb starts to move; his slow measured thrusts stroke every inch of my back passage. I can feel his cock and the vibrating love egg. My mind is struggling to make sense of the weirdness but my body has no problem. The fullness feels amazing; the intense sensations of pleasure are indescribable. I'm back on my journey to pleasure paradise.

I intentionally clench all my lower abdominal muscles to feel more. Shit! I shouldn't have done that.

Caleb lets out a low guttural curse, his pace picks up. The intense surging pleasure is heightened from his movements.

Oh god I can't stop the... oh god... oh god... I coming... as the dark pleasure detonates deep inside me it feels like a cacophony of fireworks goes off in my head.

I let out a muffled agonised cry as I unashamedly ride the waves rolling through me.

I'm vaguely aware of Caleb being right there with me.

Caleb's heavily gusting breath tickles my ear and neck. He kisses and nips my shoulder tenderly as he withdraws, I feel a gush of wetness trickle down my inner thighs, sweet lord he must have come as hard as me. A surge of smug satisfaction rolls through me at the thought.

"Well now, my naughty kitten, what am I going to do with you? Hmm" he nips my ear, my earrings clink against his teeth "you enjoyed that didn't you? Answer me" I nod my head "a little too much and now you're going to pay for that along with all your other misdemeanours. But first, let's dispense with these"

My mushy brain and sated body couldn't care less about his threat. Yeah, he can shove it in his pipe and smoke it for all I care.

Caleb raises my chest up and removes the clamps. I moan at the sensation of relief as blood rushes to my nipples. Caleb's magical hands massage my boobs before lowering me back down. He also removes the belt, the dragging silk material against my vulva and clitoris has me grinding my hips in to the mattress, as best as the restraints would allow and the gentle thrum of the vibrating egg all rekindles the flickering embers of dying pleasure. I mustn't come, I mustn't come; I recite over and over in my head. Yeah right!

I listen to Caleb moving around the room, he doesn't come near me for what seems like hours. I'm so chilled and relaxed I sink in to a light slumber.

A sharp stinging pain across my buttocks has me jerking awake, my whole body stiffens as I realise I can't move. Panic has me screaming but my voice doesn't carry, no one can hear me. I frantically fight against my restraints trying to break free. Tears leak down my cheeks as I blindly look around me. Oh god, please no more. My tightly clenched hands start to open as the pain recedes. Something is in one of my hands. It's hard and metal, a slight tinkling sound reaches my ears. It's a bell. A large warm hand caressing my bum along the welt of pain, soothes me instantly. My confused brain struggles to make sense of the building warm pleasure I'm feeling.

"I think nine more of these strikes should be sufficient kitten"

Caleb! My whole body sags with relief. My pounding heart starts to slow but then kicks up again as fear spikes and my body starts to tremble with anticipation for the next blow of the whip. Caleb doesn't fail to deliver. He hits hard and fast, no strike landing in the same place twice. The sadistic bastard sets the vibrating love egg on the top speed. By the sixth I'm crying and screaming as loud as I can around the gag. I'm screaming because I want to come so badly, my tears are from frustration. The last strike is the hardest of them all.

I feel the mattress dip. Caleb is climbing over me, the sudden removal of the vibrating egg is a shock to my system and over sensitive sex. I feel the heat of his body against the smarting skin of my arse and thighs. Caleb thrusts deep inside me. I scream from pure delight. He moves deep and hard, his hips smacking my raw bruised arse heightening the delicious dark pleasure pain deep within me.

"Please, please let me come" I cry out, the words are garbled around the gag.

My whole body is trembling with the need to climax again; my arms pull against the restraints in an effort to stave off my orgasm. Caleb's intoxicating scent fills my nostrils and I can feel his huge arms against the tops of my shoulders. In my mind I picture how we must look - me blindfolded, gagged, restrained being fucked from behind. Caleb's position over me is one of pure dominance – and I love it, a lot.

My braid is pulled, I feel Caleb wrapping my hair around his fist forcing my head back "Come, come now kitten" Caleb's low voice growls in my ear.

That completes me, I'm set free.

I soar higher than I ever have before.

Complete freedom.

My head hangs limply against my arm as Caleb works quickly to release me. The blindfold and gag are taken off first. My arms are released then my legs. I lie unmoving over the pillows. My whole body feels heavy, a dead weight and yet I've never felt so alive. My nerve endings, muscles and blood are thrumming with endorphins, it's going to be a long time before I come down from this incredible high.

A cool cream and large warm gentle caressing hands work over my lower back, buttocks and thighs soothing my hot abused skin. The stinging pain ebbing away with each caress. Caleb murmurs how pleased he is at how well I took my punishment. He whipped me harder than he had the other day, hell I've never been hit that hard in my life except when… I lock down that thought. Not going there.

Carefully Caleb turns me over, cradling me in his arms. He rains kisses over my face as his hands massage and stroke my body. Desire stirs instantly. I'm amazed at my body's capacity for pleasure… and pain for that matter. Lifting my arms, I wrap them around his neck, pulling his lips to mine. His tender kiss is so sweet, I catch and suck on his lower lip, gently biting down. Caleb takes over and claims me, again.

Moving me to lie on my back, he nudges my legs apart and settles himself between my thighs. I spread my legs wider apart to make more room. I feel his erection poking my entrance but he makes no attempt to enter, he seems content to just kiss me. I enjoy the feel of his lips against my overly warm skin. His cool breath teases my nipples before he gentle sucks on them. The overly sensitive nubs send tendrils of pain followed by pleasure straight to my core. The cotton sheets at my back rub against my tender skin reigniting the tingles of pain from the whip, this pain joins the building heaviness in my lower belly, enflaming the fresh memories of the dark pleasures Caleb bestowed on my body.

My hips start to move rubbing against him, Caleb answers by flexing his. I arch taking him deeper. A sigh of satisfaction rushes from me. I wrap my arms and legs around Caleb, feeling his hard muscled body and soft silken skin sensuously flexing and moving with mine as he takes me back to nirvana. Without words we enjoy each other through touch; our hands, mouths and the most intimate parts of our bodies. It's beautiful, it touches my soul – the dark and the light.

We come with each other's name on our lips, my orgasm is just as intense.

Rolling on to his back Caleb pulls me with him, lifting me so my sated body lies across his. Wrapping his arms around me, I nuzzle his chest, letting out a sigh of contentment I drift off listening to the steady beat of his heart, feeling protected and loved in his strong embrace.

CALEB

I listen to Skye's soft slow breathing as she drifts off to sleep. I've exhausted her. A smile plays on my lips, you could say it's out of arrogance but I would argue otherwise, fuck she's exhausted me! No, my smile is because I've finally found my other half.

Sexually we are so compatible. I haven't played like that for a long, long time and I have never, never come so hard. Hell, every time with Skye I come so hard I see stars. One thing I realised during our scene is Skye is one strong brave lady. I witnessed her struggle with and conquer her demons. There is no shadow of doubt in my mind that she has been through something very traumatic, it was terrible enough for it to induce a panic attack, twice. My mind starts throwing up suggestions but I don't want to speculate what could have happened to her because I know I will kill the bastard that hurt her. My arms pull Skye closer to me, a subconscious reaction to protect her, keep her safe.

I really expected Skye to drop the bell, I was amazed that each time her fingers opened just as quickly she clenched and fisted her hand again. The physical reaction to her internal struggle nearly had me safe wording but something stopped me, somehow I knew she had to do this for herself. It wasn't about pleasing me as her Dom, this was about her realising her deepest, darkest desires, discovering her true sexuality. Giving herself the freedom… Shit! Her safe word that's what it meant. She wanted freedom to explore and discover her sexuality without any limitations and that meant being free of her past and demons. Christ, I respected the hell out of the woman before but now… jeez it's off the scale.

Before you go all rose tinted glasses, what else have you two got in common? Yeah, go on big shot, answer that if you can.

We both share the same taste in music, she has horses – although she can't properly ride, yet. I frown, thinking back over all of our conversations. Admittedly they have mainly been with other people involved, I struggle to find something personal. We both run our own business.

Big fucking deal, she runs multiple, highly successful businesses and you can barely keep this place afloat, my conscious sneers. In a few hours you're going to be sat in front of the bank manager begging him to extend your fucking overdraft for Christ's sake. You're way out of your league man, admit it. You saw the photographs of her dressed up, everything about her screams mega wealth. You're just her bit of rough on the side. Shit, she even said it herself when you're alone together all you want to do is fuck each other's brains out. A cheap thrill. It's all about the sex, it's all it will ever be with a woman like her. You've got nothing to offer her apart from your dick and body. She's leaving tomorrow, fuck knows when she'll be back and when she is, you'll be her fuck buddy again, a secret one at that. She'll snap her fingers and you'll go running like a good little dog, wagging your tail because you'll be so pleased she's allowed you in her presence. I bet she's already laughing at you behind your back and takes the piss out of you with her friends. And what will you do when she bores of you? In no time at all you'll be crawling on your knees hoping for a few scraps to be thrown your way. Get real man! Take away the bloody good sex and what are you left with – fuck all, that's what!

Skye stirs, I loosen my arms as she stretches. She makes a cute little squeaking sound then slumps back against me. Her lips press against my skin, right over my heart. It thumps hard at the affectionate gesture.

"Hi" she whispers hoarsely, her yellow green eyes are filled with contentment and happiness.

"Hi" I whisper back dipping my head, she leans up to meet my lips. The kiss is soft and tender. I try and put a lid on my thoughts, I think I succeed but they've left me feeling unsettled. My post coitus high has long gone.

Settling back down, she rests her chin on my chest "What are you thinking about?"

"This place" I say on a whim, no way in hell am I telling her what I was really thinking about.

"Hey, tell me the story about your uncle and Joyce's grandfather" I snort a laugh at her genuine enthusiasm "come on I'm intrigued" Skye nudges me in the ribs.

"Okay" I turn us onto our sides, Skye shuffles up the bed so we are at eye level "I was fourteen or there about, so you're going to get the story from a boy's point of view" I warn her, Skye smiles and nods "my Uncle Michael liked to bet, which is an occupational hazard when you train race horses. He also liked playing cards, poker in particular. Anyway once a month Cookson would hold a poker night at the Hall. He wasn't fussy about who came, so long as you had money to gamble with you were in. Naturally my uncle went to as many as he could. He always played within his limit which was the cash he had in his pocket. On the night he lost the land we'd spent the day at the races. We had three winners, plus my uncle had placed bets on other horses and won, so as you can imagine he was pretty flushed. He made the mistake of taking all the winnings with him. He said it was just to show off, he had no intention of gambling it all. Anyway, Cookson had other ideas and according to my uncle he goaded him into betting big. Not wanting to lose face my uncle fell for it. His last hand was a full house with three aces and two kings. He was convinced he was going to win. Cookson pushed and pushed him, so in the end my uncle put all his money in the pot and offered up the field" I shift lying on my back "Cookson had a Royal flush"

Skye gasps in shock and sits up "Oh no, that's terrible. What happened next?"

"He came home, at the time he had this 'fancy woman' to use his term. Maggie, she'd stay over a couple of nights out of the week and when he played poker she'd come over and keep an eye on me. I remember sitting at the top of the stairs listening to them arguing. She really gave him what for, the last thing I remember her saying was "What about the boy? Did you ever stop to think about the legacy you'll be leaving him? He has only you and at this rate he'll have nothing" then she stormed out, slamming the door behind her. I never saw her again after that. In the morning I found my uncle sat in the kitchen, he was a broken man. He vowed to me that day he would never gamble again, and he didn't. I admired him for that"

"So how did he get use of the field?"

"A couple of days later Cookson turns up, once he'd sobered up and his cronies told him what had happened, actually they were boasting about it and Cookson's son, Anthony, overheard. Anthony went ballistic at his father, made him feel ashamed of what he'd done. So Cookson does no more than turn up here offering to sell the land back to my uncle, of course Michael hasn't got the money. In the end Cookson agreed to let him continue using the field for the horses. A few years later Cookson passed away after he set fire to the Hall, allegedly. Anthony carried on with the arrangement, actually I think he forgot about it. By then he was already working and living in the city"

"You miss him" Skye's words are softly spoken.

"Yeah, every goddam day" I sigh heavily and turn my gaze to her, my stomach twists. Christ she's so fucking beautiful "he was everything to me. The father I never had, the older big brother, my favourite teacher, he was more than an uncle to me. He taught me everything I know" Skye reaches out and clasps my hand in hers, giving it a slight squeeze, the tender look on her face and smile tells me she understands, she really does. There's no pity, just understanding. Before I can stop myself I continue talking.

"I was three when my mum died of cancer, if he hadn't taken me in I would've ended up in care. Uncle Michael fought my grandparents for custody, he won based on the fact they wouldn't have anything to do with my mum when she got with my dad. Then the inevitable happened and she fell pregnant with me. My dad took off as soon as she told him, she never saw him again. Mum went to her parents for help and they turned their backs on her when she refused to get rid of me. Michael gave my mum a roof over her head. Apparently my grandparents were very religious but Michael said they were hypocrites, didn't practise what they preached. Michael cut all ties with them as soon as he turned eighteen, he never told me why but listening to him talk I think they were very controlling, it was their way or the highway. Anyway, he helped mum get a place of her own but we spent most of our time here. Michael used to say I could ride a horse before I learnt to walk" I chuckle at the memory "I often wonder what this place would be like if he was still alive today, he had big plans"

"Tell me about your plans" Skye says after a few minutes of silence, her request surprises me "what's your ultimate dream?"

"To be the best training yard in the country" I whisper; I've never told anyone this before.

"Well since I have only ever seen Mike and Penny's ranch and this place you'll have to describe to me what the best training yard will look like" Skye's eyes glitter with interest, I can sense her excitement.

"Well, for starters I would demolish and rebuild the stable blocks, making them bigger so there's more room for the horses to move around in, I'd probably add an extra block so I could take on more horses. Then I'd build an indoor training centre along with an equine swimming pool. Finally, I'd have a purpose built track that would be used for training horses on both flat and jump"

Skye has a huge smile on her face "I have a proposition for you. How about I put the money up for…"

"Why the fuck would you do that?" I shout cutting her off, my raised voice startles Skye, her eyes go wide. All my insecurities about how different our lives are and her wealth rush to the surface and blows the lid right off the fucking box "Do you think all I'm after is your fucking money?" I leap out of bed, snatching my pants up off the floor. Skye gets off the bed and starts to quickly dress.

"That's not what I…"

"I'm not some pet project or fucking charity case, I'm more than capable of funding this myself. I will. Just because you have shit loads of money do you think that gives you a goddam fucking right to rub my nose in it" I jerk my pants on.

"I was only trying…"

"Why would you give someone, who's practically a stranger, money? You don't owe me anything" shut the fuck up and let her speak my rational mind says but my insecure irrational mind is on a roll "is it because you've had a week of mind blowing sex and the best orgasms of your life that you feel you have to offer some kind of reward to your bit of rough on the side" Skye flinches as if I'd slapped her in the face "we don't know each other. Hell lady, you even said it yourself and by Christ it's true, when we're alone all we want to do is fuck each other's brains out. Take away the sex, there's fuck all between us. So why would you offer me money?"

The confused shock and pain in Skye's beautiful face kicks me hard in the gut. Feeling guilty at being responsible for wounding her unnecessarily I turn my back on her and look out of the window. Why was I being such a fucking bastard to her?

"Obviously I made a mistake, I didn't mean to offend or upset you" at the sound of her calm husky voice I turn back round. Skye's face is white matching her knuckles which clutch her jacket tightly to her chest, I can see slight tremors rolling through her body "I apologise. I just thought…" she takes a deep breath and shakes her head "I thought, with all the things you've said we meant something to each other. That we had something more, clearly I was wrong" her voice is hoarse with supressed emotion.

"They were just words sweetheart; just fucking words any woman wants to hear" I sneer.

Skye pales even more, her gorgeous yellow green eyes suddenly look too big for her face. Without another word she turns and walks out the door.

You fucking idiot! I yank on my t-shirt and grab my boots, racing down the stairs after her. At the front door I stop to put my boots on then I'm straight out into the yard. I see the back of Skye jogging down the lane.

"Skye, wait, Skye!" I roar at the top of my lungs. She doesn't stop, not that I blame her!

"Caleb, Caleb come quick" Marty calls running out of the far stable block "somethings wrong with Wonderwall"

Shit! Shit, shit, can this day get any worse? I want to scream at the heavens, I'm torn between chasing Skye and going to see the horse.

"Quickly, something is seriously wrong" the urgency in Marty's voice makes my decision and I follow him in to the stable.

SKYE

I reach the road and chance a look behind me, there's no sign of Caleb. I don't hang around though, he made himself very clear. How could I have misjudged our situation so badly? I swipe angrily at the tears blurring my eyes. I really thought we had something that could turn into... what? I sigh. I've made a right fool of myself and I'm fooling myself even more if I thought a man like Caleb would wait for me. He's right we are practically strangers.

Still, I really, really like the guy. I've fallen for him fast and hard, much more so than I did with Clayton. Christ! I fucked the guy a couple of hours after I had met him and I didn't even know his name, I made Clayton wait a week. But Caleb's harsh words stung. I'm shocked and hurt that he thinks that of me. My wealth is obviously a huge bone of contention for him, why else would he bring it up? I reach the little church and set off towards the village. I need alone time to think, I need a hill or a mountain. I speed up suddenly remembering there's a public pathway up ahead that leads to a hill, Freya and I walked part way up it the other day before it got too much for her.

The view is breath taking, the countryside stretches out for miles. I love watching the shifting colours of browns, greens and yellows as the sun plays hide and seek with the rolling clouds, casting shadows and dispersing them just as quickly. Sitting on top of a rock with a heavy heart

I pull my phone out to check the time, I've been here an hour and I'm still no further on with my thoughts and emotions. I've shed a few tears in frustration and anger, at myself, at Caleb, at the whole fucked up mess.

I've questioned my approach; could I have done it differently? I honestly thought I had spotted the right opportunity to find out about his plans. I certainly didn't expect him to open up like he did, but I'm glad he did. I felt closer and more connected to him in that moment. Given the chance I would've told him about my estrangement from my family, I know deep down I would have told him every goddam sordid detail. Well that's not going to happen now, for some reason that makes me feel incredibly sad.

I spot two figures walking up the hill towards me, after a few minutes I recognise them. Halfway up one of them stops and scans the surroundings. Five minutes later a heavily panting Simon collapses beside me.

"You okay baby girl?" he puffs out, putting an arm around me.

I put my head on his shoulder enjoying his embrace "Yeah" I say eventually.

"Want to talk about it?" he says softly.

Do I? I ponder for a few minutes, no not really.

"Let's just say that I made a bad error of judgement and I needed time to think things through"

"Does this bad error of judgement involve Mr McHottie?" I take a deep breath and fight to hold the stinging tears back, I nod not trusting my voice "does this mean I get to bitch slap him?"

I burst out laughing "No, there's no need for that"

"Well Cinders it's time to get you ready for the ball" I look at him quizzically "Nessa has phoned, she's been invited to some pre charity drinks party and wants us to go with her, which means we have to leave in three hours" Simon stands and holds out his hand to help me up "we're going to wave the magic wand on all of this" he diva waves his hand in front of me "and show the yokels what true glamour looks like"

I grin at Simon; he never fails to lighten my mood. Although my heart still feels heavy with sadness.

Two and a half hours later I'm stood in the upstairs living room of the pub. Freya and Simon have pampered me to an inch of my life. Freya did my hair, she has quite a talent and patience for it. She straightened it — well as much as my curly hair would allow — then wove it into a complicated plait, the effect is stunning.

I have a full face of makeup, curtsey of Simon. Smouldering smoky-grey eyes and blood red lips to match my dress and jewels. I'm wearing my ruby earrings and matching choker. The satin floor length red dress fits me like a second skin. The corseted bodice cinches in my waist, emphasising my boobs and hips. The sweetheart neckline shows just the right amount of cleavage. The dress hugs me to the top of my thighs then flares out. The only decoration on the dress are the diamantes around the top of the neckline and the panels that are off the shoulder and wrap around the tops of my arms.

"Whoa, you look as if you're about to walk down the red carpet at the Oscars" Michelle says coming into the room.

"She's looks gorgeous doesn't she?" Freya says hugging herself "I need to take a picture of you, this is my inspiration"

I catch the slightly puzzled look Michelle gives Freya but she doesn't ask what she means. I know, but I'm not going to say anything. I dutifully stand still as Freya takes a picture using her tablet. Then I start messing around, posing provocatively and blow kisses. Freya giggles and clicks away.

"Fuck me it's Jessica Rabbit" Simon laughs coming in to the room "or should I be saying Bettie Page, no wait Jane Mansfield"

I flick him the finger, making Michelle and Freya laugh.

"Oh my, don't you look handsome" Michelle strokes her hand down the lapel of Simon's tuxedo jacket "wow! All you boys scrub up well" her eyes widen as Paul and Alan make an entrance. I notice Freya blushes as she looks Alan over and he gives her such a sweet smile.

"Well, we have half an hour to kill. Let's go down to the bar and give the locals something to gossip about tonight, since we won't be here" Simon says mischievously holding out his arm to me.

"Why not" I grin back.

If Caleb has issues with my wealth that's his problem, tonight I'm going to flaunt it, fuck him.

"Hang on let me change my shoes. I'm not missing this for the world" Michelle says rushing out to swap her slippers.

Michelle and Freya enter the pub first, from my position on the stairs I can hear the late afternoon crowd and it sounds reasonably busy. Paul, Alan and Simon enter next, it's as if someone has turned the volume down on all the conversations. I'm hit by a sudden bout of nerves. I take a deep breath and step through the door… to deathly silence, then sharp in takes of breath and low whistles greet me. Simon winks at me, holding out his arm, I link him and we walk round to the front of the bar. Michelle serves us our drinks; the pub is way too quiet; it feels uncomfortable. We clink glasses, the tinkling sound seems too loud. The front door opens and we all turn to see who's coming in.

"Fuck me!" Rex exclaims when he sees me.

"Language Rex" Michelle admonishes with a chuckle.

That breaks the stunned silence and everyone laughs, some come over asking if they can take a photo of our group which prompts others to do the same. Simon and I stand and pose as Paul and Alan step back, after fifteen minutes Alan signals he's getting the car.

"Have fun and see you in the morning" Freya says as we leave. I feel a pang of guilt she's not coming with us.

I tried talking Freya into coming, but she quite rightly pointed out she wouldn't be up to it. She's still too bruised and she wouldn't feel comfortable. I didn't push anymore after that, I got it. She needs time to adjust plus she wants to lose shed loads of weight first.

CALEB

Could this day get any fucking shittier? I thump the steering wheel as I head back to the yard. Wonderwall has colic, I knew it as soon as I saw the horse. I got Sally to ring Eric the vet as Marty and I tried to settle the distressed horse. Luckily his form of colic is treatable so no need for surgery thank god. Eric arrived within thirty minutes and administered a saline solution, by the time I had to leave for my appointment with the bank manager there was a vast improvement in Wonderwall's condition.

The bank manager, Mr Bellam — Mr Bell End more like — was a complete tosser. He took great delight in making me sweat before informing me that he couldn't possibly extend the overdraft. He finally relented when I explained I only needed it for a week. I hope to fucking god Bertie pays up as he promised when the horses arrive next week, otherwise I really am up shit creek without a paddle.

And to top it all off I get a phone call on my way back from Rex telling me to get to the pub pronto if I want to see something that will be the talk of the village for the next millennia, only I get a fucking puncture. By the time I get to the pub I missed Skye by ten minutes and by all accounts she looked stunning. I felt physically sick when I saw all the photos of her, she was movie star glamourous and I was reliably informed by my so called best friend that the jewels she wore were real.

The one slither of luck I had was seeing Freya, she made a note to ask Skye to come and see me tomorrow before she leaves. Freya informed me that they planned to leave early, I told her I didn't care I just need to see her. Freya promised she would pass on the message.

I hit the steering wheel again in frustration. I can't believe I've been such a fucking knob head. Why in the hell did I react the way I did to what Skye said. I never had the decency to hear her out. "That's because you're a bloody twat Raven" I mutter under my breath as I get out the car and slam the door shut.

After checking on Wonderwall and getting an update from the grooms I head in to the house and locate the fifteen-year-old bottle of scotch I brought back from Scotland. I pour myself a hefty measure and knock it back, it's quickly followed by another. Slow down, otherwise you'll be fit for no one tomorrow. With a deep sigh, I pour another and switch on the TV. I channel hop. I can't believe the crap that's on. I very rarely watch TV, aside from the horse racing there's nothing much I care for. I land on the local news and drop the remote on the sofa. I half listen to the presenter's prattle on about some scandal to do with a local councillor taking back handers. I don't know what they're so worked up about, the whole bloody lot of them are fucking corrupt in my opinion. Deciding I've heard enough I look round for the remote control.

"And finally tonight we go live to Miles Cunningham at the Savoy Hotel. I must say Miles you are looking very dapper in your tux" the female presenter gives an inane giggle.

I look at the screen pointing the control when my finger freezes on the button.

"Why thank you Penelope, I do try" Miles smiles all white teeth and fake tan into the camera, but it's what going on behind him that has my attention. Paul has just got out of a long black limousine "tonight the Savoy Hotel hosts the annual fundraising gala where several charities that help young people get a better start in life, benefit. These vary from helping young people who are at risk or living on the streets to those that are talented and underprivileged. For our viewers that don't know Indie TV

Media which is the parent company for Your Local News is one of the sponsors for tonight's event"

"I think I see Vanessa Johnson; our esteemed Managing Director has just arrived" Penelope cuts across Miles. For a split second a flash of annoyance flits across his face.

He turns to see what's going on behind him, Nessa is in camera shot moving to stand next to Simon giving room for the next person to get out of the car. Paul steps forward offering a hand. Skye merges like the goddess she is.

"Yes you're right Penelope, and she is with her very good friend Skye Darcy a renowned artist and highly successful businesswoman, who I had the pleasure of meeting yesterday" Ha! That's a fucking joke "I'm sure lots of money will be raised for these worthy causes tonight, if any of our viewers would like to make a donation details can be found on our website"

In the background Nessa is introducing Skye and Simon to various people. Paul and Alan stand off to the side, I can tell both are on high alert. Neither of them letting Skye get a few paces away from them.

"Thank you Miles, enjoy yourself tonight but not too much"

"Oh I'll try not to"

Miles and Penelope do that fake laughing thing. I throw my glass at the TV, the fucker is going to be there, with Skye, my kitten. I head upstairs taking the bottle of scotch with me, I'm going to drink myself into oblivion.

Much later, the darkness of nightfall surrounds the whole yard. No one hears the taxi coming to a stop partway up the lane. The soft thud of a car door closing as a woman gets out and walks the rest of the way up to the house. She tries the front door, it opens easily. Caleb didn't believe in locking the door since he had nothing of value. His most prized possessions were the horses; a locked door would hamper getting to them in a hurry should something happen.

The woman carefully makes her way across the living room towards the stairs. She stops holding her breath at the crunching sound of broken glass beneath her feet. No one stirs or calls out. Blindly kicking the shards aside, she carries on, carefully opening the door that leads to the stairs. She takes her shoes off and slowly creeps up, halting at each loose creaking board. She knew her way to Caleb's bedroom and makes her way without hesitation.

Caleb lay on his back, the covers pool at his waist. God, he is magnificent the woman thinks as she quickly undresses, neatly folding her clothes and putting them on the chair by the door. Approaching his bed, the woman keeps her eyes on Caleb, he is a light sleeper and the slightest noise will wake him. It's not until she stands beside him that she notices the bottle of scotch on the bedside cabinet. It's three quarters empty. A sly smile plays across her lips; tonight is her lucky night she thinks gleefully. Caleb is difficult to rouse the more he's had to drink.

Taking hold of the covers she slowly pulls them back to reveal Caleb's long heavy meaty cock. With stealth moves that would make any Ninja proud the woman places herself on the bed so she can pleasure Caleb easily. Leaning down she licks Caleb's cock from root to tip, a few more licks and swirls of her tongue has Caleb hardening, his hips surge upwards.

In his dream Skye is on her knees, arms behind her back and her talented luscious mouth is servicing his dick. The dream shifts, now she is straddling him, he's buried deep inside her hot wet cunt. Watching Skye ride him takes his breath away, her wonderful huge tits bounce and sway with her movements. He reaches for them but Skye stops him. He frowns, Skye loves having her tits played with. But that's soon forgotten when Skye rides him harder and faster. Caleb gets a strong urge to apologise for his earlier behaviour, "I'm so sorry" he tells her, Skye smiles and says it's okay, there's nothing to be sorry for. Feeling euphoric that she's forgiven him, he comes.

Elated, the woman climbs off Caleb. Apart from when he reached for her tits and she managed to redirect his searching hands, it's been easier than she expected to get what she wanted. And it was so sweet that he apologised, for what she had no idea, maybe it was because he came so quickly. She wasn't bothered in the slightest, she got what she came for, now it was time to set stage two of her plan in to action.

Taking one of his shirts out of the wardrobe and gathering her clothes she crept out of the bedroom and went to the spare room, waiting for morning.

CHAPTER NINETEEN

SKYE

I wrap my coat around me and yawn, then my whole body shakes and shivers from head to toe as the early spring morning breeze very rudely goes right through me.

"Sure you don't want to go back to bed for another hour" Paul's amused drawl comes from behind me.

I shove his shoulder and point to the SUV "Nope, just get the car open and the heating on"

"Yes ma'am" he chuckles; the chunking sound of the car unlocking gets my feet moving. I climb into the car and fasten the seat belt "do you mind telling me what you said to that TV newsreader last night, anything I should be aware of?" Paul says looking at me in the rear view mirror.

I snort a laugh; it had been a very enjoyable evening considering the despondent mood I was in after Caleb's outburst. Well, I had been enjoying it until Miles Cunningham asked me to dance.

"Miles Cunningham, the cheeky twat thought he was being clever. He started off by saying "I know who you are" and I said "Good for you". But a few seconds later he says it again so I took the bait "Go on then who am I?" I said it in my best dumb blonde voice" I grin at Paul's chuckle "Miles stage whispers "You're Mrs Blake" I gave him a surprised "No! You don't say" I will say that flummoxed him"

"I bet it did"

"Then he said "I also know you're the late Lord Belling's granddaughter" I just gave him a blank look and said "So what do you want me to do, give you a gold star for doing your homework" then I smiled ever so sweetly at him and added "Do you really think you're the only person in the village who knows all that?" Now that, took the wind out of his egotistical sails"

I smile as I watch Paul's silent laugh, his big shoulders lift up and down "Do you want me to do anything?"

"Nah, no need to put the frighteners on him. Nessa's going to do that later this morning. She wanted to know what he'd said to piss me off, so I told her. She doesn't like the little prick, her words not mine, so she's going to make sure he keeps his mouth shut. Come on we need to get going if we're to keep to schedule"

"Yes ma'am" Paul smiles and starts the car.

I lean back into the plush leather seat as we make our way to Caleb's yard. Freya, bless her, stayed up to give me his message.

"He didn't say what it was about but he looked ever so distraught, he was very insistent I gave you the message. It seemed really important to him I almost rang you"

Uneasiness settles in my stomach, I must be a glutton for punishment putting myself through this. You are, remember? My traitorous body stirs at memories of our playing yesterday. All last night I kept being reminded when I sat down, even now my arse is tender, surprisingly there's no bruising but then again that's what Caleb is good at. I'd sat for an hour watching him demonstrate the technique, how to inflict maximum pain without bruising, to a bunch of other Dom's. I force my mind to consider why he wants to speak to me, to apologise maybe?

Paul pulls up in to the yard and turns the car around so we can make a quick getaway if need be.

"Stay in the car, this shouldn't take long" I say trying to sound confident. I take a deep breath and open the door.

CALEB

"You're a piss poor excuse for a man. You had the greatest opportunity for happiness, possibly a lifetime of happiness and you sabotaged it" I berate myself holding my head in my hands sitting on the edge of the bed.

The chances of Skye coming here before she leaves are slim, in fact if I had to put odds on it I'd say hundred to one. I desperately want to apologise for what I said, my behaviour and my attitude. Christ, I really wish I could turn back time. I would keep my mouth shut and hear her out. I would love to be able to apologise to her just like in my dream.

My dream.

That was one hell of a wet dream. But was it?

A weird feeling creeps through my blood, it seemed so real.

I run my hand across my lower stomach and the tops of my thighs. Nothing, no dried semen. I throw the bed covers back and feel the sheets. They're soft and dry. I don't like this. I have the strangest sensation that something happened to me last night.

The sound of the dogs barking has me up and opening the window wider. I can hear a car approaching. Skye! She's here, she's come.

Relief, excitement and adrenaline surges through my blood, I put my jeans on only half fastening them before I grab a t-shirt and run downstairs. Shoving my feet into my boots I wrench the front door open just in time to see Skye emerging from the big black monster of an SUV. The cold morning air hits my chest. I look down at myself, realising I'm only half dressed.

"Skye, thanks so much for taking the time and coming" I say pulling on my t-shirt.

"That's okay, what is it..." Skye stops, something snags her attention over my shoulder, her eyes widen in surprise.

Frowning and wondering what it could be I turn to see what she's looking at. Holy fucking shit! My mind screams as my jaw unhinges.

Gabrielle.

Walking towards me as bold as brass. Her just fucked bed head hair and looking mussed up wearing one of my shirts all screams of one thing. I'm so shocked I'm rooted to the spot. Gabrielle sidles up next to me, snaking her arm around my waist. She smiles triumphantly at Skye.

"Good morning Ms Darcy, so good to see you again. I must say your timing is perfect, you're just in time to hear our good news" stupefied I stare down at Gabrielle as she smiles sweetly at me "honey, I didn't have time to tell you last night" she fakes a naughty giggle "but, we're pregnant!" Gabrielle announces gleefully taking my hand and puts it over her belly.

That kick starts my brain. I snatch my hand back as if I've been scolded.

"Congratulations. I'm sure you'll both be very happy together"

The vapidity of Skye's voice seizes my attention. She looks devastated, her shoulders slump as if she has the weight of the world on them. The sorrow and heartache in her eyes, floors me. Skye turns back to the SUV.

"No, wait, Skye" I call out, pushing Gabrielle away from me. Skye pauses with her hand on the door handle "she's lying. It's not mine" I say earnestly, please believe me.

"Yes, of course it is silly" Gabrielle moves towards me, I instinctively step back "remember three months ago we spent a night together just like last night" she says coyly stroking her small protruding belly.

I feel sick. My instincts were right. It wasn't a wet dream about Skye. Gabrielle, she... it was... my whole body shudders at the horror.

You need to explain to Skye why it's not yours, my mind urges me. The sound of an engine starting up spurs me in to action.

"Skye" I yell at the top of my lungs running after the car as it drives down the lane.

SKYE

Paul doesn't say a word as he drives me away. Silent grief stricken tears pour down my face. Of all the things that could have happened. Despite my vast wealth, it's the one thing I can't give him. I can't compete with Gabrielle on that score. Seeing the truth of Gabrielle's words in Caleb's face as she caressed the tiny bump of her tummy, it's too much to bear. I wrap my arms around my middle, trying to hold on.

I've lost the man who made me feel so alive.

I've lost the man who made my life whole.

I've lost the man I love.

My world collapses.

My heart shatters.

The light snuffs out.

Hello darkness, my old friend.

CALEB

Breathing heavily, I stride back to the yard. The three grooms stand silently outside the stables, watching my every move. Annoyance, rage, anger, animosity, loathing, hate – are only a few of the emotions roiling through me that I can put a name to.

"Get in the fucking house you evil lying bitch" I roar at Gabrielle "get your things and fuck off back to whichever stone you crawled out from underneath"

Gabrielle flinches, she licks her pouty Botox lips "Honey, surely you wouldn't throw the mother of your child out onto the street" she says trying to pacify and reason with me but I can see the uncertainty in her eyes.

"If you are pregnant" I roughly grab hold of the top of her arm and frog march her to the house "it's not mine" I shout pushing her through the door and slamming it shut.

So god help me, I'm going to fucking kill her. The fucking bitch has just lost me the woman who illuminated my dark world and made my shitty life worth living.

"It is yours" Gabrielle screams at me "remember, we met up to discuss the divorce settlement, we got drunk and ended up in bed, for old time's sake. We even joked about it the following morning"

"No we didn't" I growl through gritted teeth, pointing my finger in her face "do you think I'm that fucking stupid to believe you? Christ, you even believe your own fucking lies. Let me refresh your memory to what really happened. You made sure you had too much to drink so you couldn't drive. I said you could stay over and sleep in the spare room. I woke up in the middle of the night to find you straddling me" my body shudders "only last night I didn't wake up so I'm guessing you pulled the same bloody stunt, again"

Gabrielle looks defiant "Well, it's by the by" she waves her hand dismissively "the fact still remains I'm pregnant and whether you like it or not, the baby is yours"

"And like I've already told you, no it fucking isn't" I turn to the desk, opening the bottom draw and pull out the top file "you're going to have to find some other poor bastard to con into being the father" I open the file, flicking through the pages until I find the one I need "here, have a read"

I turn the file round so Gabrielle can see. Her eyes dart from side to side across the page, they widen in disbelief. Her mouth drops open.

"You... you're..." Gabrielle looks at me lost for words.

"Yeah, I'm sterile" I say with smug satisfaction "now get the fuck out"

Five minutes later Gabrielle, is out of the door. She wanted to call a taxi, instead I threw my car keys at her telling her to leave it at the train station in Henley. No way was I having her in the house any longer than necessary.

Leaning on the desk, my head hanging low I breathe through the tremors racking my body. My heart rate slows as the last of the adrenaline ebbs away "What a fucking mess" I mutter straightening. Through the window, I notice the grooms stood huddled together, each taking it in turns to look over at the house. Letting out an exasperated sigh I go to the front door.

"Sally, Marty, Davy" I call and signal for them to come in. I point to the sofa as they enter, quietly they each take a seat. I face them leaning against the desk "I owe you an explanation for the... pantomime you've just witnessed" they all remain silent. A wry smile tugs at my lips. I don't blame them "as you heard Gabrielle says she is pregnant and claims it's mine. I want to make it very clear, it isn't" I take a deep breath "I'm sterile and I've known for two years"

Sally gasps in shock, her hand covers her mouth. Marty's jaw pops open and Davy burst out laughing.

"Oh boss, that is fucking brilliant. I wish I could have seen Boomerang's face when you produced the evidence" Davy doubles up on the sofa holding his sides, soon we're all joining him.

"There's something else I need to tell you and this I do need you to keep to yourselves" I say after a few minutes, all laughter dies and they're instantly attentive "promise me not a word of what I'm about to tell you will pass your lips, until I tell you otherwise" each make a 'cross my heart' gesture and hold up three fingers in the scout's salute, Sally even mines zipping her lips, locking it and throwing away the key "Skye Darcy is Mrs Blake"

"Holy shit!"

"Good lord!"

"Fuck me!"

All chorus together.

I run my hand through my hair and grip it "And we've been seeing each other" I smile ruefully and I let my hand fall heavily to my side. Complete and utter stunned silence "Skye is a widow. Her husband, Clayton Blake, died a few days after their wedding anniversary from injuries he sustained in a car accident. Anyway, yesterday we had a misunderstanding. It was my fault. I was in the wrong, so I left a message with Freya asking Skye to call here before she left, this was so I could apologise"

"Oh no" Sally wails, tears swim in her eyes. Marty and Davy look grim "fucking Gabrielle, I hate that bloody bitch" Sally says with such vehemence, she takes me by surprise.

"That's why Skye was here and obviously I didn't get chance to say sorry" I look down at the floor, grinding my teeth together trying to quell the mixed emotions fighting to break free, on the one hand I want to tear the place apart, angry at Gabrielle. The other, I want to drop to my knees and cry for my loss. I clear my throat "as you know Skye came to look around the stables earlier in the week, she has two horses currently stabled with friends in America. She was talking of bringing them over here and asked me to train one of them" eager eyes light up "before you get too excited, after what happened yesterday and just now, I have no idea of what Skye's intentions are. So, we carry on as normal and I pray to god she hasn't changed her mind"

Sensing the meeting is over, Marty and Davy stand. Each pat me on the shoulder, a show of compassion and camaraderie. Sally waits until they've left the room before standing and approaches me.

"You love her don't you?" Sally whispers tentatively, looking me straight in the eyes.

Suddenly I feel very tired, emotionally and physically drained "Yeah, I do, Sal" my voice comes out in a hoarse whisper, I've fallen for her hard and fast, there's no turning back now, my fate is sealed. I don't hide the despair I'm feeling. Putting my head in my hands I fist clumps of hair, I feel like ripping it out to experience the physical pain that's happening in my heart "but I fucked up big time and I have no way of putting it right"

"It'll all work out, you'll see" says Sally, ever the optimist. A gentle soothing hand rubs my shoulder.

"I hope you're right, I really do because I also have no way of getting in touch with her to explain" I lift my head and let her see the agony of my misery.

"Skye's coming back. Have faith, I do" Sally leans in and kisses my cheek then leaves me to my wretchedness.

THE END

For now...